ALSO BY KAREN WHITE

The Color of Light
Pieces of the Heart
Learning to Breathe
The Memory of Water
The Lost Hours
On Folly Beach
Falling Home
The Beach Trees
Sea Change
After the Rain
The Time Between
A Long Time Gone
The Sound of Glass
Flight Patterns
Spinning the Moon
The Night the Lights Went Out
Dreams of Falling
The Last Night in London

Cowritten with Beatriz Williams and Lauren Willig

The Forgotten Room
The Glass Ocean
All the Ways We Said Goodbye
The Lost Summers of Newport
The Author's Guide to Murder

The Tradd Street Series

The House on Tradd Street
The Girl on Legare Street
The Strangers on Montagu Street
Return to Tradd Street
The Guests on South Battery
The Christmas Spirits on Tradd Street
The Attic on Queen Street

The Royal Street Series

The Shop on Royal Street
The House on Prytania

THE LADY ON ESPLANADE

KAREN WHITE

Berkley
New York

BERKLEY
An imprint of Penguin Random House LLC
1745 Broadway, New York, NY 10019
penguinrandomhouse.com

Library of Congress Cataloging-in-Publication Data

Names: White, Karen, (Karen S.), author.
Title: The lady on esplanade / Karen White.
Description: New York : Berkley, 2025. | Series: The Royal Street series ; 3
Identifiers: LCCN 2024037572 (print) | LCCN 2024037573 (ebook) |
ISBN 9780593549490 (hardcover) | ISBN 9780593549506 (ebook)
Subjects: LCGFT: Paranormal fiction. | Ghost stories. | Novels.
Classification: LCC PS3623.H5776 L33 2025 (print) |
LCC PS3623.H5776 (ebook) | DDC 813/.6--dc23/eng/20240816
LC record available at https://lccn.loc.gov/2024037572
LC ebook record available at https://lccn.loc.gov/2024037573

Printed in the United States of America
1st Printing

To my readers, whose love of my characters
is all the inspiration I need

THE LADY ON ESPLANADE

CHAPTER 1

A heavy early-November rain pummeled the windows and the roof of our town house on Broadway, pebble-sized drops falling on the streets and sidewalks, converting all flat surfaces to ankle-deep rivers. I stood inside the open front door as sheets of water cascaded down from the small overhang, splattering rain wetting my face as I breathed in the peculiar scent of moisture-laden air mixed with the odors of drenched asphalt and saturated dirt. Leftover jack-o'-lanterns from a sodden Halloween remained perched on the fraternity house doorstep across the street; they stared at me with shriveled faces, their jagged mouths black with mildew.

Hurricane season wouldn't be officially over until November thirtieth, and as in all parts of the Southeast that dipped their toes into the Gulf or the Atlantic, the collective breath that had been held here since the first of June wouldn't be completely expelled until December first. Names like Camille, Katrina, and Ida weren't mentioned out loud at all. I'd accidentally mentioned the K word and Jolene—my redheaded force-of-nature roommate—had crossed herself and then told me that, the following June, she would take me to the Mass for hurricane protection, despite the fact that neither of us was Catholic.

I'd asked her if I could borrow her waders to explore the new underwater landscape, but she'd warned me about going outside during a gully washer, because when the water rises in New Orleans it is anyone's guess what might rise with it. I closed the door, dulling the sounds and smells of the rain but not the tremor that crept over my skin at the thought of what the deluge might unbury.

I trudged up the bare wooden steps and opened the single French door to our upstairs apartment. I was greeted enthusiastically by Mardi, my adopted gray and white fur ball, despite having been absent for less than five minutes. The dog's origins and bloodline were a mystery, but he was unquestionably mine, despite Jolene's favorite-aunt status, which allowed her to dress him in seasonally themed sweaters and bandannas despite my protests. Mardi accepted resignedly. Being a Mississippi native and more Southern than Dolly Parton, my roommate believed in accessorizing and monogramming everything—including my dog.

"Still raining," I announced to the empty living room. "I hope the flooding is at least drowning the next generation of flying cockroaches."

"Honey, those evil critters would survive a nuclear explosion. I think the chemical pollution in the rain makes them bigger and gives them the kind of confidence required to open a screen door," Jolene said as she emerged from the back hallway with a life-sized Barbie head tucked under her arm. If she had been anyone else, I would have been alarmed, but with Jolene, I didn't even blink.

"What's that for?" I asked, indicating Barbie.

"I'm fixin' to send it to Charleston for Sarah, since she said she didn't have one. I wanted to style the hair first so she can use it as a model for her own. Even though you're only half sisters, y'all have the same hair, so I thought I'd practice on Barbie before I did your hair for tonight."

"Tonight?"

She raised her perfectly shaped eyebrows, a shade darker than her naturally red hair. "I know you're just trying to yank my chain, Nola. I put it on your calendar and used my good lipstick to write it on the bathroom mirror, so don't pretend you have no idea what I'm talking about. I'm going to run your bath in half an hour, so just mentally prepare yourself to get all gussied up."

I sighed heavily. "But how are we supposed to get there? The streets are flooded. And you know what humidity does to my hair."

"Bubba can plow through anything, and I'll use superglue on your hair if I have to, because until I hear otherwise, Commander's is open and we're going to be there come hell or high water."

I glanced out through the large double window over the sofa; the unrelenting rain continued to hit the glass. "But can Bubba float?" Jolene's 1989 Lincoln Town Car was a menace on the road because of its size, and it was doubly threatening when Jolene was behind the wheel. I had calluses on my right hand from clutching the passenger-side door handle. I shuddered at the image of Bubba barreling down the narrow streets of New Orleans like a speedboat in a low-wake zone and taking out everything in his path.

"I think it would be safer staying home." I smiled hopefully. "I'll let you give me one of your smelly facial masks and paint my toenails."

"Nice try, but no." Jolene looked at her watch. "You've now got twenty-five minutes. You can use the time to soak your hands in my moisturizing gloves. They look like you've been manually scraping paint from old plaster."

I looked down at my reddened knuckles and ragged fingernails. "That's because I have," I said, unable to keep the pride from my voice. I'd recently purchased a Creole cottage on the brink of demolition in the Marigny neighborhood, as my first step toward starting over and adulting in a brand-new city.

In my defense, I said, "Everybody we're having dinner with knows what I spend my time doing, and Beau will accuse me of not pulling my weight if my hands are as soft as a baby's bottom."

Despite having a graduate degree in historic preservation, I would have been in way over my head if it hadn't been for the unsolicited interference of one Beau Ryan. Granted, he was a licensed contractor and knew the ins and outs of renovating old houses, but he was also an unwelcome reminder of the parts of my past I would have rather forgotten. And as much as I liked to believe that the restless spirits that inhabited my corner of the world didn't bother me, I appreciated that Beau had risked his life to eradicate an especially vengeful one from my new home. I had returned at least part of the favor—with unexpected help from his deceased mother—during an epic showdown in the attic of his family's house on Prytania Street.

Like my stepmother, Melanie Middleton Trenholm, Beau had the ability to communicate with spirits—despite his popular podcast, which he used as a platform to debunk the many so-called psychics who gleefully took money from the grief-stricken. As a previous victim, desperate to find his parents, who'd disappeared during Hurricane Katrina, he was dedicated to preventing the fleecing of the vulnerable, while simultaneously hiding the psychic gift he'd inherited from his mother—a gift he feared, if only because he couldn't control it.

"Yes," Jolene said, "but, luckily for you, you've got me, and I've got an arsenal of beauty products to fix whatever's broken, and my reputation is at stake if I allow you to walk out the door looking like your fingers got stuck in a cotton gin. Or in an electric socket." Her gaze flicked over my Brillo-like hair, frizzed by the few minutes I'd spent in the open doorway, watching the rain. "Fortunately, I enjoy the challenge." She smiled. "I've got the perfect dress for you to wear. I found it on sale at Saks, but the color blue matches your eyes, so I want you to have it. I'm sure Beau will notice."

"In case you've forgotten, Beau has a girlfriend, and Samantha will be there tonight. Besides, you know I'm not interested in him. We don't even like each other."

"Right," she said, and let out an inelegant snort. "And it's okay to wear white shoes before Easter." She rolled her eyes. "It's not a small thing that you saved his life. He's hosting tonight's dinner to thank you, so you're going to be the star of the show. Just accept it. And you now have twenty-one minutes." Jolene placed the Barbie head on the dining table, then began walking toward the bathroom in the back hallway.

"Why don't you wear it, Jolene? Won't Jaxson be there tonight, too?" I regretted saying the words before they had even left my mouth. I didn't want to encourage her to believe that one day Jaxson would wake up and realize he was with the wrong woman. Jolene and I both knew that Jaxson had already bought an engagement ring for his girlfriend, Carly, but Jolene clung to the belief that she still had a chance as long as the ring wasn't on Carly's finger.

Jolene kept walking and didn't respond, but I knew better than to think she hadn't heard me. As sweet and kind as my roommate was, I knew it was only a matter of time before I'd find a severed Barbie head in my bed.

By some miracle, Jolene and I arrived at the restaurant, Commander's Palace, only fifteen minutes late. Jolene was firmly of the belief that it was always better to arrive late than to arrive ugly, so there was no escape from her smoothing, teasing, plucking, moisturizing, and painting my face and/or hair. Despite my worries, Bubba performed as a certified land yacht and cruised through the streets, creating wakes usually found behind bigger boats, like aircraft carriers.

Beau had reserved the restaurant's private Little Room, an intimate space where ambient noise and the footsteps of waitstaff were muffled by padded carpet. Elegant framed mirrors hung on the walls and reflected the muted light shining through the French doors and from the sparkling crystal chandeliers. Small tables beneath white tablecloths had been placed together in the center of the room to form a larger one, and menus lay on top of the place settings. Any hope I'd had that I could sneak in unnoticed and grab a chair at the far end of the table was quickly dispelled when I saw that a spot had been reserved to the right of Beau, who stood from his place at the head of the table when we entered.

"And finally—the guest of honor," he announced. Jaxson rose from his seat at the middle of the table and pulled out the chair next to him for Jolene. Carly sat across from him, and she gave Jolene a calculating glance before reaching her hand across the table to touch Jaxson's fingers. It was the same as if she'd slapped a label on him that read MINE. Jolene was so busy trying not to look smug at my proximity to Beau that she didn't notice.

I greeted Beau's grandmother Mimi Ryan with a kiss on her powdered cheek. "I'm glad you could make it," she said with a note of reproach, as expected from the family matriarch, her odd eyes—one green, one blue—crinkling at the corners and softening her words.

She sat at the opposite end of the table, next to Samantha—Sam—Beau's girlfriend and podcast partner. Sam stood and greeted me with a hug and a warm smile, and I thought yet again that we could have been friends if not for Beau Ryan. Considering that I didn't even like him very much, this was an odd sentiment, and one that I didn't care to analyze too closely.

I was happy to see Cooper Ravenel, who rose from where he'd been seated, then walked around the table to wrap me in a bear hug. Because of his job he traveled a lot, and I hadn't seen much of him since the night of the St. Louis Cathedral fund-raiser at the Ryans', when Beau had almost died. Cooper had been instrumental in saving Beau and me from the brink of disaster, which was one of the reasons he was at the celebratory dinner.

"It's good to see you," he said, his voice and touch vibrating through me.

"Same," I said, feeling everyone's eyes on us. "I hope you're in town long enough for me to show you the house on Esplanade."

"That's what I'm counting on. I've asked for no travel this coming week, so I'm all yours."

Cooper had been my teenage crush and first heartbreak, and he had recently moved to New Orleans. I was concentrating on renovating my cottage and starting my new life, and I wasn't interested in a relationship beyond friendship, but I'd be lying to myself if I said that I didn't feel an electric jolt every time I saw him. I'd yet to ask him about the scar on his face and about his years in California. If there was anything I'd learned from my stepmother, it was that sometimes not knowing was best.

"Sounds like a plan," I said as I pulled away.

Everyone took their seats except for Beau. He gently clinked his water glass—no wine or champagne on the table, in deference to me, I guessed—to quiet the chatter.

"Thank you all for coming. It was important that I gather us all together to thank those of you who not only saved my life"—he glanced at me, and I knew we were both recalling his slipping over the edge of the attic walkway as I struggled to hold on, before Cooper miraculously appeared—"but also helped my family find my long-lost sister, Sunny. As I know you are all aware, she is still processing her newly discovered identity, but Mimi and I have great hopes that she will return to us when she's ready. And we will be waiting with open arms."

"Hear, hear!" Christopher Benoit, family friend and the manager of the Past Is Never Past, the Ryans' antiques store on Royal Street, raised his water glass. The rest of us followed suit, and the sound of glasses clinking sang over the table as we turned to one another to toast the miracle of Beau's survival and the resolution of the decades-old mystery of what had happened to two-year-old Sunny Ryan.

As I sipped my water I looked around at the smiling faces, knowing that, except for Carly—whose reason for being present at the table wasn't clear—I'd found my family. Not a new family, but an extension of my beloved family back home, in Charleston—because, as Melanie and my father, Jack, had reminded me time and again, no matter where I went, there I was. And, as I was a recovering alcoholic who'd chosen for her new home a city recognized for its partying lifestyle, my family had known even before I did that I would require a support system while I tried to prove to everyone that I didn't need anyone's support but my own.

I was halfway through my dessert, crème brûlée—which I didn't enjoy as much as I should have, because I was too busy watching Sam and Beau eat their bananas Foster for two—when the lights flickered, followed quickly by a sharp crack of thunder. I looked up and met Beau's gaze, almost as if we were sharing the same unspoken thought: that just the two of us had noticed that the crystal chandelier above our table had been the only light with interrupted power in the restaurant. Everyone who lived in the coastal South was used to sporadic storms, even in November. We were even used to the electricity going out with annoying frequency. But there was also an odd static in the air, a frisson of something unknown that hovered in the room, and only Beau and I appeared to notice.

The waitstaff continued to refill water and iced tea glasses and deliver coffee in delicate china cups as if nothing had changed—as if the room hadn't just inhaled and begun to hold its breath. I picked up my glass and held it against my cheek, trying to cool my suddenly hot skin.

I was concentrating on slowing my heartbeat and was barely aware of Jaxson pulling out his chair and moving toward Carly. I half stood from my chair as Jaxson got down on one knee and produced a black velvet box. I turned to look at Jolene, whose porcelain skin had gone even paler, the carefully applied blush on her cheeks almost garish in contrast.

Everyone was rising to their feet and clapping loudly as Carly threw her arms around Jaxson's neck before delivering an intimate kiss to his lips. Jolene began clapping, too, but it looked as if her frozen white fingers might snap. I moved to her side and rested my arm around her shoulders. For a brief moment she leaned against me, before straightening and configuring a smile that even I thought looked real.

As Jaxson slid the ring onto Carly's finger I turned to Beau to ask him why he hadn't given us some kind of warning so Jolene could be prepared, but instead of watching Jaxson and Carly, Beau was staring at the floor.

Carly extended her left hand, bright light refracting through the prism of her large pear-shaped diamond. "We need to have an engagement party!"

Her eyes scanned the room before alighting on Jolene. "And I happen to know the best party planner—Jolene McKenna! If anyone can make it the party of the decade, she can!"

Jolene continued to smile, adding a nod as if agreeing to the ludicrous suggestion that she throw an engagement party for Jaxson and Carly. It was almost as unimaginable as LSU throwing a victory party for Ole Miss.

I turned back to Beau, his gaze lifting from the floor to meet mine. I held my breath in anticipation, knowing before I looked down that I would see a woman's footprints, each step marked by smeared water spots as if she had just climbed out of a swimming pool. Since I'd first met Beau, in Charleston, I'd seen such footprints often enough to know without a doubt to whom they belonged—just as I knew that Beau would do everything possible to deny it.

My eyes met Beau's again. *She's still here.* The unspoken words ricocheted from his thoughts to mine, my heart sinking as I realized what those wet footprints meant. I'd seen the footprints only once since the incident in the Ryans' attic, and I'd hoped she'd come only to say good-bye. Apparently that wasn't the case. Even though her daughter, Sunny, had been found, Adele Ryan still had unfinished business. And she needed her son's help.

CHAPTER 2

The following morning I awoke to a song playing on my iPhone. I never used music as an alarm, because it wasn't enough to wake me, and the music now playing made my sleeping brain cells tumble around one another, trying to name the song. It took me a moment to identify "Rolling in the Deep" by Adele, and another moment to recall that I didn't have any Adele songs on my playlist. It wasn't that I didn't like her music; it was just that her songs were overplayed enough that I heard them whether or not I wanted to. Like now.

My eyes popped open, my brain registering the absence of the scent of brewing coffee. I sat up and sprang from my bed, dislodging Mardi from where he lay spooning next to me. He snuffled once, then nestled back into the covers. I stared at him enviously, and not just because I wished I could go back to sleep. I crept toward my door and placed my hand on the knob as I succumbed to a sense of dread. The last time this had happened, Jolene had packed her bags—and Mardi—and headed home to Mississippi, leaving behind only a note saying she'd return soon.

I'd later learned that she'd left because Jaxson had kissed her. I couldn't imagine how long she thought she needed to recuperate after yesterday's seismic blow. My heart hurt for her, but I hadn't had a chance to speak with her yet. Cooper had driven me back to the apartment, and Jolene's bedroom door was already closed when I came in. After taking a deep breath in preparation for whatever I needed to do to be the kind of friend she'd been to me, I opened the door and peered out.

At the round dining table Jolene sat in front of her open laptop, surrounded by neat stacks of her signature Crane linen stationery with what appeared to be numbered lists in her crisp and precise handwriting covering the pages. Her hair wasn't as poofy as she liked it, but it was sprayed neatly in place, and I would have sworn that she was wearing the same outfit she'd worn the previous day. Of course, I hadn't had my coffee yet, and the lack of caffeine could have been impairing my memory. She looked up in surprise, then glanced at her *Wizard of Oz* watch.

"Good gracious! I was so lost in party planning that I lost track of the time." She jumped out of her chair and pulled an adjacent one out for me. "Just have a seat and I'll get your coffee and warm up some of the blueberry muffins I made yesterday—"

"Please don't. Really, I can do it—"

"Sit down, Nola. Or, better yet, go run a brush through that rat's nest on top of your head while I go pour you a cup and reheat those muffins." She dashed into the kitchen, the movement followed by the clanging of dishes a moment later.

"Okay," I said, pretending I hadn't heard her mention a hairbrush as I slowly lowered myself into a chair. Jolene's ordering me around was nothing new, nor was her ability to operate on very little sleep. What was new, however, was that her feet were bare. Normal for the rest of us, but for Jolene it was a clear sign that she was having an existential crisis.

As I listened to her rushing around the kitchen, I eyed the quantity of lists and notes littering the table. If Jolene had slept at all, it hadn't been for long. I imagined the desks of the D-Day planners would have been similar—but their notes would have been less complicated and definitely not on Crane stationery.

Jolene returned and placed a *Wizard of Oz* mug on the table without a coaster—the eighth deadly sin, according to Jolene—the absence of tapping from her heels now glaringly obvious. "So, Jolene . . ."

She slid her laptop across the table toward me. "Have you been following our YouTube channel? We have twenty thousand more subscribers now than we had last month. Isn't that great?"

Jolene had been hired by the Ryans' historical reconstruction and renovation company, JR Properties, as its social media and marketing guru. Her current focus was the renovation of my house, which she was using to attract clients to the company while also saving me lots of money with donations of building materials and fixtures. Beau donated his time and expertise, as well as the time and expertise of handymen Thibaut and Jorge, as a marketing expense. Jaxson, an amateur photographer and a childhood friend of Beau's, also worked pro bono on the project.

Despite feeling as if Beau had forced me yet again into the position of needing saving from myself, I had to admit that I was in an enviable situation. I was using my graduate degree in historic preservation while gaining the expertise to renovate my own house—all this while contributing to the architectural character of my new city and creating a new family and community, both necessary in my ongoing battle with my personal demons.

And now, with the popularity of the YouTube channel and other social media outlets, JR Properties was hoping to expand in a brand-new direction: murder-house flipping—meaning renovating and selling houses that would normally be unsalable because of unsavory deaths having happened under their roofs. I should have been excited that Beau had chosen me to spearhead the first project, the house on Esplanade that Cooper was interested in seeing, with an eye to purchase. And it would have been exciting—if only it didn't mean having to see more of Beau Ryan.

There was something between us, something neither of us could or wanted to name—an invisible thread born of shared childhood-abandonment issues and of Beau's need to be someone's savior, which was as strong as my need to rely only on myself. And although I would admit it to no one, a physical spark manifested itself between us whenever we shared the same space. At least we were both equally committed to ignoring it: I because I didn't need any more complications in my life; Beau because being with me opened up his psychic gift, leading restless spirits to him, even those he didn't want—including his own mother.

"We have sponsors lining up," Jolene continued, "and lots of promised freebies for your house just for the mentions. And Mimi says she'll offer a beautiful antique bed and dresser of your choosing from the Past Is Never Past in return for featuring it and the store in an upcoming episode."

"That's wonderful," I said. "Just no antiques for the guest room, for when Melanie or Sarah come to visit." My twelve-year-old half sister, Sarah, had inherited Melanie's psychic gift, and neither one would appreciate an old bed that came with previous occupants.

I took a sip from my mug and nearly choked on ice-cold coffee. I looked at Jolene to see if it might be a prank, but she was busily scrolling through the comments left under a recent video showing Thibaut and Jorge doing their wildly popular tool-juggling act on-site at the never-ending renovation of my Creole cottage in the Marigny. They had begun to include Mardi in some of the videos, which I was convinced was the reason for the sudden upswing in followers.

"Mardi is getting so much love from our viewers," she said. "I think he needs his own account on Instagram, to increase our exposure. He might even become a home-remodeling influencer! Sort of like the Kardashians, but less tacky and with more tools."

I blinked, still hoping I was being punked. When she didn't say anything, I said, "But we already have an Instagram account."

"You mean JR Properties has an account. I'm talking about Mardi having his very own account. And, by the way, they're now calling it 'the 'Gram,' so make sure you get it right when you're creating reels or captions. We don't want to lose our younger audience."

I stared at her for a moment, beginning to feel very concerned. "Um, right. Just one thing, though. Mardi's a dog—remember? He can't type."

She looked at me as if I'd just set my hair on fire. "Of course he can't type. He doesn't have opposable thumbs."

Before I could say anything else, acrid smoke began billowing from the kitchen. "Do you need to check the muffins?" I asked.

Jolene regarded me briefly before wrinkling her nose. "I think something's burning. Let me go check the oven."

When she returned, it was with a plate filled with decapitated muffins. "Someone forgot to remove the plastic wrap before putting them in the oven, so it melted all over the tops. Luckily, I was able to salvage the bottom halves." She plopped next to the plate a carton of spreadable butter straight from the fridge, a steak knife protruding from the middle of it. For as long as I'd known Jolene, she had never once put on the dining table anything that wasn't on a serving dish. Including butter. And she definitely had never served butter with a steak knife.

"Who are you and what have you done with Jolene?" I'd intended it as a joke, but its meaning flew straight over her head.

"I'm right here, Nola. Maybe you need to see your eye doctor." She returned to her seat and began to flip through the pages scattered in front of her. "Do you think Mimi Ryan would let us use her house on Prytania for the party? I'd make the food, of course, but we don't have the room here, and going to a restaurant seems so impersonal, although the Court of Two Sisters does have that large courtyard that's perfect for entertaining." She frowned. "Then again, if it rains we'll be forced to go inside, which would defeat the purpose of choosing a unique space." She reached across the table to a hand-drawn list and used her pencil to draw a line through one of the items.

"Or why don't we ask the Sabatiers if we could use their beach house in Ocean Springs?"

Jolene frowned, the perfect skin on her forehead creasing. "Have you lost your cotton-pickin' mind? After what they did to the Ryans? Let me check your temperature, because either you have a terrible fever or you've truly lost your mind."

"I'm joking. Obviously. Besides, Robert Sabatier is in jail, facing kidnapping charges for taking Sunny, and I heard that his wife, Angelina, has temporarily moved to New York to be with Michael and Sunny—although Sunny still wants to be called Felicity. Mimi said that she and Sunny are FaceTiming once a week to connect, so that's something."

"Poor Mimi," Jolene said. "All of those years looking for her granddaughter, and when she finally finds her, it seems she didn't want to be found."

"Probably because she never considered herself lost."

Jolene's eyes met mine across the table. She nodded solemnly, giving me the impression that she was back to normal and at any moment she would notice that she hadn't set the table properly. Or put on shoes. "So"—I pushed away my cold coffee and the tub of butter and indicated the cluttered table—"what are you doing?"

"I'm planning an engagement party, silly." She smiled brightly, as if I were the confused person.

"Exactly. For Jaxson. And Carly."

"I know." Her smile didn't fade, and her expression reminded me of that worn by the actresses in *The Stepford Wives*.

During my first tumultuous months back in New Orleans, Jolene had stuck by me as I navigated my new life, as well as an alcohol-addiction relapse and a heartbreak. She'd been the kind of friend who offered love and support even when they weren't deserved—the kind of friend she needed right now. "Jolene," I said softly, "you know I love you like a sister, right? So I want you to hear me when I say that I think you need some time off. Jaxson's engagement must have been a bit of a shock."

"Why would you say that?"

My gaze drifted down to her feet before taking in the butter tub and mug resting on the table, then rose to meet her green eyes. "You seem . . . disoriented."

"Do I?" Her voice sounded unnaturally high. She wiggled her toes, each nail painted a delicate pink. "If it's about the bare feet, I kick off my shoes when I need to do some deep thinking. It reminds me of when I was just a little bitty thing and I'd run out the back door before Mama could catch me and make me put my shoes on. Helps me focus."

"Then maybe you should go home to Mississippi for a bit. Take a break and schedule spa time with your mother and grandmother."

She chewed on her lower lip. "Well, I was planning on going home for Thanksgiving, and that's only a couple of weeks away. Beau said I could take the whole week off since nothing usually happens at the office over the holiday."

"Maybe he'll let you go sooner, and you can work remotely." I gave her an encouraging smile. "I'll make sure that tons of photos are taken and videos are recorded, and I'll send them to you so you can post them with your amazing commentary."

She was silent, her brow furrowed. I was already mentally clapping myself on the back when Jolene's face brightened and she slid her chair back before slapping her hands on the table. "Thank you! Despite your appalling lack of style sense, you've got good horse sense."

I stared at her. "You're welcome—I think. But thanks for what?"

"For giving me the idea of where to host the most perfect engagement party ever! Mama and Daddy are always looking for a good excuse to entertain, and they will be over the moon to have a reason to bring out the special Pickard china they only use for big family gatherings, like the Fourth of July and funerals."

"But—"

"It could be a destination engagement party! Like a destination bachelorette party or wedding, but closer to home. It's only four hours away, and we have tons of room on account of my daddy hosting hunting parties and us having so much kin that hosting Thanksgiving and Christmas is a lot like gathering the troops before a big battle—except we're friendlier. We've converted the old garçonnière into a guesthouse that sleeps twelve. And if we have overflow, there's always Grandmama's funeral home. She doesn't live there anymore because of the nightmares, but she always keeps the four upstairs bedrooms clean and ready for unexpected guests."

"But—"

"Carly already told me that she's letting me handle all the details, that she trusts me to make it the best party ever, and, thanks to you, I will!"

"But—"

"I can start the planning over Thanksgiving. We can throw the party right before Christmas so Mama won't have to do any extra decorating since the house will already be sparkling like a float in the Christmas parade. She'll want to add tulle and glitter for the special occasion, and of course red roses—I wonder how hard those are to come by in December. I bet Grandmama knows, since people die in December, which is highly inconvenient, but they still want roses at their funerals, but—"

"Jolene." I said it louder than usual because she was on an over-caffeinated train of unfiltered thought that could go on for hours and I was going to be late for work. I was an architectural historian for a civil engineering firm, and though my employers were very accommodating with my schedule, allowing me to fit my office hours around the renovations of my house, they had their limits.

Jolene stopped midsentence, her green eyes widening. "Why are you shouting? You've made me forget what I was saying."

"Good, because I need you to have a long think about this whole engagement-party idea. I know any party you planned would be the most amazing party ever, but I'm wondering if your efforts would be better spent elsewhere—like on organizing the house-blessing party for when my house is finally done. You've mentioned doing that before." I gave her an encouraging smile.

Her shoulders dipped. "But I already—"

I held up my hand. "I know. Why don't you drink a tall glass of water and then go lie down? I'll call Beau and tell him you'll be coming in late this morning, all right?"

"But I've already made my bed."

"Of course you have," I said under my breath. "I haven't made mine, so feel free to use it. We can talk again after work. I'll order pizza. We can put on one of your gooey face masks and have a good chat, all right? Hopefully by then the caffeine will have worn off and you can think clearly."

She lowered her eyes. "All right. Maybe I need to go back to Mississippi early regardless. Nothing like being home to restore the soul, you know?"

"Yeah. I know." I gave her a lopsided grin. "Cooper was supposed to drive me home to Charleston for Thanksgiving, but now he has to fly to Malaysia on business and won't be able to. A plane ticket's not in my budget, and I refuse to accept another penny from my parents. It's no big deal—I'll be seeing them for Christmas."

She perked up. "Then you need to come with me! Mama would love to have you! And you can meet the rest of my family!"

I imagined Jolene times ten, and I'd be lying if I said I didn't find the thought more than a little intimidating—and exhausting. "Wow, that's really generous, but I'd planned to use the time to catch up on work and install plumbing fixtures in the downstairs bathroom at my house. Definitely another time, okay? I'd love to meet your family, since I've heard so much about them."

"Okay." She gave me a tired smile, and I noticed how her usually fresh lipstick had faded to a pale rose.

"How long have you been up?"

Jolene glanced at her watch. "I'm not sure I ever went to bed. I had all of these party plans running through my head and I needed to write them down before I forgot them, so as soon as you went to bed I made a pot of coffee. And then I think I made another. It's all sort of fuzzy right now. . . ."

I took her elbow and pulled her from her chair. "You'll feel better after you've had a good sleep." I led her to my room and tucked her into my bed after removing an unhappy Mardi. She was already asleep before I'd pulled the covers over her. I grabbed my clothes for work, then tiptoed out of the room, carrying Mardi so he wouldn't jump back into the bed. I was eager to feed and walk the dog, then get to work before Jolene awoke and realized she'd gone to sleep with her makeup on.

I was halfway to the kitchen to brew a fresh pot of coffee and fill Mardi's bowl when my cell phone rang. "Hi, Sarah. Shouldn't you be at school?"

I could picture her rolling her eyes. "I am. But I snuck my phone into school so I could excuse myself to use the bathroom during class and talk to you in private. I don't want Mom to hear."

A smattering of gooseflesh erupted down my spine. "Oh, okay. What's up?" I forced a light tone. "You want me to tell Jolene you don't want the Barbie head?"

"Um, no. It's something else."

I waited for her to continue, the gooseflesh rippling along my skin as a ball of dread congealed in the pit of my stomach.

"I got a phone call from Great-grandma Sarah. On Mom's land-line. The one that's not plugged in or anything."

My gaze drifted to my own unplugged telephone sitting on top of the ancient teacher's desk in the dining room. Melanie's deceased grandmother Sarah had called me on that phone, too, but mercifully she had been silent ever since the spirit showdown in the Ryans' attic. I'd tried hiding the old phone in the back of my closet, but it kept reappearing on the desk, in the exact spot from where it had been removed. I'd considered taking it to a dumpster, but I had chosen not to when the phone had stopped ringing. After listening to my sister, I was rethinking my decision.

"Yeah? Did she have anything interesting to say?"

"Hang on." Her words were muffled, as if she was holding her cell phone against her chest, and then all I could hear was the sound of a distant door clanging shut, followed shortly afterward by a toilet flushing and water running. "That was close. I had to duck into a stall. That was Holly McCormick, and if she'd caught me she would have gone straight to the head of school's office."

"So, what did Grandma Sarah have to say?" I tried to keep the impatience out of my voice.

She paused, and I could hear her breathing into the phone.

"Sarah?"

"Do you remember that fortune teller we saw at Jackson Square that day we all had lunch at Muriel's?"

"Yeah. It was right before we saw the wet footprints and you saw Beau's mom. Adele."

"Like the singer." Sarah's voice was so quiet I could barely hear her.

"That's right. And Adele said something to you."

"She told me that she wanted to help Beau."

"And she said to decide what's worth the fight and let the rest go—among other things. I remember."

"Yeah, well, Grandma Sarah said that again today on the phone."

I closed my eyes, wondering why I had bothered to wake up today.

"She said that you needed to go talk to Madame Zoe about Buddy. I have no clue who she was talking about, and I was hoping that you might."

I cleared my throat. "Madame Zoe is the fortune teller. Buddy is Beau's dad. Madame Zoe stopped by a few weeks ago. She didn't stay to chat, just long enough to say that Beau needed me and that I needed to bring him to her so they could talk about Buddy. Madame Zoe apparently knew him. He also disappeared during Katrina."

"He's not dead," Sarah said matter-of-factly.

"I sort of figured, since we haven't seen his footprints following us around, although I'm not sure why he's stayed gone all this time if he's still alive. I'm sure that's part of Beau's anger toward his parents."

She didn't respond. "Sarah? You still there?"

"I'm here." I listened as she breathed in, then out, my nerves on high alert.

"There's one more thing she wanted me to tell you, and I don't know how you're going to take it."

I sat down hard in my recently vacated chair, my knees wobbly. Mardi stopped whining for his food and rested his head and paws on my feet. That was the thing about dogs. They were better than most people at sensing things that we couldn't see or feel—or that we preferred to pretend weren't there.

"She kept saying the word 'bones,' and then there was a sound like . . . sucking mud—like when we'd dig for clams in the marsh."

"'Bones' and sucking mud," I repeated. A flash of lightning flared from the window, followed by a roar of thunder. Mardi shuffled under my chair for protection but returned his paw to rest on my foot.

A song began blasting in my ear, drowning out Sarah's voice. "Do you hear that?" I shouted. If she replied, I couldn't hear it. The call ended, abruptly stopping the music. I placed the phone on the table, not wanting to drop it from my shaking hand, the familiar tune still in my head, its words on a seeming loop. "Rolling in the Deep" by

Adele. I wanted to believe that it was a coincidence that Beau's mother's name was Adele—but as my father, Jack, had often said, there was no such thing as coincidence.

I closed my eyes as a burst of hard rain pelted the window, suddenly reminding me of something Jolene had told me. *When the water rises in New Orleans, it's anyone's guess what might rise with it.*

CHAPTER 3

Heavy rains continued throughout the day and into the next, forcing my boss to cancel my scheduled fieldwork to evaluate an old sugar plantation in Plaquemines Parish—which was probably a good thing, since I hadn't figured out how I was supposed to get there. By choice I didn't own a car, mostly because I was a reluctant and newly relicensed driver, so when traveling to adjoining parishes—a requirement for my job—I was dependent on other drivers, usually Jolene. Eventually I'd have to get a car, because being driven by Jolene was almost as nerve-racking as driving myself.

Although Jolene had gone to work she still hadn't seemed herself. At least she hadn't again mentioned giving the engagement party at her parents' house in Mississippi. I hoped that meant that she'd decided against it, but I was too afraid to bring it up again.

When Cooper called I smiled dopily at my phone as I answered. He didn't waste any time before getting to the point of the call. "Are you up to go look at some houses? I know our official house hunting isn't supposed to start until tomorrow, but I figured with all this rain your Plaquemines Parish excursion would be postponed."

My smile broadened. "You remembered." It was rare to find a man who not only listened to the minutiae of one's life but also paid attention.

"I have a mother and a sister. I learned the hard way the consequences of not listening."

His sister, Alston, was one of my best friends from Charleston, and I could only imagine the passive-aggressive punishments.

"Plus, I find your life interesting."

"I was already going to say yes, Cooper. You didn't have to sweeten the deal with flattery."

He chuckled. "I'm serious. You're a *fascinating* person. I've always thought that."

I was glad he couldn't see my flaming cheeks. "Yes, well, we can at least go see the house on Esplanade, since JR Properties owns it and I have the keys. And since I'm leading the renovation, I'll be able to give you a good idea of what it will look like when it's all done. Just let me know when you'd like to go, and I'll be ready."

"I'm actually in your driveway. I was hoping you'd say yes."

"Oh. Wow. I can be ready in five."

"Perfect. I'll meet you at your door with an umbrella."

I ran to my room to grab my backpack, and then to the coat-tree in the living room for my ancient rain jacket, passing the large hall mirror on my way. I stopped in horror at my reflection. I was wearing the usual fieldwork uniform of long-sleeved T-shirt and baggy jeans, ratty hair in a ponytail, and no makeup. Before I'd met Jolene I would have kept going looking like this, but I couldn't help but feel guilty at the thought of discarding all her tutelage—not to mention her oft-repeated adage "It's always better to arrive late than to arrive ugly."

Muttering to myself, I ran to Jolene's room, resisting the impulse to call her for guidance. I was a grown woman, and I had been practicing good grooming habits and makeup application under Jolene's watchful eye for months now. Surely I was capable of making myself presentable in five minutes.

Twenty minutes later I was running down the stairs, sliding my hair tie over my high ponytail and ensuring that the lipstick I'd used to swipe my lips was tucked into the pocket of my dress—a pullover navy one I'd borrowed from Jolene's closet. It had a simple round neckline with no collar, zipper, or buttons—but it did have two deep pockets, which was the sole reason I'd selected it. I left my backpack, instead choosing to bring the crossbody purse that had been made for me by Paige Mukowski, the young woman masquerading as Sunny Ryan. Paige had disappeared on the same night her secret was discovered, but despite her duplicity, I firmly believed that she wasn't a bad person.

I knew what it was like to be in the kind of situation in which no choice was a good one, and what lay behind doors A, B, and C was all equally terrible. I also knew that Paige had never intended to hurt anyone. She'd been raised in the foster care system and had wanted only to find a family to call her own—even if it belonged to someone else.

I jogged down the stairs, my feet buried in a borrowed pair of yellow patent leather rain boots. I hoped that they would distract Cooper from noticing any of my hastily-applied-makeup errors and the amateur hairstyling attempt. I was contemplating whether I should ask Jolene for a large Barbie head for Christmas when I opened the door to find Cooper waiting patiently under a large umbrella.

"Sorry it took me so long," I said. "Saying good-bye to Mardi always takes a while." That wasn't a lie.

Cooper smiled, and something inside my chest squeezed. "It was worth the wait." He placed his hand on the small of my back as he guided me toward his car, being careful not to let any rain hit me.

As he typed the address of the house on Esplanade into his GPS app, I said, "I should probably drive, since I know where we're going, and you should be focusing on the neighborhood instead of the road." I held my breath, hoping he'd say no.

"Thanks, but you can't drive." He started the engine, then pulled the car out onto the street.

"What? Have you been talking to Beau?" I couldn't keep the indignation from my voice. "He's the one who's always forcing me to drive even though I've made it clear that I'm not—"

"No. It's not that at all. It's just that this is a rental, and only my name is on the agreement as an authorized driver."

"Oh. Of course. It's probably for the best anyway. With me behind the wheel I'm liable to kill us both, and then you'll never get to see the house."

Cooper didn't smile, his grip on the steering wheel tightening as he focused on the road in front of him. "You shouldn't say that."

I looked at him, studying the odd set of his mouth. It was the sort of grimace one wore when delivering bad news. "I was only joking."

"I know." The *swoosh-swoosh* of the windshield wipers filled the silence, his grim expression giving me pinpricks of apprehension. He looked at me, and I saw again the scar on his chin, something he hadn't had when I'd known him in Charleston. I touched it gently with my finger, and he turned his head away, his gaze focusing on the rain pelting the car's hood. I dropped my hand.

"How did you get that? Shaving incident?" I'd wanted it to sound flippant, to lighten the suddenly serious mood, but when he looked at me again, his stricken expression told me that I shouldn't have said anything at all.

"Bad traffic accident in LA," he said, so quietly that I could barely hear it over the sound of the rain hammering the top of the car.

"Were you driving?" I wasn't sure why I asked. Probably because my aversion to driving was due to an accident I'd caused while behind the wheel.

Yeah. I couldn't hear the word, but he nodded his head once.

"Was anyone else hurt?"

He pretended he hadn't heard me, and I was glad. I shouldn't have asked him, as everything about his body language had told me to back off, but there was a mystery there and, as with my dad, it was against my nature to let a mystery go, no matter how much I knew I should.

Cooper swerved around a pothole on Carrollton before expertly maneuvering back into his lane. "Wow," he said. "That was huge. Don't they spend any money on road improvements here?"

"Not that I know of," I said, realizing that the previous topic had been closed indefinitely. "There's a great Insta account devoted to the potholes and other hazards on New Orleans streets. I'll send you a link. It's always good for a smile while you're waiting on the side of the road for a tow truck."

He laughed. It sounded a little forced, but his expression had returned to normal. We spent the rest of the short drive talking about his new job and his sister, Alston, who kept promising to come visit but hadn't yet. As he turned right on Esplanade I indicated how far down the avenue he needed to go, then pointed out the bright blue shotgun house with the Classical Revival architectural details I'd fallen in love with on my very first visit. There was something special about an old house, its timeworn existence evidenced by its drooping eaves and peeling paint, its fading patina like an elderly woman's old lipstick.

Cooper put the car in park, then unbuckled his seat belt before turning to face the avenue. His gaze took in the street, including its wonky intersection with Bayou Road and the eclectic display of styles and color palettes of the houses that lined the avenue. "I like this," he said. "I like this a lot. It reminds me of Charleston. Old trees, incredible architecture . . ."

"Eyebrow-singeing heat in the summer, flying cockroaches . . ." I added.

He grinned. "Yeah. Just like home."

I wasn't a real estate agent, but my stepmother was, and she would be disappointed in me if I didn't emphasize the selling points of the house's location. "This grand boulevard was the Spanish citizens' response to St. Charles Avenue, which was the exclusive domain of the new Americans back in the day, which is why there's this gorgeous neutral ground and old-growth oak trees. You can tell just by the paint color choices that this isn't the Garden District—or South of Broad," I added, as a nod to his Charleston neighborhood.

"True." He spun in a half circle to take in the neighboring houses, stopping to peer down the street. "What's in that direction?"

"City Park. If you're still a runner, it's only about one and a half miles in that direction, and in the other direction there's a straight shot to the US Mint building, which now houses the jazz museum."

A dark gray Honda sedan traveling on the same side of the street as the house slowed its pace as it approached us where we stood on the neutral ground. I wouldn't have even noticed it except that its two occupants, a teenage girl and a woman who appeared old enough to be her mother, were looking at what I now considered to be my house. They didn't stop, but as soon as they were past the house the car sped up. "Uh-oh," I said. "You might have some competition."

"Bring it on," Cooper said. "I don't think many buyers are as committed to renovation as I am." He faced me. "And that's just one of the reasons why I love this house. But best of all, I'd be really close to your cottage in the Marigny."

"How did you know that?"

"I Googled it. I like the thought of you being nearby."

"Oh. Okay." I fumbled with the house keys to hide my acute awkwardness. I needed to dissect his implication, but I knew that deep analysis would wait until the wee hours of the morning as I lay awake with his words and their potential meaning haunting me like a little sheep refusing to be counted.

We climbed the porch steps and, after two tries, managed to unlock the door. Pushing it open, I said, "Ignore the furniture and décor. It has a sort of hoarding-grandma's-garage vibe, but it's all going away."

Cooper followed me into the living room, the first in a single line of rooms leading to the rear of the home, a typical shotgun house. "Just don't do anything until I've made my decision," he said. "There might be a few pieces here and there that I'd want to . . ." He stopped as his gaze fell on a cracked-leather footstool with what appeared to be real alligator feet, then traveled to the collection of taxidermied animal heads hanging on the walls. "Never mind," he said as he bent to examine a yellowed lace doily on the headrest of an overstuffed floral armchair. Straightening, he looked at me with a grimace. "Nothing that a match and lighter fluid can't fix."

I suppressed a laugh. "To be fair, in one of the bedrooms there are a few larger antiques that are quite nice. Whatever you decide about the house, you can certainly make an offer for any of the furniture for your new home—assuming you don't already have a houseful in storage somewhere."

The stiff expression he'd worn in the car when he'd been talking about the scar on his chin settled on his face again. He turned toward one of the floor-to-ceiling windows, where sunlight now spilled through its open louvers. I'd removed the heavy draperies, since they seemed to be more dust and mothballs than velvet, and to allow natural light to illuminate the beautiful architectural details of the ceiling cornices and thick baseboards.

Cooper shoved his hands into his pockets and peered outside. "I sold everything when I moved. I wanted to make a clean break."

Before I could ask him why, he tilted his head. "Do you smell perfume?"

I nodded, glad it wasn't just me who'd noticed it. I wasn't interested in a personal haunting, but I could probably handle a general one. Recent experiences had soured me on hangers-on who had something they wanted to tell only me.

He continued. "It reminds me of a perfume my grandmother wears—definitely not a scent you smell very much anymore."

"True. I'm not sure who it belongs to, but I don't get any negative vibes. In the interest of full disclosure, you might also hear the sound of small running feet. It's apparently a little boy, according to Beau, but we don't know who he is or why he's here."

"What about the perfume wearer? Any guesses as to who she might be?"

"It could be the woman who was murdered in the house. I think I read that her name was Sybil. She was in her sixties. That was over eight years ago, so it could be her. Her son, daughter-in-law, and granddaughter disappeared and have never been found, but I don't think it would be any of them, since there's no evidence that any of them are dead."

Cooper nodded as he slowly walked around the perimeter of the room, studying his surroundings. "So there weren't any witnesses to Sybil's murder?"

"Just a bird. Zeus. But Zeus hasn't spoken a word since."

Cooper looked at me with raised eyebrows. "Interesting."

"Very," I said. Turning to face the room, I imagined I was Melanie showing a house to a client. "So, it's a small house with a quirky yet iconic floor plan. It's what's called a camelback shotgun because an upstairs room was added to the back of the house, with stairs leading from the kitchen. The only bathroom is at the end of the house, on this floor, only accessible through the kitchen and bedrooms."

"Not really made for today's living, but it's your job to convince me, right?"

Before I could reply, my phone buzzed. "It's Jolene," I said to Cooper. "Is it okay if I answer? It's probably just to ask me what I want for dinner."

"Sure. I'll just keep exploring the house if that's all right."

I gave him a thumbs-up and answered the call.

"Good news!" Jolene's cheerful voice sounded normal, making me hopeful that she'd recovered from her earlier funk.

"Yeah? Did we get that new sponsor—the bug control people?" Having bug control was as important as, if not more than, having a roof if you owned a house in New Orleans.

"I'm working on it, and I'm very close."

As Jolene spoke, I walked toward the back of the house, to the larger bedroom, where I remembered seeing a few pieces of furniture that might be salvageable. The room appeared to have been emptied of all personal items, presumably by the last owners, Honey Meggison and Joan Wenzel, widowed sisters in their mid-to-late sixties, and stepdaughters of the murdered woman found with the parrotlet Zeus in the house. They had hung on to the house for eight years, never giving up hope that their half brother, Mark, along with his wife and child, would one day return—or be found.

A dark walnut bed with knobby spindles and a curved headboard but missing a mattress and bedding had been shoved against one wall, possibly to remove the rug whose shadow remained on the sun-bleached wooden floor. I tried not to think of why the rug might be missing, my imagination going straight to the infamous unsolved murder.

Opposite the bed sat a marble-topped dressing table, its oval mirror speckled with age. A narrow drawer sat above the kneehole, while two larger ones were located on each side of the opening, drawing my attention. One by one, I slid them open to see what might have been left behind. If everything hadn't already been cleared out by either the police or the family, it was unlikely that anything left would have any value. Still, I had to look—if only to tell the junk-collection company what to expect.

Jolene continued. "When I mentioned your address, they hung up on me. I called back until they finally answered, and they swore up and down that the call was accidentally dropped. Whatever. They're working up a proposal and will e-mail it to me. Apparently, none of the salespeople or technicians want to come out to give me a proper quote. That just grinds my grits."

To be fair, my house did have a well-deserved reputation for being haunted. But, thanks to Beau, all the spirits were gone now. The UPS guy still did only drive-by deliveries, during which he slid packages out of the truck without coming to a complete stop, but at least the birds and insects had returned to my yard to sing their daily choruses.

"But in the meantime," Jolene continued, "I've got something even better! I've found you a car!"

"A car?" My enthusiasm was several levels below hers. I pulled open the final drawer, empty except for a single pair of men's white boxer shorts. I didn't examine them closely enough to determine whether they were clean before slamming the drawer shut.

"You should be excited, Nola. You'll have your own car, so you won't have to beg people for rides. Don't get me wrong. I enjoy your company and I don't mind driving you. It's just, well . . ." She paused. "It's Bubba."

"Bubba? Has he finally gone to the junkyard in the sky?" I turned toward a chest of drawers and began opening each one. Except for an impressive collection of mismatched socks, the drawers were stuffed with an odd assortment of household junk. I'd make sure to mark the furniture "as is" when the estate sale happened so that deciding what to keep and what to give away wouldn't be up to me. My precarious early childhood had included living in a car for three months, so discarding anything that might be useful later was harder for me than for most.

"I won't tell him you said that. Hopefully he'll last another fifty years or so—assuming you're not a frequent passenger."

I approached a freestanding armoire, its sparse style and small size narrowing its approximate vintage down to the 1920s or '30s. An empty keyhole was set conspicuously in one of the two doors. "What's that supposed to mean?" I pulled on the door's teardrop-shaped knob, to no effect. Frowning at the object, I then dug my fingertips into the edge of the door and tugged, my efforts rewarded by what sounded like the clinking of colliding wooden hangers and the thunk of a small, hard object falling to the bottom of the armoire.

Peering into the narrow opening between the doors, I didn't see the brass bar that should have been there if the doors were locked. This meant that the doors were merely stuck—not an unusual thing, considering that the doors were wooden and the house was in a humid climate that could rival that of the Amazon.

I turned to the single nightstand, which stood on its side next to the bed, and slid open its top drawer in search of anything I could use to pry the doors open. It wasn't that opening the armoire would be instrumental to assuring Cooper's interest in the home, but it would be for my peace of mind. I had inherited my father's need to solve problems. I was like a cat waiting at a baseboard for a mouse that had disappeared. There was a solution for every problem—although, as I'd learned from working with Melanie and Beau, it wasn't always a logical one.

I raked my hand through a pile of paper clips in the top drawer. "You do know that cars are inanimate objects, right?" Examining the back of the drawer, I found a collection of rubber bands and a roll of postage stamps, as well as a receipt from the now-defunct K&B pharmacy; it was for a prescription refill for the same arthritis medication my grandmother Amelia took. I shoved everything back into place before closing it.

"Says the girl who has never owned a car," Jolene continued. "Bubba and I have gone through a lot together. And he survived decades with pristine armrests until you became a frequent passenger. Now there are fingernail marks etched into the vinyl all over the armrests and side door. It's like some rabid raccoon has been living in my car. And believe me, I know what kind of damage a rabid raccoon can do. My cousin Gwen—you know, the one in Greenwood? She went away to Ocean Springs for the weekend to visit a friend who was feeling poorly, and while she was gone a raccoon and its four babies chewed through the screen of a window she used to leave open for ventilation in the attic, and the raccoons took up residence. Lordy, it was like someone had tried to dress an angry cat and put curlers in its tail."

"Thanks for the visual, Jolene. Very helpful. So, what you're telling me is that you are no longer willing to drive me when I need a ride?" Hearing myself, I winced, realizing how selfish I sounded.

"I'm not saying that," she said without sounding offended, which only made me feel worse. "You know I love you, which is why I'm being a mama bird and pushing you out of the nest because you refuse to fly. It's for your own good. You'll thank me later. Promise."

I sighed into the phone. "So, what is this car and how much is it?" I opened the crossbody bag, wishing I'd brought my backpack, which contained the small toolbox that had been a gift from Melanie. As different as we were, I'd begun to appreciate some of my stepmother's idiosyncrasies, like using a labeling gun and having an organized underwear drawer but carrying random items in my bag—which had paid off more than once. Like now. At the last minute before heading out the door, I'd grabbed a screwdriver and thrown it into the purse, next to the roll of breath mints Jolene insisted I always carry.

"It's a red 1967 Mustang convertible. Fully restored." She sounded like I'd just won the lottery.

Cradling the phone between my shoulder and my ear, and being careful not to scratch the polished surface of the armoire, I used the flat head of the screwdriver to pry open the doors. The wood protested with a short creak and moan as the doors swung open, a scent of stale perfume billowing out like an exhaled breath.

"Nola? You still there?"

"Right. Sorry. The car sounds old. And expensive. You know I can't afford—"

"It's free! You just need to transfer the title and get it insured, and it's all yours. Grandmama got it from Ida Peacock when her husband, Dew, passed on. He loved that car more than anything else—including Ida, according to her and just about everybody in town—and he wanted to be buried in it. Ida didn't want to go to the expense for 'that damn car'—those are her words, not my grandmama's, who doesn't cuss—and she didn't want it sitting in her garage and acting like a slap in the face every time she saw it, so she just gave it to Grandmama to offset the funeral costs. But Grandmama said she's too old to be driving a red car and offered it to me."

"Then you take it," I said distractedly as my gaze traveled over the interior of the armoire, taking in a small, mirrored door with yet another empty keyhole. The mirror was head height, making me think it had been meant for knotting a tie or combing hair. The door was shut fast with no knob, making me guess that the absent key doubled as the knob, and when I tried to insert the flat head of the screwdriver it was clear that this particular door was locked.

Squatting, I reached into the back recesses of the armoire in search of a key, but instead of finding one, my fingers touched cool, hard glass. I recalled the sound of something falling when I pried open the door, and when I drew out my hand I found myself holding an old bottle of perfume. The dark brown, viscous contents were half-gone, and when I pulled off the brass cap the spray nozzle was clogged and sticky. I lifted the bottle to my nose, the lingering scent vaguely familiar.

"I can't accept a new car, Nola. Bubba would never forgive me. It would be like having an affair, and I'm not a cheater."

I closed my eyes, trying to place the scent, only partially listening to Jolene. "You're not married, so that wouldn't count as cheating."

"I'm going to pretend you didn't say that. And are you even listening? I'm offering you a free car—and not just a free car but a really cool vintage Mustang in mint condition. All you need to do is drive down with me to Mississippi to collect it, and it's all yours!"

The sound of small running feet rumbled in the adjacent room. My head jerked up, smacking the bottom of the top shelf of the armoire, making the hangers shimmy. "Cooper?" I called, even though I knew it couldn't have been him running in the next room. I'd heard the sound of bare feet against wooden floors. Bare, small feet that didn't belong to Cooper. I'd heard them before—the first time I'd been to the house with Beau.

"Nola?" Jolene's worried voice called through the phone. "Is everything all right?"

"Hang on a sec." I tiptoed to the door, then peered out into the adjacent room. As I turned to go back into the bedroom, I stepped on something. Lifting my foot, I spotted a stubby brass key—an old-fashioned kind usually found with antique furniture. Like an armoire.

"Thank you," I said to the emptiness.

"You're welcome," Jolene replied. "I'm thinking the best time would be Thanksgiving. You can bring your laptop and work in the car on the way down. . . ."

I tuned her voice out to concentrate on jabbing the key into the keyhole inside the armoire. The lock turned without any resistance. Gently pulling on the key, I opened the door and looked inside, blinking twice to register what it was I was seeing. A pair of lifeless blue eyes in a pale round face met my gaze. The object the eyes were connected to fell forward, somersaulting off the shelf upon which it had been resting, then hit my foot with a soft thud. It rolled forward, coming to rest at my feet, the sightless eyes staring up at me in silent supplication.

CHAPTER 4

I must have screamed, but I was so preoccupied with getting out of the room as quickly as possible that I couldn't say for sure. Only the pain from my forehead—I hit the doorframe on my way out—was proof of my panicked state. I'd made it to the kitchen before I collided with a large, solid human body—a body with two strong arms that immediately wrapped around me.

I buried my face in the broad chest, a familiar male scent breaking through my fear with a mixture of comfort and rightness. "Beau?" I muttered into his chest, unable to open my eyes.

"It's me," he said, instinctively patting my back and not asking for an explanation. This was the way it was between us; there was an unspoken understanding that was as comforting as it was confounding.

"Is everything okay? I thought I heard a scream."

Beau's arms dropped to his sides as I pulled away, not completely sure why I felt guilty. We both turned to see Cooper standing in the doorway between the dining room and the kitchen.

"Yes," I said. "There was . . ." I jerked my head in the direction of the back bedroom, not yet able to form coherent thoughts.

Beau took my hand in a solid grasp and began leading me toward the rear of the house, my forehead pounding where I'd smacked it. We stopped inside the second bedroom, taking in the open armoire and my purse, which I didn't remember dropping.

Cooper walked past us, then stopped in the middle of the room. "What's this?" He picked up the object of my terror and held it up.

I stayed back as Beau joined Cooper. "Looks like an antique doll," Beau said. "My grandmother has an impressive collection at the store." He took it from Cooper's hand and flipped the doll over before lifting the strawlike hair from the nape. "I can tell from the markings that it's a Madame Alexander doll, and definitely post-1940, since the dolls weren't marked before then, just their clothes."

"So you still play with dolls?" Cooper asked.

"Funny. Nola didn't tell me you were a comedian."

Cooper slid his gaze to me. "Nice to know she talks about me. The list of all my good points must have been too long."

Beau took his time smoothing down the doll's dress before turning it around to face us. "Actually, I can't say that she's ever mentioned your name once in the years I've known her."

I snatched the doll from Beau so he and Cooper would stop puffing up their feathers, or showing their rumps, or whatever was the human male equivalent to an animal dominance dance. "Is it worth anything?"

Beau shrugged. "Could be. You should ask Mimi, who's the real expert. I only know what Mimi's told me when she's sent me to auctions to bid on them. This one looks to be in pretty good condition, though, which will always put it in a pricier bracket. Where did it come from?"

I pointed at the armoire, the mirrored cabinet yawning open. "It was in there, behind the locked door—except there wasn't a key inside it."

"Where'd you find the key?" Cooper asked.

I opened and closed my mouth several times, trying to find the best way to answer the question. "I heard small feet running on the wooden floors, and when I went to investigate I stepped on the key."

"It must have fallen from the top of the doorframe ledge," Beau said. "It's a common place for hiding a key."

"Right," I said. "And denial isn't just a river in Egypt. Look, Cooper isn't a stranger to things that go bump in the night. He knows Melanie—remember? And if he's seriously considering buying this house, we need full disclosure of any . . . problems the house might have."

Our attention was drawn to a steady *drip, drip* from a corner of the room where a growing puddle had begun to spread on the uneven floor, accentuating the warping of the wood. Puckered plaster surrounded by yellowed and peeling paint ringed a hole in the ceiling through which rain entered the house unfettered.

"Exactly." Beau walked over to the corner and peered up at the ceiling. "Obviously a new roof and fixing the floors will be part of the renovation—which, incidentally, we haven't yet started—so if you're squeamish about old houses that need a lot of work, this isn't the house for you."

"Nola? Are you there? Do I need to call nine-one-one?" Jolene's voice came from my phone where I'd dropped it outside the doorway. I rushed to pick it up and turned on the speaker. "Sorry—I, uh, left my phone in another room. Beau and Cooper are here, so I've got to go. We can finish our conversation later, okay?"

"Sure. But did you hear the last thing I said?"

My mind tried to rewind to the moments before the doll fell at my feet. I gingerly touched the sore spot on my forehead, where a lump had begun to form. "About the Mustang?"

"No. About the story on the news this morning. It's been a real gully washer for the last week, so it's not totally unexpected, but a construction worker at the old Charity Hospital site found a human bone stuck in mud near the back entrance. He thought it might be from a nearby cemetery, since every once in a while some of the residents float out of their resting places during heavy rains, but the cemetery director said it didn't come from him, so—"

"Jolene," I interrupted, "is there anything important I need to know right away, or can this wait?"

"Sorry. It can wait. I just thought you'd find it interesting."

"Later, all right?"

"Fine. Last thing—if you need to borrow my rain boots, they're in the back of my closet, on the left side."

I looked down at my feet, warmly ensconced in Jolene's yellow boots. "Okay. Thank you. I think I will."

"Say hey to Cooper and Beau for me, all right?"

"I will. I've got to go n—"

"And if you don't think it will be too awkward with the two of them fighting over you, there's a great little place for lunch right down the street from where you are right now—Café Degas. It's Wednesday, which means they're open, so you're in luck. Did you know that Degas lived with an uncle and his family for a few months in a house on Esplanade? He—"

"See you tonight, Jolene." I ended the call, then turned back to where the two men stood in front of the armoire, pretending they hadn't heard Jolene talking about them.

Cooper was holding the perfume bottle I'd apparently dropped before fleeing; he had pulled off the stopper so he could wave its scent in the air between him and Beau. "I definitely recognize this perfume. I remember buying it for my grandmother every Christmas when Gwynn's had the gift sets."

"Yeah. And the lady of this house liked it a lot, too." I walked past Cooper with the doll, then shoved it back onto its little shelf and closed the door. "Why don't you put the bottle back inside as a special gift for whoever buys the armoire?"

Beau strode over to the armoire and removed the doll. "It's just a doll, Nola. No need to be creeped out about it. I need to bring this to Mimi so she can decide what she wants to do with it."

"I didn't say I was creeped out."

His eyes softened. "You didn't need to."

I felt Cooper shift on his feet as a small electric jolt shot through me. Glancing back to the leaking ceiling, I said, "Yeah, well, maybe we should be a little creeped out. This room could have been the murdered woman's, and this doll was locked inside the armoire without a key to open it. Sounds creepy to me."

Cooper faced Beau. "Why don't you go take your doll to your grandmother while Nola shows me the rest of the house and tells me the renovation plans? It was nice seeing you again."

"Actually, I stopped by to talk with Nola. We need to go over our reno specs, and Jolene mentioned that Nola wouldn't be doing fieldwork today because of the weather, so I figured this would be a good time. I thought maybe we could grab lunch and talk while we ate."

"That's a great idea," Cooper said. "Since I'm extremely interested in buying the house, I'm thinking I need to be part of the discussion."

Before I could say that I thought the three of us having lunch together was a terrible idea, a loud crack of thunder sounded above us, followed by a fresh burst of rain. The lights flickered, and my phone buzzed in my hand. I flipped it over to see the music app loading, and then the sound of Adele's "Rolling in the Deep" blasted from the speaker.

I attempted to shut off the music, and when that didn't work I turned the volume down to the lowest setting, which also had no effect. Desperate, I powered off the phone, Adele's singing coming to an abrupt stop.

My eyes met Beau's. "That was Adele. It's happened before. With the same Adele song. But I don't have any of her tunes in my music library."

"Hey, look at this." Beau and I turned to where Cooper was crouching in the middle of the room beside a set of wet footprints—too big to be a child's and too small for a man's—distinct from the growing puddle in the corner. He stood, pointing at the fading trail they made to the doorway, where they disappeared just past the threshold.

We sat at an interior table at Café Degas. The simple décor—including a tree emerging from the middle of the floor, and a French tricolor window hanging over the exposed kitchen area—came as a surprise, considering all the accolades the restaurant had garnered since it was opened in 1986. But, as my dad would always say when we went out to eat in Charleston, we weren't eating the furniture.

Cooper, Beau, and I ordered drinks immediately—a Fauxjito for me—even though it was the middle of the day. Despite our self-proclaimed immunity to paranormal phenomena, we were all a little off-kilter following the morning's events.

Cooper finished his drink with a large gulp before placing the glass on the table with a thunk. The pretty paisley-patterned tablecloth was covered thoughtfully with a sheet of glass, which I, for one, was especially thankful for, since Melanie said I still ate like a toddler.

"So, what was that all about?" Cooper asked. "Is that another ghost attached to the house, or something else?"

Beau stared down at the ice in his glass. "I'm not sure—"

"It's his mom," I interjected. "I'm pretty sure she's the woman you saw at the Ryans' house, the one who told you to go to the attic the night Beau almost died."

Cooper leaned back in his chair. "I know you keep saying that, but the woman I saw wasn't a ghost. I mean, she wasn't transparent or anything, and she spoke to me."

"But she was soaking wet," I said, "and it wasn't raining. I'm no expert, but I know that spirits appear in many forms, and that night Adele needed help to save her son's life."

"Adele?" Cooper's gaze flicked over to Beau.

The muscles in Beau's hand flexed. "Yeah. Like the singer. But that doesn't mean . . ."

I opened up the photo album on my phone and flipped through the pictures until I found the one I was looking for. I had snapped a photo of a framed picture of Adele with a much younger Beau the last time I was at Mimi's house. "Is this the woman you saw?"

Cooper took my phone and stared at the screen, his face blanching. "Yeah. That was definitely her." He gave me back my phone, with an apologetic glance at Beau.

"It was dark—remember?" Beau said. "And if her hair was wet—"

I squeezed Beau's arm. "Stop, okay? Cooper's a friend. He's also pretty good at solving puzzles; just ask my dad. Sometimes it helps to get a fresh perspective on a problem—"

"There's no problem, Nola, no mystery to be solved here. I wish you would just drop it."

The server appeared to take our order, before discreetly backing away at the tone of Beau's voice. I smiled at her, hoping she wouldn't take too long to return, because I was starving.

"I'm sorry, Beau. I know you don't like to admit it, but your mom is still here." I slid my chair closer to him, placing my hand on his arm. "Do you remember when you came to see me right after you got out of the hospital? After you left, I saw the wet footprints."

He stared at me in stony silence.

"But before the footprints appeared, I had another visitor. Madame Zoe. She's a fortune teller in Jackson Square."

Beau shook his head. "I don't—"

I cut him off. "She said you wouldn't know her. But she knew Buddy. Your father."

"Then why wouldn't she come to me first?" He raised his empty glass and signaled to the server to bring him another drink.

"Because, according to her, you'd fight the information that she would tell you—but it's something you need to know."

"That's ridiculous. Why would she tell you first?"

"Probably because Nola is one of the few people who could actually knock some sense into you and make you listen." Cooper folded his hands on the table and smiled. The server cautiously approached the table again and delivered a second round of drinks, but now she stood next to Cooper instead of Beau. "Ready to order?"

Beau glowered at her. Instead of asking her to come back again, even though we hadn't yet opened our menus except to look at the drinks, I gathered them up and handed them to her. "We'll all have today's lunch special. And water for the table." I gave her my friendliest smile as she backed away from the table and headed toward the kitchen.

Beau took a sip from his drink. "So, what did this Madame Zoe say?"

Unable to meet his eyes, I studied the paisley pattern beneath the glass table topper. "She said you'd need my counsel after hearing what she has to say. I don't have a clue what this is all about. All I *do* know is that Sunny's been found but your mom's still here. We all believed that was the reason why Adele was hanging around, but we were wrong. I'm guessing Adele's still being here has something to do with your dad. If she has information on what happened to him, or if he's still alive, don't you want to know?"

Glancing up, I met his eyes but had to look away quickly. His expression was too much like that of a lost child who suddenly found himself alone in the middle of a city sidewalk. "For the record, Grandmother Sarah called my sister to impart the same information about you going to see the fortune teller. I'm thinking that maybe we should go talk to Madame Zoe."

"'We'?"

I shrugged. "Grandmother Sarah and Madame Zoe's idea, not mine. You can go it alone if you want, but she said you're stubborn, like your dad, so if I have to drag you, I will. You're kinda big, but I bet if I need help, Cooper will be happy to volunteer to assist me."

Cooper gave me a lopsided grin. "Anything I can do to help, Nola."

The waitress, still leery of Beau's glowering expression, appeared with the soup course. We ate in silence until Beau cleared his throat and slid papers out of the satchel he'd brought from his truck. "So, if the two of you are done ganging up on me, let's talk about the house on Esplanade and the renovations. I've got a lot of great ideas but would welcome your input." He paused, then looked up at Cooper. "From both of you, assuming you're serious about buying it."

"As a heart attack," Cooper said, meeting Beau's eyes.

"Fine. And for the record, Louisiana law doesn't require me to tell you that there was a death on the property, but you seem to be already aware. Just Google the address if you want to know all the sordid details."

"I already did. There's a great site called DeathInHouse.com. It's only eleven dollars and ninety-nine cents per search. Didn't tell me anything I didn't already know. Except . . ."

"Except?"

"The running feet. Nola said it's a little boy, but the child who's been missing since the murder was a girl."

Beau nodded. "Yep. My guess is that whoever the boy is predates the murder. You might be able to find out more from the previous owners, Joan Wenzel and Honey Meggison. The house has been in their family since it was built. They might have an idea."

"I just might do that," Cooper said. He slid back his chair. "If you'll excuse me just for a moment, I need to visit the restroom before we get into this. I don't want to interrupt once we get started."

After he had left the table, Beau turned to me. He seemed to be waiting for something.

"What is it?" I asked.

He paused as if measuring his words. "Can I ask you something?"

For reasons I couldn't explain and didn't want to examine closely, my cheeks flushed. "That depends. About what?"

"Cooper."

"Cooper?"

"Yes. How well do you know him?"

I narrowed my eyes. "Why? Jealous?"

"Why would I be jealous?"

I decided to overlook the hidden insult in his question. "His sister is one of my best friends and she tells me everything, so I'd say I know him pretty well. We also dated for a minute when I was in high school and he was at the Citadel."

Beau's eyes shifted from me to the direction in which Cooper had headed. "Does his sister really tell you everything, or just what Cooper has told her?"

"I guess. I mean, Alston and Cooper were pretty close growing up, so I imagine he tells her everything." I sat back in my chair, feeling an uneasiness creeping over me. "What are you getting at?"

His gaze moved to a spot behind me. "Did she ever mention if Cooper had a significant other?"

"Like a girlfriend?"

"Probably something more serious, like a fiancée."

Icy chills tiptoed across my bones. "No, she didn't, maybe because she knows my history with Cooper and how devastated I was when he left."

"Uh-huh." His eyes didn't return to my face.

"Beau—what are you trying to tell me?"

He seemed reluctant to meet my eyes. "There's a woman here. I've been trying to ignore her, but she's very persistent. She's been standing behind Cooper's chair since we sat down."

"Okay," I said slowly. "What makes you think she's a significant other?"

Beau eyed me steadily as he spoke. "She's wearing a big diamond on her left hand and she definitely wanted me to notice it. She's also . . ." He stopped. Frowned.

"She's also what?"

"Angry. Maybe at Cooper. I'm not sure."

"Can you ask her who she is and why she's here? Ask her why she's angry."

His face seemed to close, like a curtain being drawn across a stage. "I'd rather not."

I raised my eyebrows. "Excuse me?"

"I don't want to engage. It gives unrestricted access to other spirits, who think they can just barge in and talk to me at any time, and unless you want me to burst out singing an ABBA song and slap my hands over my ears, you should respect my wishes."

I leaned forward so the server couldn't hear me hissing at him. "If by 'other spirits' you mean your mom, all I can say is that you should be ashamed of yourself. She saved your life, or have you already forgotten? And excuse me for pointing out the obvious, but maybe if you'd been listening to her all along, you wouldn't have almost died, and maybe—just maybe—you would have known about Sunny when she first showed up, and you probably would have found out what happened to your father by now."

His face darkened, his expression almost like a slap. "You have no idea—"

He stopped abruptly, shifting his focus back to his renovation notes when Cooper returned to the table.

"So, where were we?" Cooper asked.

I picked up my water glass and took my time emptying it.

Beau cleared his throat. "We were just saying that if you're really interested in the house, you might want to talk with the sellers. Since they're related to the original owners, they might be able to give you a bit of background on who lived there before and how the living spaces were utilized."

"Sounds great to me," Cooper said. "I share Nola's passion for old houses and appreciate that they're not just places where people live. They're vessels of history, really. And the sisters might be able to shed some light on who the barefoot little boy might be. I'm okay with sharing the house with him"—Cooper moved his chair closer to the table—"as long as he's friendly."

Cooper jerked his head, glancing behind him as he rubbed his neck—the kind of thing people do when they sense someone standing behind them. While I watched, a thin line appeared on his jaw, starting as a dot and then expanding to something darker and wider—a red scratch that could have been caused by an unseen fingernail.

"Cooper . . ." I began, my words forgotten before they left my mouth, as a loud clap of thunder shook the restaurant and the vase on our table fell over and shattered, scattering water, flowers, and glass onto Cooper.

CHAPTER 5

The following morning I was met at the corner of Royal Street and Canal, the pickup point I'd designated with twelve-year-old entrepreneur Trevor Williams. I'd first met him during a run through Washington Square Park, where I'd found him on a bench, selling various items that I didn't know I needed until I saw them and heard his sales pitch. They included my bike and the flowered basket he'd found to put on it—at an extra charge. Trevor was small for his age and therefore appeared more vulnerable and needy than he actually was. He most definitely used this to his advantage, his appeals always leading me to spend more money than I could afford on things I didn't need.

The rain continued to soak the city, concealing treacherous potholes from drivers and pedestrians alike, the saturated earth reminding everyone that this part of the world existed below sea level, the vengeful Mississippi River and the jealous Gulf fighting a constant battle with the land over ownership. As I looked around me now, it appeared the water was winning.

Trevor carried a ginormous blue and white golf umbrella with the name of a golf course in Dunwoody, Georgia, emblazoned on the top. I never asked Trevor where he procured his wares, but I believed him when he told me he never stole anything. He was incredibly smart for his age, and I expected that forgetful tourists were responsible for most of his inventory, and for the growth of his savings account. The account had been set up for him by Christopher Benoit, who'd become a mentor for the fatherless Trevor. The young boy lived with his grandmother and some of his nine siblings in a house in the Bywater, and I'd never met any of them, despite frequent attempts on my part. Even Christopher had given up trying to set up a meeting. In any case, Trevor now worked at the Past Is Never Past, doing odd jobs, learning about antiques, and saving money to buy his own home computer.

"Good morning, Miss Nola." He greeted me with his trademark smile. I'd told him many times to call me just Nola, but he said his meemaw had drilled good manners into him and he wouldn't want to disappoint her. He moved the umbrella to cover us both, lessening the sound of the rain bouncing off the shiny yellow hood of my rain jacket. Its previous owner had bedazzled a pink unicorn on the back, and Trevor had sold it to me for only twenty dollars—a considerable deal—since he hadn't had any other takers.

"I'm thinkin' about buildin' me an ark and selling tickets if this rain don't stop," he said, still grinning.

"Please reserve a seat for me." I frowned at the waves of water splashing up onto the sidewalk from a passing car. "I'm wondering if I should let you keep the bike for today and try walking. If I ride into one of these potholes, I might not be found until summer."

"You need a car," he said, his expression thoughtful. "You know how to drive yet?"

"Knowing how and actually doing it are two different things, Trevor. But I do think you're right. Jolene said she has one for me, but I'd have to go to Mississippi to pick it up."

His nose wrinkled. "Like Bubba? That's a lotta car, Miss Nola."

"Agreed. The car she wants to give me is a Mustang. It's real old, though—like, from way before I was born, even. I think she said 1967."

His eyes went wide. "A Mustang? Like, a Ford Mustang? And she wants to give it to you?"

"It belonged to a man who died and his wife wants to get rid of it. Why? You know about old Mustangs?"

Trevor stared at me like my hair was on fire. "Uh, yeah, like everyone in the entire world with half a brain does. Is it a convertible?"

I thought for a moment. "Yeah. I think so. Why?"

He pretended to swoon, tilting the umbrella so that it sloshed rainwater on me.

I grabbed hold of the umbrella to pull it back over my drenched face. "Let's talk about the car another time, okay? I need to get to my house before we both drown. I think I'll walk my bike so I'll have it when I need to come home. This rain has got to stop sometime, right?"

"Yes, ma'am," Trevor said, "but I got somethin' for you just in case."

I held the umbrella while he slid off his backpack. The Tulane logo was emblazoned across the front, the backpack so new that the white lettering of the logo was still solid and bright. "Nice backpack," I said. "What happened to your old one?"

"Sold it for sixty bucks," he said proudly. According to Christopher, Trevor was a born salesman, and it wasn't hard to imagine him selling a ratty old backpack to a tourist or student who seemed desperate enough. I knew better than to ask him where the new one came from. There were some things I was better off not knowing about, such as the presence of wandering spirits that I blissfully could not see. I suppressed a shudder as I recalled the scratch on Cooper's cheek; I was still trying to come up with a logical explanation for something that defied logic.

"Good for you," I said, watching as he pulled a small rainbow-colored umbrella out of the backpack.

He popped it open and I saw that it had a headband attached to it. "It's hands-free!" he announced with a bright smile.

"For me?" I asked, touched that he would think about me navigating my bike in the rain.

He nodded. "It's yours," he said, handing it to me while taking the larger umbrella. "For fifty bucks."

I blinked. "Fifty?"

"Yes, ma'am. If you was anybody else, I'd charge you a hundred, but because we're friends, you get a discount."

"Uh-huh. What kind of a markup is that?"

"A hundred percent. I got it for free." His smile didn't dim, nor did he seem embarrassed to admit that he was fleecing me. "Mr. Christopher is teaching me a lot about business, so I know that's a good profit."

"It sure is." I almost wanted to teach him a lesson on extortion, but then I remembered the beautiful breakfront in my kitchen and how he had helped create it from a discarded piece of furniture and had given it to me without charge, and instead I said, "Well, I don't carry that much cash on me, so I guess it's going to have to be a no from me."

He continued to smile brightly. "No problem, Miss Nola. I trust you. You can pay me later."

I glanced again at the swollen river that had once been a street, and I realized I'd need both hands to push the bike. Turning back to him, I said, "Well, in that case . . ." I began adjusting the headband over the hood of my rain jacket, grateful that Jolene wasn't there to use colorful adjectives to describe my appearance.

"I'll give you my friends-only discounted interest rate of six percent."

"Six percent? What do you charge people you don't like?"

"A lot more. Don't forget my convenience fee for bringin' it to you."

I was getting increasingly soaked standing in the rain and arguing with him, so I decided to let it go.

We said good-bye and I began pushing my bike through standing water toward my house, absurdly grateful for the umbrella hat that kept the rain off my face without obscuring my vision and allowed me to keep both hands on the handlebars so the bike wouldn't get washed away by what I could swear was a current.

Despite the gloom, my mood brightened as I neared my under-renovation house in the Marigny neighborhood, the usual two ancient pickup trucks parked in front alongside a dumpster brimming with empty paint cans, circa-1974 light fixtures, and the laminate wood paneling that someone without any sense of history or good taste had glued to the upstairs walls. I smiled as I saw my Charleston green–painted front door, along with the palmetto-tree door knocker that Melanie had given me as a nod to my hometown. I'd realized as I'd painted the door that, with the continuing renovation, I'd have to repaint it, but I couldn't wait. The start of my new life had already been postponed too long. I might not have running water in the upstairs bathroom, or operational windows in most of the house, but at least the front door made it look as if my house was a real home.

I'd dragged my bike up onto the porch and was reaching for the doorknob when one of my contractors, Thibaut Kobylt, carrying two large mixing buckets filled with water, opened the door and almost ran me over.

"Good morning!" he called from the porch as Jorge, with two more full buckets, ran out the door behind him.

"What's happening?" I asked as the men emptied their buckets into the street, reflecting the feeling in the pit of my stomach. This couldn't be good.

Jorge shook his head, to mean either that he didn't understand me or that I didn't want to know, before hurriedly following Thibaut outside toward the back of the house.

A familiar engine roar followed by the scrape of steel bumper against concrete curb alerted me to Jolene's arrival. I watched from the porch as she elegantly exited the car, opening her umbrella at the same time without getting wet—a trick I'd yet to master, despite her patient tutelage—before she headed to the trunk of her car.

Since I still wore my umbrella hat and bedazzled raincoat, I jogged down the steps to help. She peered out from under her umbrella as I approached, the quick blinking of her green eyes the only indication that she'd noticed my outfit. Reaching into the voluminous trunk—big enough to carry seven bodies and the shovels needed to bury them, according to her funeral-director grandmother—Jolene grabbed the handle of a thick fabric-sample book and handed it to me before taking one herself, then slammed the trunk shut.

We hurried up the porch steps, pausing to catch our breath and take off our wet jackets. "If I'd known you were coming this morning I would have caught a ride," I said. "I had to walk my bike all the way from Canal Street, and I'm soaked through to the bone. I might have a touch of hypothermia."

Jolene took in my old high school sweatshirt, which was layered over two sweaters, both older than the sweatshirt and both with a fair share of moth holes. "Bless your heart, Nola. I'm happy you consider us such good friends that you didn't feel the need to dress up for me." Pushing open the front door, she added, "I had to drive to Metairie first thing to pick up these fabric samples, or I would have offered." Jolene shook out her umbrella and leaned it against the house as I removed my headband and placed it carefully on one of the two rocking chairs I'd painted to match the front door.

I followed Jolene inside, noticing her perfect and somehow completely dry hair. "At the very least I could have saved you from looking like a clown who escaped from the circus," she said.

"Please notice that my boots match my jacket." We both looked down at the small puddle around my borrowed yellow boots, a small wet pool spreading on the tarp placed in front of the door to protect the wide-plank wooden floors that I had painstakingly hand sanded and stained.

I was spared another *bless your heart* by the front door's opening, revealing Jaxson carrying his camera. He closed the door and grimaced. "Beau's on the way. It seems either a water pipe has burst or part of the new roof patch has failed. Or both. Don't worry—we'll figure it out and get it fixed."

I frowned. "Don't worry? I can literally hear my bank account hemorrhaging. Something tells me that neither one of these disasters is in my renovation budget. And why did Beau call you and not me?"

"Because he didn't want you to get upset," Jolene and Jaxson said in unison.

"Upset?" I raised my voice to be heard over the pounding rain and the hammering that had started on the roof above us. "Why would I be upset?" I shouted.

Jolene gently took my elbow. "Let's go sit in the kitchen, where we can talk." She led me to the back of the house, to the only room that looked as if any work had actually been done to it. The hand-tiled backsplash that I had copied from a picture in the Preservation Resource Center's member magazine, *Preservation in Print*, was my pride and joy, despite its current position, floating in the middle of the wall. Cabinets that I'd helped sand by hand and stain sat beneath the tiles, but there were no countertops yet, as Jolene was currently working on getting a steep discount from a local stone supplier. If I weren't so broke, I would have told her to get them at any cost. I needed just one thing to be settled in my life so I could stop feeling as if I were stranded on a raft out at sea, with only the barest glimpse of land to offer encouragement.

A circa-1920s porcelain-enameled-top table that Trevor had found in a dumpster stood in the center of the floor, with an assortment of metal and vinyl-upholstered folding chairs settled around it. The table was nicked and scarred, but Trevor promised me that he'd work his "Trevor Transformation" magic on it. I couldn't wait to see what he'd do with it, and I could only hope that I could afford it.

Jolene walked to the table, where Jaxson waited to push in her chair. Being too agitated to sit, I paced the room as my panic grew with each bang on the roof.

Jaxson placed his camera on the table before sitting. "In answer to your question, Beau called me to take pictures of the damage, since I'm the official renovation photographer. If there's something any of the contractors did wrong, we need to document it so they can make it right."

"But it's my house! He should have called me first."

Jaxson nodded. "I agree. But"—he shifted uncomfortably in his chair—"he said you were a little . . . confrontational in your last discussion, and he wasn't in the mood to deal with you right now."

"Not in the mood . . ." I repeated, just as a loud bang sounded from the top of the house, and what appeared to be an entire section of roof tiles fell past the kitchen window to the small backyard.

I turned my back to the window, unwilling to witness any further destruction of my dream that refused to come to fruition despite my best efforts.

"Sometimes what we think is the worst that can happen turns out to be the best." Jolene smiled brightly, and if I didn't like her so much I might have wanted to slap her into next week—another helpful phrase I'd learned from her.

"How so?" I asked, silently congratulating myself for keeping my voice calm.

"Well, now you can come with me to Mississippi for Thanksgiving, since it appears that we still have a ways to go before the finishing touches—unless you think you can get a new roof installed before the holiday."

"Wait—you're going to Mississippi for Thanksgiving?" Jaxson smacked his hands on the table.

"Um, I haven't decided," I said. "I can't go home to Charleston, so I was planning on staying here, but Jolene wants me to go to Mississippi with her."

Jolene looked at Jaxson for the first time, making me aware that she'd been avoiding eye contact with him. Not that I blamed her. Unrequited love was painful to witness. "My grandmama has a car for her. All Nola has to do is pick it up and drive it to New Orleans. It's a vintage Mustang."

"Wow!" Jaxson said, his expression mimicking Trevor's when I'd told him about the car. "Actually, this might be serendipity. I need to interview the brother and aunt of one of my clients, and they're unable to travel, so I said I'd go down to talk to them the week of Thanksgiving, since I'm apparently free. My parents, for the first time in their lives, have decided they want to go away for Thanksgiving and have booked a Caribbean cruise for just the two of them. And Carly's family is hosting a huge family event at their beach house in Alys Beach, in the Florida panhandle, but I'm not invited. It's strictly family, and since Carly and I aren't married yet, I'm out."

He shrugged, obviously not too upset about his exclusion. "I don't really mind. I like her parents, but I think an entire week with them might be a challenge. Plus I've got to do this interview, so it all works out, right?"

I could almost hear Jolene's mind spinning like a pinwheel in a hurricane. "That's perfect!" she said. "Because I know Nola wouldn't be comfortable driving the car by herself, so you could ride with her back to New Orleans. I would do it and let you drive Bubba, but Bubba can be temperamental and responds best to me. And I know Mama will be thrilled to have you both for the holiday."

With a heavy sense of resignation, I sat down at the table, the metal chair squeaking beneath me.

"We really need to find new kitchen chairs," Jolene said with a frown. "Every time someone sits, it's like a baby pig squealing for his mama."

I leaned on the table, my chin in my hands. "I haven't committed to going to Mississippi—yet," I said. "I'm fine staying here and eating a turkey sandwich while catching up on paperwork, and I'd really like to be here fixing things. I don't want this to be like Jack and Melanie's house, where the renovations just go on and on."

Jaxson gave me a sympathetic smile. "I hate to break it to you, Nola, but owning an old house is—"

"Like digging a hole and emptying your bank accounts into it," I finished, repeating something my stepmother had said often ever since I'd known her—not that it had stopped me from falling in love with old houses, because, despite Melanie's constant disparagement of her historic home, we both understood that an old house was much more than just brick and mortar. It was a piece of history you could hold in your hand, a time capsule filled with memories that connected different generations of people who'd lived between its walls. All while at the same time being a sick infatuation with something that could never love you back with equal intensity.

"I was going to say it's like a long-term marriage," Jaxson said. "For better and for worse. And sometimes the worse happens more and seems to last longer than the better. So yeah, I get it. I don't think it's possible to live in a place like New Orleans without that love of historic spaces that we instinctively get with our first breath. Which is why I'm saying you should go to Mississippi for Thanksgiving. It's only for four days, right? Let Thibaut and Jorge figure out what to do here, and the break will give you and Jolene time to do some creative brainstorming about making the house stunning."

"Absolutely," Jolene said, a little too enthusiastically. "There's room in Bubba's trunk for all my fabric and paint samples. And don't forget that Mama and Grandmama can give us expert advice. I'm not too proud to say that my grandmama's funeral home is the most *beautifully* decorated funeral home in the entire state of Mississippi."

"Right. You've said that before, and I will take it under consideration, but there's still so much to be done before the house-blessing party in January." Turning to Jaxson, I said, "Jolene's already made the menu and planned the decorations, so I need to make sure the house is ready."

"Well, my brother Luke, the priest, is still planning on invoking the house blessing, so if God and Jolene both have it on their calendars, it will happen."

It appeared as if Jolene might hyperventilate at the thought of spending the holiday with Jaxson, but she was saved the humiliation by the sound of the front door opening and Beau bellowing my name.

We all turned as Beau entered the kitchen, his hair and jacket dripping water onto the floor, his eyes hard as his gaze found me. Before I could say anything, Beau plunked the Madame Alexander doll on the table.

"Is that a Madame Alexander Pussycat?" Jolene seemed genuinely excited.

"You know what that is?" I asked.

"Of course. Doesn't every little girl want a Madame Alexander doll?"

I stared at her blankly. "Actually, until yesterday I had never even seen one."

"That's so sad. You were more deprived than I thought. My grandmama gave me my Pussycat doll when I was five, and I treasured it—at least until I burned off all its hair when I was learning how to use a curling iron, and my little brother decided it would be the perfect size for target practice."

I was trying to process what Jolene had just said, but Beau interrupted my thoughts. "Was this supposed to be a joke?"

Jaxson leaned back on the two rear legs of his chair, the metal protesting loudly. "Yo, bro, does your girlfriend know you still play with dolls? Seriously, where did you find that?"

There was no amusement in Beau's eyes. "In an armoire in the house we're flipping on Esplanade." Turning back to me, he said, "I went out of my way to bring this doll to Mimi to see if it might be worth anything, but when I returned to get it from my truck's backseat, where I thought I'd put it, it wasn't there. So I went all the way back to Sam's apartment, where I figured I must have left it, but it wasn't there, either. And when I got back into my truck to return to the house on Esplanade to look there, the doll was in the driver's seat—in the exact spot where I'd been sitting."

I looked at the empty eyes, imagining something sinister in the blank stare that sent shivers tripping down my spine. Something about the corrupted innocence of childhood made it so much creepier.

I tore my gaze from the doll to look at Beau. "I have no idea how that got in your seat, but I promise you I had nothing to do with it. I have better things to do than head out in the rain to prank you. Did you ask Sam about it?"

"I did. She had nothing to do with it."

"So you believe her and not me?"

He narrowed his eyes. "I don't know what to think. Maybe we should be asking Cooper about it."

"Really?"

"Yeah, really. It seems he has a few secrets he's been keeping to himself."

I glanced at Jolene and Jaxson, who appeared not to be listening while actively doing so. "Well, then, he wouldn't be the only one, would he?"

"What's that supposed to mean?"

Jolene placed a calming hand on my arm, forcing me to take a deep breath before responding. "Look, Beau. We're all friends here, right? Nobody's judging anybody. I just wanted to point out that it seems pretty clear that your mom is still hanging around because there's unfinished business. And until you accept that, she will remain to literally haunt you until you ask for her help in finding your dad, or whatever it is she needs to talk to you about."

Beau continued to glare at me, so I continued. "We're your friends, Beau. And we understand what kind of burden your gift—or whatever you want to call it—has been to you. But you have to understand that it doesn't always have to be a burden. Maybe it can help you find the missing pieces of the puzzle of what happened to your family during Katrina."

I should have stopped there. I wasn't his girlfriend. In fact, I wasn't even sure we had a relationship—at least not one that could easily be defined by the word "friend." Shared experiences should have qualified us as friends, but since most of those hadn't been the positive kind, I hesitated to call him one. But because of a lifetime spent not knowing when to be silent, I continued. "As soon as this rain ends, I think we should take a trip to Jackson Square for a visit to Madame Zoe. She knew your dad. She told me she could help. And I'm here and willing."

Beau's silence extended to an uncomfortable length of time, but I resisted the urge to shift in my chair. I cleared my throat. "Maybe you want to discuss this with Sam first?" For some reason, her name stuck in the back of my mouth.

A loud bang sounded from the roof, but Beau didn't acknowledge that he'd heard anything. Narrowing his eyes again, he said, "If my dad's still alive, then he knows where to find me. I'm completely capable of living my life without interference from Madame Zoe or anyone else."

I opened my mouth to remind him again of how his mother's interference had saved his life, but just then my phone rang. Except it wasn't my usual ringtone, and my phone wasn't the only one ringing.

The four of us exchanged glances as our phones vibrated in our hands, the song "Hello" ringing out of all of them in unison. Jaxson looked from Beau to me, and then at his own phone. "It says UNKNOWN. Should I answer it?"

Beau shook his head. "No."

"Is that . . . ?" I began.

"It's Adele." Beau hit the End button on his screen, silencing everyone's phone. "I have to go," he said.

He had reached the doorway when stupidity or stubbornness made me call out to him, "Let me know when you're ready to go see Madame Zoe. You owe me one—remember? Asking me to rekindle a relationship with the guy who'd betrayed me was a much bigger ask than my suggestion that you talk to your mother."

Beau turned around, his face unreadable. "It's not that easy, Nola."

"Nothing ever is."

He gave me a long, lingering look before exiting the room. Jolene, Jaxson, and I sat in silence until the front door slammed, and the doll Beau had left on the table collapsed backward, her pale blue eyes staring up at the ceiling.

CHAPTER 6

It finally stopped raining three days later. The bright fingers of golden sun peeking between my drapery panels prodded me awake, along with Mardi's happy yipping. He hated the rain almost as much as I did, having come to us with an aversion to precipitation that no amount of culinary persuasion or doggie rainwear could assuage. If he could hear raindrops splattering against the pavement or grass, he'd refuse to go out at all. Jolene and I had concluded that either he had the largest bladder on the planet or he'd managed to find a hidden spot indoors that we wouldn't find until we could smell it.

Cooper had flown to London the day after our lunch at Café Degas, so I hadn't had a chance to talk to him about the woman Beau had seen or about the scratch on his chin. I had dialed Alston several times to ask her, but I had ended the calls before the first ring. If there was something Cooper wasn't telling me, I needed to hear about it from him and not from his sister or in a text. I told myself I was being considerate and not cowardly, although I knew my habit of ignoring unpleasant things in the hope that they'd go away on their own was partially responsible and had nothing to do with good manners or courage.

I threw my legs over the side of my bed and smelled the aroma of fresh coffee drifting under my door as my feet searched for my slippers. My phone rang as I tripped over a fluffy dog eager to get outside into the sunshine, then stumbled out into the dining room. I sat down at the table, in front of a steaming mug of coffee and a waiting plate with a homemade biscuit already slathered with butter and strawberry preserves.

I looked down at my phone to see who was calling so early. My family and friends knew not to call before they could be sure that I'd already had at least my first cup of coffee. Assuming it was a sales call, I was preparing to end it when I saw Beau's name and number. He'd been ignoring all my calls and texts since I'd last seen him at my house. All my questions and concerns about the water—a combination of a broken water pipe and a faulty roof repair—had been redirected to Thibaut, which I took to mean that Beau didn't want to give me the chance to broach the subject of his parents again. My indignation over his cowardliness at least partially masked my own.

I took a fortifying sip of my coffee, then answered. "If you're calling about your doll, I've got her—although I should say Jolene has. I will warn you that Jolene has hand laundered and pressed Pussycat's ensemble and has made the doll a new outfit more appropriate for the season. And if you don't come and pick it up soon, Jolene might make me a matching outfit, and I don't think I have it in me to say no when she asks me to wear it."

There was a long pause before Beau said anything. "That's nice." I could hear a smile in his voice, and I wondered if he might be picturing me in a pink sunbonnet and a white lace pinafore. Without preamble, he said, "What are you doing tonight?"

"Excuse me?"

As if I were hard of hearing, he repeated the question, slightly more loudly.

"Why?" I drew out the word.

"Mimi's having special guests at dinner tonight and she would like for you to join us."

"Oh," I said, feeling oddly deflated. Not that I'd expected him to call and apologize or tell me that I was right about his mom. Unless he'd been hit on the head by a falling meteorite and no one had told me. "That depends. Who're the special guests?"

"Camille LeBlanc. And her husband, Henry."

I frowned at my phone. "Is that someone I should know? I'm not the best with remembering names, but I think I'd remember hers, because I'm guessing she's named after Hurricane Camille, right?"

"I doubt you've ever met, and I'm not sure about the hurricane thing. You can ask her about it when you meet her."

"Well, aren't you the confident one? I didn't say I was going. So, who is this Camille LeBlanc?"

There was a long silence before he replied. "My mother's best friend. They grew up next to each other in Hoover, Alabama, and were college roommates at Auburn. Camille was my mom's maid of honor at her wedding. Camille and Henry moved to New Orleans about a year before Katrina. She's my godmother."

I took a sip of my coffee to give me time to process what he'd said. "Okay, so it's kind of weird that I haven't heard their names before if they live here and there's a close family connection."

"They were one of many families who evacuated after the storm and didn't come back. And then, with my sister's kidnapping and my parents . . . missing, we got distracted and pretty much lost touch. But Camille and Henry recently moved back and reached out to Mimi to reconnect."

"And Mimi wants to have them over. Makes sense. But why invite me? And why isn't Mimi calling me herself?"

I heard a drawer slamming and silverware rattling on the other end of the line. "Why isn't Mimi calling me herself?" I repeated.

"Because it wasn't her idea to invite you."

"Ah. Okay. So are you saying you might need a little emotional support?"

"Maybe." His voice sounded forced, as if his lips were blocking the way.

"And how does Sam feel about that?"

"She doesn't have to know that I invited you, okay? It's best to keep that to ourselves."

I took a moment to consider what that was supposed to mean. "Won't Sam want to know why I'm wearing a vest with a leash?"

"Very funny. Look, if you don't want to help out a friend—"

"Oh, so we're friends now." I wanted to pull back the words, knowing I'd approached dangerous territory.

"We've always been friends, Nola. Maybe more than just friends."

I didn't say anything, half dreading and half anticipating what he would say next.

"Because of all we've been through together. Sort of like soldiers who've fought battles shoulder to shoulder. I'm actually glad that Sam wasn't with us in the attic while we were fighting Antoine, because now when I'm with her I'm not bombarded with bad memories."

"Uh-huh. So I'm like a PTSD trigger."

"Exactly. I mean . . . no. That's not what I meant. It's just that when I'm with Sam my thoughts go where I want them to, but when I'm with you they get a little more . . . visceral." He paused. "Your presence does something to my brain. Like, it weakens the doors I've built between this world and the next. Your presence is . . . distracting. And not in a good way."

I recalled what he'd once said to his mother on a disconnected phone in the middle of the night, when he'd presumably been sleepwalking. *She's dangerous. I can't afford to lose my focus. I can't ever let that happen again.*

"Wow, Beau. You really know how to make a girl feel special. Has anyone ever told you that you have a lousy way of asking favors from a friend?"

"Look. I'm sorry. I'm not . . . I'm not good with words. But you know what I mean. You understand and appreciate my psychic abilities. And whether that's the reason or not, you seem to make them stronger."

I took a deep breath and wondered if it was his Y chromosome that made his reasoning so obtuse as to defy understanding. "Then why do you want me to come to dinner to meet your mother's best friend?"

"Because I'm thinking that's why Mom's still here. She needs me to pass some information on to Camille. They were best friends until the day my mother disappeared. There must have been something unsaid between them, maybe some parting words that Mom thought important enough to hang around to deliver." He paused as if searching for his next words. "You make me stronger. My psychic abilities, I mean. I need to help Mom get this done so she can move on and leave me alone."

"Uh-huh." I chewed on my lower lip. "Can I bring Jolene? I might also need an emotional-support person."

"Sure. No need for vests, though, all right? I'll pick you up around six o'clock."

"I'll ask Jolene to drive. Should I come early so we can talk about Madame Zoe and your—"

"See you tonight," he said before the phone went silent.

Jolene knocked on my bedroom door for the third time in fifteen minutes. "Are you sure you're all right?" she asked, the last word extending into three syllables.

"I know how to get dressed, Jolene. I've been living with you for a while now." I gave a cursory glance in the mirror, pausing long enough to drag a brush through my hair. I frowned, watching my halo of curls expand around my head. Even though it was November, humidity in New Orleans was still a thing, and a daily threat to those of us with overexcited hair follicles.

"Do you at least need me to do your hair? I've brought my hair spray just in case."

I frowned into the mirror, realizing that not even a can of Jolene's miracle hair spray would be enough. In desperation, I grabbed a hair tie from my wrist and swept my hair back. "No, I'm good. But thanks."

I flicked a cookie crumb from the collar of my navy blue blouse—a gift from Jolene, so I figured it worked—then tucked the blouse into my pants before sliding my feet into the low-heeled pumps I'd borrowed from her.

"Come on," I said, walking quickly past her and not making eye contact. Allowing her to catch me would mean at least a half hour of accessorizing and tweaking, and I wanted to hurry up and get the evening over with. I hadn't been back to Mimi's house since the night of the fund-raiser and the showdown with the evil spirit of Antoine Broussard in the attic, and I wasn't thrilled about returning.

I slowed down long enough to give Mardi a good scratch behind his ears and promise that Jolene and I would be home before he had time to miss us. I'd made it to the French door at the top of the stairs when Jolene said, "No need to rush like there's a sale on Crisco down at the Walmart, Nola. Antoine is no longer there to mess with you—remember? And if he wants to try something, I will be happy to open up a can of whoop-ass on him on your behalf."

I stopped to look at her, amazed yet again at how perceptive she was. "I'm sure that won't be necessary, but thank you." I turned and walked down the stairs.

"And you look real nice. I like what you did to your hair."

I kept moving while waiting for a *bless your heart.* Instead she said, "I'm right proud of you, Nola. You've come a long way since your camo-and-jeans phase. I think we're ready to move on to accessorizing and nails."

I kept facing straight ahead so she wouldn't see me roll my eyes. "Let me master driving first, okay? Then we can go on to the next big hurdle."

"Sounds like a plan," Jolene said as she shut the door behind us. Her jangling keys let me know that she was locking the dead bolt. We'd already been broken into twice, and we weren't taking chances.

I waited near Bubba as Jolene approached. "And don't think I couldn't feel you rolling your eyes, Nola Trenholm."

Before I could ask her how she could possibly feel my eye roll with my back to her, she said, "It's a gift."

She unlocked her car door and slid in before leaning across the front bench seat to unlatch my door. I sat down, then immediately jumped up with a shout. "What in the . . . ?" I plucked the creepy doll off the seat and plopped it into Jolene's lap. "Why is this here?"

Jolene's eyes met mine. "I thought you'd put her there."

"No. Definitely not."

Jolene blinked, then turned around to place the doll carefully on the rear seat. "Well, then. Beau wanted to show it to Mimi, so it's a good thing we remembered to bring it."

"Right," I said. "We won't talk about how the creepy baby doll got into your car with all the windows closed and the doors locked."

Jolene put Bubba in reverse and began backing out of the driveway. "Please don't call her creepy. Some little girl once loved her, and it's sad that the doll got forgotten on the shelf of an armoire in an empty house. But you're right, Nola. My brain is already full to bursting, what with my job, trying to dress up your house while working around the hole in your roof, and planning an engagement party. If I have to worry about this, too, my head might explode. There'd be red hair everywhere."

I found myself grinning despite the violence of the image. "Yeah. What a mess." I gripped my armrest as a pickup truck's horn blared as it barreled up behind us, brakes squealing as Jolene slowly pulled out onto the street. I kept my gaze focused in front of us so I couldn't see any interesting finger gestures from the truck's driver.

"Just thinking out loud here," I said, "but what if the doll belonged to the little girl who disappeared? I think Lynda was her name.

If we find out that's the case, maybe it will lead us to figuring out what happened to her and her parents after her grandmother's murder."

Jolene nodded solemnly. "And if that's her doll, and it keeps showing up, then it probably means she's no longer with us."

We rode in silence as we considered the implications, until we reached the intersection of Broadway and St. Charles Avenue and I clenched my eyes shut out of habit. Jolene seemed to assume that she had the right of way regardless of traffic light color or oncoming streetcars. It was just better not to watch.

"That poor, sweet girl." Jolene turned to me. "How do you plan to find out if the doll belonged to Lynda?"

"I think I need to speak to her two aunts. Maybe they'll have pictures of Lynda. My brother JJ's comfort item was a kitchen whisk. Every picture of him as a child shows him clutching that whisk. Not sure if Honey and Joan would have any pictures of their niece, since they were estranged from their brother, but I can ask. Beau mentioned that the aunts asked him to meet with them—maybe I can tag along."

"What about Sarah?" Jolene asked as she swerved around a pothole, nearly sideswiping a bicyclist.

"She didn't have a comfort item. I guess she didn't need one since she always had 'imaginary friends' to keep her company."

Jolene took a sharp and sudden right off St. Charles. I closed my eyes, not wanting to see a flying bicycle or pedestrian, and opened them only when I hadn't heard a thud against the car's hood. "Maybe you should invite Sarah back for a visit. She might could tell you what you need to know about that doll and the family who used to live in the house on Esplanade." The front tire thumped against the curb as Jolene parked in front of the Ryans' Italianate home, the familiar ornate architecture reminding me of a wedding cake.

"Or," she said, unbuckling her seat belt, "you could ask Beau."

"Well, we are supposed to be doing this murder-house-flip business together, starting with the house on Esplanade, but so far his only interest has been in the nuts and bolts of the renovation part, which I don't think is unintentional. Like, he wants to pretend that any lingering residents aren't part of the process."

"He's really good at denial, isn't he?" Jolene asked.

"Most definitely. It's beyond aggravating."

Jolene looked at me without moving or opening her door. "Is that so? It reminds me of someone else, too."

"Funny." I swung open the heavy passenger-side door, using both hands. I got out and slammed it shut, then began walking toward the hourglass gate in front of the house.

"You forgot Pussycat," Jolene called after me.

"Oops. Since you're on a first-name basis with her, could you bring her, please?"

She grabbed the doll from the backseat before locking up the car and following me to the gate, carrying the doll on her shoulder like a real baby. "If I hadn't just seen my own Pussycat on my bed when I was at my mama's, I could swear this is the same doll. I mean, it's from a different year, but it's the same model. Still, it feels . . . different. Maybe they used a thicker plastic or something, because this one's heavier for sure."

"Maybe Beau can use it for a doorstop," I said as I stepped up onto the curb.

"Why all the hate, Nola? It's just a baby doll."

"It's creepy. I'm actually glad I didn't have a mother who thought I should have dolls as a little girl. I think she saved me from a lot of therapy."

As I unlatched the gate, I looked up at the sound of rustling leaves from a live oak. Jolene stepped past me and began moving down the walkway while I stopped to watch the green leaves twitch in a wind that seemed to surround only the one tree. The other trees and plants in the yard—and my hair—remained unmoved by whatever unseen force shook the leaves of the old oak.

The gate clattered shut behind me. I turned, feeling the temperature plummet, goose bumps tiptoeing along my neck and arms beneath my coat. Taking a step forward, I heard an unexpected *splat* and looked down at my feet, knowing what I would see reflected in the pale lamplight. A trail of wet footprints led up the walkway toward the marble front steps, coming to an abrupt halt in front of the double doors of the house on Prytania.

Oblivious to the unseen presence, Jolene rang the doorbell. "Here we go again," I muttered as I followed the footprints up to the house.

CHAPTER 7

The front door opened and we were greeted warmly by Christopher. He was impeccably groomed, as usual, but his amber eyes were red rimmed, as if he'd been crying.

"Is everything all right?" I asked, glancing in the direction of murmuring voices in the parlor.

"It's a good day, Nola. For Mimi especially. I haven't seen her this happy since we thought Sunny had returned. But today, having Camille here—well, it's a bit like having a piece of Adele back again."

Christopher's gaze drifted to the doll and his smile fell. "Is that a Madame Alexander?"

Jolene nodded excitedly. "It is. I figured you'd probably know. Nola hasn't a clue." She sent me a sidelong glance. "Nola found it in the armoire at the house on Esplanade. Beau wanted to show it to Mimi, but he keeps misplacing it."

Christopher's eyes met mine. "I see," he said, as if he did. "May I?" he asked, reaching for the doll. "I'll put it somewhere safe for now if that's all right. Mimi's a bit occupied right now."

Jolene eagerly relinquished the doll, and we watched as Christopher opened the lower cabinet of a demilune chest in a small alcove next to the door. He absently wiped his palms on his pants before turning back to us. Feeling someone watching me, I turned toward the portrait of Beau's grandfather and Mimi's husband, Charles. His spirit—presumably now at rest—had been a benign and helpful one, but that didn't stop me from being disturbed by the feeling of eyes in the portrait following me.

"One seltzer water and one Sazerac coming right up, ladies." Christopher was well-versed in our drinks of choice, as well as knowing that Jolene had to be cut off after one cocktail. The three of us had learned that the hard way. "Shall we?" he asked, leading us into the front parlor filled with elegant antiques and the white marble fireplace upon which rested the familiar bust of the Roman god Bacchus.

I was relieved that plastic sheeting shielded the arched opening between the parlor and the dining room, where scaffolding covering the walls could be seen through a crack along one edge. My heart beat a little more slowly as I noted there was no swinging chandelier and no demonlike presence projecting itself from the ceiling. I still woke up at night with a scream in my throat, having not quite recovered from that awful time when Jeanne and Antoine Broussard had been sent to the light, and Beau had almost died.

The unanswered questions from that event filled my dreams, clinging to my subconscious like burrs, unwilling to let me go until I could figure out why Adele was still earthbound and what had happened to Beau's father, Buddy. I hoped that was all. I really, really hoped that was all. My well-being was dependent on my staying sober, and sleepless nights and restless ghosts were not conducive to the tranquil and sober life for which I had moved to New Orleans.

Sam waved from where she sat next to Mimi on the sofa and widened her eyes as if to indicate that we had a lot to discuss in private later. Not for the first time, I thought that Sam and I could be good friends except for the minor detail of her being Beau's girlfriend. Mimi rose and greeted me with a kiss on each cheek. Her unusual eyes—one green and one blue—bored into me before she took my hand and turned to a middle-aged couple seated in the pair of salmon-colored velvet Biedermeier chairs by the fireplace. Beau stood next to them in conversation before Mimi interrupted.

"Camille and Henry, I'd like you to meet a good friend of ours, Nola Trenholm."

The woman—Camille—appeared to be in her mid-to-late forties. Her petiteness was emphasized by the extremely tall man standing next to her, presumably Henry. He was about the same age as his wife, and as blond as she was dark. Camille wore round tortoiseshell glasses that seemed too heavy and big for her nose. She pushed them up with her left hand as she reached to shake my hand with her right.

"Beau's been telling us all about you," Camille said, with a small yet warm smile and the soft handshake usually given by elderly women or young children. Her accent was definitely Southern, which made sense since Beau had said she was from Hoover, Alabama, where she'd grown up with his mother. The way she spoke made me think of newscasters who'd taken elocution lessons to learn how to drop their regional accents, but telltale signs always remained to give them away. It made me wonder where she'd been since leaving New Orleans after Hurricane Katrina.

Camille regarded me with bright green eyes fringed with thick black lashes, the single standout feature that made her memorable. As soon as I shook her hand her gaze shifted to the floor. With her beautiful eyes downcast, Camille disappeared into her beige cardigan and matching beige turtleneck and pants. The only areas of color that weren't beige, besides her brown hair, were her brown loafers.

"That's a bit worrying," I said, "so please let me know if you need clarification on anything."

Camille laughed, the sound confined mostly to her throat, as if she were afraid of being heard. "I'm sure that won't be necessary."

"And you must be Jolene," Henry said, stretching out a hand to my roommate.

"Yes," she drawled.

I had to look at my friend to make sure that low, sultry voice was hers. Her cheeks had pinkened, and when I turned toward Henry I understood why. He was what my grandmother Amelia would call "movie-star handsome," or what Jolene would call a cool drink of water.

Henry was a cross between Ryan Reynolds and a blond Tom Cruise but taller, and better-looking—if that was even possible. He wore a light blue button-down oxford-cloth shirt beneath a navy cable-knit cashmere sweater that accentuated his summer-sky blue eyes. Maybe it was the mental mention of my grandmother, an avid bird-watcher, that made me see Henry and Camille as cardinals, the male all showy in his scarlet plumage and the drab female meant to blend into the background. It may have been my childhood, spent in the shadows of my mother's addictions, that made me warm to Camille, or maybe an instinctive distrust of any good-looking male (*Thank you, Michael Hebert*) that made me shift away from Henry and embrace Camille.

Mimi put her arm around Camille's shoulders and gave a gentle squeeze. "We've been sharing stories about Adele. She knew Adele long before Buddy did. She has photo albums at her parents' house in Alabama, and she's going to ask them to send them. I think Beau would enjoy seeing them."

Christopher joined us. "And I remember working with Adele and Camille at the Past Is Never Past during the short time they lived in New Orleans before the storm. Never a dull moment with those two, that's for sure. I also remember that Camille had an encyclopedic memory of every piece of inventory."

"That's right," Mimi said. "And she could add up an entire column of numbers without a calculator. After a while I stopped double-checking her totals, because she was never wrong."

Camille looked down at her feet as a blotchy red stained her cheeks.

"Well, that's one thing she can do better than me," Henry said with a chuckle. He was the only one who laughed.

Mimi hooked her arm through Camille's. "I've recently installed a small greenhouse in my back garden and am testing my green thumb with orchids. They're extremely temperamental, so who knows how long I can keep them alive? But they look so lovely. We've got another half hour until dinner, so why don't I take you back to show you?"

Camille glanced at her husband as if asking for permission.

Henry waved his hands in their direction. "Oh, go on. We men would prefer to talk football—am I right?" Henry didn't wait for Beau or Christopher to respond before he scooped a handful of nuts from a crystal dish on a side table and plopped down on the vacated sofa.

As Sam, Jolene, and I followed Mimi and Camille from the room, I could hear Beau suggesting that Henry remove his feet from the inlaid wooden coffee table and then apologizing that they hadn't considered adding a Barcalounger to the parlor room's décor.

Sam and I shared a glance, choking on our laughter.

"Y'all hush," Jolene whispered from behind us. "He might have been raised in a barn and doesn't know any better."

We followed Mimi into the backyard and into a greenhouse that was only about fifteen feet square but that someone with an eye for architecture and an appreciation for historic vernacular had given an Italian Renaissance roof that matched that of the house, including a widow's walk and oval windows. The glass windowpanes were set in copper frames, the patina of which would change to an antique blue-green hue over time.

"Did you design this?" I asked Mimi, taking in the freestanding wood-and-iron shelves and the potting bench along one short side of the structure.

"Actually, no. Beau did."

I looked at her. "Beau Ryan? Your grandson?"

Jolene poked me in the ribs, causing me to yelp. Every time I told her not to poke me with her finger she insisted that she wouldn't need to if I would simply remember to be polite.

Mimi chuckled. "Yes, Beau. I suppose I'd been mentioning for years that I wanted to try my hand at growing orchids but wasn't sure how to go about it. He must have been working on the design and ordering materials while he was in the hospital, recuperating from his, er, accident, so it was all ready to go last weekend, when he and Christopher installed it. It went up very quickly. Unlike the orchids."

She frowned at a row of pots that displayed not even a single stem protruding from the soil they contained.

"I don't think orchids are supposed to grow that fast."

"Oh, I know that," Mimi said with a dismissive wave. "It's just that, well, I was hoping to have some blooms by Christmas—as a sort of present to myself."

"Adele loved orchids." Camille's voice was so quiet that I wasn't exactly sure who'd spoken until she spoke again. "She carried orchids for her wedding bouquet."

"She did," Mimi said. "I was relieved that she settled on white orchids instead of blue and orange, like she originally wanted."

Jolene's eyes lit up. "War Eagle!"

Camille smiled, her face transformed, giving a hint as to what she might look like if she wore colors besides beige. "War Eagle," she replied.

"I love Auburn," Jolene said. "Mostly because I hate Alabama and Auburn's their blood-sworn rival. But then again, everybody hates Alabama. They have the most obnoxious fans. I remember—"

"Is Auburn where you and Henry met?" I asked, cutting Jolene off before she went down her list of SEC teams. College football was her favorite subject, next to makeup.

Camille shook her head. "Henry went to Alabama. We met at a fraternity mixer after the Iron Bowl. He was the best-looking guy I had ever seen, and he was surrounded by all these pretty Chi Omegas, but for some reason he noticed me." She shrugged and looked down at her feet. "He was mad because Auburn had actually won for a change, and he was threatening to go down to Toomer's Corner and poison those cherished oak trees."

"And you talked him out of it?" Sam asked.

She shook her head. "No. It was Adele. I was jealous at first, because she was so gorgeous and I knew I wouldn't stand a chance if she showed any interest, but Henry only had eyes for me." Her smile seemed sad, and I thought it was because of the memory of her long-lost friend. "Besides, Adele didn't like Henry all that much."

"Because he went to Alabama?" Jolene asked.

Camille grimaced. "I think it was because Adele had met Buddy and they were dating long-distance at that point. Henry wasn't Buddy. That was probably the main reason. Even when Buddy was away with the Army and they didn't see each other for a year, he was everything to her."

"Not to mention that Henry's a bit of a jerk," Sam muttered in my ear. She yelped, presumably another victim of Jolene's sharp index finger.

I brushed my hand across the smooth yellow pine countertop surrounding a pretty round porcelain sink painted with pink peonies, the small cracks in the enamel identifying it as an antique. "This is stunning," I said.

Sam moved to stand next to me. "Did Beau pick this out, too?"

Mimi shook her head. "No. I'd been keeping it in the storeroom at the shop, waiting to find the perfect place to use it. Adele chose it for Sunny's playhouse. We were going to build one right here. Then, well . . ."

"Katrina came," Sam said. "And everything changed."

Mimi nodded somberly. "So many people just . . . gone. Like Buddy, and Adele." She took Camille's hands. "I'm just so happy to see you again. We weren't even sure what had happened to you and Henry. We tried to find you, but everything was such a mess after the storm, and Adele and Buddy were gone, searching for Sunny—" Her voice caught. She dropped Camille's hands and retrieved a watering can from a shelf.

Mimi stuck an index finger into the soil in one of the pots. "I never know when I'm supposed to water them. Too little, and they shrivel. Too much, and they drown. . . ."

"It's all my fault." Camille's voice was so quiet that I wasn't sure she'd said anything at all.

Mimi quickly set down the watering can before turning to embrace her, cradling her head as if she were a child. "Oh, sweetheart, please don't say that. How could you even think that?"

Camille pulled away, using the sleeve of her cardigan to wipe her eyes. "When Sunny disappeared, Buddy was frantic. It was clear that the police weren't doing enough to find her, and there was a big storm coming—although nobody knew just how big." She glanced up at Mimi before continuing.

"I told him that if he kept badgering the police they'd arrest him for harassment and put him in jail, and then he couldn't be any help at all. So I suggested that he go out on his own and look for Sunny." Camille clenched her eyes tightly. "He didn't want to leave Adele and Beau, but I promised him that Henry and I would keep them safe." She gave a choking sob, the tears flowing freely now. "But I was wrong, wasn't I? I should have known that Adele loved him too much to let him go alone." Facing Mimi, she said, "Adele knew that Beau would be safe with you. I even told her where I thought Buddy had gone, so she'd have a place to start. If I'd known neither one would come back, I would have never—" Her words were swallowed by more sobbing.

Mimi drew her into another embrace. "You couldn't have stopped her. Believe me. I tried. So did Beau. That's why he's still conflicted about her love for him. He doesn't think that a mother who loves her child could ever willingly abandon him." Mimi gently pressed Camille away from her to look her in the face. "And regardless of who suggested where Adele should go look for Buddy, she would have made the same decision. Because you're right—she knew Beau was safe with me. But Buddy and Sunny were out there, someplace where they definitely weren't safe. As a wife and mother, Adele did the only thing she could think of to try to bring them back."

"It's not like she had a choice," I said, my eyes stinging.

Sam rubbed her hands over her face. "Try telling that to Beau. I've stopped trying."

Jolene crossed her arms. "I know. And so has Nola. But that boy's as stubborn as a mule stuck in cement."

Camille pulled away again, then cleared her throat. "Would you excuse me, please? I need to use the ladies' room. No need to show me the way—it's been a while, but I remember where it is."

Wearing a wobbly smile, she let herself out of the greenhouse. Mimi was the first to speak. "She must miss Adele terribly. They were both only children, so they considered themselves like sisters. They say blood's thicker than water, and I think a close friendship like that becomes like blood. It breaks my heart that she's been holding herself responsible all these years. We made the best decisions we could at the time. But sometimes wrong decisions made before a storm hits can turn out to be worse than the actual hurricane."

Sam slid her arm through Mimi's. "I think we need to take you inside."

Mimi patted Sam's hand. "I'd like a few minutes alone before going back inside, if that's all right. Could you please tell Lorda in the kitchen to go ahead and put the food on the table and let everyone know that we'll be eating in ten minutes? I'm afraid it's just my jambalaya and fried okra again, but it's Camille's favorite, so I thought it was appropriate."

"No apologies needed," Jolene said. "I'd walk a mile barefoot over hot coals to eat your jambalaya on any day that ends with Y. Take as long as you need. We'll even help Lorda, if only to keep Nola from eating all the corn bread before it makes it to the table."

"Funny," I said, grateful for the soft smile on Mimi's face.

We left Mimi and headed to the kitchen, where Lorda, the Ryans' longtime housekeeper, was taking out of the oven a baking pan filled with golden yellow sweet corn bread. I began salivating as soon as I saw it.

"I'll be right back," I said to Jolene and Sam. "I'll let the guys know that dinner will be out shortly." I headed through the kitchen to the back hallway, noticing that the powder room was empty as I passed it. I entered the parlor expecting to see Camille, but though the men were exactly where we'd left them—including Henry, with his feet still propped up on the coffee table, the almost-empty bowl of nuts now in his lap—there was no sign of her.

"Has anyone seen Camille?" I asked. Beau and Christopher stood as I entered, while Henry remained where he was and put another handful of nuts into his mouth.

"She went that way," Henry said with a full mouth, his index finger pointing toward the foyer.

"Thanks," I said. "Mimi sent me to tell you that dinner will be ready in ten minutes."

I left them and headed to the foyer, stopping abruptly at the foot of the stairs. The old baby doll that I'd seen Christopher place inside the cabinet sat propped on the third step, its heavily lashed eyes focused on the front door. Holding back a ripple of revulsion, I picked it up, careful to keep it away from my body. My gaze traveled to the cabinet door, and I felt an odd relief that it was partially open, which had to mean that someone—an actual living, breathing someone—had opened it. Or it hadn't been closed properly, so the doll fell out, and someone, possibly Camille, had put it on the step.

I glanced up the elegant staircase with its turned wooden spindles. It was none of my business why Camille was upstairs. But that didn't stop me from wondering. My only excuse was that I'd inherited my author father's curiosity and his propensity to question everything. Except he was a writer, so that kind of odd behavior was understandable. I had no excuse. But I couldn't stop myself from climbing those stairs any more than I could tell my eyes to stop being blue.

I put my foot on the bottom step, telling myself that I was just doing as Mimi had asked, letting Camille know that it was time for supper. I'd barely made it halfway up the stairs when I heard the sound of a door closing, the latch clicking into place with slow deliberation. I stopped and waited, hoping it was someone who should be upstairs—like, a living, breathing someone.

Camille appeared at the top of the stairs. She pressed her hand against her chest when her eyes locked on mine. "You scared me."

"Sorry. I was sent to tell you that supper's almost ready. I thought you were in the powder room."

A small, pale hand grasped the banister. "It was occupied, so I used the hall bathroom upstairs. I spent a lot of time here when I lived in New Orleans, so I knew where it was. I didn't think Mimi would mind."

"No, of course not."

Her gaze settled on the doll. "Is that yours? I was wondering why it was left on the steps."

"Not exactly, but I did bring it to show Mimi."

Camille nodded. "Mimi's always been an expert on all things antique. Adele so admired her." She was looking at me oddly, as if I had food on my cheek. I rubbed my face with the back of my hand just in case.

"Mimi has so many talents, doesn't she?" Camille's gaze traveled to the doll again, then back up to me. "I think she calls it psychometry, right? Is she still doing that?"

Mimi's psychic talent wasn't exactly a secret, so I wasn't surprised that Camille would know about it.

"Yeah. Occasionally." I held up Pussycat. "But that's not why I brought this over. I was hoping Mimi might know if it's valuable. I found it in an armoire in a house Beau and I are getting ready to renovate."

"Oh, right. For the murder-house-flip show. Mimi was telling us a little bit about it before you and Jolene arrived."

"Well, it's not a show yet. Right now we're just making an episodic series on our YouTube channel, but we're hoping to get it picked up by one of the home-improvement channels. Beau and I will be using the Esplanade house for the first project."

"That's so cool." Camille smiled, transforming her face, and I wanted to tell her that she should do it more often. Her gaze drifted back down to the doll. "I remember there was a room up here where Mimi kept the personal effects of missing people and murder victims that she'd gotten from clients who wanted to know what had happened to their loved ones. I was hoping there might be something from Buddy and Adele, something that Mimi could use to find them. But I'm sure she's already tried, right?"

"You'll have to ask her about that, but I do know she used psychometry when we were trying to find Sunny."

"Oh, yes. Sweet Sunny. I remember her so clearly. She was truly a ray of sunshine to her family. It broke my heart when I read that she'd been found but that she'd chosen to continue living in New York. Mimi said that they're talking on the phone at least, but it's not enough, is it?" Her lips turned up in a sad smile. "It's why we came back, you know. That news article. I subscribe to the *Times-Picayune* online so I can keep up with what's happening in my favorite city, and I never expected to see an article about Sunny. It hadn't occurred to me that Adele and Buddy might still be missing after all this time. Thinking that the Ryans were once again all together helped me sleep at night, I guess. What we don't know can't hurt us, right?" She pressed her lips together like a person who hasn't been given many opportunities to talk and finds themselves with a willing listener.

"I'm curious, Camille—why did you stay away so long?"

Her mouth twisted. "The memories, I suppose. Of New Orleans. I could only imagine how much the storm had changed what we remembered and loved. We'd only called it home for a short time, but I'd never really felt attached to a place like I did here. I thought it would be too painful to come back. And now that I'm back I realize

I wasn't wrong. Mostly, though, I didn't think Mimi would want to see me again."

"Why not? Because of what you thought was your role in what happened to Adele? I hope you listened to what Mimi had to say. There is no blame. Adele would have gone looking for Buddy and Sunny even without your suggestion. Mimi knows this. And you need to accept it, too." I grimaced. "I know. Easier said than done. If my parents could hear me now, asking someone to take my advice without question, they'd probably die laughing."

I was rewarded with one of Camille's rare but beautiful smiles. "You're right. I do think Mimi is glad I'm back. Who knows? Maybe Henry and I can help her find Adele and Buddy. I realize that many people have been searching since they disappeared, but sometimes it just takes a new perspective."

"Very true," I said. "And I know that Beau and Mimi will appreciate the help. There's just . . . one thing you might want to know. It's not my place to tell you, so you'll have to ask Mimi."

She closed her eyes briefly. "About Adele? Mimi already told me how everyone believes that she's dead." Camille shook her head. "I just refuse to believe it. Maybe that's what Mimi and Beau need to accept so they can sleep at night, but I can't." She pressed a small fist to her chest. "I'd know it—right here. And until I have positive proof that she's no longer alive, I have to have hope."

Now I looked away, unable not to imagine the dying hope in the eyes of the storm's survivors as the waters receded and the seasons changed and time passed with no news of loved ones who were no longer there.

Camille took a deep breath. "Maybe if we focus on finding Buddy, he'll know where Adele is. Because wherever he is, I know that Adele won't be far away."

She said it with such conviction that I had to believe her. I thought of Madame Zoe, and of the fortune teller's message to Beau about his father. I opened my mouth to tell Camille but stopped. It wasn't for me to share—assuming there was anything to share. After I eventually dragged Beau to see Madame Zoe, I'd suggest that he share any findings with Camille. Like Camille had said, sometimes answers could be found if the puzzle was looked at from a new perspective.

I appreciated her optimism. "Well, then. Let's focus on finding Buddy. We can ask Mimi if she gleaned anything from Buddy's possessions. Maybe something will spark an idea she hadn't considered."

"That's a good plan. I can ask Mimi in the morning. Henry and I will be happy to do the legwork, since you have your hands full with the new YouTube project and your own house renovation."

"Oh, I don't mind. I've somehow managed to include several extracurricular activities around my real job." I kept a straight face as I recalled my ill-fated dates with Michael Hebert, the endless procession of restless and unfriendly spirits I had to deal with, the Barbie-head makeup-and-hair instructions from Jolene, and a visit from my family, to name just a few.

"Yes, well," Camille said, "we'll see. Henry and I don't have jobs yet, so we might have more time than you. But it's good to know we can rely on you if we need help."

She took a step down, making me realize that I was blocking her way. I turned and headed to the bottom of the stairs, still holding the doll. I approached the cabinet where I'd seen Christopher put her, and then I paused. A familiar set of wet footprints led across the marble tile of the foyer before coming to a full stop at the bottom of the stairs.

Camille appeared not to have noticed, as she walked past me and into the parlor. I shoved the doll back into the cabinet and hurried to follow her. The sound of something clattering onto the floor behind me made me turn. I darted my eyes around, expecting to see someone. Or some*thing*. But the foyer and staircase appeared empty. Which, as I'd long since learned, didn't mean they were.

"Aren't you coming?"

I swung around at the sound of Beau's voice from the doorway.

"You're usually like a boll weevil in a cotton field when there's food on the table, so I was sent to see if anything was wrong. . . ." His voice tapered off as he spotted the footprints. We both noticed the small object lying on the floor near the last set.

Remembering the sound of something hitting the floor behind me, I bent to retrieve the object. Holding it up, I said, "It looks like—"

"An earring," Beau finished. He took it from me and shook it so that its myriad gold circles within circles would clink softly together.

Our eyes met over the earring. "I've seen it before," I said. "Twice." The first time had been in Jackson Square. The second, in front of my house when the fortune teller had come to see me to tell me that Beau needed to talk to her. "It's Madame Zoe's. But I think your mom brought it for you to see."

"No, that can't be right. She's not talking to me tonight. I could have sworn that was what was supposed to happen, but my mother hasn't passed on any messages as far as I can tell."

"That's not true." I tapped the earring, making it shimmy. "This is a message from Adele. Maybe she got tired of trying to get through to you, so she's trying me now, in a way I can understand. And I think she's trying to tell us that you need to go see Madame Zoe."

"Are you two joining us? Mimi sent me to come find you before the food gets cold." Camille stood in the doorway, her beige sweater making her nearly blend in with the wall.

Beau's fingers instinctively closed around the earring, hiding it from sight. "Yeah—sorry."

He placed his hand on the small of my back, leading me forward, but not before I noticed that the footprints that had been there just seconds before had completely vanished.

CHAPTER 8

Why do you enjoy torturing me?" I asked as Beau secured my seat belt where I sat behind the wheel. We were on our way to see Honey Meggison and Joan Wenzel to find out if the doll I'd found in their previous home had once belonged to their missing niece, Lynda. If the doll was worth anything, it would belong to Honey and Joan. Whether or not it was valuable, if it had been Lynda's, it should remain with them anyway in the hope that they might one day return it to her. Regardless, I was eager to get it out of my possession. The not knowing where it would show up next had begun to unnerve me.

Unfortunately, the doll had disappeared from the demilune chest again while we were at dinner, before I'd had a chance to show it to Mimi. Despite a search, the doll had failed to materialize. It seemed as if it could reason on its own and knew better than we did where it belonged. The very thought made me shudder. I knew the doll would show up again sooner or later, so Beau and I continued with our plans to visit the two sisters to confirm ownership, so I'd at least know whose mailbox to shove it into when it decided to make another appearance.

The other disappointment of the evening was Adele's failure to communicate with Beau despite all his machinations to make it happen. He remained in the dark as to why she remained earthbound.

"I wouldn't call making sure you are proficient in a life skill torture." Beau reached toward me and snapped the bright red rubber band on my wrist. "Remember what this means."

"I know, I know. Fear can't win," I said, repeating the words he'd said to me when he'd given me the rubber band from his own wrist. He'd used it to remember what his dad had taught him—that whether we felt afraid didn't matter. What mattered was that we didn't allow our fear to get between us and our objectives. My only argument was that my becoming a proficient driver was more Beau's objective than mine.

"You're getting your own car—remember?" he said, reminding me that I really should make it my goal. But bad memories of my first motor vehicle accident, when I was a newly licensed driver back in Charleston, still made me freeze at the wrong moments, like when approaching a four-way intersection or merging onto the interstate. Despite all the encouragement and lessons Beau had given me, I still couldn't erase the trepidation I felt when getting behind the wheel of any vehicle that had an engine or more than two tires.

"Not that I want it. It's sort of being dumped on me."

"You poor thing. A classic Ford Mustang convertible in pristine condition. I don't know how you're holding up with that kind of burden."

Ignoring him, I adjusted the rearview mirror, letting out an involuntary shout as the mirror reflected the rear seat. Following my gaze, Beau turned to see the doll sitting up like an actual child, its blue gaze focused straight ahead.

My eyes met Beau's with the unasked question.

"I didn't put her there." He reached back and grabbed the doll. She expelled a subdued "Mama" when he tilted her forward, which was more terrifying than cute.

I held up my hands. "I promise I didn't have anything to do with it, either. Trust me." I pointed to my backpack, which I'd tossed on the passenger-side floor. "Put it in there. At least we have it to show Honey and Joan."

Beau nodded as he shoved the doll into the backpack and zipped it closed, unceremoniously pressing down on the head to get it to fit. Valuable or not, neither one of us wanted to look down and see that face peering up at us.

I turned the key, my nerves jumping at the sound of the engine rumbling to life. My phone connected automatically to the Bluetooth, prompting the unsettling realization that I spent way too much time with Beau and his truck. Only relatives and the best of friends should have automatic connection rights to Bluetooth and Wi-Fi. I was definitely not a relative, and although I wasn't sure how to classify our relationship, we certainly weren't the best of friends.

I had just made it to Carrollton Avenue when my phone rang and Sarah's name came up on the dash screen. I hit the Answer button on the steering wheel. "Hey, Sarah. I'm driving and this is hands-free, but I think Beau might have a heart attack if I don't focus on the road. Actually, I might have the heart attack, but whatever. Is this quick, or do I need to call you back?"

"Does that mean Beau's there?" she asked.

Beau leaned forward. "Right here, Sarah. So make it G-rated, all right?"

I shot him a look while Sarah laughed. "I'm not even thirteen, Beau. I know nothing."

I rolled my eyes. "Right. So, what is it?"

"Mom said you're not coming for Thanksgiving."

"I know—I'm pretty bummed. But I can't get there without asking for money, which I'm not going to do, and besides, I've got lots of work here. Thibaut's teaching me how to repoint bricks so I can work on the exposed chimneys in my house after I finish the bathroom tiling project that's been waiting for me to free up some time."

"Yeah, wow. Sounds thrilling." I pictured her rolling her eyes. It was no longer clear who'd learned it from whom. "So, I was thinking, since I'm still just a kid living with parents, I don't have any problem asking them to buy me a plane ticket to visit you for Thanksgiving."

"That sounds like fun, but Jolene is trying to convince me to drive down to Mississippi with her for the holiday and to pick up a car. I'd much rather install bathroom fixtures and repoint chimney bricks, but Jolene keeps asking. I haven't yet agreed to go, since I'm dying to finish my renovations, and I'm not sure who's going to win this argument."

"Well, that's a no-brainer. I've met Jolene. So, can I go, too? Remember how much fun we had at the Sabatiers' beach house? Please, Nola? You're my favorite sister and I really want to go." I imagined her using the same puppy dog eyes Mardi used on me when he was begging for another treat or for a scrap from my plate.

"I'm your only sister, which by default makes me your favorite," I pointed out. "I'll think about it, okay? But the answer is probably going to be no. I'll call you about it later. I'm supposed to be driving right now." My finger hovered over the Disconnect button.

"One more thing—I promise I'll be quick. Grandma Sarah called me again."

I glanced at Beau. "Yeah? Anything new?"

"I think so. I didn't understand the first thing she said, but maybe you will. Something that sounded like *timespick* something. I have no idea what that meant, but she kept repeating today's date, like she wanted to make sure I remembered it."

"Could it have been the *Times-Picayune*?" Beau asked.

"Yeah, that sounds right. Isn't that the New Orleans newspaper?"

"Yes," I said. I'd listened to the local news on the television only briefly as I got ready that morning, and I couldn't remember anything notable. "What else did she say?"

Beau grabbed hold of his armrest as I slammed to a stop at a red light that seemed to have appeared out of nowhere.

Unaware of Beau's unnecessary histrionics, Sarah continued. "She kept talking about an earring—a big gold hoop one, with, like, smaller hoops inside of it. Any idea what that means?"

I felt Beau staring at me, but I didn't turn my head. "Yeah, I think it means that Beau and I should go see Madame Zoe."

I looked up in time to see a sign indicating the turnoff for I-10. Without using my blinker—something I'd picked up quickly during my brief forays into New Orleans driving—I drove across three lanes so I wouldn't miss it.

Beau jerked forward. "She'll call you later," he said before unceremoniously ending the call with a hard press of the steering wheel's End Call button.

"What?" I asked as I headed the truck in the direction of Old Metairie, where the two sisters lived. "If you don't like the way I drive, you shouldn't have forced me."

Despite my death grip on the wheel, and that my speed was a solid ten miles per hour below the limit, his face was completely blanched. He pointed to an upcoming exit. "Take this one."

"But that's not what the GPS says—" I began.

"We're getting off the interstate and we'll drive the back roads. I'm not going to call you a menace, because that's what you want. And then you'll have it as an excuse to refuse to try again, and I'm not going to allow that."

"Fine." I exited the highway before turning right into a shopping center parking lot without using my turn signal, then stopped the truck and got out.

Beau joined me, his expression probably matching mine. "What are you doing?"

I walked past him and climbed into the passenger seat. "I'm waiting for you to drive the rest of the way. Since you know what's best for me."

"That's not what I meant." He got in behind the wheel. "I just think you're being a little pigheaded about the whole driving thing. You've told yourself for years that you're a horrible driver, so that now you believe it." He threw the gearshift into drive and pulled out of the parking lot, jerking the steering wheel in righteous anger.

"Sort of like you telling yourself that you understand your parents' motives and nothing anyone can say or do can convince you otherwise. Even though you have the ability to actually talk to your mother and get an answer, you have shut down all communication. And yet you call me the pigheaded one."

We drove in silence the rest of the way, Beau clenching his jaw, his knuckles white on the steering wheel. He didn't speak until he'd pulled onto a residential street and stopped the truck at the curb. "I see what you did there."

"Yeah. Sometimes being pigheaded can be an asset."

He gave me a sidelong glance but didn't smile. "You think I should go see that fortune teller."

I pressed the heels of my hands into my eyes, if only so I wouldn't smack him on the head. "Seriously? You were abandoned by your parents. I get that—believe me. Seen it, done it, been there. Even bought the T-shirt. But it's not like they left you on the side of the road, you know? They made sure that you had family who loved you and would keep you safe while they were gone. Your parents had another child who was out there somewhere, taken by strangers to who knows where. They were desperate to find her. Together. Because they loved each other and didn't want either one of them to face alone whatever it was they were going to find. They did what they did because they loved your sister and because they loved you. They had no idea that Katrina would happen."

I took a deep breath, willing myself to calm down. This wasn't about me. At least it shouldn't be. "When my mother, Bonnie, overdosed, all she left me was my father's name on a crumpled piece of paper. I was on my own. I'm not trying to give you a sob story; you know it all already. I just want you to realize that your parents were light-years ahead of mine in terms of parenting skills. From where I sit, your parents did nothing wrong."

Beau stared out the window as if I hadn't said anything. But his fingers played with the rubber band on his wrist, so I knew he'd heard every word. I thought about touching his arm, but I stopped myself before I made it all more complicated than it needed to be. Gently, I said, "How many ways do you have to be told something before it sinks in? I feel like I should apologize to all the rocks out there for comparing them to you. I just don't understand what else you need to hear to be convinced that there are answers to the questions you've had since you were a little boy. And there are people such as Madame Zoe who are offering their help. I honestly don't know what else I can say to you. I swear, if I looked up the word 'mulish' in the dictionary, your picture would be there in the definition. And 'intractable.' 'Immovable.' 'Obdurate.' 'Asinine' . . . "

"Stop. Okay? Just stop. You have no idea. . . ."

I smacked my own forehead now. Not interested in hearing his explanations for acting like a stubborn toddler yet again, I flicked on the radio just to get him to stop talking. Adele's rich voice, singing "Rumour Has It," filled the truck, the volume on the radio getting louder and louder on its own until Beau shut it off.

Beau drew a deep breath. "Fine," he said. "You win."

"No, Beau. You win."

He turned the key, shutting off the engine before sitting back and not speaking to or looking at me for a full minute. Finally he turned to me. "So, when do you want to go see Madame Zoe?"

"I think you meant to ask *When are you available?* since I'm doing this for you and not the other way around. Just to be clear as to whose favor it is, like that whole thing about you not saving my guitar in the house fire back in Charleston."

"Because I thought saving your life was more important."

"Hey, I didn't ask you to save me—remember? I could have done it on my own, but I would have grabbed my guitar first. But whatever. We're even now. So, when are you available to go see Madame Zoe? I can do it Saturday morning if that works for you. I assume she's in Jackson Square every day, but that's just a guess. I figure we'll find out when we get there."

He stared at me for a while before answering. "Fine. Saturday morning. I'll pick you up at nine. We can grab coffee and a beignet while we wait around if she's not there."

"Great," I said, afraid to say more. That had been a lot easier than I'd anticipated. I'd imagined having to use sleeping pills, rope, and a wheelbarrow to get him to agree to see the fortune teller.

"But you owe me," he said, then got out of the truck, slamming the door behind him and cutting off my words of protest.

CHAPTER 9

By the time I caught up to Beau, he was halfway up the walkway in front of a pretty white-brick single-story home that appeared to date back to the 1930s. On either side of it, enormous McMansions that had been built too close to the street and were too big for their lots towered over the little house like vultures over roadkill. As a card-carrying old-house hugger, I cringed as I imagined the older houses that had occupied those lots and had formed a cohesive architectural vibe—something the two monstrosities had destroyed, and then essentially rubbed salt into the wound with their complete disregard for the neighborhood aesthetic.

I continued up the walkway toward a round columned portico covering the curved redbrick steps that led up to the front door of the white house. Original diamond-paned windows graced the fanlight and sidelights surrounding the door, and a black iron gas lantern hung down above it. The portico was devoid of cobwebs, or debris of any kind, giving me a hint to the fastidiousness of the home's occupants—or at least one of them. A window with black shutters sat on each side of the door, and a carport to the left housed a late-model maroon Cadillac sedan.

The yard was freshly mowed, the hedges neatly trimmed, but in the back I could spy a garden that appeared to adhere more to the natural school of thought. My guess would be Mrs. Meggison—Honey—who wore purple and black nail polish, along with a long gray braid, and not her sister, who favored Ferragamo flats and kept her platinum blond hair in a trim bob. There was no question as to which sister was responsible for which part of the yard.

Beau and I crunched up a path of smooth white stones, the front door opening before we'd reached the steps. Honey stood there to greet us, her lips highlighted in fuchsia lipstick, a purple silk turban wrapped around her hair. A bird we'd seen before—a parrotlet—sat on her raised forearm.

"Joan is getting the tea tray ready, so Zeus and I thought we'd be the ones to welcome you to our home."

"Mrs. Meggison—" I began before a flash of bright blue feathers zipped past me, forcing me to duck as the small bird winged his way to Beau.

"Zeus, come back here!" The woman began fluttering her hands as she descended the stairs toward Beau. He was making an attempt to cover his head with his arms as the parrotlet circled him, searching for a place to land.

"He won't hurt you. Just put your arms at your sides and he'll settle down on one of your shoulders." Joan Wenzel stood in the doorway now, her platinum hair like a football helmet gleaming in the sun.

Beau did as Joan had suggested, but he kept his eyes tightly shut as if afraid the bird might not have been paying attention to the "He won't hurt you" part.

"I don't know what's got into him," Honey said as we all watched the bird settle on Beau's broad shoulder and begin letting out erratically spaced noises that could have been words.

"What's he saying?" I asked.

"I wish I knew," Joan Wenzel said as she calmly came down the steps and approached Beau. "He hasn't spoken in the last eight years—ever since he came to live with us. Except for the one time when Zeus first met you, he hasn't uttered a single syllable."

She held out her hand with the index finger extended like a small branch. "Come on, Zeus. I'll put your perch near Mr. Ryan inside, I promise."

As if the small bird actually understood, he nodded his head once before hopping over to the offered finger. Beau slowly opened his eyes to find the bird looking directly at him. "Can't you just put him back in his cage?"

Zeus let out a long, pain-filled caw.

"Zeus doesn't stay in a cage, except for when we leave the house," Mrs. Wenzel explained, with what I thought sounded like an air of disdain. "He's more like a pet cat than a bird, and he uses a litter tray in the kitchen and sleeps on his perch in Honey's bedroom." She led the way into a low-ceilinged foyer and then to a step-down living room.

After seeing the outdated, overly worn, and just plain ugly furnishings in the Esplanade house, I was pleasantly surprised by these simple and bright interiors. The floral upholstery, ruffled drapes, light-colored wicker furniture, and celery green wall-to-wall carpet gave off *Golden Girls* vibes, but the hand-knit throws, the polished silver frames holding family photographs, and the stack of books next to the plush velvet armchair gave it a homey, almost cozy feeling. And the lack of dead animals' body parts used as furniture legs made it all much more inviting.

"What a lovely home," I said, sitting down on a palm frond–patterned sofa cushion.

"You sound surprised," Mrs. Wenzel said as she picked up a teapot and filled a cup with steaming liquid. She handed it to me without asking if I wanted it. She filled another and handed it to Beau while Honey moved a tray of small pastries toward Beau and me on the sofa.

"I made these from scratch using my grandmother's recipes," Honey said. With a black-tipped fingernail she began identifying the sugary confections. "Brown-butter tart, chocolate ganache tart, kouign-amann, and, of course, cheese straws." Cupping her hand to the side of her face, she whispered, "Those are store-bought. No matter how hard I try, I can't make them any better. Just don't tell Joan."

Not wanting to disappoint, I accepted a plate and helped myself to a variety, belatedly noticing that everyone else had placed only a single pastry on their plates. After taking a bite of a decadent tart, I reluctantly placed it back on my plate. As I wiped my fingers on my napkin, I allowed my gaze to drift to the photographs covering every available flat surface.

The subject of most of them was a young girl with light brown hair and an almost elfin face with a pointy chin and wide blue eyes. The pictures started when she was a baby, continuing through toddlerhood, up to around age four. My perusal came to an abrupt stop when I spotted what I'd been hoping to see. I walked over to the mantel and picked up an oval silver frame containing a posed studio shot of a man seated in front of two women—one a generation older than the other—and a young girl. This photo stood out as the only one I saw that included the man—presumably Lynda's father, and Joan and Honey's half brother, Mark. Most of the rest of the photos showed the girl by herself or with the young woman I assumed to be her mother, Jessica. A handful depicted her with the older woman, who I guessed was the murder victim, Lynda's grandmother Sybil.

But it was the doll the little girl clutched in the photograph that had caught my attention. It was undoubtedly the same doll that had been tormenting me, but in the picture it was dressed in a pale blue smocked dress with a white Peter Pan collar.

Honey stood next to me. "That was taken about a month before . . . before the incident."

"They're a beautiful family," I said, my attention focused on the doll. "And I'm pretty sure that's the same doll I found in the armoire. Was it Lynda's favorite?"

Honey took the frame from me, her fingertips gently brushing her niece's image. "Unfortunately, yes. Mark bought it as an investment, expecting it to remain in the unopened box on a shelf and out of reach. Either he wasn't clear about his intentions or Jessica couldn't say no to sweet Lynda when she asked to play with it, but the doll became her favorite toy. She and her mother made clothes for it, and it went everywhere with her." Honey replaced the frame on the mantel. "Mark was furious, and it was the source of many disagreements between Mark and Jessica. We loved him, of course—he was our brother. But Joan and I realized very early that he wasn't the most forgiving person. He found fault with everything Jessica, Sybil, and even little Lynda did. It was hard to witness, but we did our best to stay out of their affairs."

"Is that why there aren't many photos of Mark?" I asked.

"It's not for us to know what goes on in a marriage," Joan said as she poured herself another cup of tea. "All we know is that Jessica and Lynda moved into the house on Esplanade with Sybil when Lynda was just a baby. We assumed Jessica needed her mother-in-law's help caring for Lynda. Mark also owned a beautiful lakefront mansion, and he lived there most of the time, while Jessica and Lynda made their home on Esplanade. That at least allowed us to forge a relationship with our niece. And Sybil. That was when we understood that we'd been unfair to her. Our mother had been dead a long time, and Sybil had been a loving and loyal wife to our father. It was only right that she should inherit the house."

Honey raised a tissue to her eyes and sniffed. "If only we hadn't wasted so much time. But we didn't know . . ."

"Of course not," I said gently.

Beau stood to retrieve my backpack, which he'd slung over the back of his chair. "There's one way to find out for sure if it's the same doll." He unzipped the top, then reached inside. He'd managed to reveal just the head of the doll before Zeus sprang from his perch and began hurtling through the air in excited spins and loop-de-loops as if he were riding on an invisible roller coaster.

"Zeus!" Joan lifted an arm in an invitation for him to land, only to have to duck as the bird made a good approximation of a death dive in her direction. He rose toward the ceiling before making a loop and preparing for another dive.

Joan grabbed a cable-knit throw from the back of the reading chair and tossed it over herself and her sister, both of them sinking to the floor beneath it as Beau stood in the middle of the room, holding the doll. The bird focused on him and the doll, making a beeline toward them with a sharp snap of wings, then doing a reconnaissance circle around Beau before landing on the doll's head.

I dropped to my knees and crawled toward the backpack, which had fallen at Beau's feet; I retrieved it before retreating a few steps. The room was filled with the staccato sound of continuous pecks at the doll's blond curls. I held the backpack open and carefully approached Beau.

"Throw it in here!"

"Be careful not to hurt Zeus!" Honey shouted.

I could almost hear Beau gritting his teeth as he moved toward me, holding the doll with an outstretched hand and picking up a folded newspaper from a side table with the other. When the doll was positioned over the opening in the backpack, he dropped the doll inside while using the newspaper as a barrier so that I could zip the backpack closed without suffering an attack from Zeus. The bird, now apparently exhausted from what I could describe only as a demonic episode, collapsed on Honey's extended arm and closed his eyes.

"What in the—" Beau began, then stopped himself before he offended any delicate sensibilities. "Is that what you meant when you said he wouldn't hurt anyone?"

Joan and Honey had emerged from under the knit throw and were standing with their arms linked. Honey's turban had slipped down the side of her head, but not a hair on Joan's head was out of place. I made a mental note to ask her later what hair spray she used so I could tell Jolene.

"He's never acted that way before. Not as long as we've had him, anyway," Honey said as she softly stroked the bird's side with a bent knuckle. "I don't know what got into him."

"What are you going to do with the doll?" Joan asked.

"Hang on to it," Beau said.

"Toss it into Manchac Swamp," I said at the same time.

Our eyes met over the backpack. It wasn't moving, but I imagined little plastic fists beating at the canvas from inside.

"We'd like for my grandmother Mimi Ryan to take a look to determine if it's valuable. We'll let you know if it is, and give you first refusal, of course."

"Thank you," Joan said, her eyes not moving from the zipped backpack. "We tried to solicit your grandmother's help before. We know about her psychometry. It's why we were at the antique shop the first time we met. It's not something my sister and I are supposed to believe in, but we have reached the point where we will try just about anything to get answers. And if Mark, Jessica, and Lynda are still alive, we want to see them again. We won't be here forever."

Zeus continued to sleep cradled against the soft fabric of Honey's caftan as her fingers gently stroked his tiny head.

We returned to our seats, except for Beau, who began examining the framed photographs that filled the deep sill in front of the picture window, which was almost as wide as the room. "I'm not going to take the doll out again, but from what you could see, do you think that was Lynda's doll?"

Joan and Honey exchanged a glance before they nodded in unison. "Yes," Joan said. "Lynda cut off one of the curls on the doll's forehead. I remember it because it made Mark so angry. And that doll"—she pointed to the backpack—"is missing the curl on the right side of her forehead."

Beau nodded, then continued to pick up frames, study them, and then return them before moving on to the next. "Was the doll in the house when the crime was committed?"

Honey shrugged. "We're not sure. Today is the first time we've seen it since . . . well, since *it* happened. But I do remember searching the house before we put it on the market, to make sure nothing valuable was left behind. I don't know how we missed the doll."

"It was in a locked cabinet inside an old armoire. Maybe that's why?" I asked.

"No." Joan shook her head adamantly. "That door has never had a key as long as I can remember, and it's always remained locked. Neither Lynda nor anyone else would have been able to hide the doll there."

Something about Beau's body language made me watch him as Joan talked, so I saw when he picked up a frame and tucked it inside his shirt. I stared at his back to get him to look at me and offer some kind of explanation, but he just continued looking at the photographs in frames and replacing them on the sill.

I turned back to Joan. "I'm surprised Lynda didn't take her doll with her, since it was her favorite. Did she sleep with it at night?"

"Yes," Joan answered. "She never went anywhere without it. Her Annabelle—that's what she named her." Her lips turned up in a sad smile. "All this time we thought they were together, especially because it was nighttime when the intruder broke in, and she would have been in bed, with Annabelle tucked beneath her arm just the way she liked."

"You're sure it was an intruder?" Beau asked.

Joan nodded. "It's all speculation, but that's the scenario the police put together. Mark was a very wealthy man and wasn't shy about showing it. He carried a lot of cash and enjoyed flashing it around town, which, naturally, made him a target for those looking for easy prey. It's thought that he was visiting the house on Esplanade and was followed to the house by one or two people intent on robbing them.

Sybil must have surprised the intruders, which led to the struggle and her violent death."

Honey shuddered. "The crime scene was . . . extensive. Sybil's room was upstairs, but nothing was disturbed up there. It seemed she surprised the intruder as she entered Jessica's downstairs bedroom. This meant that they had to pass through Lynda's room first." She closed her eyes. "I'm just so grateful they didn't hurt her. Because when they entered the back bedroom—"

"The murder room," Mrs. Wenzel clarified. "Where Sybil was butchered."

"She means she was stabbed to death," Honey said, her hands twisting nervously in her lap.

"Butchered," Mrs. Wenzel repeated. "Lynda's bedroom was supposed to be the one upstairs, but she was afraid to sleep up there. She said it was haunted."

I made a point not to look at Beau, knowing we were both recalling the sound of disembodied little feet running through the house, and the armoire key that had seemingly dropped from an invisible hand.

"And no leads from the crime scene?" Beau asked.

"No. There was a lot of Sybil's blood, of course, and also a small drop from Mark. The detectives thought it may have been from a defensive wound. But that's all. When the police had finished their investigation, we boxed up pretty much everything except for the furniture and took it all to a dumpster. I'm just not sure whether we should be happy you found Annabelle. Because I don't know what it means." Honey dabbed at her eyes. "We'd really appreciate it if you could let your grandmother hold the doll. Maybe she'll be able to answer our questions."

"I will," Beau said. "I'll let you know." He turned to me. "We need to get going."

I looked with longing at the tray of pastries, and at my pastry with only a single bite taken. "Yeah. We should. Thank you for the refreshments." I slung my backpack over my shoulders.

"Would you like to take any of the pastries home with you?" Honey asked.

"If it's not too much trouble," I answered before she'd finished speaking.

Honey gently placed Zeus on his perch and left the room while Joan led the way to the front door. Beau paused in the doorway to give the diminutive bird a hard stare before following the older woman.

"You might not recall," I said to Joan as I adjusted my backpack—I didn't like the way I could feel the shape of the doll through the canvas—"but do you happen to remember if either your stepmother or your sister-in-law wore a particular perfume?"

"Oh, yes. I do remember. I'm not sure if Jessica did, but Sybil certainly did. She never went anywhere without a spritz or two. It always seemed as if Lynda was covered in it just from Sybil hugging her. It certainly took the guesswork out of what to get her for her birthday and Christmas."

"Was it by any chance Youth-Dew by Estée Lauder?"

Her eyes widened. "Yes. Yes, it was. How did you know that?"

"There's a bottle of it in the armoire where we found the doll."

"You smell it at the house, don't you?" Joan asked quietly.

"Yeah," Beau answered. "We both do. We smelled it outside the house the first time we visited, and then again in the armoire where we found the bottle."

She nodded before glancing behind her shoulder. With a lowered voice, she said, "If you wouldn't mind telling me first anything you might discover about the doll? Honey is . . . a bit excitable. She's always had delicate nerves, I'm afraid. Ever since childhood. We were both traumatized by our mother's death, but Honey more so because she was so young. I've always protected her from anything unpleasant, and we've both grown used to our roles."

"Of course," Beau said as we all turned to see Honey approaching with two brown lunch bags folded neatly at the top.

"I wrapped them individually in foil so you can freeze them if you like."

"Thank you so much." I took my bag, thankful for the foil if only because it would slow me down and keep me from eating them all at once.

"We'll be in touch," Beau said.

We'd said our good-byes and had almost reached the truck when Honey came running after us, waving the newspaper that Beau had used to protect us from Zeus. "I think you forgot this."

"Actually, it's yours. It was on a side table."

She thrust it at him so he was forced to accept it. "I know. But take it anyway. I don't want Joan to know I'm talking about her." She glanced over her shoulder toward the picture window. "She's always been so sensitive, and I didn't want to upset her further. Talking about Lynda is very hard for both of us, but especially for Joan. She's always been such a mother hen, and I her dutiful chick." Honey smiled. "It's because of our mother dying so young, and Joan just had a natural instinct when it came to nurturing. It's a shame she never had any children of her own, because she would have made an excellent mother. Because I'm the artistic one, she thought I needed special handling, but sometimes I think it's the other way around."

"So if we find out anything about the doll, you want us to tell you first," Beau said.

"Yes. If you would be so kind. I took the liberty of writing down my cell number, just in case you need it." She shoved it into my backpack, and made no move to head back to the house.

"Is there anything else?" I asked.

Her eyes, beneath thinly penciled eyebrows, met mine. "Lynda was right. About the house being haunted. We probably should have told you before you bought it, but we thought it might turn you off. It's a little boy, and he likes to cause mischief, but he's a happy little soul. We think it's a great-uncle who died when he was six years old, during the influenza epidemic of 1919. His name was Patrick." She smiled again. "I just thought you should know."

"Thank you," Beau said. "You weren't legally required to tell us anything, so we appreciate it. I'm sure Patrick and I will get along just fine."

She clapped her hands like a little girl, the gold bangles on her wrists jingling in tandem. "I was hoping you would say that. We felt so bad selling the house with him trapped inside without any friends. It's good to know he won't be lonely."

We said our good-byes again, then watched as she seemed, in her long caftan, to float back to the house before we headed to the truck parked at the curb.

Beau cleared his throat. "There's something I need to tell you."

I braced myself. I didn't believe—hadn't even considered—that he would make any sort of declaration to me, or about me, or, well, anything to do with me, but still I found myself quieting my footsteps so that I wouldn't miss a single word.

He stopped by the driver's-side door but didn't open it. "If Cooper is seriously interested in the Esplanade house, I need to make a full disclosure."

I mentally sorted through all the things that could be so fundamentally wrong with a historic house that they would be detrimental not only to its renovation and restoration but also in finding a buyer who was interested in either one.

"It's termites, isn't it?" They were my biggest fear, up there next to black mold and a crumbling foundation, the trifecta of what could make the difference between restoration and demolition. For preservationists like me, any of those three issues was enough to make our knees shake.

"I wish. It's a bit more, um, complicated than that."

I stared at him in silence, my mind flicking through my grad school textbooks, searching for something else that could derail the project. The mental reel stopped abruptly as I thought of one thing that wouldn't be found in any historic-preservation textbook. "We already know about the ghosts of Sybil and Patrick. They seemed pretty harmless to me. Even Cooper didn't think they were anything to worry about."

"Right. And I agree." He shifted his weight on his feet, then looked past me to the closed door of the house we'd just left.

"Is it the woman you saw at Café Degas?"

He shook his head. "No. I've only seen her that once, and that was while Cooper was with me. I have a feeling I'll only see her again when I'm near him, which I'm happy to avoid."

I frowned at him, but I was too anxious about what he wasn't telling me to be angry. "So . . . ?"

"It's a male spirit. An adult male. Definitely not a kid; older than me. Forties, maybe. Judging by his clothing, my guess is contemporary, like, anywhere from the eighties or nineties to now. Guys' fashions don't really change that much, so it's hard for me to tell. And I couldn't really get a good look at him. I sensed his presence the very first time I entered the Esplanade house. I felt that he's somehow connected to Honey and Joan. That's why I was looking so closely at their photos."

"Okay," I said. "But since Cooper and I and the majority of people can't see him, then it doesn't matter, right? Melanie and Jack have lived with the benign ghosts in their Tradd Street house for years. There was a pretty nasty one that Melanie got rid of, but the rest of them just sort of rub along nicely with the living."

Beau nodded. "I know. But Sybil—the one with the perfume—acts like a protector, sort of like she's shielding the living and any benevolent ghosts, like the little boy, from him. Because this adult male entity is definitely not a nice person. Or he wasn't a nice person, and death hasn't improved his disposition."

"So as long as she's there, everything's fine, right? If she's happy to stay and protect the rest of us, more power to her, right?"

Beau's brown eyes bored into mine, sending an electric pulse through my blood. "I'm not so sure. He's getting stronger with each new person who walks through the door. That includes you, and Cooper, and any of the workers we hire for the project. He feeds off your energy and is getting stronger and stronger. I barely noticed him the first time I entered the house, and now I feel his presence like a sharp blade being held to my throat."

I stepped back. "Like Antoine?"

"Yeah. And the stronger he gets, the more he'll be able to manipulate the physical world in a negative way."

"So we need to find out who he is, so we can get rid of him."

"'We'?" A quick mouth tilt momentarily softened his grim expression.

"Well, we do have a good track record. And I'd hate to throw in the towel without a fight on our first murder-flip project." An involuntary shudder rippled through me as a flashback to the night in the Ryans' attic played in my head.

He frowned and scratched the back of his neck. "I'm not sure, Nola. We barely survived the last time—remember?"

"Oh, I remember. Trust me. But I'd like to believe that our experience has made us stronger. And smarter. So we can be more prepared next time."

His gaze locked with mine. "My gut tells me that I should say no, that you and I shouldn't be working together, and that what happened in Mimi's attic was an anomaly or we just got lucky. Because . . ."

He stopped, but I knew what he'd been about to say—the same words I'd heard him say to his dead mother over the phone. *I want her too much. She's dangerous. I can't afford to lose my focus. I can't ever let that happen again.*

"Because . . . ?" I prompted.

"Because it could be dangerous. You need to have a talk with Cooper and let him know. I need you both to go in with eyes wide-open."

Beau held open the passenger-side door while I climbed in, and shut it before walking around the truck, opening the driver's-side door, and sliding behind the wheel.

We drove in silence, neither of us wanting to take the risk of turning on the radio. We hadn't gone far when I began to feel tiny pricks of awareness on the back of my neck. Like the feeling of someone watching me. I turned to look, expecting to find the baby doll propped against the leather and staring at me. But the space was bare except for a Saints baseball cap and a reusable grocery bag from Whole Foods.

I jerked my gaze to Beau. Dark beard stubble peppered his chin, highlighted by the pallor of his skin. His eyes were trained on the rearview mirror, and he was looking at something in the empty backseat.

"What is it?" I asked.

"Nothing," he said. "Nothing at all." He pressed his foot down on the accelerator as if trying to outpace whatever it was he was seeing. As if we both didn't already know that the only way to fight one's demons was to face them.

CHAPTER 10

Jolene and I stood outside the Lucy Rose boutique on Magazine Street, peering into the front window. "Come on, Nola. I am absolutely positive that we'll find something in here for you to wear tonight. I never leave this store empty-handed."

With multiple shopping bags draped over her arm, she pulled open the door. Eyeing my pitiful lone and very small bag, she said, "I know you can do better than that."

I'd been to the Magazine Street shop of the renowned New Orleans native and jewelry designer Mignon Faget and purchased pretty, dangly fleur-de-lis earrings for Sarah. They were the first Christmas present I'd bought this year, and I was feeling proud of myself for starting before December. Melanie usually had all gifts purchased, wrapped, and labeled by October, so I had a long way to go, but at least this was a start.

Jolene continued. "They have the *cutest* clothes and accessories. I know we'll find the perfect outfit for you. And then we can go to Petcetera to get something festive for Mardi for Thanksgiving. Do you think I should ask Mama to set a place for him at the table? You know how he likes to be a part of the action."

I'd given up trying to say no to Jolene's invitation to go with her to Mississippi for the upcoming holiday. It wasn't worth the cold coffee and burnt muffins that had been my morning staples until I'd finally agreed. And as Jolene pointed out, my Creole cottage had been waiting for a makeover for more than five decades; it could wait a little longer.

Delaying work on my house was made somewhat more palatable by speaking with Thibaut, who let me know that the roof issue was more extensive than previously thought and that repointing the bricks would have to be put off for now. At least I had that to look forward to. That and redoing my spreadsheets, which I updated daily and helpfully tacked onto the kitchen wall to keep Thibaut and Jorge on track. There was still some debate about scheduling potty breaks, so I left them off. For now.

Jolene immediately headed over to a rack of clothing marked SALE. Watching Jolene shop was like watching Michelangelo sculpt his *David* or Leonardo da Vinci paint his *Mona Lisa*. She was swift, methodical, and thorough as she flipped through hangers, pulling out a lilac cashmere cardigan with the precision of a scientist pulling out DNA from a smear of blood.

Reaching into her animal-print handbag—which matched her shoes, naturally—she retrieved a cell phone–sized plastic folder containing swatches of fabric. I'd seen her whip it out in the other stores we'd already visited and I'd been afraid to ask, but my curiosity won out.

"Okay. I give up. What is that?"

Her green eyes widened with surprise as if I'd just asked if she might be pregnant. "It's my colors." Her face softened with understanding. "I keep forgetting that you were raised mostly in California, bless your heart. But don't worry—we can fix that. Remember my aunt Janie I told you about? I'll make an appointment with her for you to have your colors done when we're down for Thanksgiving. It will change. Your. Life."

"Wow. Hard to believe I've survived this long without having my 'colors done,' whatever that means. Maybe Sarah would like to have hers done, too." My younger sister had been added to the ever-growing list of people invited to Mrs. McKenna's Thanksgiving table, and if I had to submit to getting my colors done, then there was no reason why Sarah couldn't share in the misery.

"That's an excellent idea," Jolene said, with so much enthusiasm that I was sure she would have clapped her hands if they'd been empty. "You will both thank me. Knowing which colors flatter you the best is a lifelong skill."

"Like potty training," I said with a smile, repeating what she'd once told me about learning how to drive.

"Exactly." She returned the color swatches to her bag and slid the hanger back onto the rack.

I headed over to a jewelry display and picked up a pair of copper-colored bangles. Holding them up for Jolene to see, I said, "What about these for tonight?"

"They're very pretty. But if you don't find a dress to wear, I think people will be too distracted by your naked body to notice them."

I rolled my eyes. "Can't I just borrow something from your closet? If I buy something new, chances are I won't wear it again, and borrowing something would save me money." I had just received a small raise, so I wasn't panicking about paying my rent, but I was tired from shopping and wanted to go home, so I threw that last bit in to garner sympathy.

Her sigh of disappointment carried the same weight as one Melanie would give my dad when she'd notice that the dresser drawers she'd organized and labeled were once again in disarray. "Don't you like dressing up just a little bit? We're going to the Saenger Theatre. Have you seen it? I think it might even be illegal not to wear lipstick and heels."

At my doubtful look, she added, "Well, if it's not illegal, it should be. And afterward we'll be dining at Arnaud's, and Cooper will be joining us, so I know you'll want to look your best."

I put the bangles back and picked up a large padded headband studded with multicolored rhinestones. "I thought the purpose of dressing well was to make you feel beautiful on the inside."

Jolene studied me for a moment, taking in my jeans, the scuffed ankle boots that I'd borrowed from Melanie years ago and kept forgetting to return, my old Ashley Hall school cardigan, and my trusty frayed backpack. "That's very true. But right now you're looking like someone whose roof is leaking, who can't afford to go home for Thanksgiving, and whose love life is as complicated as two spiders trying to square-dance." She stopped speaking and I waited for her to say another *bless your heart*, but instead she reached over, plucked the headband out of my hands, and returned it to the display. "It's rare that I turn down something sparkly, but I think this looks too much like part of a Mardi Gras costume. It would certainly draw attention, but not the *right kind* of attention."

"Like wearing a dress that has both a low neckline and a high hemline?"

She beamed at me. "Exactly. I'm glad you've been paying attention." She turned back to the sale rack. "Now let's find something pretty for you to wear. I'm thinking blue to match your eyes, so you look like Princess Elsa instead of something the dog dug up out of the yard."

Jolene dragged me through three more shops on Magazine before we found something we both agreed upon and I could afford. When we made it back to Bubba and loaded our bags into the trunk I felt like I'd just survived a bloody battle. I slid into Bubba's passenger seat, grateful for the extra legroom afforded by the older-model car, and kicked off my boots to wiggle feeling back into my toes.

As Jolene pulled out of her parking spot amid a series of sharp horn honks from an approaching car, she said, "Are you excited about tonight?"

I was eager to attend a performance of *Beetlejuice* at the historic Saenger. The theater was a testament to all I held dear in terms of historic preservation. Hurricane Katrina had almost destroyed it, and it had remained closed for eight years, but during that time it had been lovingly restored to its 1920s art deco splendor, and it had returned to being a mainstay of New Orleans' cultural backbone. It was the rest of the evening that I was worried about.

"We'll have to hurry. I'll take care of feeding and walking Mardi while you get started." Jolene sent me a quick side-glance. "Don't worry about washing your hair. I'm thinking a high ponytail would be perfect with your new dress, since it will highlight the cutout in the back, and making a ponytail smooth is always easier when the hair isn't freshly washed."

"How do you know all this stuff?"

"Trial and error, Nola. Just trial and error. You have to go through a lot of *awful* before you can get to *just right*." She turned to me briefly, but long enough for me to understand that she was talking about more than just hair and makeup.

I was reminded yet again how easily her bright external persona hid her sharp mind and accurate assessment of people and situations. It was a secret very few were privileged to unravel. I had long since determined that I was very fortunate to have Jolene McKenna in my life—and not just for the coffee and fresh baked goods.

"I added Cooper to the dinner reservation, so now it will be a table for nine. Arnaud's seemed okay with the odd number."

"Thanks for doing that. I wouldn't have asked, but I haven't seen him for a week and he's headed out of town again tomorrow. At least you can still be my date for the theater. And I'll make sure you're on the end and not next to Carly or Jaxson."

She smiled without saying anything and I knew she was probably thinking that she wouldn't mind sitting next to Jaxson, even though we both knew that would be a terrible idea.

The entire outing had actually been Samantha's doing. Her goal was to help Beau move forward by reconciling with his dead mother. With Adele's best friend now within reach, it was Sam's hope that Camille would have the answers Beau had been waiting for, and she wanted to throw them together in as many situations as possible. Sam had roped me into helping her with a plea that I was better at planning than she was. What she'd really meant was that I had access to the queen of planning and entertaining, Jolene. So, of course, the guest list had grown exponentially. In addition to Camille and Henry, it included Sam and Beau, Carly and Jaxson, and, because Cooper wasn't supposed to be back in time, Jolene and me. When Cooper had called and said he'd gotten an earlier flight and could make it to dinner at least, our numbers had swelled by one.

"Don't worry about me," Jolene said. "It'll be fun."

"Fun" wasn't the word I would have used to describe the gathering in the lobby of the historic Saenger on Canal Street, but I was willing to try. I was hoping for a chance to speak with Cooper later, at dinner, to ask him about the unhappy woman Beau had seen at Café Degas. I wasn't looking forward to sharing an evening with Henry LeBlanc, but at least I could look forward to getting to know Camille better, and hopefully helping Beau to find answers to questions he had about his mother.

Everyone in our group arrived within five minutes of one another and waited in the preselected spot in the lobby so Sam could find us and distribute our tickets. Even I had to admit that she and Beau made a cute couple as they grinned at each other in a private joke and he bent down so she could say something into his ear. We all turned at the sound of a wolf whistle as Henry and Camille approached. Camille had her arm linked with one of Henry's, and from his unsteady gait it was clear that he'd been drinking.

"Whoa, sexy!" he said, looking at me. His open perusal left me feeling naked, and I found myself wishing I hadn't already checked my coat. I'd been more excited about wearing my new dress than I'd wanted to admit. It had a large keyhole opening that exposed the upper part of my back, and the hemline was above the knee—both acceptable to Jolene—and the sapphire color was, according to Jolene, on my color wheel. But that excitement quickly dwindled as I found myself being embraced by Henry, his fingers lingering on my bare skin and his lips leaving a wet spot on my cheek.

"How nice to see you again." I tried to pull away, but he held on. Not wanting to cause a scene, I turned my head, trying to avoid the wafting alcohol fumes from his mouth. I hadn't felt a desperate need for a drink since the debacle of Michael Hebert's betrayal, but tonight I found myself craving the sort of emotional buffer only alcohol could give me, and the potent smell of gin on Henry's breath didn't help. The tighter he held me, the worse the craving got. I wouldn't even have to ask my therapist about this visceral reaction. I already knew it had little to do with the unwanted attention—although that was definitely a part of it—and more to do with the tension I always felt when Beau was near. It was like a persistent itch I couldn't reach.

"Let the lady breathe." Beau's tone was jovial, but the hand on Henry's shoulder wasn't. After a brief resistance, Henry released his hold on me and I stepped back, teetering on the borrowed high heels Jolene had said I needed to "complete the look." Beau steadied me and then shed his jacket to place over my shoulders.

"You looked cold." His eyes met mine, and I felt the familiar buzz that sparked between us at inopportune times. Like now. It reminded me of how much our thoughts always seemed to run in tandem.

I glanced up to find Sam's eyes on us, and quickly stepped away. "Thank you," I said in the direction of Beau's shoulder, and turned to greet Camille.

She gave me an apologetic smile. "I'm sorry about that. I told Henry to go easy on the celebrating, but I guess he didn't listen." She looked down at her feet, as if this were somehow her fault. "I'll make sure he doesn't drink any more tonight and that he doesn't sit next to you. I really am sorry."

"Please don't worry. I'm fine." I almost added *as long as it doesn't happen again*, but she already looked so beaten that I couldn't. "If you don't mind my asking, what's the celebration all about?"

"Oh, sorry. I thought Mimi or Beau or someone else would have already mentioned it."

I wanted to tell her to stop apologizing, that she wasn't responsible for everything and everyone, but I was afraid that would make her apologize again. "No. I haven't heard from Mimi, and when I saw Beau yesterday he didn't mention anything. What is it?"

"Henry and I both have jobs! Mimi said she could use more inventory and front-office help at the Past Is Never Past, and she hired us both. We're so grateful for her generosity. Of course, we worked at the shop before, so it's not like we're newbies, and Henry and I already understand the antiques business, so it makes sense. It will certainly save time on training." Two creases formed the shape of the number eleven between her eyebrows. "Of course, I'll need Christopher to show me how to use the new computer, but everything else looks to be pretty much the same as before. I hope he doesn't mind." She gave me a worried look.

"I'm sure he doesn't. Christopher has been nothing but kind and patient to Trevor, the young man he's mentoring. He's such a quick study. If either you or Henry need help with anything and Christopher isn't available, Trevor will most likely be able to assist."

Camille frowned again. "Yes, well. We'll see."

I wanted to ask her what she meant, but Jaxson and Carly were approaching Jolene, and I figured Jolene would need some moral support, so I excused myself and headed over just as Carly was planting air-kisses on both of her cheeks.

"Nola!" Carly shouted as I approached, and then enveloped me in a hug saturated with a fragrance composed of vanilla and spice and something that I couldn't identify but was undoubtedly expensive. Carly was an attorney for a private law practice, and everything about her was expensive, including the strapless cocktail dress of emerald green and the diamond pendant necklace that sparkled almost as much as the diamond on her left hand.

Jaxson gave me a warm hug in greeting. He was a New Orleans native and an old friend of Beau's. Despite working as a public defender, he was as kind as he was funny. The only thing to dislike about Jaxson Landry was his choice in fiancées.

I turned back to Jolene, who was listening to Carly bemoan all the wedding details she had to take care of. I wanted to point out that her mother was heavily involved in the planning, as was the team of wedding planners her mother had hired, but I doubted she would hear my sarcasm, and she might even continue talking about the wedding. Although Jolene was smiling and nodding, her eyes had become glassy, like those of a taxidermied deer whose last vision was of a bullet.

The lights dimmed, letting us know that it was time to find our seats. As we began to file into the auditorium, Carly was still talking to Jolene. "I wanted to make this more formal, but I guess now would be a good time to ask you to be my maid of honor."

Jolene continued to smile, but I wondered if anyone else noticed that her expression was that of a person stuck in the middle of a highway with a tractor trailer barreling toward her.

Carly didn't stop talking, oblivious to Jolene's sudden muteness. "You're so amazing at planning and organizing, and you understand that it's the unique little details that make an event special, so of course I thought of you! And because I'm so busy with work and travel, I appreciate that you won't need a lot of instruction and oversight, which is more than I can say for the planners my mother hired."

Jolene's smile didn't falter, but she still seemed to be unable to speak.

"Our first order of business will be to plan a luncheon to surprise my other bridesmaids with a formal invite to be a part of our big day." She hooked her arm through Jaxson's. "This will be so much fun!"

Jaxson looked everywhere except at Jolene's face as he led Carly into the auditorium.

Jolene and I followed them to our seats. I turned to Jolene to ask her to say something but was interrupted by Henry. "What time is intermission? I'm going to need another beer pretty soon. I don't know how long I can stand sitting in this monkey suit, either."

"Henry," Camille said, a warning in her soft voice, "we're all here to have a nice time. Please behave yourself." She ushered her husband into our row, thankfully putting him on the far end, and then followed him. Next were Sam and Beau. I grabbed Jolene's arm and made her slide in next to Beau, followed by me and then Carly and Jaxson.

Jolene's smile appeared frozen, and she still hadn't said anything, despite an urgent finger poking from me. Turning to Carly, I took a deep breath. "You know, I don't think Jolene will have time to be your maid of honor. She's so busy doing the social media for JR Properties for both my house and now the new one, on Esplanade. She also hasn't agreed. I think she's too nice to say no—"

Carly cut me off. Leaning forward to look past me at Jolene, she said, "You'll do it, right? Please? I really need you—you really are the perfect person for it." She reached around me to take Jolene's hand and squeeze.

With the same *I'm about to get hit by a truck* expression, Jolene said, "Of course I will. I'm honored."

I sat back in my plush red velvet seat, aware of the chatter of the people around me and the general commotion of people taking their seats in the rows around us, and of a peculiarly silent Jolene.

I leaned close to her ear. "You okay?"

Still smiling, she nodded, then directed my attention to the startling ceiling, which mimicked the sky and was filled with stars and moving projections of clouds. Pointing at the architectural surround, she said, "I feel like I'm in Italy."

I let out a sigh of relief that she was still capable of speaking. A mute Jolene wasn't something I could even comprehend. "I've never been, but I imagine this is what it looks like in person." I followed her gaze, knowing that she shared my appreciation for old buildings. The design of the theater when it opened in 1927 was meant to recall a Baroque Italian courtyard, complete with Greek and Roman statues set in alcoves and on top of faux walls. The meticulous restoration had replicated the original design right down to the color scheme, carpeting, lighting fixtures, and marquees.

"I've always wanted to go to Italy," Jolene said. "Until I came to New Orleans for college, I'd never been out of Mississippi. Maybe I'll get the chance to go someday."

Carly leaned forward again. "Jaxson and I have decided to go to Italy on our honeymoon! We'll send lots of pictures so you can pretend that you're there."

Jolene nodded, her smile a bit wobbly. I restrained myself from throwing an elbow into Carly's side and instead sat back in my seat. As the massive red velvet curtain rose, I prepared to enjoy the performance. I'd talk to Jolene later, in private, and help her to understand that she hadn't actually agreed to Carly's request; that the word "yes" had never crossed Jolene's lips; and that she hadn't said or done anything that could possibly make Carly believe that Jolene had committed to participate in her wedding in any capacity. I needed to make it clear that she would be Carly's maid of honor over my dead body. Or Carly's. Because that's what best friends were for.

Halfway through the first act, I became aware of someone attempting to exit our row and I instinctively moved my legs to the side. The person was already out of the row and heading back to the lobby before I realized it was Beau. The white of his shirtsleeves almost glowed in the darkened theater, reminding me that I still wore his jacket over my shoulders.

I mostly returned my attention to the performance, keeping half-aware of any movement from the aisle so I'd be ready to move when

Beau came back. Except he didn't. I leaned forward to see if he'd returned from the other direction, but his seat remained vacant. Unable to relax now, and wondering if he'd forgotten he'd given me his jacket and was looking for it, I got up and made my way to the aisle and then up to the lobby.

The lobby was empty except for a couple of ushers, and a man and woman having a heated argument near one of the backlit marquees. I waited for a few minutes, thinking that Beau might be in the bathroom. I was about to approach a male usher to ask him to go check when, through the glass front doors, I caught sight of Beau standing on the sidewalk.

The chilly night air hit me as I stepped outside. The steady hum of Canal Street's traffic masked my approach, and he jumped when I touched his arm.

"Sorry," I said, drawing back. "I called your name, but I guess you didn't hear me." I slid the jacket from my shoulders. "Here. You must be freezing."

"I'm fine. You keep it." He settled it back on my shoulders, and I enjoyed the brief warmth of his hands before he withdrew them.

"Are you not enjoying the show?" I asked.

He seemed surprised by my question. "The show?" He shook his head as if remembering why we were there. "No. I mean, yes. The show is fantastic. It's just"—he indicated the Saenger behind us—"the theater. It's had a, um, long and tumultuous history."

"Ah. Right. Like old houses."

"Or really any old building where people have lived moments of their lives. Or died—as in hospitals. They all come with a host of unsettled spirits with unfinished business. And once they spot me—"

I held up my hand. "I get it. Melanie and my aunt Jayne have the same issue. You're like a beacon in a dark night. I guess we should be glad you didn't jump up and start singing 'Dancing Queen.'"

Beau smiled at me as we both recalled Melanie's proclivity to sing an ABBA song to make the ghosts leave her alone. He lifted his arm, and a red rubber band was visible beneath his shirt cuff. "I've got this. It's a little more subtle and, I'd like to think, just as effective. Warding off the unwanted attention is exhausting, though, so I decided I needed some fresh air. Guess I've been gone longer than I thought."

I met his eyes, knowing that what he'd just told me was only half the truth. "It's about tomorrow, isn't it? About seeing Madame Zoe."

His eyes became guarded. "Why would you say that?"

"Because I'm right, aren't I?"

He brought his face closer to mine. "But how would you know that?"

I didn't pull back. "Because whether we want to admit it or not, there's some sort of annoying psychic connection between us. I know I'm not alone in wishing that weren't the case or that it would just go away, but there it is."

A corner of his mouth tilted up. "Yep. There it is." His expression became serious again, his thoughts turning inward.

I touched his arm briefly, and my fingers lifted as soon as I felt the familiar zing. "I've discovered that not knowing the truth is usually so much worse than finding it. Because when you've found it you can deal with it and move on. I didn't know my mom was dead for two weeks. She just didn't come home. That wasn't all that unusual, but it was strange for her to be gone for that long. When the police knocked on my door and told me, it was a relief, really. Because then I knew and didn't have to worry about where she was or if she was hurt and wanting to come home. She was gone and I had no other choice but to move on. So I did."

"Does your dad know all this?"

I shook my head. "Not all of it. I left out the worst bits. Why make him suffer, too, you know?"

He nodded slowly. "I'm afraid of what I'll find out about my parents. All these years, I've been telling myself a certain narrative. Finding out that the truth doesn't match that narrative will mean that I've been lying to myself for so long."

"We all lie to ourselves about something, Beau. It's human nature. It makes the hard pills easier to swallow. But I think it's these lies that hold us back, you know? Not just emotionally, but . . ." I shrugged. "But everything, I guess. Your career, your everyday choices. Your relationships."

His eyes met mine again. "Yeah. All that. It's just . . ." He inhaled. Exhaled. Like someone getting ready to jump into an icy-cold pool. "It's just that I feel like I'm all alone in this. Yes, I have Mimi, but her focus is her son, regardless of how much she loved her daughter-in-law. It's not the same as a sibling who shares both parents. But Sunny won't return my phone calls even though she's speaking to Mimi. She's my sister, and I really think we should do this together. Not just for me, but for her, too. Surely she's wondered about what happened to our parents since she found out who she really is. I know she doesn't remember them, but . . ." He stopped.

"But they're still her parents. And you're her brother."

"Yeah." His voice held all the heartbreak of a boy who believed he'd been deserted by the two people who were supposed to love him best, and then by his sister. My own heart echoed with a familiar ache of desertion, and before I could remind myself that this was Beau, I moved closer, put my arms around him, and pulled him to me. I lay my head against his chest, feeling the beat of his heart beneath my ear.

"You're not alone, Beau. I'm here. Always."

I felt his hand on my head, stroking my hair softly. "I know."

We stood like that for a while, unable or unwilling to pull apart.

"I was wondering what was taking you so long."

We dropped our arms and stepped back at the sound of Sam's voice, the action making us look guilty of whatever it was she thought we were doing.

"I was returning his jacket . . ." I said.

"We were just talking . . ." Beau said at the same time.

Sam pressed her lips together, ignoring me and focusing on Beau. "I can see that. The show's almost over. I've got a headache, so I've called an Uber to take me home. Sorry to miss dinner at Arnaud's. Beau knows it's my favorite restaurant."

A white Camry pulled up to the curb. Sam looked at her phone, then at the license plate and driver, before opening the door and sliding into the backseat.

Beau grabbed the door. "Sam, please don't leave like this. . . ."

Sam leaned toward the front seat and spoke to the driver. "Please go—I'm ready."

With a quick look of apology, Beau slid in next to Sam in the backseat, then closed the door behind him. The Camry pulled onto Canal Street and drove away, leaving me standing on the sidewalk, where I stayed until I realized how cold I was and went back into the theater.

I returned to my seat and pretended to watch the rest of the performance, clapping when I was supposed to but unaware of anything except for the feel of Beau's jacket over my shoulders and the memory of the sound of his heartbeat close to my ear.

CHAPTER 11

Cooper was waiting outside the theater as the audience spilled out of the doors at the end of the performance. His hands were shoved into the pockets of a navy blue wool overcoat, and a plaid Burberry scarf hung from his neck.

Seeing him was like drinking a cup of hot coffee on a cold morning, and his smile as I approached definitely did something to my heart rate, but I wasn't wearing my smart watch, so I couldn't check to be sure. He held my shoulders as he bent down to kiss my cheek, his lips lingering long enough that I could feel his warm breath on my neck—and that certainly made my blood swish a little faster.

"Nice jacket," he said, indicating Beau's jacket, which I'd draped over my arm after I retrieved my coat.

"Beau let me borrow it. He had to leave early—Sam had a migraine." I decided to go with the same story I'd told the rest of our party.

"Probably for the best. I hear Arnaud's is very haunted."

"Really? Anybody in particular?"

"Considering parts of it were once opium dens and houses of ill repute, it shouldn't come as a surprise if some of the hangers-on are pretty happy where they are. But the original owner, known as the Count, is seen in the main dining room, surveying his domain. All of the spirits are friendly, at least—as far as I've read."

"Oh, you read up on it?"

He smiled down at me, and my heart may have sped up another beat or two. "Of course. I always like to be prepared."

I stepped closer to him, enjoying his warmth. With the tip of my finger, I brushed the scar on his chin. "You don't need a roof or walls to be haunted, you know. I've come to believe that we create ghosts out of our memories and our grief for things we've lost. Or opportunities. Or people."

His eyes met mine. "Nola . . ." he began.

"Come on—the Uber's here," Camille said from behind us.

"We're missing some prime drinking time," Henry said, heading toward a light blue SUV.

"Let's walk," I said to Cooper. "It's only a few blocks." My toes groaned at the suggestion. As Jolene had put it, I was wearing a pair of her "sittin' down" shoes, meaning they were for decorative purposes only. But I was eager to speak with Cooper alone, to ask him about the spirit of the woman Beau had seen behind Cooper at Café Degas. There were plenty of Band-Aids and ice at the apartment.

"Come on, Jolene," Carly called. "We'll let the boys sit in the back so you and I can talk wedding details."

Jolene looked at me with an expression of horror.

"Why don't you come walk with us?" I suggested, ignoring her four-inch stilettos. There were enough Band-Aids and ice for both of us.

"I'd love to," she shouted, with a little too much enthusiasm. "We've been sitting so long, and I would appreciate stretching my legs."

"Let's go," Henry said, his hand pressing firmly on Camille's back. "Drinking time's a-wasting."

Cooper gently took my elbow and then Jolene's and started walking before the SUV's door had shut.

"Thank you," Jolene said. "I don't know if I could have survived the four blocks, so thank you. I might be crippled for a month from walking in these heels, but it will be worth it."

"Not a fan of Henry's?" Cooper asked.

I turned so I could meet Jolene's gaze.

"Well, he's certainly easy on the eyes, but I don't think both his oars are in the water—you know what I mean?"

"So I'm guessing it's Carly you're avoiding?" Cooper said.

I elbowed him gently in the side. "Let's talk about more pleasant things, okay? Like your trip to London. Or even how pervasive mildew can be. Just anything else, please."

Cooper chuckled as we continued down North Rampart, our conversation about nothing at all.

We arrived at the restaurant at the same time as the Uber, so we were all escorted into the main dining room together. I tried to ensure that Jolene was seated between Cooper and me to prevent her having to converse with either Henry or Carly. But somehow she managed to sit next to Jaxson, with me on her left and Cooper on my left. The table was round, so conversation among the entire party would still be possible, but at least this way Jolene had a better chance of enjoying her meal.

I looked around me at the august space in one of New Orleans' premier and historic eateries—which was saying a lot, considering both adjectives could describe many of the restaurants in the Big Easy. Arnaud's had been around since the turn of the previous century, and it had survived the Volstead Act through the sheer cunning of its owner, the Count. A massive restoration in the late seventies had ensured that the original chandeliers, iron columns, and cypress paneling remained. The old ceiling fans also stayed—and were reportedly as temperamental now as they'd been back when the restaurant was new.

Beautiful beveled glass windows had replaced a wall of pebbled glass—a change that I didn't hate even though it meant exchanging something historic with something that, well, wasn't. Above us, an exact replica of the original tin ceiling graced the entire main dining room. But the details I'd been most excited to see since I'd first read about the restoration, when I was an undergrad at Tulane, were the original small Italian tiles that covered the floors throughout the restaurant, with patterns and colors varying from room to room. They were almost as iconic as the restaurant itself.

"May I interest you in a cocktail?" Our server, dressed immaculately in a black tuxedo and bow tie, stood next to the table, looking at me expectantly.

"Maker's Mark on the rocks for me," Henry interjected. "And make it a double."

The server smiled, then returned his attention to me, apparently adhering to the ladies-first rule. "Seltzer water with lemon, please."

"What?" Henry asked with exaggerated surprise. "You can't order *seltzer water.* This is New Orleans!" He turned to the server. "She'll have what I'm having."

I shook my head. "No, I'm fine with the seltzer water."

"The lady will have a double bourbon," Henry said, his voice loud enough that other diners turned to stare.

"No, she won't." Cooper remained seated and didn't raise his voice, but that didn't make him any less menacing. The scar on his chin whitened against his flushed skin, the only indication that he wasn't as calm as he otherwise appeared. Cooper turned to the server. "She'll have the seltzer with lemon, and so will I."

Henry started to say something but was stopped by his wife's hand on his arm. I studied Camille for a moment, surprised that she had the ability to rein in her husband. I didn't know a lot about marriage except what I'd seen between Jack and Melanie (a lot of which made me want to cover my eyes and block out sound), but they probably weren't the norm—at least not according to the true-crime shows I binged with Jolene. The main takeaway was that it was impossible to know exactly what went on in a marriage unless you were one of the two people involved. As far as Camille and Henry went, I was happy not knowing.

Fortunately, since almost all of us had just seen the same theatrical production, there was plenty to talk about while we perused the menu. I'd already decided on the Shrimp Arnaud to start, and the Crabmeat Karen for my entrée. I wanted to go ahead and select my dessert to make sure they wouldn't run out, but the desserts weren't printed on the menu.

Conversation flowed, Carly talking about her wedding, and Camille discussing her excitement about working in the antiques business again and about how surprised she was that Christopher still worked at the Past Is Never Past, since he'd been there when she'd worked at the shop before Katrina. She almost seemed disappointed.

Thankfully, Henry grew quieter the more he drank, and he stopped trying to convince me to have a drink, too. Jaxson and Jolene were strangely silent, probably because Carly was happy to do all the talking. When she mentioned wedding-dress shopping I felt Jolene tense beside me. I turned to Camille and, talking over Carly, said, "I'm sorry Beau had to leave. I know he wanted the chance to talk with you about Adele, since you knew her longer than he did."

"We don't talk about Adele," Henry slurred. "Right, Camille?"

Camille stared at her plate. "We don't," she said quietly. "It's too painful."

"Yup," Henry said, followed by a loud burp. "Too painful."

I was saved from responding by the sound of my phone buzzing in my purse. I discreetly slid it out and saw a text from Beau. Can you talk.

"Everything all right?" Cooper asked.

"Yeah. I just need to make a quick phone call."

Cooper stood to pull out my chair as I excused myself, and I made my way to the ladies' room. Beau picked up on the first ring.

"Seriously?" I said before he had a chance to say anything. "This whole evening was meant to get you together with Camille so maybe she'll help you find out what your mom is looking for and give you any information she has about where your dad went. But you left, and I have no idea what you want me to ask her. I have your jacket, by the way."

"I'm sorry. Really. I just . . ." I heard him breathe out. "Anyway, that's why I'm calling. My jacket has my wallet and driver's license in it, and I left my car parked near the restaurant. I thought I'd call an Uber so I can meet up with you to get my jacket."

"Well, you'd better hurry. They're getting ready to serve dessert. It's late and I need to get home. I can't sleep in tomorrow morning because we're meeting Madame Zoe—remember?"

"Hard to forget. My phone keeps zinging with reminders from you."

"You're welcome. Now hurry up and get here so you can ask Camille whatever it is you need to know so tonight's not a complete waste. Well, aside from the show and eating at Arnaud's. I've got to get Jolene out of here before her face is permanently frozen in that weird smile she's been wearing all night."

"Uber's on its way. I'll be there as soon as I can. I'm coming from Sam's, so it will take about fifteen minutes longer, but I'll tell the driver to hurry."

I'd just tossed my phone back into my purse when Camille opened the bathroom door.

"We were wondering where you'd gone," she said. "The waiter removed your dessert before you'd had a chance to eat it, but Cooper asked him to bring it back in a box for you to take home. I thought that was very nice of him."

"It was." She made no move toward a stall or the door. I had doubts that Beau would get there in time to talk to Camille, and because he and I were seeing Madame Zoe the following morning, I decided to talk to her myself. "Camille, I'm sorry, since I know you find the subject of Adele too painful, but there are so many unanswered questions. If you don't mind, I have a quick one."

She looked at me, her eyes wounded, as if she already knew what I was going to say.

I hurried before she could ask me to stop. "I know that Beau would ask you this himself if he were here, but is there any reason you can think of why Adele, presuming she's dead, would still be here? Can you think of any unfinished business that would keep her here?"

Her face paled, and her distress was like a blow to my gut. "I'm sorry. I didn't mean—"

She held up a hand. "No. Really. It's all right. I understand. Beau lost his mother—and father—when he was still a young boy. He's looking for answers. As we all are." She looked down at her feet. When she looked up again, the glare on her glasses hid her eyes.

"Maybe there's something you remember? Anything Adele might have told you before she disappeared?" I hesitated, unsure of how to say what I needed to say, what Beau would want to say if he were there. I took a deep breath. "Beau knows his mother's no longer alive. He also knows she's not resting in peace."

Her eyebrows rose over the tortoiseshell frames. "What do you mean?"

Again I hesitated. I didn't want to share anything that wasn't mine to share, but there were still a few things that could be considered public knowledge. "He keeps seeing wet footprints that seem to follow him. I've seen them, too. So have others, including Sam. We're pretty sure they're Adele's, because they belong to a woman, they're always dripping wet, and they usually appear in conjunction with Beau. We used to think she was looking for Sunny, and now that Sunny's been found we're wondering why she's still here. That's why Beau is hoping you might know something. Or remember something. Or even have some clue about where Buddy might be. Maybe Adele's still being here has to do with Buddy."

Camille's brow puckered, which, along with the glasses, made her look like a wizened owl. "I've already told Mimi what I remember, including the places I suggested that Buddy look for Sunny. And that's it. Mimi has tried touching some of Buddy's belongings, but they aren't telling her anything—or anything she can use. She says that whatever vibrations she's getting are all garbled and disjointed, almost like he's speaking a foreign language that Mimi can't understand."

Camille clasped her hands together. Softly, she said, "Whether or not Mimi and Beau want to admit it, even just to themselves, if Buddy wanted to be found he would have come home by now. As for Adele, if she were dead I'd know it. I would." Camille removed her glasses and used her knuckle to wipe at the corners of her eyes. "She was like a sister to me. I'd know." Just like she'd done before when talking about Adele, she pressed her hand against her heart.

Her hand remained where it was, causing her to look like a child making a wish—like me on every Christmas Eve, wishing my mom would be there the next morning. "So you suggest they just sit and wait?"

She gave me a sympathetic look. "Yes. I do. So does Henry."

The door opened again, and a stranger entered the bathroom. I caught the door before it could close; I needed to hurry so I wouldn't miss Beau. Turning back to Camille, I said, "Thank you for sharing that. One more thing—do you remember if Adele or Buddy were into psychics or fortune tellers?"

She frowned, shook her head. "Not that I recall. Maybe for fun, but not because they believed in that sort of thing. I think Mimi was about all they could take of the psychic world."

"Maybe," I said with a quick nod. "Thanks again for sharing that." I let the door close behind me and rushed back to our table to retrieve Beau's jacket.

"Are you leaving now?" Cooper asked, standing as I approached.

"No. I just have to meet Beau to give him this." I held up the jacket.

"May I drive you home afterward? We didn't get a chance to really talk, and I'm leaving again in the morning."

I glanced over at Jolene, who, despite her smile and vivid hair, looked like a frozen mannequin, with too-white skin and unfocused eyes. "I think I should go home with Jolene. She . . . doesn't seem herself."

Cooper followed my gaze, then shoved his hands into his pockets with a resigned sigh. "I get it. Can I call you? I'll be in Los Angeles, but it's only a two-hour time difference, so I won't have to wake you up."

He looked so hopeful that I stood on my toes and gave him a soft kiss on his mouth, making him smile. "What was that for?"

"For understanding. And just . . ." I shrugged. "Just being you." I stepped away and held my hand up to my ear with thumb and pinkie extended, like an old-fashioned phone. *Call me,* I mouthed, then headed outside to the sidewalk.

Beau was just stepping out of his Uber as the restaurant door closed behind me. "Perfect timing," I said. "Everything okay with Sam?" I didn't say I was sorry for causing her quick exit because I hadn't done anything wrong. This time.

He avoided my eyes. "Yeah. All good." He pointed to his jacket, draped over my arm. "Can I have that? Sam's waiting and I need to get to my truck." He reached for the jacket, but I held it back.

"Hang on—I need to say something first."

"Okay," he said, dropping his hand.

"Since you bailed on me, I took the opportunity to speak with Camille. She has nothing to add to what we already know. I asked her if either of your parents spoke with a fortune teller, and she said she didn't think so. She also mentioned that when Mimi touched some of your dad's belongings all she got was garbled words. She also believes that your mom is still alive, despite what I told her about the wet footprints. Camille didn't seem to be aware of your psychic abilities, so I didn't say anything."

"Thank you. I don't mind Camille knowing—after all, she knows about Mimi—but I don't want Henry to know. He'd probably hound me so that I'd help him find some source of money. Christopher told me that he's that kind of guy."

I nodded. "Yeah. I agree. Although I like Camille."

Beau inclined his head toward the restaurant. "What does Jolene think? I trust her intuition when it comes to people."

I thought for a moment. "Let me try this word for word: 'That man's as useless as a milk bucket under a bull.'"

Beau gave a soft laugh. "Good to know I wasn't off base with my initial reaction." He glanced at his watch. "I need to go. Sam's waiting."

"Of course. Here." I lifted the jacket from my arm, fumbling it as it got stuck in the straps of my purse before slipping to the sidewalk. Beau grabbed it quickly, but something fell from a pocket and clattered to the ground. I picked it up, examining it closely before handing it to Beau. It was a ring box from the famed Adler's Jewelry.

He took it from my outstretched hand. Unable to restrain my curiosity, I said, "Is that—?"

Beau cut me off with a curt nod, then tucked the box back into the inner breast pocket of his jacket. "I wish I had my mom's ring, because it was a family heirloom. But . . ." He shrugged.

"It's none of my business," I said, already walking away. "I'll see you tomorrow morning. Nine on the dot. I'll be waiting for you in my driveway."

I turned and ran back into the restaurant before I said anything else.

CHAPTER 12

Despite my wish for rain to delay our visit to Madame Zoe, the vivid autumn sun glared brightly from a cerulean sky. I held the travel coffee mug that had been a gift from Jolene and read CALIFORNIAN BY BIRTH, SOUTHERN BY CHOICE; I was desperately hoping to absorb caffeine after a sleepless night.

I'd tried to slip out the door without Jolene noticing, but she apparently had eyes in the back of her head. She'd pointed to the French door and given the command "Stop." I'd stopped at her authoritarian tone, and so had Mardi, sprawling on the floor between me and the door.

I'd been impressed despite my annoyance. "Did you teach him that?"

"No. Whoever his previous owner was must have. I was trying to get a roach to stay still while I went for the bug spray, and let's just say that Mardi did a much better job than the roach." She bent down to give Mardi a scratch behind one floppy ear. "Makes me wonder what else he knows and who he belonged to."

"Their loss, our gain," I said, remembering all the posters we'd spread around town after we'd found him and how we'd hoped that despite our best efforts an owner wouldn't be located. I reached for the doorknob and pulled on it, but instead of moving out of the way, Mardi looked up at me and did a half growl, half bark. I turned to Jolene. "Could you call off your dog, please? I have to meet Beau in exactly five minutes."

"Not looking like that." She reached down again and patted Mardi's head. "Good boy. Ain't nobody looking like they just rolled out of bed is leaving this apartment. It reflects poorly on me." Mardi seemed to smile as he looked up at my roommate, then rose to his feet and moved to his monogrammed doggie bed.

I sent a surreptitious look at the unguarded door. "Don't even think about it," Jolene said. "I don't know what else Mardi knows, but I don't want to give him any of the attack commands my uncle Boo uses as a prison guard down at Angola." She shuddered. "That could get ugly. So why don't you just come with me and I'll fix you right up and you'll only be a few minutes late?" She glanced at her watch. "Maybe a few more, since you're lollygagging."

I knew it would waste more time if I argued, so I went with her to the makeup table in her room, where she did something called "color correcting" on the bruise-colored skin under my eyes. "I wish you'd tell me what's wrong," she said as she selected a small makeup brush from her stockpile. "Even if there's nothing I can do, it sometimes helps just to tell someone."

She dipped the brush in some yellow goop in a compact, then gently dabbed it under my eyes.

"I think Beau proposed to Sam last night. And it's not like I have feelings for him—I mean, besides finding him annoying and authoritative and bossy. But not, like, anything that would make me not sleep if he and Sam were engaged, you know?"

I caught the look of concern in Jolene's green eyes before she turned away to dab more goop on the brush. I waited for her to share one of her usual pearls of wisdom that made me feel better. Instead, she said,

"I guess it's a good thing you're coming to Mississippi with me for Thanksgiving, then. Time away will give you a new perspective."

"I don't need a new perspective. I see twenty-twenty. Beau and I . . ." I paused, trying not to remember how warm and safe I'd felt in his embrace at the Saenger the night before. "We have a shared history of parental abandonment, so of course we feel a bond. But anything else . . ." I made a gagging noise, something I'd learned from Sarah and I knew was immature for a woman my age. Anything to distract Jolene from her line of thought.

She picked up a hairbrush and began brushing my hair into a high ponytail. "Just because we tell ourselves something isn't true doesn't make it any less true."

"I guess you're right. Which means that now would be the right time to talk about you planning the engagement party for Carly and Jaxson, and how there is no way on earth I will allow you to go wedding-dress shopping with her—regardless of who she's marrying. She doesn't treat you the way you deserve, Jolene. You are nothing but nice to her, and she's, well . . ."

"Not," Jolene finished, smoothing a bump in my hair. "My mama often says that it's those who are in the most need of love who are the hardest to love. I haven't quite figured out why Carly is the way she is, but one thing I do know is that she needs a friend."

"Well, you're a better friend than I am."

"Don't say that, Nola. You're an amazing friend. Besides, you haven't seen my voodoo doll collection."

I looked at her in alarm and didn't relax even when she smiled. There were so many things about Jolene—like her apparent lack of need of sleep—that could be explained only by voodoo or witchcraft that I couldn't completely dismiss her comment as a joke.

She studied my head from all directions in the mirror. "I've been thinking about something you said in the car on the way home last night. How Beau wishes that his sister would play a part in his search for their parents."

"Yes?" I said warily, my gaze meeting hers in the mirror. "She's blocked his number and has made it clear that she doesn't want to talk to him."

"Right. But she hasn't blocked your number. As far as you know."

"Not yet, but I'm sure she considers me guilty by association. Besides, I don't have her phone number."

"No, but Sam does. She's the one who called her about the fundraiser party—remember? I'd bet she hasn't deleted it."

"You have a short memory, Jolene. Don't you remember what happened the last time Sam and I tried to work behind Beau's back?"

"Do you mean how you returned Sunny to her family, so that she now has a relationship with her grandmother? Beau was mad at you for almost five whole minutes."

I sent her a long stare in the mirror. "It was longer than that. Besides, if Sunny won't speak with Beau, I'm positive she won't want to speak with me."

"How will you know if you don't try?"

I stood quickly. "Thanks for the primping, but I'm late and I need to get going."

After a brief scratch beneath Mardi's chin, I grabbed my backpack and headed toward the front door. In her own words, Jolene was as stubborn as a spot on a ladybug. In any case, I knew this wasn't the last I would hear on the subject.

Beau was waiting in his truck in the driveway when I emerged with a fresh 'do and with my face completely color corrected. As I climbed into the passenger seat, I said, "Sorry I'm a little late. You could have come in and waited, you know."

"I know. I just didn't want to interrupt Jolene's momentum and spoil the final result. You look really nice, by the way."

The compliment took me by surprise, making me fumble the words I'd been rehearsing all night, and then forget them completely. "Thank you," I said instead. "Jolene did it."

"I know. I can tell."

I wondered if he'd intended that as an insult. Maybe it had been meant to put us back into our old and familiar pattern. Before he could say anything that might take us down a road I didn't want to travel, such as the reason why Sam had abruptly left the theater or why he had been carrying a ring box in his jacket pocket, I said, "Can I see the photo you stole from Honey and her sister?"

He didn't seem disconcerted that I knew. "I didn't steal it. I was just borrowing it without asking permission. There's a difference. And I have every intention of returning it, so it's not technically stealing. As soon as I make a copy of it I'll find a way to put it back." He indicated for me to open the glove box. "It's the photo the sisters used for their real estate ads for the Esplanade house—I recognized it from the one that sparked my initial interest in the property—which means it's recent. They must have wanted a memento to take with them after they sold it."

"But why would you . . ." The question dissolved on my tongue as I brought the picture closer to my face. A white, smoky image appeared in one of the floor-to-ceiling windows of the front room. Although the edges of the cloud were smudged, two figures could be clearly seen. One, smaller than the other, looked like a young boy wearing short pants and suspenders. The face of the other was that of a middle-aged woman, her knee-length floral-print dress modern. Her hand rested on his shoulder in a maternal gesture.

I looked at Beau. "I'm guessing that's Patrick, the little boy who died in the influenza epidemic in 1919, and I think I recognize the woman from another photo I saw at the sisters' house. It looks like—"

"Sybil," Beau finished. "The woman murdered in the house. She's even wearing the same dress in the photo with Jessica and Lynda."

"You told me before that you thought Sybil was acting like the protector of the young spirit. This sort of proves it, doesn't it?"

He nodded. "And I think this is who she's protecting him from." He pointed to a corner of the house where tall bushes and other vegetation blended with shadows.

"I don't see . . ." I stopped, the shadows morphing into the cohesive shape of a head, torso, arms, and legs. I could now clearly make out the dark shadow figure of a man. I drew back, a cold fear spreading from my neck to my back. Even though the face had no features, I felt the menace of two eyes staring at me from the photograph.

I shoved the photo back into the glove box. "That's awful. Terrifying, really. We need to show that to Cooper before he makes any final decisions about the house."

"Agreed."

"Who do you think that could be?" I rubbed my arms, which were now covered with goose bumps.

"I don't know. I've only felt him in the house, but he's pretty much left me alone, I think because of Sybil. She's protecting me, too."

"Unless you decide to confront him."

He gave me a sidelong glance. "Yeah. Unless I confront him."

"Are those the only spirits in the house?"

He nodded again. "As far as I can tell. Unless there are others who keep hidden because they're afraid of . . . whatever that is."

I thought for a moment. "But that could be good news, right?"

"What do you mean?"

"Well, since you don't sense Jessica, Lynda, or Mark, they're possibly still alive, right?"

"Possibly. Or not. Not everyone who dies comes back. Haven't yet figured out why, but that's my understanding."

"There's only one way to find out for sure."

He gave me another sidelong glance. "Yeah. I was thinking the same thing. I just don't know if I'm ready for that."

"Problems don't go away just because you ignore them, you know."

Beau barked out a laugh and edged out of the driveway onto Broadway. "Right. Coming from the poster child of avoiding unpleasant things . . . Otherwise, we would be talking about Cooper and why you haven't yet asked him about the angry woman I saw hovering around him."

"It's because I haven't had a chance because he's been so busy traveling, and then last night . . ."

"Exactly," Beau said with infuriating calm. "Because if you really wanted to hear the answer, you'd find a way to ask."

I started to tell him he was wrong, then stopped, knowing I'd lost the argument before it had even started.

We drove in silence until we'd reached a parking garage in the Quarter, not far from the Past Is Never Past, then walked the short distance to the cathedral and Jackson Square. Despite it being November, the temperature hovered in the mid-sixties, and the blue sky and bright sun promised a beautiful fall day. Vendors had set up shop around the iron fence surrounding General Jackson on his horse, and a few of them had customers getting their silhouettes sketched or having their tarot cards read. It seemed every season in New Orleans was tourist season.

I turned to Beau to ask him about his suggestion that we have coffee and beignets before we met with Madame Zoe, but I stopped midsentence as I followed his gaze to where the fortune teller sat in front of the iron fence. She was perched behind a round table covered with a black satin tablecloth sparkling with scattered glitter that made it mimic the night sky. Two empty chairs sat waiting on the side of the table opposite her. The crystal ball I remembered from my visit with Sarah and Jolene sat in the middle of the table, a shape or movement causing ripples inside the clear glass before vanishing so quickly that I thought I had imagined it.

"That's Madame Zoe . . ." I began.

"I know." He took a step forward, then stopped to look at me. "You coming?"

I nodded, and because it seemed like the right thing to do, I slid my hand into his. He reached into his jeans pocket with his other hand and withdrew a small gold object. When we stood next to the table, he dropped it onto its surface. "I think this is yours?"

She looked up and smiled, showing white, even teeth, not a single one gold or missing. I wasn't sure if street performers had benefits, but Madame Zoe definitely visited a dentist on a regular basis. Or maybe I was just projecting my own stereotypes. Or, as Jolene might tell me, I was overthinking so that I could distract myself from facing something unpleasant.

The woman grasped the earring with fingers that had long, manicured nails painted a dark purple. Without expressing surprise at its sudden appearance, she said, "It is. Thank you." Indicating the two chairs opposite her, she said, "Please sit."

While we made ourselves comfortable on the too-small wooden folding chairs, Madame Zoe lifted her headscarf and reattached the earring. She shook her head, displaying the matching pair on her ears.

Her dark eyes studied me. "Adele said it would take longer for you to convince Beau to come."

Beau leaned forward. "You've spoken to my mother?"

Their gazes locked. "Yes. The same way she speaks to you. Except you don't listen."

His knee bounced against the table, making it shake. It was a nervous habit I'd come to recognize. I placed my hand on his knee, and he stopped. "What did she tell you?" he asked, his tone defiant.

Madame Zoe sat back in her chair, her earrings reflecting the sun. "The same thing she would tell you if you would stop being so stubborn and listen."

His leg tensed as if he were preparing to stand, so I squeezed, eliciting a scowl in my direction, but he remained seated.

"And what would that be?" I asked, because Beau remained silent.

Madame Zoe focused her unsettling gaze on me, making me want to bolt. But I remained seated, rooted by the warmth of Beau's leg beneath my hand. "I need you each to place a palm on the crystal ball, and don't move it. The small fingers on your hands should touch."

"Do we really—" Beau began, but I cut him off with another sharp squeeze of his leg, this time using what little fingernails I had to get his attention.

I did as the fortune teller asked, and after a pointed look at Beau, he did the same, but with a heavy sigh. I stretched my pinkie close to his, and after a brief hesitation Beau touched mine with his.

Ignoring Beau, Madame Zoe placed both her hands on top of the ball and closed her eyes. She took two deep breaths, then opened her eyes again and stared into the crystal ball. Odd streaks like contrails began to form inside it. Or like apparitions flitting past a doorway. "She talks about a girl named Emmaline. She wants Beau and Emmaline together, because Emmaline makes Beau stronger in all ways that matter—and not just his ability to see that which others cannot." Madame Zoe frowned. "But Beau is afraid to be stronger. He's afraid that he won't be able to control his gift if it becomes bigger than he is."

I pulled my hand from Beau's knee and placed it in my lap. "Are you sure she didn't say 'Samantha,' or 'Sam'?" I wanted to ignore Madame Zoe's theatrics and dismiss her lucky guess as thorough research. With the increase of my presence on social media, due to the success of Jolene's YouTube channel, anyone with access to a computer could find out that Emmaline was my given name. "It's just that those who've been able to . . . speak with Adele say she is hard to understand. Like she's speaking through water."

Black streaks swirled inside the ball, like droplets of ink added to water. As I watched, the stain spread, obscuring the inside of the glass and turning it opaque.

"How well did you know my parents?" Beau asked, a slight belligerence to his tone. I didn't fault him for it. He'd gone through so much since his parents' disappearance. It was almost absurd that he might finally find them through a fortune teller named Madame Zoe in Jackson Square.

"Your mother was a regular. She only brought your father once, and he was as skeptical as you are. He didn't return. Your mother came to me often before the storm. And then once afterward, for help finding her little girl." Her face wrinkled in concentration. "Sunshine, I think. The little girl's name was something like Sunshine."

"Sunny," Beau said, his tone dismissive. "A lot of good that did."

"I can only tell you what I see. As I explained to your mother, how you choose to interpret that information and what you do with it is completely up to you." She tapped her long fingernails against the globe. "Adele didn't come to me after that. Not alive, anyway." Her face softened as she lifted her eyes from the ball and looked at Beau. "I'm telling you things that you already know. Things you know in your heart."

"Things I know in my heart," Beau repeated, his mouth turned down as if he'd just eaten something rotten. "Even though—"

"Even though others tell you differently. Some people will think they are being truthful because they cannot face the truth. And others . . ." She stopped and frowned at the ball, which now resembled my little brother's Magic 8 Ball, its obsidian surface missing only the small window and the triangle-faceted die with raised white lettering spelling out rote, noncommittal responses.

"Reply hazy. Try again," Beau said, quoting one of the twenty responses available from the iconic toy. Despite his flippancy, he didn't remove his hand from the crystal ball.

"And others because they don't want to face the truth," Madame Zoe continued, as if she hadn't been interrupted.

"The truth?" Beau said. "I've accepted that my mother is dead. If you can tell me where her remains are, so my family can lay her to rest, then this visit won't be a total waste. Or tell me where my father is. Because I'd like to stop this hocus-pocus right now and get on with it."

"It doesn't work that way. Spirit only shows me a part of the message. The rest is up to you. Buddy is alive. But you already know that. He's just . . ." She squinted at the globe, as if trying to discern a picture in the churning blackness inside. Madame Zoe shook her head.

"He's lost. He . . ." She peered into the crystal. "You need to find him. There are those who mean him harm if you do not."

"Right. Did you get that from the Magic Eight Ball? You had a fifty-fifty chance of guessing about my dad. Now tell me something that you couldn't easily guess or find out, and then maybe I'll listen to what else you have to say." Beau tensed, preparing to pull away from the table.

Her gaze turned to me. "Your sister. I saw her before. She has a strong gift, yes?"

I nodded, not surprised that she would remember Sarah from when we visited Jackson Square the previous month.

"Adele speaks to her, too. She's told you about the newspaper. It's important."

I focused my attention on Beau for corroboration, but his attention was locked on the fortune teller, whose gold earrings seemed to wink at us as if the universe and all things unexplainable were including us in a joke we didn't understand.

She sat back, and I watched in fascination as the blackness inside the globe disintegrated into a smudge of swirling smoke before evaporating completely. Her shoulders dropped and she closed her eyes with exhaustion.

"What else?" Beau demanded. "Can you ask Adele where to find my dad?"

Madame Zoe looked at him through weary eyes. "No." She blinked slowly. "But you can."

Beau jerked back in his seat. "No. There has to be more"—he pointed his chin in the direction of the now-clear crystal ball—"in there."

With a tired voice, the woman said, "You have a gift, Beau. Use it." She reached for the hem of the sparkly tablecloth and draped it over the ball.

"So that's it?" Beau said. "That's all you've got? That and a dollar will get me absolutely nothing." I hoped that Madame Zoe would hear the desperation beneath the belligerence in Beau's voice.

The fortune teller untethered a small leather bag that was looped around her rope belt. "Before you leave, I have something for you." She untied the top of the bag and emptied the contents onto the table.

It was an assortment of smooth and rough stones of varying hues and sizes. They seemed to slither together on the cloth, their gentle clink and shine making me want to touch them.

With her finger, Madame Zoe slid a smooth green stone toward Beau. "This is jasper. It will promote courage and quick thinking. And it will support you through times of stress. All of these things will be important to you."

Beau sat back in his chair and crossed his arms. "Uh-huh."

Ignoring him, Madame Zoe plucked a purple crystal from the table. "This is amethyst. It's used for increasing psychic awareness. Your power is strong, yet you turn away from it, hoping your light will diminish. It won't. If you hone your abilities, you will be able to protect yourself and others. The amethyst can be carried or worn, but I also suggest you place it under your pillow while you sleep for best effect."

She reached her hand into a tattered Kate Spade tote at her feet and pulled out a small cloth bag. After picking up the green and purple stones, she slid them inside the pouch and handed it to Beau. He stared at it for a long moment without moving. I didn't want to hurt Madame Zoe's feelings, so I was reaching for it when Beau finally took it.

"Thank you," I said, feeling like the mother of a toddler who needed to be reminded of his manners.

"I have some for you, too." Using her index finger to shuffle through the stones on the table, she selected a smooth black one, the dense color clouding the sun's reflection. "This is an obsidian. To help process emotions and experiences, and aid in letting go of people and things that plague us. Including unhealthy habits that wait inside us, looking for a weak moment."

Our eyes met over the stone, and I wondered how she knew. It wasn't that I hid the fact that I was a recovering alcoholic, but I didn't advertise it, either.

She returned to the small pile of stones, flicking through them until she selected another one, then slid a smooth pink stone in my direction. "This is rose quartz. It is used mostly for love and romance."

I held it up between my thumb and index finger, admiring the way the sun pierced the murky pink stone, which clarified the light as it passed between my fingers. Madame Zoe sent me a meaningful glance. "It enhances connections and restores harmony in relationships. It also provides comfort and calm during times of grief." She dropped both stones into another small bag and handed it to me.

I took it, feeling confused. "I'm not sure if any of that applies to me, but thank you."

"You are still grieving for someone you lost long ago. You will continue to grieve until you've made your peace with her."

Blood ran to my head in a hot rush. "How . . ."

It was Beau's turn to place a calming hand on me. "It's time to go." He stood, taking my elbow so that I stood at the same time. Madame Zoe remained seated, as if too exhausted to stand. To Beau, she said, "I gave stones to Adele. For protection and clear thinking."

"Not that it did any good," he said, reaching for his wallet. "How much do I owe you?"

"Nothing. Consider it a gift from your mother. And maybe think about inviting me as a guest on your podcast to see if I'm a fake? Later, of course, after all of this makes sense. Because it will. The universe has a way of settling into its cracks eventually."

Beau shoved his wallet back into his jeans. "I have no idea what that means, but whatever. This has been very entertaining at least."

She opened her mouth in a broad smile, as if she'd just been let in on a huge joke.

"Thank you," I said, remembering the manners Melanie and my two grandmothers had drilled into me since I'd first arrived in Charleston. Whether or not Beau wanted to admit it, Madame Zoe knew things any normal person couldn't have known. And she had given him answers—or at least a path to answers. I could only hope that the cracks in the universe she'd mentioned weren't on a fault line and that the ground beneath our feet hadn't already begun to shift.

CHAPTER 13

I jogged to keep up with Beau as he left the square, not slowing down even when a group on a guided tour crossed his path. I muttered apologies as I followed in his wake and grabbed hold of his jacket when I got close enough.

"Where are you going?" I asked, distracted by the sweet smell of powdered beignets wafting from Café du Monde.

"To the truck. I still have the newspaper Honey gave me."

"Right," I said, pretending I hadn't forgotten. Too much weird stuff was happening, and it was messing with my brain. Still walking fast, he turned to me. "Take this," he said, handing me the small cloth pouch from Madame Zoe.

While jogging to keep up, I took it from him and shoved it into my backpack with mine. When we reached the truck I tried to hide my heavy breathing, embarrassed at how out of shape I was. I'd stopped my daily runs in Audubon Park, needing more time before seeing Michael again or being reminded of the first time I'd seen him there. I'd find a new route or the courage to return. Eventually. Maybe tomorrow.

Beau jerked open the rear door, then groaned.

"What's wrong?"

He reached inside and yanked something out to show me. I knew before I saw the round head and sightless eyes that it was the creepy baby doll.

"I thought you were bringing it to Mimi."

"I did. But apparently it didn't want to be there." He tossed it onto the seat, unperturbed by its potential value. He leaned inside to look on the floor before sliding into the rear seat for a closer inspection. "I could have sworn I put the newspaper back here before we left the house."

"Has anyone else been in your truck since then? Besides me."

He thought for a moment before his face relaxed. "Sam," he said. "After I dropped you off, Sam and I ran to Fresh Market in Metairie for some groceries. She must have picked it up when she grabbed the bags from the backseat."

"Why would you go all the way to Metairie instead of going to the Fresh Market on St. Charles?"

Beau exited the backseat and closed the door. "Because that one used to be Bultman Funeral Home. I prefer my grocery shopping without lost spirits who want to ask me why there are bananas in the viewing room."

We both climbed into the front seat, and he started the engine before backing out of the parking space. "Crap," he said, noticing the clock on the dash. "I'm supposed to meet Thibaut at another job site to get his take on things. He's doing me a favor working on a Saturday."

"That's fine," I said. "Do you have time to drop me off at Sam's apartment? I can get the newspaper and let you know if I find anything. I'll take an Uber back home or call Jolene. She's always looking for a reason to take Mardi for a car ride—he really loves it. She even bought him a pair of red Doggles to protect his eyes when he sticks his head out of the window." I buckled my seat belt casually, not wanting Beau to jump to conclusions about any ulterior motives I'd have to talk to Sam.

"Are you sure?"

I shrugged nonchalantly. "Cooper's in London, and I've got nothing planned today except for some catch-up on paperwork. I'm not allowed near the cottage until the roof is intact and the water damage is fixed. They've got huge fans blowing twenty-four seven to dry it out completely so I don't have any mold issues. Would I be wrong to think that Jolene is behind all of this so that I have no choice but to go with her to Mississippi for Thanksgiving?"

He grinned as he pulled out of the parking garage and onto the street. "No. Not at all. But I'm glad you're going. Someone needs to act as chaperone."

"Are you afraid Jolene will throw herself at Jaxson?"

"Actually, I'm thinking it's the other way around."

"You see it, too?" I asked. "Even though Jaxson and Carly are engaged?"

"You don't have to be psychic to see the obvious, Nola. There's a weird dynamic between those three, and I'm not even going to try to understand it."

"Funny, because . . ." I stopped, realizing that I'd been about to say that Jolene had said the same thing about Beau, Sam, and me. Not in so many words, and with a much thicker Southern accent, but the meaning was the same.

"What's funny?" he asked, turning to drive through the gated entrance to an apartment complex parking lot on Annunciation Street in the Lower Garden District. The guard at the gate waved us through despite the sign clearly saying that IDs were required for entry. Apparently Beau was enough of a frequent visitor to make him exempt.

"Nothing. Just something that Jolene said, but I can't repeat it, because it wouldn't be as funny without her saying it."

He pulled into a brick courtyard with a fountain that had two spitting fish in the middle. "Nice touch," I said. As he drew closer, I noted the mid-1980s style of the three squat buildings in front of me, each with pedimented gables and columns to give at least a nod to actual architectural thought. Iron balconies lined the three stories of each building, clashing with the Greek Revival style of the rest of the buildings, so I could give them only two points out of ten for trying.

Beau stopped the truck and turned to me. "I know what you're thinking."

"Yeah? And what would that be?"

"That you wouldn't live in this kind of building if your life depended on it. You'd prefer mold on your rafters to a roof without a history."

"You know me too well." I'd meant it as a joke, but he didn't smile.

"And in that I think you'd be right."

I opened my door and slid out of the seat to the ground. "Make sure to text Sam to let her know I'm coming. I don't want her answering the door dressed only in Saran wrap."

His fingers were already flying on his phone screen. "Got it." When he was finished, he looked up at me where I stood, lingering with my hand on the open door. "Is there anything else?"

"So, last night . . . the ring box. Did she . . . ?"

"Say yes? No."

I hoped he couldn't see the relief on my face. "I'm sorry," I said, wondering how much of me he really knew.

"I didn't ask her. Yet. We did a lot of talking, and then . . ." He stopped, shrugged. "And then we made up."

"Got it," I said, smiling to cover the rising nausea in the back of my throat. "I won't say anything, then. Don't want to ruin the surprise."

"Thanks." He held up his phone. "Good news—she has the newspaper, and she's expecting you. She's in apartment 3B."

I gave him a thumbs-up, then shut the door behind me and headed toward the white-painted double doors next to a brass plaque with elegant script reading *AUDUBON PARC*—spelled with a C, just in case anybody got confused about whether they were in the actual Audubon Park, with a K.

The doors opened into a lobby decorated à la Holiday Inn 1980, with lots of floral upholstery and with sad reproductions of well-known paintings nailed high on the walls, as if someone who was really tall and had no clue had been in charge of their placement.

A metal elevator sat in the left wall, inside a box of vinyl wallpaper border meant to make the space resemble a green arbor. I pushed the call button and stepped inside. My slow progress to the third floor gave me plenty of time to read all the neatly printed flyers affixed to the elevator's laminate walls, advertising social events: S'MORES! SECRET SANTA! BOOK CLUB!

I imagined living in a place like this had its advantages, especially socially. Not having to worry about lawn care, exterior paint, and a leaking roof would definitely free up a lot of time. But I doubted the low popcorn ceilings and the particleboard doors ever spoke to any of the residents. Just as I was sure that beneath the wall-to-wall carpeting there were no hardwood floors that bore the marks of past generations. And I was doubly positive that no one who lived here, current or past, ever thought that the building had chosen them.

The elevator doors slid open with a *bing*, and I exited into a short corridor. I followed a sign to apartment B, and I knocked on the door after staring at the doorbell for a full minute and wondering if it would be rude to ring it.

The door swung open, allowing the scent of simmering food to float out of the apartment. Sam smiled, her warmth a far cry from her disposition the last time I'd seen her, at the theater—when she'd stormed away and gotten into her Uber.

"Come on in," she said, holding open the door and looking like a J.Crew catalog model, with her slim corduroy pants, her striped oxford-cloth shirt, and a sweater knotted loosely around her shoulders. Her shiny brown hair was pulled back into an effortless messy bun held together with a massive tortoiseshell clip. "Excuse me just for a minute—I need to check the grillades. They should be just about done simmering."

"Smells delicious," I said as I closed the door behind me and followed her inside, happy to be on a neutral footing after the previous night's awkward parting. I stepped over a pair of Beau's running shoes, left in the small entranceway, and I wondered if they'd been put there on purpose.

Sam stood in front of an older electric stove, lifting the lid of a Dutch oven. "I'm making Beau's favorite, grillades and grits. It's Mimi's recipe, flavored with onions, celery, and green peppers—what she calls the 'Holy Trinity'—plus plenty of garlic, since that's what Beau likes. Not to mention a whole lot of love."

In my chest I felt a thickness that could have been heartburn, even though I hadn't eaten anything. Sam scooped a large spoon into the pot, then held it out to me. "Here, give it a try and let me know what you think." She waved her hand at the steam coming off of it. "Make sure you blow on it first so you don't burn your tongue."

The look in her eyes made me do a quick scan of the counter for a bottle of rat poison or anything else that might contain arsenic. I started to refuse, but she pressed the spoon closer to my mouth, leaving me without a choice. If I was going to ask her for Sunny's phone number, I had to play nice. And hopefully not die trying.

"That's amazing," I lied. It could have been sawdust.

"I'm glad you like it," she said, settling the lid back on the pot, then lowering the heat on the burner. "I'd invite you to stay, but Beau and I have plans for an early supper, and then . . ." She shrugged, the Cheshire cat grin on her face telling me everything I would rather not know.

"No worries," I said with forced cheerfulness. "Jolene and I are going out, too."

She looked at me expectantly. My roommate and I usually spent Saturday nights wearing green-goop facial masks and eating takeout while bingeing true-crime shows on the Investigation Discovery channel. "There's a new bar on Magazine we want to check out. Some of Jolene's friends from work might be there, so . . ."

"Sounds fun. What's the name of it?" At my blank stare, she added, "In case Beau and I want to go sometime."

"Oh, um, I don't remember. Jolene's driving, so all I have to do is get in the car."

"Right." She leaned against the counter, her arms crossed. "It's nice of you to be Jolene's wingwoman. She's such a beautiful person, inside and out, and it's hard to watch her throw herself at a guy who's engaged to someone else."

I started to say that Sam and Beau weren't engaged yet but stopped. She wasn't talking about me.

"I've seen a few of the comments on the YouTube channel where she and Jaxson share screen time, so I know it's not just me."

"There have been comments?" I was embarrassed to admit that I gave our channel only a cursory glance every once in a while. YouTube was a black hole, and every time I settled in to watch an episode I got sucked in, swept toward suggested channels about cute dogs and restoring old houses. Watching YouTube videos was a great way to waste time—for a person who had time to waste. Which I didn't.

"Lots. Don't worry—whoever is in charge of the channel deletes them as soon as they appear, but I guess a few have slipped through the cracks. Same with a bunch of anonymous ones from people claiming they know where Mardi came from. Probably just scammers looking to make a buck, which is why, I'm assuming, they're taken down so quickly."

"Wait—what? Someone says they know where Mardi came from?"

"Yes. I'm sorry—I thought you were the one taking them down."

I shook my head. "No, Jolene's in charge of all the social media for JR Properties, so I don't have to be involved at all. I just show up when asked to pose with Thibaut and Jorge or while using donated tools or hardware."

"Oh. Then I guess you'll need to ask her about it. Like I said, I'm sure it's just a scam." She looked at me expectantly. "So, Beau said you needed a newspaper?"

"Yeah. He left one in his truck and he thinks you might have picked it up with the groceries."

"Right," she said. "I wish he'd told me earlier, because now there are tomato sauce cans and beer bottles on top of it." She stepped on the pedal of a tall stainless steel garbage can and peered inside. "I can just make out a corner of it. Could you grab the rubber gloves on the sink and hand them to me?"

"I don't mind digging for it. Let me."

She didn't argue, so I reached inside and pulled the newspaper out from beneath several empty beer bottles of Beau's favorite brand. It was still folded, as if it had just been left on a doorstep, then placed directly in the recycling bin.

"I can look through it here and pull out what I need if you think you might read the rest of it."

"Considering it's a few days old, not likely. Take it—it's yours."

"Great. Thanks." I tucked the paper beneath my arm, then washed my hands in the sink. "There was one more thing I wanted to ask you."

"About Beau?"

"What? No. Although if you're wondering what Beau and I were doing outside the theater—"

She held up her hand. "Don't bother. He already told me. About your mom. I hope you don't mind."

"Of course not. It's not really a secret. But it does help knowing someone who has faced similar issues. It's hard to explain what I'm feeling to someone who was raised by two parents in a happy household."

"I get it. No explanation needed. I'm just sorry I overreacted." She gave me a warm smile. "I'm a little sensitive when it comes to Beau. I know that he's 'the one' for me. I've felt that since the first time we met. Trust me—I kissed a lot of frogs before I found Beau, so I almost feel like he's the dessert, you know?"

I nodded in agreement so I wouldn't have to tell her that I knew exactly what she was saying.

"I want us to be friends," she said, "after all we went through to find Sunny. Not that mistakes weren't made, but I thought we made a good team."

"We did. We do," I added, not mentioning how Beau almost died because of the plans that Sam and I put into motion. "And that sort of brings me to the second thing I came here for. Sunny's phone number. I'm hoping you still have it."

She seemed surprised. "Of course I do. We talk. Regularly."

It was my turn to be surprised. "Oh. It was my understanding that she'd blocked Beau's number and was only speaking with Mimi."

"Yeah, well, I'm not Beau. And no, Beau doesn't know that we talk. I think it would hurt his feelings—you know how men are." She gave a small laugh. "It's hard, because I don't even know why she's okay talking with Mimi but won't talk to Beau. It's not like he had anything to do with her kidnapping. I think it's because she truly loves the family who raised her and she thinks it's disrespectful to want to know her biological family. And yes, Mimi is her biological grandmother, but Sunny and Beau share the same parents."

I looked at Sam with disbelief. "Have you tried pointing out to her that the family who raised her *is* the family who kidnapped her, regardless of their intentions and how much they actually knew?"

"I'm not an idiot, Nola. Of course I have. But you of all people should understand her point of view. For the last thirteen years of your life, you've been welcome in a new family who didn't know you existed. I'm sure there have been times when you've felt angry with your mom for not telling you that you had a father and that he hadn't abandoned you, because he didn't even know you were born."

At my blank look she said, "I'm sorry. Beau and I talk about anything and everything. Even you."

I wasn't sure if I should be pleased or alarmed to know that Beau talked about me. Or that he even thought about me when we weren't in the same physical space.

Sam continued. "I've been trying to get Sunny back to New Orleans—just for a visit—but I haven't had any success."

"Well, then. This kind of makes it easier. If I'd known that you were still communicating with her, I would have approached you before now."

"Wow. Now I'm intrigued."

I hesitated, remembering the repercussions from the last time we collaborated behind Beau's back. But this was different, I assured myself. This wasn't a plot to extort information or to feign affection with an ex. This was about the reunion of a brother and sister and the hope that they could work together to find out what happened to their parents. Surely nothing bad could happen with such honorable intentions.

"I think we need to force a meeting between Beau and Sunny."

I waited for Sam to shake her head or hold up her hand or do anything else to make me stop, but she only nodded. "I agree. They're siblings, and it's not their fault that they're estranged."

"To be fair," I went on, "this was Jolene's idea, and after seeing Madame Zoe today—"

"Wait—you went with Beau to see Madame Zoe?"

"Yes. He didn't tell you?"

"He said he was going to see the fortune teller, but he didn't mention that he was going with you."

My face flushed as if I were lying, even though I wasn't. "I guess that was because Madame Zoe approached me first and told me to bring Beau to see her. He didn't take it seriously anyway. Maybe he didn't want to waste your time."

Her light brown eyes considered me, taking in my reddened face and noticing the way I stammered my explanation. I imagined my constant feelings of guilt stemmed from my mother making me lie to the police and her various dealers once I was old enough to talk. Even when I was telling the truth, saying that I had no idea where she was, I still felt like a liar.

"What did the fortune teller say?"

"That Beau should ask his mom where to find Buddy."

"Sounds pretty simple to me," Sam said. "But Beau doesn't see it that way."

"I think she's right. Adele is still here for some reason, and my best guess is that it's because she wants to reunite Buddy with his family. And if Madame Zoe is right, Beau needs to find his father before others who mean Buddy harm do. I have no idea if we should take that with a grain of salt, but that's what she said. Regardless, I think Beau's reluctance to ask for help from his mother has more to do with his anger at both of his parents for deserting him than with anything else. It doesn't take a therapist to see that Beau needs closure. Even if that means confronting his father—assuming he's still alive—and finding out why he's never come back home."

"Fear of rejection, then?" Sam asked.

"I hadn't thought of that, but yeah. That makes sense."

"Either way, in typical Beau fashion, he's being stubborn and just needs a little push in the right direction. From the right people."

We smiled at each other, and I thought once again how Sam and I could be very good friends. Except for that one thing that started with the letter B and ended in the letter U.

"Exactly," I said. "And I can't help but think that Sunny might have a trump card up her sleeve to move this all along."

Sam grinned. "I was thinking the same thing. She was too young when she was taken, so nobody has any idea if she's inherited any psychic abilities. It's not out of the realm of possibility." She pressed her lips together, her eyes narrowing. "We need to come up with a plan," she said. "Do you have a few minutes to plot out our next moves? We have to hurry, since I don't know when Beau will be back—but he'll text first."

"Sure," I said, feeling annoying tendrils of doubt accompanied by a fleeting memory of Melanie and Jack telling me about the importance of learning from my mistakes.

"Great. Come on," she said, heading into the living room area, which was furnished with tasteful finds from Pottery Barn and Restoration Hardware. She worked in PR and communications for the Ritz-Carlton downtown and apparently made more money than I did with my graduate degree in historic preservation.

I sat down on a brown leather sectional with throw pillows that probably cost more than the couch in my apartment. Technically they did, since that couch had been inherited when I signed the lease.

Sam pulled a notepad and pen from the drawer of a floor-to-ceiling bookcase and sat down next to me. I again noticed her gnawed fingernails—her only imperfection. It made her easier to like. She put the number one inside a circle at the top of the page, and next to it she wrote *Call Sunny.*

"I can do that," she said. "She already knows me, so it won't seem weird. We'll have to make up some story—like, Mimi is really sick and wants to see her one last time?"

"Well, that escalated quickly. That seems a little . . . drastic. Plus, all she has to do is call Mimi and we're busted. Maybe something more subtle, like her mom's best friend has moved back to New Orleans and wants to meet her?"

"That's pretty lame. All she'd have to do is talk to her on the phone."

I stared down at the almost-blank page as Sam tapped the pen against her leg. In my head I turned over and discarded scenario after scenario, looking up only when I realized that Sam had stopped tapping and was watching me. Our eyes met, and I felt a tremor of unease. "What?"

"Have you spoken with Michael lately?"

I stood. "Nope, nope, nope. I see where you're going with this, but no. Not going to happen."

She stood, too. "I'm not asking you to rekindle your romance. I'm just asking you to use your history with him to solicit his help. Sunny said they're sharing an apartment in New York, since they're still basically siblings. She still goes by Felicity Hebert. He owes you, right? And he owes the Ryans. It should be an easy yes for him. He's probably been trying to come up with a way to make it right. And here's his chance."

I thought about the Michael Hebert I'd fallen in love with, before either of us had known about his family's involvement in Sunny's kidnapping, or that the girl he'd called his sister and who had been renamed Felicity wasn't related to him at all. And before I'd known that he was pursuing a relationship with me only because his uncle had told him to.

I sat down, cushioned in the buttery-soft leather of the couch. "Please don't make me do this. Anything but that."

Plopping down next to me, she said, "Sure. Just give me a better idea."

We both stared at the notepad for a long time before Sam lined out the words she'd just written and wrote next to them *CALL MICHAEL*. After placing the pen and notepad on an antique captain's chest being used as a coffee table, she turned to me. Gently, she said, "I don't think Beau's the only person who needs closure."

When I didn't argue, she stood. "It's getting late. Beau should be home any minute. He probably forgot to text me. I'll call you tomorrow to talk about the rest of the plan." With a conciliatory smile, she said, "I've got a batch of homemade pralines in the kitchen. Why don't I wrap some up for you to take with you?"

"Is that like the nurse handing me a lollipop before giving me a shot?"

"Pretty much."

I waited while she placed the pralines on a paper plate and tucked them in with foil. Handing the plate to me, she said, "Hey, did I miss anything at dinner last night? I'll probably run into Camille and

Henry at some point, since they're living here now, and I want to be prepared. I've asked Beau, and he's described them with adjectives like 'nice' and 'normal.'" She rolled her eyes.

"Men," we said simultaneously, and then laughed like conspirators—which, I guessed, we were.

"My first take is that Camille is cowed by her husband in just about every way, including physically. I hope, with her spending more time around Mimi, she can blossom a bit. Henry's a bit of a blowhard. I'm not really sure what Camille sees in him except that he's really good-looking. Jolene said she wouldn't kick him out of bed for eating crackers, if that says anything. Although she's pretty sure he only has one oar in the water."

"Good to know. I've learned to trust Jolene's opinions."

"Me, too."

We said our good-byes, and I ordered my Uber on the elevator ride down. After settling myself on a faux iron bench by the front door to wait for my ride, I sent a quick text to Sarah.

I have the newspaper is there a pic with article?

Her response came quickly. Yes on top right of page

Do you know which page?

Her response was an eye roll emoji.

Assuming that meant no, I began on the first page, under the *Times-Picayune*'s banner, which now included THE NEW ORLEANS ADVOCATE printed beneath it in smaller type. After a quick perusal of a headline about the as-yet-undefeated Saints and their chances of making it to another Super Bowl, I started flipping through the paper, focusing on articles containing pictures in the top-right-hand corners of the pages on which they appeared. I was distracted by an article about the crime rate in the Quarter and the ongoing redevelopment in the Central Business District, including Tulane University's expansion from its Uptown campus and its massive investment in the downtown biomedical corridor.

I glanced down at my phone to check my Uber's progress—apparently it was stalled in traffic on Tchoupitoulas—then settled back in my seat and returned to the newspaper. I wouldn't freely admit it to my contemporaries, but there was something relaxing and engaging about reading print on actual paper.

A stiff breeze blew through the courtyard, whipping the paper from my hand and making me scramble to collect the pages—a distinct disadvantage of a physical newspaper, I thought as I snagged a double page off a fake evergreen topiary. I shoved it under my arm before dropping to my knees to grab another page, which had scooted under the bench and was trapped by one of the legs.

Clutching the newspaper, now wadded and crumpled, I sat back down. I was wondering whether it was worth trying to reconstruct the newspaper or if I should just read it as it was when my gaze fixed on the top right of one errant page. SUSPECTED KATRINA VICTIM FOUND, the headline shouted. And beneath, in smaller type: CHARITY HOSPITAL RENOVATION UNCOVERS LONE SKELETON.

Pinpricks tickled the back of my neck as I scanned the article about the ongoing redevelopment of the beloved hospital, which had been in existence since 1736 and located at the current site since 1834, and was fondly known as "Big Charity" until it was closed following Katrina, in 2005. I swallowed, my mouth suddenly dry. For reasons I couldn't yet explain, goose bumps spread down my spine and all four limbs as I speed-read the article, quickly summarizing the main takeaways—something I'd learned to do in graduate school.

In the ongoing final phase of Tulane's plan to take over most of the enormous hospital and turn it into a multiuse complex, unforeseen delays, including the recent heavy rains, had extended the building's renovation. Work resumed last week, including the removal of debris from the flooded green space in front of the hospital, which was where the remains were found by a construction worker. What appeared to be a human skull had been exposed by the rising water table, which halted work until the police were notified.

Early reports confirmed that the remains were not recent and might date back two decades, to the aftermath of Hurricane Katrina. Workers initially believed that the skeleton was fake and had been put there as a joke, until they dug further and spotted a wedding ring and an engagement ring still on a finger on the left hand. Authorities were sharing a photo of the rings in the hopes of finding relatives before further analysis could be made for positive identification.

It wasn't until a picture was referenced that I remembered that a picture was what I was supposed to be looking for. My gaze shifted to the top-right-hand corner of the page, to two photos. One showed the art deco hospital that took up an entire city block on Tulane Avenue, and the other was a black-and-white photo depicting two rings: a wide wedding band and an accompanying ring with a hollow cavity that had once held a large stone in an antique flush setting. From what I could see in the second photo, the rings were made from either white gold or platinum. The photo of the wedding band had been enlarged to show an eternal floral pattern marching around the circumference of the ring, the edges showing fine milgrain work. I squinted, trying to make out the repeating motif in both the wedding ring and the engagement ring. I held my breath, not trusting my eyes. As I recalled ridiculing Melanie for doing exactly what I was about to do, I opened the camera on my phone, then took a picture and expanded the photo on the screen.

I remembered what Beau had said about wanting to give his fiancée the family-heirloom ring that had been worn by his mother. He hadn't described it, but my heart and my head agreed that if he had, he would have described this engagement ring. Because there, entwined with roses and vines and surrounded by filigree ornamentation, were the etchings of an hourglass.

I tried to tell myself that an hourglass wasn't an unusual symbol for eternity, that it could have different meanings for different couples. Until I read the caption beneath the photograph.

"Inscription inside the wedding band reads *The past is never past; our love is eternal as time.*"

I read it out loud twice, and I felt more and more lightheaded as I looked at the picture, unable to block out mental images of the finger from which the rings had been removed; the violence of whatever force had removed the gem from the engagement ring; and of the eternal love that had come to a shattering end.

No, no, no, no, no, no, no, no. The litany continued in my head as I stared at the photograph of the two rings. Finally the Ryans would have closure. They would be able to place Adele's remains in the family vault, content with the knowledge that she was home at last. But the questions would remain. Of how she'd ended up on the grounds of Charity Hospital. And why.

I recalled the stack of newspapers that would accumulate on the side table in the back sunroom of Mimi's house until she had time to read them all from cover to cover, so there was a good chance she hadn't read this issue yet. Or maybe she had, and the rings weren't Adele's, so the photos hadn't meant anything to her. Either way, I needed to make sure she'd seen it.

At the sound of crunching gravel I looked up to see a car matching the make and model of my Uber ride. Gathering all the newspaper pages in a tight hold to make sure none flew away again, I opened the door and slid inside.

"Nola?" A middle-aged woman with purple hair and wearing a clump of Mardi Gras beads around her neck turned to face me with a smile.

"Yes—and I need to change my destination."

Her smile faltered.

"Don't worry—it's still uptown." I pictured my current five-star Uber passenger rating being downgraded to a four, and I tried again.

"I'm so sorry. It's . . . it's urgent." I gave her the address and waited as she punched it into her GPS.

My phone binged with a text message, giving me a brief respite from my unease. My chest tightened again when I saw that it was from Cooper. I've decided to buy Esplanade house.

Now it was my stomach that tightened. Before he made any irrevocable decisions, I needed to show him the picture of the two ghosts and the evil entity that would be his roommates if he decided to proceed with the purchase of the home.

I responded quickly. Let's go see it again together and talk. When will you get back?

I'm taking earlier flight. I miss you. Call you when I land.

A pleasant warmth replaced my earlier apprehension. Miss you, too. Before hitting Send, I paused, then added a kissing-face emoji.

I sat back and stared out the window, the glow from Cooper's text fading as we drew closer to the house on Prytania, then disappearing as the driver pulled up to the gate, an hourglass displayed prominently in the middle. I thanked the driver and got out, then waited at the gate as the car pulled away. I looked up at the beautiful house, trying to absorb the fortitude that had kept it intact through both external and internal storms for over a century. I think that was why I loved old houses, because of all the lessons in survival they offered if we were astute enough to listen.

Then I pushed through the gate and headed up the walkway.

CHAPTER 14

I expected to see Mimi or Christopher when the door opened, but instead I found myself looking into Trevor's annoyed face. "Yes? What do you want?"

I stared at him, wondering if he didn't recognize me, or if the polite boy I'd once known as Trevor had become a zombie.

"Trevor! Don't . . ." Christopher stopped behind Trevor as he recognized me. "Thank goodness it's you. Although this young man still needs to apologize. I know I've taught him better than that." He folded his arms across his chest and waited for Trevor to speak.

"Sorry," Trevor mumbled.

"Excuse me?" Christopher prompted.

"Sorry, sir!" he said, more loudly now, then abandoned his post and stomped across the foyer in the direction of the kitchen.

I stepped inside and Christopher closed the door behind me. "Is everything all right? I don't think I've ever seen Trevor in a bad mood before."

Christopher leaned forward to peer into the parlor, then pulled me aside to speak quietly. "Henry and Camille have moved in while they search for an apartment, and Henry's managed to crawl onto everyone's last nerve—even Trevor's. Mimi invited Trevor over for supper, so I drove him after his shift at the store. Henry was getting in the way in the kitchen, so I suggested we play cards with Trevor, to keep them both occupied until it was time to eat." He shook his head. "It's pretty bad when I'm playing cards and someone cheats, and Henry was blatantly cheating—against a twelve-year-old boy! Playing Go Fish! I mean, who does that?"

I looked past Christopher and into the parlor, where a small television set had been placed next to a PlayStation on a Georgian bookshelf with cords snaking out from behind it to where Henry sat, cross-legged, on top of the antique coffee table. His hands furiously moved the buttons on a white plastic game controller while he shouted at the TV screen. I didn't know how old Henry was, but he was definitely too old for that kind of behavior.

"Did you suggest that they play video games together?"

Christopher frowned. "I did. But Henry wouldn't let Trevor have a turn."

I paused for a moment to let that sink in. "Well, then, I don't blame Trevor for being ticked off. I would be, too. Where's Camille?"

"In the kitchen, helping Mimi. Are you here for supper? Mimi didn't mention that you'd be coming."

I pressed the sloppily refolded newspaper against my chest. "She isn't expecting me. I just need to talk with her, but I don't want to interrupt. It's, um, kind of important, but it should wait until after she eats." I studied Christopher for a moment. "Actually, I have an idea. Maybe if I show you first, you can tell me if it's important or not. Do you have a minute?"

He lifted his eyebrows. "Sure." He peered into the parlor, where Henry was oblivious to the world outside the primary-colored one on the screen, in which cartoonish characters shot at each other with random objects. "Follow me."

I passed the parlor without Henry even looking up, then walked down the back hallway to where Mimi's late husband's library remained in preserved pristine condition. I stood in front of the dark mahogany Edwardian-period partners desk. Scratches and faded patches on its leather top were a testament to the work that had happened on the desk in the century since it had been crafted. Like true antique dealers, the Ryans and my own family believed that antiques, if not too fragile, were meant to be used and enjoyed—with respect. Antiques weren't antiques simply because they were old but because they'd played a part in the lives of the people who'd once owned them. Only true aficionados knew the difference. Or those, like Melanie and Beau, who hated antiques for the same reason.

Christopher moved aside a brass lamp and a marble bust of Winston Churchill to give me space on the desktop. I folded the newspaper on the crease so that the page in question faced up, and then I pointed to the picture. "Do you think Mimi knows about this yet?"

He slid a pair of readers from his jacket pocket and placed them on his nose before leaning over the desk, bracing himself with his hands on the edge while he read. And then, just as mine had been, his attention was brought up to the top-right corner and the picture of the two rings, and his elbows gave way.

He managed to catch himself and sit down heavily in a nearby chair, taking the page with him.

"Are they Adele's?"

Christopher nodded. "I'd recognize them anywhere. They're one of a kind. Mimi's father-in-law had them made for his bride, and then, after Mimi was married, she wore the rings until Buddy proposed to Adele. They didn't fit Mimi anymore, so she'd stopped wearing them, and instead of resizing them, she thought it would be best if Adele wore them. They fit her perfectly." His voice cracked on the last word.

"Is there a photograph of the rings?" I asked. "Or some insurance documentation for proof? The authorities will want all of that."

Christopher nodded as he stood, placing the newspaper page back on the desk. "There's this, although it doesn't show a close-up of either ring." He'd moved behind the desk, to a matching credenza where a double five-by-seven-inch hinged frame had been placed next to a bronzed baby shoe. Both photographs in the frames showed a bride and groom in full wedding regalia, one in sepia and the other a color picture from the late 1980s. Christopher reached across the desk to hand the frame to me while he knelt in front of the desk, slid open its middle drawer, and stuck his hand inside. After a pause, I heard a click and then watched as Christopher pulled open a file drawer inside a leg of the desk. He began riffling through files while I examined the photographs.

I was startled by how much Beau resembled his great-grandfather, and not just in stature. He definitely had the same jaw and defined cheekbones. The smile the man in the photo wore was the same smile I'd seen on Beau's face dozens of times. I took a breath, then moved to the photo of Adele and Buddy. My heart burned—actually *burned*, as if it were on fire. It wasn't so much the image of the groom that absorbed my focus, although the familial resemblance between Buddy and Beau was unmistakable, too. It was of the glowing bride. Adele. The woman whose ghost I'd been chasing.

She was beautiful, of course, as only brides on their wedding day can be. But looking into the young, open face of the woman beneath the lace veil revealed something almost ethereal about her. If it were possible to accept that there was such a thing as a love that never dies, her face alone would make you a believer.

"Here." Christopher handed me a large brass-and-wood-handled magnifying glass.

I sent him a grateful look before using the magnifying glass to examine the left hand on each of the brides. They were both wearing rings, but it was apparent that even with a lot of magnification the rings wouldn't be identifiable. One was almost completely hidden by the flowers in the bride's bouquet, and the other by the bride's veil.

"We do have this." Christopher placed a multipage tri-folded document with a Lloyd's of London logo stamp on the desk in front of me. "We have the original in a safe off-site because of fire concerns, but this policy describes the rings and includes photos, so there shouldn't be any confusion."

"Lloyd's of London? Are they really that valuable?"

"Well, the bands are platinum, so they're worth a bit. But it was the diamond that made the engagement ring exceptionally valuable."

"The stone that's missing," I said.

He nodded. "It once belonged to an Indian maharaja before being purchased by the future Edward VIII when he was still quite young—prior to his association with Wallis Simpson, and long before his famous bow to the other king here in New Orleans in 1950, the king of Mardi Gras. The provenance is documented, which adds to the value, but basically, while still Prince of Wales, Edward lost the diamond in a poker game in Paris, to a businessman from New Orleans who subsequently lost it, in a horse race, to Beau's great-grandfather. His fiancée told him she'd only accept it on the grounds that he never bet again. As far as I know, he didn't. From every source, theirs was a great love story."

"'Our love is eternal as time,'" I quoted from memory. "And now the diamond is missing."

"It would seem so. And I doubt water, regardless of how strong the current, could have removed it from its setting."

"Presumably postmortem, right?"

He didn't respond right away. "Presumably."

I swallowed, letting that sink in. "Someone will need to call the coroner, or whoever is in charge, and let them know that we believe the remains are Adele's. Mimi will want to be there. Whether or not the police will admit into evidence her reaction upon touching the rings, she'll want to hold them. To be sure."

"Of course. But someone needs to tell her. And Beau. They should be together."

"Tell me what?" Mimi's voice came from the doorway, where she stood in her sensible shoes and a silk dress over which she wore a purple apron with the words ROUX GURU printed on it. Her smile faded when she spotted the newspaper. "What's this all about?"

"Mimi, should I go ahead and boil the . . ." Camille came up behind Mimi, then stopped, her gaze moving from face to face. "Is everything all right?"

Mimi had picked up the newspaper, her eyes drawn to the photographs of the building and the rings. Her hands shook and a mewling sound, like that of a wounded kitten, came from deep in her chest; it was a sound I'd never heard before and didn't want to hear ever again. Her knees wobbled, but Christopher held her steady while I set a chair behind her. She sat down and, the paper held tightly against her chest, began to rock back and forth, keening softly. I wanted to tell her that she could scream. That for this it was more than okay to scream until there was nothing left.

"I'll get her some water," I said, turning to go.

Camille held me back, her expression one of alarm. "What's happened?"

"I think they've found Adele. The remains are skeletonized, but they're wearing Adele's wedding rings."

She jerked back as if I'd slapped her. "But it might not be her, right? I mean, they'll need to check the dental records to be sure, won't they?"

Camille's face had gone red, and tears began to pool in her eyes and spill down her cheeks. I touched her arm for reassurance. "Of course. There's still a chance it's not her."

She nodded, using the sleeve of her shirt to wipe her eyes. "I think I've begun to accept that she's no longer alive. But to have proof . . ." She shook her head, then moved to kneel next to Mimi and put her arms around her.

Feeling redundant, I turned to Christopher. "I'll call Beau and tell him to get here as soon as he can." Then I headed toward the kitchen to get a glass of water, pausing in the hallway to pull out my phone.

I hit Beau's number and let it ring eight times before dialing again, telling myself that he and Sam were busy eating grillades and grits and not doing anything else that would prevent him from picking up his phone.

Giving up after the second try, I sent him a text, using all caps like Melanie, but I was doing it on purpose.

URGENT. MIMI NEEDS YOU.

I stared at my screen for a full minute, waiting to see the dots in a bubble indicating that Beau was texting me back. When the screen remained blank, I shoved my phone back in my pocket, then pushed open the kitchen door.

A large covered pot on the stove frothed under its lid and bubbled over. I reduced the flame, then reached toward the cabinet where I knew the glasses were kept. A muffled sob from behind me spun me around. Trevor stood by the refrigerator, his arms hugging his middle as he struggled to hold back tears.

I went to him and put my hands on his shoulders. "Trevor? What's wrong?"

"Beau's mama. She's dead, ain't she?"

I dropped to my knees. My heart hurt at this street-smart kid crying over someone else's pain. I nodded. "I think we've known it for a while, but now we might have proof."

He looked away to wipe at his face with the heels of his hands, then turned back to me. "My granddaddy and uncle ain't never been found, neither. Or they be buried but nobody knows who they are. They be gone, but Meemaw likes to pretend they comin' home soon."

His body was stiff as I put my arms around him. I held on until I felt the shift in his spine, and his arms came around me as his head lowered onto my shoulders and he began to sob out loud. The waves of hurt and destruction from Hurricane Katrina continued to be as real and solid throughout the city as if it had happened yesterday, affecting even those who hadn't yet been born when the storm decimated the city.

Despite all the strides in the redevelopment and rebuilding of New Orleans that had transpired over the last two decades, shadows of loss haunted the streets and people. Katrina was a wound that refused to heal long after the levees were rebuilt and the last victim was claimed.

I waited until Trevor's sobs subsided and he pulled back before I stood, being careful to ignore his reddened eyes and the wet spot on my shoulder.

"You gonna call Sunny now? Beau and Miss Mimi gonna need her back."

Yet again, I was amazed at the astuteness of this twelve-year-old. I wasn't sure that even my brother, JJ, who was the same age, would have thought the same thing. "Yeah, that's my next phone call." I moved to the sink, where I soaked a paper towel in cool water, then filled a glass from the bottled-water dispenser. No one drank New Orleans tap water, even in times of distress.

"Here," I said, handing them both to Trevor. "Wipe your face, and then go give this glass to Miss Mimi, all right?"

He nodded. "Do I have to talk to Henry?"

"No. Are you mad because he wouldn't let you play video games?"

"And because he lies."

I raised my eyebrows. "Yeah? Like, about what?"

He shrugged. "Stuff at the shop. Like, I'll put something in the stockroom, and when Christopher can't find it Henry blames me because he's moved it."

"I'm sorry. Would you like me to talk to Christopher about it?"

He thought for a moment and looked up at the corner of the room before shaking his head. "No. Christopher says that I need to learn how to fight my own battles. So I'll do it. Just gotta make sure Henry isn't listening." He leaned forward to whisper in my ear. "He likes to spy on people."

"That's not good. Let me know if you need an adult to step in."

After a brief hesitation, he nodded, then left the kitchen, headed for the study.

I pulled out my phone again and opened the contacts app. I had yet to permanently delete Michael Hebert's contact info, although I'd blocked his number more than once. We had had the opportunity to talk amicably at his parents' beach house in Mississippi the previous month, but that had been before I'd discovered the truth about his family's involvement in Sunny's kidnapping. We hadn't spoken since he and Felicity/Sunny had escaped to New York City, where Felicity had been living before she'd discovered her true identity.

My thumb remained poised over his number while I gathered courage; then I quickly tapped on it before I could talk myself out of it. He answered in the middle of the second ring.

"Nola."

"Hello, Michael." I waited for him to say something. When he didn't, I said, "I need to speak with Sunny."

"She still goes by Felicity. And why do you need to speak with her?"

I decided that being direct would be the most efficient way to get what I needed. "Because we're pretty sure her mother's body has been found. I don't know any of the details yet, but I know there will be a funeral after the coroner releases the remains. Beau and Mimi need her here."

There was a pause, and then: "Hold on. Let me get her."

I heard muffled voices in the background, and then a female voice came on the phone. "This is Felicity Hebert," she said, her voice almost confrontational. Not that I blamed her. She'd been lied to her entire life and probably wasn't sure whom she should be angry with. She might even blame me for my role in her adoptive father's incarceration and the family's turmoil and stress over his upcoming trial for kidnapping and related charges.

"Hello, Felicity. This is Nola Trenholm. We didn't get a chance to speak when you were here—"

"I know who you are. Please tell Mimi that I will be there as soon as I can. Can I send you my flight details? I don't want to burden Mimi right now."

"Of course. I'll even pick you up at the airport." I didn't consider how I didn't have a car until the words were already said. Maybe Jolene could drive. Or Cooper. I'd think about it later.

"Thank you. I'll have Michael give me your number so it's on my phone."

"Okay. And please give me yours—" I stopped because she'd already disconnected the call.

I texted Christopher to let him know that Felicity would be coming and I'd keep him posted, and then I headed to the front door to call an Uber. After ordering my ride, I followed the sounds of the video game and the regular outbursts from Henry, who was still sitting on top of the coffee table. I was debating whether I should let him know about the drama unfolding in the library when I caught sight of a reflection on the floor next to the Aubusson rug in the parlor.

It was a small puddle of water in the perfect shape of a woman's footprint and it faced into the room. I looked down to see a trail of fading footprints leading from the hallway where I'd just been and stopping in the threshold of the room where Henry was oblivious to everything except his game. Even to the scrutiny of a curious ghost.

Adele was still here. I could feel her right here in the foyer, where the temperature had suddenly plummeted. I watched as Henry shivered, his only motion beside his frenetic movements on the game controller.

If only I could speak with Adele, I'd get the answers now. But I wasn't the one with the gift. I could ask, but I wouldn't be able to hear her answers. But Beau could. When Beau had asked Madame Zoe if she could ask his mother where Buddy was, the fortune teller had told him no, but that Beau could. I didn't know if he had, but I doubted it. I tiptoed across the foyer, remembering something else that Madame Zoe had said. Something about how Beau needed to find his father before others, who intended Buddy harm, did. I clenched my eyes, feeling exhaustion in every limb. I was way too tired to consider the implications of what Zoe might have meant. I'd think about that later.

I quietly let myself out of the house, then headed toward the gate to wait for my ride. I held on to the iron hourglass as I shut the gate softly behind me.

CHAPTER 15

My hair was still half up in pink foam rollers when my doorbell rang the following morning. I let out a short expletive, knowing it would irritate Jolene, since it was her fault I wasn't already outside, waiting on the doorstep.

"If I thought I could wrassle you to the floor, I'd be washing your mouth out with soap right now." She unclipped one of the curlers and slid it from my hair, yanking it from my head.

"Ouch," I said as she moved on to the three remaining ones. She removed them all at the same time, along with most of my scalp.

"Sorry," she said, her smile in the mirror telling me she wasn't. "I'll go get the door. Do not leave this room before I get back and can finish."

I stared in horror at my reflection. My face looked small and pale beneath the massive cloud of dark curls. "I look like that clown from *It*," I called after her.

"Oh, ye of little faith," she said, her voice almost drowned out by Mardi excitedly barking to let us know that someone had rung the doorbell, in case we'd missed it. "You'd need red hair for that." Her footsteps and Mardi's yelps faded as the two of them descended the stairs toward the front door.

Before I had time to wonder how I was supposed to interpret that, my phone buzzed with a text from Sarah.

You up?

I responded with an eye-roll emoji.

Tell Jolene Mom took me shopping have
two new dresses and shoes with small heels

I smiled at the phone, picturing Melanie trying to guess what would be appropriate for a tween girl to wear for Thanksgiving with Jolene's family in Mississippi. I felt a small pang and found myself wishing I could have been with them.

I'm packing Grandma Sarah's brooch

I recalled the navy, green, and gold jeweled, peacock-shaped brooch that had belonged to Melanie's grandmother and Sarah's namesake. It was a beautiful piece of jewelry that deserved to be worn. But I also remembered that she'd worn it for the same reason Beau always kept a rubber band around his wrist.

I'm also bringing ten rubber bands
just in case

I stared at my phone, a sense of unease erupting in my gut. Is there something I should know?

She waited a moment before responding. Don't know yet just want to be prepared

Prepared for what?

Gotta go mom's calling

I looked up as Jolene walked into the room, closing the door behind her. "Wow," she said. "You weren't kidding. Don't worry. Give me five minutes and you'll be beauty pageant–worthy."

I grabbed her wrist as she reached for the hair straightener. "Please, no. How about just 'I'm going to see a house before heading to the airport' hair?" I pointed to my head. "I need at least three-quarters of this to go away, and you have three minutes to make it happen."

Her look of disappointment quickly changed to one of determination. "Challenge accepted. Although I do think a bit of fullness here on top—"

"No."

Something in the tone of my voice made her pause. With a resigned sigh, she began wielding the flat iron and a comb with rapid, precise movements like a seasoned surgeon's. She stood between me and the mirror so I couldn't watch, but when she was finished she stepped back. With a deep cotillion bow (in which she was well versed), she said, "Voilà. My work here is done."

My hair had been coaxed into a vision of smooth glossiness, the ends bent upward in a chic flip. "You really are a miracle worker," I said, starting to stand.

"Not so fast." She lifted an industrial-sized can of Aqua Net and began coating my hair, face, and vanity in a cloud of hair spray. I closed my eyes, knowing I was at the mercy of a professional, having seen her nail a fleeing cockroach in its tracks from five feet away with a stream from that same nozzle. I wasn't sure if it was the stickiness or the overwhelming scent of the spray that had caused the insect's demise, but it was definitely dead long before I'd found the courage to gather it in a wad of toilet paper and flush it down to its just reward.

I staggered from the room coughing and hoping my tearing eyes wouldn't make my mascara run.

When I entered, Cooper stood, dislodging Mardi, who'd been happily snuggled in his lap—something Mardi didn't do with just anyone. Cooper wore a navy cable-knit pullover on top of a crisp white button-down with khakis and loafers, which was all so different from the jeans and boots Beau wore most of the time. Although I had no idea why I was comparing the two men.

Cooper had been such an important part of my early years in Charleston—when, for the first time in my life, I had a family and a home and felt loved and protected—that seeing him now, after only a few days apart, made my heart beat a little faster. Until that moment, I hadn't realized how the events of the past few days had worn on me, or how Sarah's text had thrown streamers of worry and apprehension over my morning. Now, all of a sudden, Cooper was there, looking like the answer to all the questions I wasn't even aware that I had.

He tilted his head, seeing in my eyes a need that even I didn't yet recognize, and he held out his arms. "Nola," he said. I allowed myself to be folded into his embrace, nestling into his warmth like a stray animal finding the comfort of home. "Is everything all right?"

I nodded, then shook my head against his jacket, not yet willing to pull back. "They think they've found Adele, Beau's mother." In as few words as possible, I told him about the discovery at Charity Hospital—for now leaving out Sarah's phone call with her dead grandmother and my visit to Madame Zoe. I'd fill him in later. It wasn't that he didn't already know about Sarah's abilities, or about any of the woo-woo stuff that usually happened around my family and me. His presence reminded me of the normal world, the one without wet footprints, and phone calls from the dead on disconnected landlines, and gold hoop earrings that dropped out of the air. And an angry spectral woman who lingered without detection until Beau saw her. But until I told Cooper about her, this was my safe place, there in his embrace, for however long I could make it last.

I continued. "They're analyzing the remains now, but Mimi will know if it's Adele before they do. She and Beau are supposed to go to the coroner's office to retrieve the wedding rings today. Mimi's already identified them in a photograph, but she'll know for sure when she holds them."

I felt Cooper nod before resting his chin on top of my head. I never remembered how tall he was until we were standing close, like now. He and Beau were approximately the same height, but Beau seemed taller in my mind—maybe because Beau and I were together a lot, so I was constantly reminded of how he towered over me. I just needed to spend more time with Cooper so I could adjust my frame of reference.

His voice rumbled in his chest beneath my cheek when he spoke. "Maybe Mimi will be able to see what happened to Adele. I doubt that will be easy."

"It won't be. That's why Beau's going with her. Not that it will be easy for him, either, but being together will help. There's nothing worse than hearing bad news by yourself, without anyone to lean on."

He held me tighter in unspoken understanding.

"I texted Felicity to see if she wanted to go, too," I said. "To support Mimi. I know Mimi and Beau would wait if she did. Felicity responded with a quick no. And then, an hour later, she texted that going to the funeral would be about all she could handle."

"Because seeing the Ryans will trigger her PTSD from the night of the fund-raiser?"

I shrugged. "Who knows? I don't think she was aware of the demon battle going on in the attic, but finding out that she isn't who she thought she was could still be a bit of a mental challenge." Reluctantly, I pulled away. "Speaking of which, we need to get going so we have time to look at the house again before heading to the airport." When I'd told him about my offer to pick Felicity up from the airport, and my plan to take an Uber, he had immediately offered to drive.

"Coffee, anyone?" Jolene emerged from the kitchen holding two monogrammed go-cups, bright pink and lime green. She said their embellishments ensured that they would be returned.

"Thank you," we said in unison as we each took a cup. Being Jolene, she knew that Cooper took his coffee black and I took mine with lots of cream and sugar.

Cooper dropped down onto his knee and held up a hand to Mardi. "High five," he said. Mardi tapped his paw against Cooper's palm. "Down low," Cooper commanded, lowering his hand so that it was palm up, and Mardi placed his paw in Cooper's outstretched hand.

"Good boy," Cooper said as he used his free hand to vigorously scratch behind Mardi's ears, taking them one at a time so as not to spill his coffee. He stood and shared a look of adoration with my dog. "Whoever owned him before spent a lot of time training him. I wonder what other tricks he knows."

I remembered what Sam had told me about the deleted comments on the YouTube channel. Turning to Jolene, I said, "Samantha told me that there had been a few comments on the channel about Mardi's previous owner but that they were taken down pretty quickly. Was that you?"

Her expertly shadowed lids covered her green eyes, then snapped open in a small blink. "Of course it was. I think it's just someone looking to cause trouble. You know how hard we tried to find his previous owners. And he wasn't chipped! That alone tells us that whoever had him before didn't deserve him. Besides, he's ours now and his name is Mardi Lee Trenholm. He has the monogrammed bed, bandannas, and sweaters to prove it."

In a show of solidarity she picked Mardi up, and he rewarded her by snuffling against her neck. "See? He belongs to us now."

"I couldn't agree more," I said, bending toward Mardi so he could lick my face. "But if they post any more comments, could you please let me know? I'd like to figure out who's behind them, just in case. I hate surprises, especially the kind that spring out from behind a door, you know?"

"I will. Promise. I was just trying to save you some aggravation from someone who's probably a troll and just looking to make someone else's life as miserable as theirs must be. I'll pray for them. But I will also open up a can of whoop-ass on them if they don't quit."

"Well, then," I said, heading toward the door, "let's hope that whoever it is takes a hint so we don't have to see what that is, because it sounds serious."

"Oh, it is. Believe me." Jolene followed us to the top of the stairs, then watched as we descended to the front door. "Just ask my cousin Clyde. He wouldn't stop beheading my Barbie dolls, so I put a mess of fire ants in the back pockets of his Wranglers. He couldn't sit down for a week, bless his heart. Let's just say he never did it again."

"Good to know." Cooper opened the door, and I looked up to say good-bye and saw Jolene waving Mardi's paw. I blew them both a kiss and stepped out into the cool autumn sunshine.

A brand-new sporty navy Audi sedan sat in the driveway. "Is that your rental?" I asked, stepping close to admire it. He opened the passenger door and the distinct scent of new leather wafted out at me from the cream-colored interior. Obviously the car of a single man without kids or animals. I bit the inside of my cheek to get myself to stop thinking like Melanie.

"Nope. It's mine. I ordered it online and had it waiting for me at the airport when I landed. Do you like it?"

"It's very sexy." I looked up at Cooper and stopped myself from adding *Like you.* That wasn't the kind of thing I would say to a member of the opposite sex, regardless of how much I might think it. I couldn't imagine that hanging between us on the ride over to the Esplanade house and then to the airport.

"Thank you. I don't know about 'sexy,' but I do know it drives like a performance car, which I enjoy."

"I hope it has all the latest safety features, since you're going to be driving it in New Orleans. And may I suggest throwing a couple of extra spare tires in the trunk?"

He laughed and then took my elbow to stop me as I moved to step inside. "You need to practice. And yes, it does have all the latest safety features, because I'd hoped that you would be a frequent passenger. Or driver. You really do need practice, Nola. Especially if you're getting that Mustang after Thanksgiving."

I looked at the car and then back at Cooper. "But it's brand-new. And I'm not the most confident driver."

"I know. But you will be. And I trust you."

I bit my lip. "Are you absolutely sure?"

"Absolutely," he said, guiding me toward the driver's side and pulling open the door.

I slid inside, feeling the soft leather beneath me and trying not to be intimidated by the flat digital instrument panel in front of me. "I feel like I'm in the cockpit of a plane. And I'm feeling really stupid because I don't see where to insert the key."

Cooper walked around to the passenger side and sat down beside me. "I've got the key fob in my pocket, so just put your foot on the brake and push the ignition button." He indicated a discreet button on the dash. The engine purred to life, the sound almost unnoticeable inside the car—unlike Bubba's engine, which made occupants feel as if they were riding under the hood.

"I could get used to this," I said.

"Good." Cooper looked at me and smiled, and I was surprised by the ensuing flash of heat that washed over me. We were just friends, I reminded myself. I must have been feeling lonelier than I'd thought. "Give me your phone and I'll get it hooked up with Bluetooth so you can use CarPlay for hands-free calls and messaging. You can even play your music without looking away from the road to change tracks."

Just as he was finishing, my phone rang through the car's impressive speakers, playing "Tubular Bells," the theme from the movie *The Exorcist* and the new ringtone that Sarah had programmed into my phone during her last visit so that I'd know it was her when she called. She said it was because we were near Halloween at the time, so the ringtone needed to be spooky. I had to ask her how to change it, because it was now almost Thanksgiving.

"I'll be quick," I said, hitting the green Answer button on the phone screen.

"Did you forget something?" I asked Sarah. It had barely been an hour since we'd finished texting. Maybe she was ready to tell me what I was supposed to be prepared for.

"Yeah. Grandma Ginny had a strange dream last night," she said, referring to Melanie's mother.

"Okay. Was it about me?"

"Not technically."

"All right. So what was it about?"

"She said I was riding in a really big old car, and I was behind the wheel like I was driving. I think she was talking about Bubba, because she mentioned that the windows had those manual thingies."

"You mean window cranks?"

"Yeah, that's it."

I sighed. "Go on. And please hurry."

"So, I was driving along when all of a sudden there was, like, a loud squealing and a big bang, and then everything went black and she woke up."

"Well, that kind of makes sense, doesn't it? Aren't you nearing your midterms?"

"Funny. Anyway, I've been trying to figure it out, and it occurred to me that her dream couldn't be about me, because I don't know how to drive."

"Like I said, maybe it was metaphorical and it actually was about you. Hey, can I call you back? Cooper and I are on a tight schedule."

"Ooh, Cooper." Sarah made obnoxious smooching noises into her phone. "He is smokin' hot."

"Just so you know, he's sitting next to me and you're on speaker."

Long pause. "Oh. Hi, Cooper."

"Hi, Sarah." He somehow managed to keep a straight face as he spoke.

To interrupt the awkward moment, I said, "I've really got to hurry, so if you could tell me what—"

"So, what I was trying to say, metaphorically or not, is that I don't think the dream was about me because I don't drive." She paused again. "But you do."

"True, but I wouldn't worry, because Jolene doesn't let me drive her car. She says it takes me too long to park it, because I drive around the block until I find two spots next to each other. So I'm thinking it was metaphorical and about you. And you should probably hang up and get studying." To soften my words, I said, "But I promise I'll be careful."

"Just in case you didn't know, if you've got an airbag and a deer jumps in front of you, it's better to plow head-on into the deer instead of swerving to avoid it, because the airbag will do less damage than rolling your car. I saw that in an injury-lawyer ad."

"I'll keep that in mind."

"Okay. One more thing. Jolene says she's going to have my colors done. Should I be scared?"

"No, Sarah. It's supposed to be fun. Or 'life-changing,' according to Jolene. We'll talk about it later. Now go study."

I pressed the button on the steering wheel to end the call and turned to Cooper. "Maybe I shouldn't drive."

"If you're really worried, then don't. But it seems to me as if your grandmother's dream wasn't about you at all, and that maybe you're looking for an easy out." Before I could argue, he held up his hand. "Which is totally fine with me. I'm here to help, and not to pressure you in any way. Just remember that if you ever want the independence of being a confident driver, you have to actually get behind the wheel and practice."

I stared at the interlocking rings of the logo in the middle of the steering wheel. "Yeah. You're right. One hundred percent." I turned my head and met his gaze before shifting the car into drive. "Let's do this."

CHAPTER 16

We made it to Esplanade Avenue without incident, although I did notice Cooper gripping his door handle as I attempted to parallel park in front of the house. He winced at the sound of scraping but didn't say anything as I felt the rear wheel hike itself up on the curb.

"That's good enough," he said. "Remind me to get you a set of curb feelers for your new car. And maybe for mine, too." He said it lightly, but his voice sounded a little shaky.

I wasn't surprised to find Thibaut's truck parked on the street, since I knew he and Beau had gone over the preliminary plans for the renovation and that Beau was eager to get started while we waited for the roof shingles for my house. Because the universe apparently hated me, the historically accurate shingles matching the ones we'd already installed on the rest of the roof were out of stock at the manufacturer, with a six-month wait. Thibaut was calling every supplier he could get ahold of throughout the country and having them sent piecemeal until he had enough to complete my roof.

Cooper exited the car while I took a few moments to figure out how to put it in park. After parking, I crossed the street, barely avoiding a collision with a bicyclist. I joined him on the neutral ground for a view of the house. "What do you think?" I asked. "Still like it?"

A crooked smile lit his face. "I know there's a ton of work to be done, but look at those bones! And that pediment and fan window! I think my favorite features, besides that hidden dormer, are the double-hung sash windows in the front that open all the way to the ceiling. Have you tested them yet to see if they work?"

"Not yet, but that will be part of my job."

He nodded. "Those old windows really are an engineering marvel, aren't they? With their system of pulleys, cords, and weights hidden inside the jambs to help open and close them. And great for creating a cross breeze on a hot day."

"If you don't mind the bugs. Beau and I will be installing central air, so you won't need windows for ventilation—just to show off at parties during cooler weather. Don't worry—it will be factored into the selling price, so you won't be hit with a surprise."

I felt his eyes on me, so I turned to face him.

"So, you and Beau work pretty closely together."

It wasn't a question, but I felt compelled to answer him anyway. "Yes. Beau's being very generous, allowing me to use him as the general contractor for my cottage so I can afford the renovations. Because of Jolene and her social media talents, we've received a lot of sponsors—and free stuff. Which is pretty great since I'm basically broke right now. I'm also now working freelance for JR Properties, for their new venture in flipping murder houses—which was Mimi's idea, by the way."

He raised his eyebrows. "Murder houses? Like, houses where there have been murders? I already know about the woman who was killed here."

"Yeah. Speaking of, there's a little more to that story you need to hear." I took his arm and, after checking the street for bike and car traffic, led him to the house. "Before you decide on anything, I've got something to show you." I'd brought the framed photo of the house in my backpack—with a promise to Beau that I'd find a way to get it back to Honey and Joan—for Cooper to see. If this house had picked him, he needed to go into it with eyes wide open.

As we climbed the front porch, Cooper sniffed the air. "Do you smell that perfume?"

I nodded. "Youth-Dew by Estée Lauder."

"Yeah, that's it. Both of my grandmothers wore it."

"I think everybody's grandmother wore it. But perfect timing, since that's part of what I need to tell you."

He opened the door and held it for me. "I find the scent comforting, which is a good thing."

I followed him inside, where the sound of sawing could be heard from upstairs. "Probably just Thibaut cutting into a wall to find out more about the plumbing and electrical systems," I said. "Hopefully he'll have good news, but be prepared: Restoring old houses always comes with equal measures of love and heartbreak. Regardless, anything we find will be part of the full disclosure in any contract we give you."

"No worries," he said as he followed me to the stairs. "I trust you and your judgment. Whatever it is, we'll make it work. And that pretty much sums up life in general, doesn't it? Equal measures of love and heartbreak."

I paused to face him, thinking he'd just handed me the perfect opener to ask him about the phantom woman. Beau's words about me being the poster child for avoiding unpleasant things still stung. "Speaking of full disclosure—"

The sound of small, quick footsteps clattering down the stairs stopped me. We turned in unison to see nothing at all, but I felt a waft of air followed by a chilly breeze as the footsteps ran past us and then faded away.

Our eyes met. "Did you . . ." I began.

"Hear steps and feel a cold breeze? Yeah. They took me by surprise but definitely weren't scary. I can live with that and the perfume, if that's what you were worried about."

"I wish." I slid off my backpack and pulled out the framed photograph. Handing it to Cooper, I said, "There's at least one more spirit you need to be aware of."

He took the frame and studied the photograph. "It looks like a recent photo of the house. I don't . . . Oh, wait. I see them now. The woman and the boy in the front window."

"Yeah, the sources of the perfume and the running steps. That's not who I'm worried about. Look closer."

He squinted, bringing the photograph right up to his face. I knew the moment he'd spotted the third spirit. His eyes widened and he gave a sudden involuntary jerk, dropping the frame. "I'm so sorry," he said, bending down to retrieve it. He turned it over, revealing a small scratch in the silver at the top of the frame. "I don't know what happened. It was almost like someone shoved me."

"We don't know who that is, but we're fairly certain that the little boy is a great-uncle of the previous owners and died in the influenza epidemic in the early part of the last century. The woman is most likely Sybil, who was murdered in the house. As to the identity of the creepy guy?" I shrugged. "I don't have a clue, and neither does Beau."

Cooper was still studying the picture. "That guy is really terrifying," he said, tapping the spot where I could sense the male specter glowering from the picture. "Does Beau have any idea why the, um, spirits are here? I'm not sure what to call them while having a normal conversation."

"I get it. Luckily, with Melanie as my stepmother, 'ghost' is just a part of my daily vocabulary. But to answer your question: I'm guessing that Sybil would like to move toward the light, but either she can't because the dark spirit is holding her here, or she's staying to protect the boy because he can't find the light yet. I've been wondering about that myself, and I think that, since Lynda was a child when she lived here, maybe the boy considered her his companion."

"They do say that children have more open minds and can see what we adults can't."

"True. And animals, too. I'm thinking that this little boy—Patrick—is looking for Lynda. Maybe he just wants to know that she's safe."

Cooper nodded. "It's hard to think about children as ghosts, but it's especially hard to think that they're earthbound because of unfinished business. That should be an adults-only thing."

"Agreed. And speaking of unfinished business—"

"Do you smell that?" Cooper's nose wrinkled as the stench of something rotting and putrid seemed to smother us in an invisible cloud.

I put my hands over my nose, desperately sniffing the soap smell lingering on my skin. "Yeah. It smells like . . ." I was about to say "death" but was interrupted by a deep voice above us.

"Are y'all coming up, or do I need to come down there?" Thibaut's towering frame loomed over the upstairs railing.

The foul odor disappeared as if an invisible vacuum had sucked it out of the air. "We're coming right up," I said, giving myself points for at least attempting to talk with Cooper about the woman and ignoring the sweep of relief the reprieve brought me. It wasn't the subject of the woman haunting him that I was anxious about. It was the fact that he hadn't mentioned her to me. Not that I was avoiding anything. I'd tried. I'd attempt to ask him again. Later.

I led the way upstairs, climbing to the top of the steps, to the camelback room. The stairs were narrow and steep and had to be climbed one foot at a time. The room had last been used as a bedroom, occupied most recently by the murdered woman, Sybil.

Cooper and I found Thibaut at a wall where a large rectangular hole had been made in the plaster. He wore clean coveralls and a white T-shirt that strained around his heavily muscled and tattooed biceps. His full tool belt lay on the floor with a handsaw, and his bald head was hidden inside the wall, where he was apparently inspecting the mechanicals.

He removed his head from the wall and turned to greet us. Despite his imposing size and bulging muscles, I knew he was a teddy bear at heart. He'd gone to jail for the manslaughter of his wife, and her family wouldn't allow him to contact his only child, a son named Gregory, whom he referred to as "Greggie."

"Hey, boss," he said to me. "I was hoping to see you today. Saves me a trip to ask Beau to relay a message."

"I hope it's good news." Thibaut was the only person I knew who didn't believe in owning a cell phone. Considering how many text interruptions I had in a day, I wouldn't say I disagreed with his philosophy.

Cooper approached with an outstretched hand. "Good to see you again, Mr. Kobylt." They'd met when my family had come down to visit for fall break, and I mentally gave Cooper ten extra bonus points for not only remembering Thibaut's last name but also for knowing that my contractor deserved the show of respect of adding "Mr." to his name.

"Likewise." Thibaut reached out for Cooper's hand, and I might have winced when I saw them shake.

Cooper grimaced as Thibaut squeezed his hand, but he was stoic and didn't pull away. "Nola keeps telling me that you're the best contractor in New Orleans. I figure you'd have to be for her to allow you within a mile of her house with a hammer or saw. Glad to have you on board, working on my house."

"It's not yours yet," Thibaut said as he continued squeezing Cooper's hand.

"No, sir. Not yet."

"Thibaut," I said, looking down at their hands; I could see the tips of Cooper's fingers turning a pale pink from lack of blood flow. "I don't . . ."

Ignoring me, Thibaut said, "I need you to understand something, young man, so listen up. You hurt Miss Nola, you answer to me. I've already been to prison, and I ain't afraid of going back. And I know about swamps 'round here where they ain't never going to find what's left of your body once I get through with you."

Thibaut dropped Cooper's hand and I silently applauded Cooper's stoicism, but I did see him flex his fingers to restore blood flow and movement. "Yes, sir. You'd have to wait in line behind Jack Trenholm, though. He gets first dibs on anyone who hurts his daughter. He throws around the words 'castration' and 'disembowelment' whenever he can, so I'm well aware of the consequences." His face became serious. "But I promise you that I have no intentions of ever hurting her again."

Thibaut's brow creased up to the crown of his bald head.

I moved to stand between them. "That was a long time ago—when I was in high school. We were both young and stupid. Water under the bridge. We're just good friends now."

"Hmm." Thibaut considered Cooper with narrowed eyes. "Nola tells me you're interested in buying this house. You have a degree in historic preservation or something similar?"

"No, sir. Not even close."

"Good. We got enough of them types swarming around Nola's house already." He gave me a wink that, coupled with his bald head and tattoos, made him look more than a little bit like a pirate.

"I'd rather rely on professionals," Cooper said, still flexing his fingers. "If I need brain surgery, I'll ask a brain surgeon instead of trying to do it myself. Same with restoring an old house. I'd prefer to trust an experienced contractor to do the job. I don't think rewiring an entire house should be left to anyone else."

Thibaut clapped Cooper on the back, making the younger man jerk forward, but he held his ground. "I think we'll get along just fine. And just call me Thibaut. No need for 'Mr.' Any friend of Nola's is a friend of mine."

"Good to know," Cooper said, looking relieved.

"So, what have you found?" I asked, resisting the impulse to cross my fingers behind my back.

"Knob and tube wiring, which we expected, and which is fixable. Also lead pipes in the plumbing, which will need to be replaced. But no mold and no asbestos—which already puts us way ahead of your house." He gave a little chuckle but quickly sobered when he noticed I wasn't laughing.

Cooper nodded. "So basically a straightforward renovation involving updates for current living and maybe a little reconfiguring of the floor plan." At my pointed look, he added, "With a sensitivity to the historical character of the house."

"Yes, sir. And hold your hands over your ears while I say this, Miss Nola, but there's an old house on Moss Street that's been condemned for multiple code violations, and they're getting ready to tear it down."

"Couldn't they save it?" Cooper asked.

"Nope. It's not located within a local historic district and it's not a local landmark, so they didn't need to get demolition approval from the Historic District Landmarks Commission. It's a darned shame. As soon as they announced the scheduled demolition, scavengers with crowbars began circling it for the transoms, millwork, cypress built-ins, and iron fireplace grates. I'd rather see those things reused in other buildings than in a dumpster—that's for sure. But it'll be like clowns at a wig sale, so I'm gonna head over there as soon as we're done here. I'll admit to having jimmied a door to get a better look inside, and there are some beautiful crystal doorknobs and porcelain sinks that you might want for this house or Nola's."

"Thanks," I said. "But I'm glad you didn't get arrested for trespassing."

"Like the New Orleans police don't have anything better to do than stopping a person from salvaging what's left of a condemned property. If you ask my opinion, I think they should be holding open the door and helping carry stuff out."

"I'm not going to argue with you. Just be careful. I have no idea what I'd do without you."

His smile softened his harsh features, allowing me to see his inner teddy bear. "Don't worry. I'm careful. I've got eyes in the back of my head. It's one of the many things I learned while in prison, along with carpentry and electrical systems."

"Good to know."

We said our good-byes, and then Cooper and I made our way downstairs, pausing in the bedroom, where the door to the armoire remained open. "Hang on," I said, going to close it.

The little mirrored door inside, where I'd found the creepy doll, was closed, the key protruding from the keyhole. I considered just closing the main door and walking away, but I was too much like my father to leave a potential clue to a mystery unexamined. I turned the key, then took a deep breath before tugging the door open.

I screamed as a hand touched my shoulder.

"Sorry—I didn't mean to startle you." Cooper's expression was apologetic, but it still took me a few moments to find my breath to speak.

"That's all right. It's just that I was half expecting to find that doll in here. It keeps . . . appearing where it's not supposed to be."

His brows rose. "Interesting" was all he said, which made me like him even more. He peered around me into the armoire. "Empty," he said. "Except for the perfume smell." He indicated the stoppered bottle on the bottom shelf. "Did you want to leave that in here?"

"Yes. Leaving it gives me one less inanimate object to worry about."

"Got it." He closed the small door and turned the key, then closed and latched the main door. "Do you have time to walk through the rest of the house with me?"

I checked my watch. "We have two hours before Sunny's plane lands, and it's only about thirty minutes to the airport, so we're good."

"And it's a small house," Cooper said as he gently placed his hand on my lower back to guide me out of the room.

After a quick tour, during which we paused in the kitchen to determine which of the vintage appliances still worked, we exited the house and stopped again on the neutral ground to view the house.

I turned to Cooper, trying not to notice the scar on his chin. "So, what do you think? Of course you'll want to have your own inspection before you sign anything, but I believe you're aware of most of the kinks."

"And the things that go bump in the night."

"Those, too." I bit my lip. "Remember, you don't have to do anything right away. Most people would want to wait until the reno is complete, because there's no real way of knowing right now what sort of unforeseen costs might still be hidden."

He nodded, his gaze focused on the house. "I'm well aware." He was silent a moment before turning to me. "Maybe you'll understand this better than most, but when I first saw this house, I had the strangest feeling that it had picked me, you know?"

A spark of mutual understanding arced between us as our eyes met. "I know exactly. Come termites or failing roofs, we're in it for the long haul. I think it's like finding the person who's the right fit, where you can imagine spending your entire lives together."

"Yeah," he said. "Exactly."

I leaned forward and kissed him gently on the mouth, then immediately pulled back, watching him. I had once loved Cooper with my whole young heart. My feelings had softened over the years, leaving me with a deep affection for him that could possibly turn into something more. Someday. I couldn't deny that there were sparks—remembered or new—regardless of whether I wanted there to be. I only hoped that Cooper wasn't a mental self-defense to distract me from my unreconciled feelings for Beau. Because that was a truly horrifying thought.

Cooper leaned down and cupped my head in his hands, bringing me closer for a deeper kiss. I had just closed my eyes when a car drove past and someone shouted from its open window, "Get a room!"

Embarrassed, I stepped back. "We should get going," I said, taking hold of Cooper's arm and heading toward the car.

He held the driver's door open for me. I shook my head. "No. Not on the interstate. I'm not ready."

"Yes, you are. You've got lots of experience driving around town. You know all the rules. It's just a matter of building up your confidence. Think of all the things you've accomplished, Nola. By the sheer force of your will. Like getting sober. Nobody did that but you. And I imagine that was a whole lot harder than driving is. And I'm here—right next to you."

"Yeah. And I saw you clutching the door handle, too."

"Sorry. I won't do that again. I think your nervousness fed my own and vice versa, so that you became even more nervous."

"But it's your new car—"

"With every safety feature available today. You're safer in my car than in just about any other car around."

"Except for Bubba."

He considered that for a moment before nodding. "Except for Bubba. But that's only because he's a nearly swimming pool–sized block of steel. Fortunately, there aren't a lot of cars like that still on the road today. Imagine the damage."

"I don't have to imagine. I've seen what Jolene can do to a mailbox."

I slid behind the steering wheel. Cooper closed the door and walked around to the passenger side while I buckled up and readjusted my seat and side mirrors a couple of times, then experimented with the lumbar support and heated-seat settings just to be sure they hadn't changed. I was more nervous about driving on the interstate than I wanted to admit. I waited until Cooper was buckled up before pressing the ignition button. I remembered to turn on my blinker to alert oncoming traffic that I was pulling out, then looked up to double-check the rearview mirror. For the second time that morning, I screamed.

The familiar blank stare of the antique doll met my gaze. Cooper reached behind and snatched it from the backseat, the movement making it say "Mama." He held it away from him. "I think that sound might be even more terrifying than finding it in my backseat. Behind locked doors."

"Are you sure they were locked?" I asked hopefully.

"Unfortunately, yes. I heard the beep after I hit the button on the key fob. If a door had been opened without the key, it would have set off the alarm and we would have heard it."

I sighed. "You couldn't have lied to me just this once, huh? Because I'd be happy thinking some sick individual had placed the doll in your backseat—or even Beau, for reasons I can't fathom. Anything except . . . what it is."

Cooper tucked the doll beneath his seat, being careful not to tip it forward, so that it remained silent. "I would never lie to you, Nola."

I almost asked him then about the woman, and about the scar on his chin. I knew from his reaction when I'd first asked about the scar that the two things were related. But I needed to focus on driving, so now wasn't the time. But later. Definitely later.

"What do you think it means?" he asked. "Does Beau have any ideas?"

"No. We keep attempting to give it to Mimi for a value appraisal and so she can use her psychometry on it. But it keeps . . . escaping."

Cooper nodded slowly. "I'm wondering . . . is there any rhyme or reason to its appearances?"

I thought for a moment, trying to recall the many—too many—appearances of the doll. "Not that I can tell. It seems like it just wants me to see it. And Beau, too. We seem to be only a few of a handful of people lucky enough to be graced by its presence."

"Interesting." He programmed his GPS app so that it displayed directions to the airport on the screen in front of me. "You ready?"

I nodded. Then, after checking all my mirrors twice, I pulled out onto the road and headed toward the interstate.

CHAPTER 17

Thready late-morning traffic accompanied us as we headed up the entrance ramp to the highway. We'd barely reached the top when a song started blasting from the car speakers. It took me a moment of listening to the opening lines to recognize the Adele song "Water Under the Bridge."

Cooper leaned forward and hit a button on the steering wheel, turning off the sound. "I'd recommend that you don't listen to any music while you drive, so you can concentrate. Give it a few weeks of driving by yourself before you introduce music. Adele's perfect for starters. Or ABBA. Then you can ease into the heavier stuff, like Foo Fighters or Ozzy."

"Except I didn't turn it on. And I definitely don't have that song on my playlist. Maybe it's on yours?"

"Adele? Um, no. Not that there's anything wrong with her music; just not something I listen to."

"So what do you listen to?"

He settled back in his seat, which in turn made me relax and loosen my hold on the steering wheel. "Oh, lots of stuff. I like jazz and the blues—it's one of the reasons why moving to New Orleans was so appealing. And bagpipes."

I almost swerved out of my lane. "Bagpipes? As in Scottish Highlanders in kilts?"

"Is there any other kind?" He didn't wait for my answer. "They're kind of soothing, actually. Once I move into my temporary apartment, we'll have a quiet evening at home and I'll play some of my favorite bagpipe music."

"Sounds exciting," I said, and I meant it, but not because of the bagpipes. "I didn't know you'd found an apartment. Wasn't Jolene supposed to be helping you find something? She didn't mention it."

"That's because I haven't told her yet. A coworker of mine is moving to Mandeville but he's locked into a year-long lease on a two-bedroom apartment. So I offered to accept a sublease from him. I haven't seen it in person, but he sent me pictures. It's new construction, so it's not really our taste, but it's got modern plumbing and a microwave, which is about all I really need right now. It's right on the parade route, so, come Mardi Gras, we'll have a perfect vantage point."

"Sounds great." I tried not to read anything into the mention of the words "our" and "we." I wanted to sneak a look at him to gauge his expression, but I didn't want to risk it.

I followed the GPS toward the Louis Armstrong New Orleans International Airport. It was pretty much a straight shot on I-10, but I didn't want to leave anything to chance. I was a nervous driver, and taking a wrong turn would mess with my equilibrium and fragile confidence. I managed to keep my calm despite a tailgating pickup and a tractor trailer hugging the line next to me. When the large truck finally pulled ahead and the pickup sped away, I surreptitiously wiped my palms, one at a time, on my jeans.

"I've been thinking about the entities in my house," Cooper said.

"'*My* house'?"

"Yeah, well, I just need to meet with Beau and get the paperwork started so I can make it official, but for now I'm calling it mine.

Which means that whatever is still in there has become my problem. If I were in Charleston and getting ready to buy a haunted house, I'd call Melanie. But here, I only know of one person like that who might be able to help me."

"Beau."

"Yeah. I don't want to waste my time Googling psychics when I've seen him work and know he's legit. I'm just not sure how to approach him."

"He can be a bit prickly about his abilities. Hopefully, now that we're close to putting his mother to rest, he can come to terms with his gift. Kicking and screaming, sure, but he will. If Melanie, who has spent most of her life singing ABBA out loud to block out the voices, can do it, anyone can. I'll be happy to talk with him on your behalf if you like."

"No. But if you could go with me when I approach him, I'd appreciate it."

"Done and done. But let's wait until after Adele's funeral. I don't want to throw anything else at him right now."

"Of course. Any idea of when that will be?"

"No, but Christopher said that with all the publicity, they'll want to close the case as soon as possible. I hope that means the coroner's office is working overtime, because the entire Ryan family has been waiting for two decades for closure."

"That's assuming there won't be a criminal investigation, right? If an expensive diamond is missing, and she was found where nobody expected to find her, they will probably want to investigate."

I flipped on my blinker to change lanes at the first sign indicating the airport. "Yeah, probably. But after all this time, I'm doubtful any clues as to what happened to her will remain."

"Unless Mimi sees something when she holds the rings."

"Right," I said. "We can only hope."

"In the meantime, I'll start digging into what's going on at the Esplanade house to lay some groundwork before we approach Beau.

I hope he appreciates that I'm meeting him halfway. I thought I'd re-create our evenings at your parents' house on Tradd Street when we'd draw up elaborate charts and index cards and lay them all out on the dining room table—remember?"

"I do. And sometimes we'd play backgammon, and I'd always beat you."

I felt him looking at me, but I didn't dare turn my head. "Funny, that's not how I remember it. I recall winning every game except for the times I let you win."

"I know you only said that because my hands are practically glued to this steering wheel and I can't hit you. Just wait until I get out of the car."

He laughed. "Anyway, I won't go into detail now because you're driving, but I've gone ahead and started making index cards in my head about all the things we do and don't know about the identities of the three entities in the house."

"Sybil, Patrick, and some guy."

"A really angry guy. I'll research the archives and look at previous residents of the home to try to figure out who it might be. I'm leaning toward the father of the older sisters, whose second wife wasn't immediately accepted by his daughters. Maybe he's still angry about that. Until I can do more research, the only other man who I know had a relationship with the house is Mark, Lynda's father and Jessica's husband. But we don't know if he's dead. We don't know if any of them are dead. They're just . . . gone."

"The house was built around the turn of the last century, so you'll need to track down a lot of people. But it was held in the same family the entire time, which should make it easier."

"I'm hoping," he said. "Getting ahold of the police reports from the murder is on my first index card. Speaking with the two sisters . . ." He paused, and I felt him looking at me.

"Honey Meggison and Joan Wenzel," I supplied.

"Right, Honey and Joan. From what you've told me, they sound like they'd welcome a fresh look at the case."

"Yeah. I know they didn't have a great relationship with their half brother, but they were very attached to their niece and sister-in-law. I think their loss hurt them deeply, but I didn't get the sense that they felt the same about their half brother."

"And then there's the doll, which is the subject on my next index card." He leaned over and stuck his hand beneath his seat. "No worries—it's still there. Thankfully." Sitting back, he said, "What do you know about it?"

"It did belong to Lynda. Mark bought it for her, but only to sit on a shelf and not be played with, since it's a collector's item. According to the sisters, it would make Mark really angry if he caught Lynda playing with it. But she loved it and they couldn't keep it away from her."

"So why didn't Lynda take it with her when she left?" Cooper asked.

"That would be the million-dollar question, wouldn't it?"

Cooper was silent as I signaled again to take the upcoming exit to the airport access road. "I just can't stop wondering what kind of guy buys his young daughter a doll and gets angry when she wants to play with it. He sounds like a jerk, which could actually be a clue. Maybe he was a jerk to the wrong people. Maybe business associates. What line of work was he in?"

"Honey mentioned that he imported textiles from the Middle East. He was a very wealthy man, with a big mansion on the lakefront, but his wife and daughter preferred to live with his mother in the little house on Esplanade. That says a lot about the man, doesn't it?"

"Sure does."

"You're working on the next index card in your head, aren't you? I can already see the title in your bold all-caps handwriting: *JERK FATHER*."

He laughed. "You know me well."

That would have been the perfect opening to ask him about the woman, except we were practically already at the airport and I wanted to make sure we had enough time to talk. Instead, I said, "I'd like to know why that doll keeps following me around. Maybe little Patrick is a prankster? Or Sybil? Or some other spirit we're not aware of. We need to let Mimi get her hands on it, but that will have to wait. But 'creepy baby doll' can be the next index card heading following 'jerk father.' If you have a cleaning lady, you might need to explain to her what you're doing so she doesn't get freaked out."

I began braking as I steered the car toward the exit ramp, but instead of feeling the car's transmission downshift, the engine seemed to be revving. I glanced at the speedometer and saw the needle moving higher instead of lower.

"You need to slow down, Nola. You're exiting the highway, and there's a red light ahead."

I stomped my foot on the brake. "It's not working."

"Try again."

"I am, I am!"

"Okay. You're doing great. The light just turned green, so prepare to turn right. Don't worry about the blinker. Just worry about staying on the road. And not hitting anything. I'll be your GPS telling you what to do."

I nodded, my teeth clenched. "It's going faster and my foot's not on the pedal! What do I do?"

"Just stay calm and listen to my direction. We can circle the airport until we run out of gas or the computer glitch works its way out. There are multiple lanes, so all you have to do is avoid other cars and the construction cones, okay?" He didn't mention the temporary concrete barriers that had been placed along the shoulder of the road for the never-ending airport expansion. He didn't need to.

A fetid stench rose from the car's floorboards and blasted from the air vents. Bile rose in my throat.

"What the . . . ?"

I didn't hear whatever Cooper was about to say. A movement in the backseat caught my peripheral vision and forced an involuntary glance in the rearview mirror. A man sat in the middle of the backseat, his face obscured by a shadow that oozed out of him like black tar. I felt his eyes looking back at me, his gaze laser hot on my skin. And then he smiled. Wet lips and yellowed teeth were all I could see before Cooper shouted. I jerked my face forward. A concrete barrier loomed in front of the car. It wasn't a deer, but the car had airbags. With my hands firmly planted on the steering wheel, I kept the car heading straight toward the immovable concrete. Then the only sensation I was aware of was hearing the sounds of metal crumpling and my own screams following me into deep, dark blackness.

CHAPTER 18

I woke up to an overpowering aroma of flowers that couldn't quite erase the smell of bleach and antiseptic. Squinting at blinding overhead fluorescent lights, I was aware of soft conversation around me and of the sound of metal chair legs screeching on tile. For a moment I thought I was back in school, but then I heard Beau's voice.

"Nola?"

My eyes focused on his worried face. I blinked twice. "I guess I'm not in heaven, then."

Beau frowned, and then I heard Mimi's voice. "Jolene, please push the button to let the doctor know she's awake."

Mimi's face replaced Beau's and I felt her warm hand covering mine. "You had us worried, Nola. You have a concussion and you've been in and out of consciousness. How do you feel?"

My brain flashed to the last things I could remember: the stuck brake, the concrete divider. The man in the backseat who wasn't supposed to be there. And Cooper.

I struggled to sit up, and Jolene appeared to put more pillows under my head. She smoothed my hair back and gave my shoulder a brief squeeze as she pulled away. "I've been dabbing a little color on your lips and brushing your hair so people know you're still alive. Let's just say that the lighting in here doesn't do anyone any favors."

"Thanks," I said, not bothering with sarcasm. "Where's Cooper?"

Jolene patted my shoulder. "He's fine. He was seated far back enough that he only has minor bruising on his chest from the passenger-side airbag. He refused to leave your side until your doctors forced him to go home and rest. He said he'd be right back. Most of the flowers are from him, but the rest of us did our share. The pink peonies are from me, because they're such cheerful flowers." She bent toward the table next to me and began rearranging the flowers. "I hope you don't mind, but I put a small vase of them here because the color is very flattering." She gave me a perky grin, which didn't completely conceal the worry in her eyes. "The red roses are from Cooper."

My momentary relief was replaced by a new panic. "What about my parents? Do they know?"

Beau stood at the foot of the bed, looking like he hadn't shaved or slept in days. "We've been trying to reach them, but their phones might be turned off."

I clenched my eyes shut in an attempt to think beyond the throbbing headache and the barrage of images that I couldn't stop from flashing through my brain. "That's because they're supposed to be in California for JJ's cooking competition. Their phones would have been turned off during the flights, and I know that they'd be careful to leave them off while at the competition. If any of the judges hear a single vibration, they'll throw you out. Did you leave messages?"

"No. I didn't think that was how they should learn that their daughter was in an accident," Mimi said. "And then, when it looked like you'd be in the clear, Jolene, Beau, and I decided to wait until you could call them yourself. I know how you hate it when people try to interfere."

If my head didn't hurt so much, I would have smirked. "That's a relief. I don't need them to worry, and I don't want to ruin JJ's big event. I'll let them know what happened later. Like, when all the bandages are off."

"Are you sure?" Mimi asked. She sat in a bedside chair, and I noticed a bag of needlework tucked beside her as well as a Ken Follett novel lying dog-eared at the foot of my bed. She also didn't look as if she'd slept in days, and rampant flyaways covered her usually sleek bun, making it look like a ball of yarn after a litter of kittens had attacked it. "I argued with Beau and threatened to call them myself, but he reminded me of your . . . propensity to get a little, er, upset when others do something on your behalf." Her gentle smile softened her words. Marginally.

"What about Sarah? Did anyone tell her?"

Jolene shook her head. "I didn't think you'd want your parents to hear the news from her. I know she's staying with a friend's family while your parents are gone, and she's got midterms, so I didn't want to worry her, either."

A petite woman with dark hair and eyes and wearing a pale pink lab coat entered the room, along with a middle-aged man in green scrubs—presumably a doctor and a nurse. The woman slid a clipboard from a pocket at the foot of my bed and began reading over my chart as the nurse moved around to the side of the bed to check something on the machinery hanging from the wall.

The doctor looked up and smiled at me, and I noticed the strand of pearls around her neck and the matching pearl stud earrings. "Good afternoon, Miss Trenholm. I'm Dr. Longo. You've been unconscious for a day and a half, so it's good to see you with your eyes open. How are you feeling?"

I gave myself a mental inventory, starting with the scratchiness of the bandages on my head and the general soreness in my arms. It wasn't until my assessment had reached my right leg that I knew something was wrong. "Why can't I move my foot?"

"Because your ankle is broken, so we've immobilized it in a splint. You're very fortunate that that's the only thing you broke. Along with the concussion and the abrasions on your arms, that's the extent of the damage. You could do an Audi commercial showcasing the safety of their cars. If you'd been in something smaller, or without all the new technologies, it would be a different story. Although, to be honest, I've seen the damage caused by a car hitting a concrete wall at sixty miles an hour, and the type of car and the safety features usually don't make a difference. You and your friend are very, very lucky. Or you have an amazingly alert guardian angel."

I clenched my eyes shut again, trying to separate the unending parade of images that flashed in my head like a TikTok video. Maybe it was the mention of an angel, or just the memory of a pair of arms bracing me against the seat. Was there music? Cooper had turned the stereo off. I remembered that. But there had been music. A lullaby humming in my ear. I heard it now, like the soundtrack to the mental video replay. And the distinct scent of Youth-Dew perfume.

Something else the doctor said finally caught up to me. I pressed my eyes wide open as if to make sure I was actually awake and not dreaming. "Wait—I was unconscious for almost two days? So who picked Felicity up?"

"Beau did," Mimi said. "When you didn't show up or answer your phone, she called me. She said she'd take an Uber, but I told her to wait and that I'd send Beau." She grimaced. "I don't like driving on the interstate anymore, and I thought it would be a good opportunity for Beau and his sister to talk."

"And it was," Beau agreed. "It's what we should have planned on doing in the first place." He began walking in a tight circle, pulling his fingers through his hair. "I should have insisted regardless of what Felicity said. And then you wouldn't—"

"Stop. Please. No one could have known. It was . . ." I was about to say *no one's fault*, but the image of the man in the backseat stopped me. "It was an accident," I said instead.

Beau ended his pacing and looked at me closely. "An accident," he repeated.

"Yes. So, was Felicity okay with it when she saw you?"

He reluctantly pulled his gaze away from me and resumed pacing. "To be honest, she was a little annoyed at first, so I asked if she was hungry. I figured we were in New Orleans and food is the perfect way to build bridges, so I took her to Camellia Grill for lunch, because sharing a chili cheese omelet is a great way to start a conversation. And I was right." He shot an apologetic glance at his grandmother. "I told her that we didn't expect her to cut ties with the Sabatiers and that I was sure we could find a way to coexist with them."

Mimi shifted in her chair to give him a hard look. "You didn't—"

Beau interrupted her. "Because we want her in our lives, and if that's a condition of having her be a part of our family again, then Mimi and I will adjust. I also explained that our hands were tied regarding the kidnapping charges, because that's a federal offense."

I pressed my head against my pillow and closed my eyes, trying to process the deluge of information.

Cool fingers stroked my cheek. "I think Nola needs to rest," Jolene said softly. "I'll stay and keep everyone updated. And I'll make sure that she calls her parents," she added, with a hard edge to her voice.

"I don't have time to rest," I said. "Sarah's arriving tomorrow, and then we're driving to Mississippi. I still need to clean up my room before she sees it and tells Melanie." I attempted to sit up and throw off my covers, but the nurse held me down with a firm hand and a smile that clearly said he wasn't to be messed with.

"Oh, no, Miss Trenholm," the doctor said. She was smiling, too, but it was the kind of smile Jolene gave me when she caught me sneaking out the door without lipstick. "I'm afraid that for the next ten to fourteen days you will need to keep your leg elevated above the heart for twenty-three hours a day. Absolutely no weight on it whatsoever—and definitely no traveling."

"Two weeks? And then I can walk on it?"

"Not quite. If you follow my instructions, in two weeks we can put your foot in a removable boot, but even then you won't be allowed to walk on it." She smiled at me like a mom speaking to a toddler who wants to dive into the deep end of a pool without knowing how to swim.

She handed my chart to the nurse and leaned over me to shine a light in each of my eyes. "Everything looks good here, but we'll want to keep you for another night for observation and to run a few more tests. Standard protocol for concussions. We'll send you home with pain meds, as well as a schedule for upcoming appointments with a doctor and a physical therapist. If you do everything you're supposed to, you may be able to begin weight-bearing exercises as soon as four to six weeks, depending on how well you follow instructions." She sent me a look as if she thought I might argue.

"So can I ride my bike? That's not a weight-bearing exercise."

She didn't respond right away, maybe because she was waiting to see if I was joking—which, for the record, I wasn't. "You are technically correct. Riding a bike is not weight bearing, but falling off is, and it's not recommended unless you'd like to compound your injury and break something else."

She took my chart back from the nurse and jotted something down before sliding it back into the slot at the end of my bed. "Do you have any more questions for me?"

I had several, but I knew without asking that her answer to all of them would be no. I shook my head.

She said good-bye before giving Jolene an odd wave, then left, the nurse staying behind to check my vitals and perform other annoyances.

Jolene frowned down at me. "I wonder if they'll let me bring a pretty scarf to drape around your neck to soften the harsh light. I'll ask Sherri."

"Sherri?"

"Yes—Dr. Longo. She and I were sorority sisters at LSU. It's such a small world!"

"I guess that explains the pink lab coat and pearls," I said. "Could you please find my phone? I think it's best to wait until JJ's competition is over before calling Melanie and Jack, but I need to call Sarah. Or maybe you should call Sarah. She's going to be so disappointed not to be going to Mississippi with you. I can handle Melanie and Jack."

"Not as disappointed as I am. At least Jaxson will still be going, so he can drive your car back."

I tried to sit up, but Jolene gently held me down, reminding me of how her petite exterior disguised a warrior woman who could change a flat while wearing heels and repel an intruder with nothing more than a giant plastic Barbie head.

I vigorously shook my head. "Oh, no. Nope, nope, nope. If I could think clearly, I might be able to come up with a creative way to tell you what you can do with that car that doesn't involve it being anywhere near me. Like—"

"Don't say something you'll regret," Christopher said as he entered, carrying a bouquet of happy-face balloons. He was followed by Cooper, who looked as ragged as Beau but appeared to have at least changed his clothes since the accident.

I looked around at the crowd gathered in my hospital room. "Who's minding the store?"

Christopher chuckled. "I guess you're feeling all right. I don't know anybody else who would worry about practical matters right after waking up from a coma."

"I do," Beau and I said in unison.

Christopher made room on a small table by the window for the balloons. "To answer your question, Camille and Henry." He shared a quick glance with Mimi. "Or mostly Camille, I should say. And Trevor will be there after school to manage them. I'm actually on my way there now. I just wanted to stop by and see how you were. I'm glad to see you're awake."

"We all are," Mimi said. "And I should be going, too." She rose and began gathering her things.

Cooper moved to the side of my bed, and I reached for his hand.

He looked exhausted, the pallor of his skin highlighting the pink scar on his chin.

"Are you mad about your car?"

Cooper sighed, sat down in the chair vacated by Mimi, and put his elbows on the edge of the bed, momentarily holding his head in his hands. "I don't care about the car. It's insured and replaceable. You're not. I have no idea what happened, but it wasn't your fault. I'll let the insurance adjusters figure out what went wrong. All I care about is that you're okay."

"I know what happened," I said quietly, pulling him closer. "There was someone—"

The nurse reappeared, interrupting me. "Okay, everyone. Time to give the patient some privacy and rest. You can visit again later."

I started to protest, but I stopped when I saw what the nurse was carrying. I squinted at it, trying to figure out why he might be holding the doll that I remembered Cooper sticking under the car seat before the accident.

"Where did you get that?" Beau asked, holding out his hand.

The nurse eagerly relinquished it. "It was propped up outside your room. I thought one of you had left it there. It's scaring the other patients, so I was hoping one of you could take it when you go."

"It was in the car," Cooper said. "Maybe one of the EMTs brought it in?"

The nurse shrugged. "That's possible. I just need to make sure it goes away."

"Don't be ridiculous," Mimi said. "It's an old Madame Alexander doll and might be quite valuable. Here, let me see it."

She put down her needlework bag and reached for the doll, grabbing it before Beau could stop her. Mimi froze in place with her fingers clutching the doll's arms. Her eyes rolled back in her head before she sank to the floor, still holding the doll, its eyes wide open and staring directly at me before it uttered the only word it knew. "Mama."

CHAPTER 19

It's a good thing Bubba has such a big backseat," Jolene said, looking at me in her rearview mirror. "Beau suggested putting you in the bed of his truck, but I thought you'd be more comfortable in here."

"I was joking." Beau turned around to look at me in the backseat, where I sat sidewise to keep my leg elevated. "But not about you laying off of Jolene's muffins. It's going to be a struggle getting you up the front steps."

"Don't make me stop this car, Beau Ryan," Jolene said from the front seat. "If you can't be nice, I'm going to let you out on the side of the road."

"Again, joking," he said. "I thought we all could use a little levity right now."

He turned around while I studied the back of his neck, noticing that he'd had a haircut, the paler skin on his neck making him look somewhat vulnerable.

As if reading my mind, he rubbed his neck. "Mimi asked me to cut it for the funeral."

With an eyebrow raised in question, Jolene looked at me in the rearview mirror and I shrugged. Even I couldn't understand the weird connection Beau and I seemed to share. It was better left unsaid.

"Has the date for the funeral been set?" I asked.

"Yes," Beau said. "Mimi said that the coroner expects to release the body later today, so she's scheduled the funeral for Wednesday."

"What about the wedding rings? Has she . . . ?"

"No. She goes today to pick them up. Felicity and I are going with her. Camille wanted to go, too, for moral support, but I told her it should be just family."

"I really wish you'd take me to my apartment. I'll be fine there. Really. I'm a runner, so I've got great quads and can hop around until I'm allowed to put weight on my foot. Uber Eats and Jolene's stockpile of food in the freezer will ensure that I don't starve. And Cooper and Jolene will both be back on Sunday, so it's not like I'll be alone for very long."

"You need one of those 'Help me; I've fallen' necklaces—you know, like in the commercials?" Jolene's eyes met mine in the rearview mirror. "My grandmama has one just in case she gets too deep of a whiff of formaldehyde and falls onto the embalming table, or worse, and I'm sure I don't need to tell you how much peace of mind that gives us."

"I'm sure. But I've got my Apple Watch, so I can just call for help if I need it—which I won't, because I know how to be careful. I wish you'd talk to Mimi again."

"Have you ever tried arguing with my grandmother?" Beau asked. "She's insisting that you're better off with people around to help."

"But I don't need any . . ."

He held up his hand. "I know. You don't need any help. I tried to tell her that. It's like arguing with a brick wall."

"Well, that explains a lot," I said, staring at the back of Beau's head. "Speaking of Mimi, how is she?" The last time I'd seen her, she'd been put on a gurney and was being taken to another hospital room, her protests carrying down the hallway to me.

"Embarrassed, mostly. She said the doll may or may not be worth anything, but she doesn't want to see it ever again. She said there's more to tell, but she only wants to relive the experience once, so she's waiting until you, me, and Cooper are all together. When is Cooper leaving?"

"He's flying to Kuala Lumpur tonight." I grabbed the back of the front seat to brace myself as Jolene took a sharp turn before bouncing over the curb. "He said he'd stop by Mimi's sometime this morning. I'd call to find out when, but I need both hands right now."

Beau grinned as Bubba swerved again, clipping the edge of a large pothole and rattling my teeth.

"Has anyone heard from Sarah?" I asked. "She was so disappointed when I told her she wouldn't be going to Mississippi, and now she won't answer my texts or phone calls."

Jolene and Beau shared a glance, but before I could question them Jolene bumped the two right tires over the curb and put the car in park. "Oh, look—we're here!"

Mimi and Camille came bustling out of the front door of the house on Prytania and headed down the walkway. "Your welcoming committee is here!" Jolene said as she opened my door.

Beau retrieved my crutches from the trunk and leaned them against Bubba. I was attempting to exit the car by myself when he reached in and lifted me out. After studying the steps leading up to the front walk, and then the marble steps under the portico, he said, "I might as well carry you all the way inside. I hope my back can handle it."

I gave him a small punch on the shoulder. "Be careful," I said. "The next time I'm going to hit you where it hurts."

"Don't get me too excited, Nola. I might trip."

I hit him again, harder this time. He carried me the entire way into the house while Camille and Jolene brought in the crutches and my overnight bag. I heard the sound of a video game from the parlor, and as Beau brought me closer I was surprised to see the backs of two females, one brunette and one blond, sitting on the sofa, facing the game. Henry, his arms crossed over his chest like a sulking little boy, sat in one of the two matching side chairs, frowning at the two people on the sofa.

"Hey, Nola," he said with a brief nod in my direction, before returning his attention to the screen. It didn't surprise me that he hadn't rushed outside to help.

"Surprise!" Sarah jumped up from the couch, dropping a game controller on the floor, and ran to embrace me.

The girl I recognized as Felicity stood, too, making room for Beau to place me on the sofa before positioning me, while Mimi retrieved two cushions from a side chair and propped them under my legs. "How's that?"

"Fine. But"—I turned to my sister, noticing the peacock brooch on her cardigan and the red rubber band around her wrist—"what are you doing here?"

"Aren't you happy to see me?"

"Of course I am. It's just . . . Does Melanie know you're here?"

She rolled her eyes. "I'm not stupid, Nola. She still thinks I'm driving to Mississippi with you and Jolene. And as long as you don't tell her, I won't mention the ankle thing." She smiled sweetly, her hands folded in front of her like a choirboy's.

I frowned. "But where will you stay? You can't stay by yourself at the apartment."

"That's why I've invited her to stay here with us," Mimi said as she placed her arm around Sarah's shoulders. "I don't agree with keeping Melanie and Jack in the dark, but I know you two will find a way to tell them sooner rather than later, yes?"

Sarah and I nodded, and I was fairly confident that my sister was crossing her fingers behind her back, too. "I'm not keeping them in the dark, Mimi. I just know how . . . excitable they can be, and I don't want to ruin JJ's big event. Which is exactly what would happen, because my parents would be on the first flight to New Orleans, and it's completely unnecessary. I know I'm in excellent hands. I just hate intruding on your grief."

Mimi's expression softened. "I welcome the company during this difficult time. Having something with which to occupy myself would be the distraction I need while saying good-bye to our darling Adele."

"Of course," Camille said, moving to Mimi's side and gently squeezing her shoulders.

"And you must be Felicity," I said to the young blond woman who looked almost exactly like the imposter we'd known as Sunny. Same yellow-gold hair and round blue eyes. Same elfin chin and warm smile. Which had been the point, I supposed. "I'm sorry about not picking you up at the airport as planned."

"Are you kidding me? I'm so glad you're okay—except for the ankle thing, I mean." I noticed that she clutched both game controllers despite Henry's hovering and avid interest in claiming one. "It's good to officially meet you. We didn't really get a chance the last time I was here."

"There was a lot going on." I didn't feel it necessary to bring up the occurrences of the evening of her last visit, which included the appearance of an evil spirit and the chandelier crashing onto the dining room table. "I'm sorry we're meeting at such a difficult time."

She looked at Mimi and then Beau before returning her gaze to me and drawing in a deep breath. "We've agreed not to look at it that way. I think we all feel that even though Adele is no longer alive, being together to lay her to rest is bringing us more comfort than grief, so we are choosing to feel joy today instead of sadness. If I have learned anything in the last month, it's that we get to choose how we interpret each day and each event. It's hard to survive in this world of constant turmoil if we don't, you know?"

I nodded, deciding that I liked this young woman very much. I hoped we could become friends. I'd already determined that we were destined to become close when I'd noticed her clutching the game controller simply to annoy Henry.

Camille moved to stand behind me. "Can I get you something to drink? Another pillow for behind your back? Mimi and I have rearranged the library into a cozy bedroom for you. The pullout couch is very comfortable—Henry tested it just to be sure."

"That's very nice of you," I said, skirting the comment about Henry testing out my sleeping space. Despite Jolene's claim that she wouldn't kick him out of bed for eating crackers, I would for much less.

"I've asked Camille to stay with you while I go to my appointment with the coroner. Uncle Bernie has agreed to meet us there."

"Uncle Bernie?" I said. Bernie was actually Jaxson's uncle, but a friend of the Ryans, and also a retired New Orleans police detective. He'd been a huge help in discovering the real identity of the Sunny imposter.

"Yes," Mimi said. "Jaxson reached out to him after Jolene told him about the discovery at Charity. He made a few phone calls on my behalf, to speed things along, and arranged for a private meeting with the coroner."

"Speaking of which," Beau said, "we need to get going."

Felicity handed her game controller to me and the other one back to Sarah. "Here—you can take my place and finish beating Sarah."

"Thanks," I said, fairly sure that her motivation was to keep it away from Henry, confirming my suspicion that we were going to be friends.

As soon as they left, I handed the controller to Sarah. "Can you put this thing on pause? I don't think I can concentrate, and I'd hate to make Felicity lose."

Henry left shortly afterward, with a mumbled comment that he was headed to the store to fix whatever mess Camille had probably left for him to deal with. Camille's smile didn't fade as she turned to me. "Can I get you a sandwich or something? Mimi said you need to have food in your stomach before you take your pills, and it's about time for your next dose."

"Yes, I'd appreciate that. Thank you. And anything you want to make is fine with me."

"I'll help," Jolene announced as she followed Camille toward the kitchen. "And she really will eat anything you put in front of her. I think she has a hollow leg, because she has the appetite of a linebacker but the figure of a movie star."

The sound of the women laughing faded as they moved toward the back of the house.

Sarah stood and unplugged the controllers from the game console before wrapping them together with the cords and stuffing them under the sofa.

"Is that necessary?" I asked.

She gave me the look of disappointment that Melanie would give me when I kicked my shoes under my bed or hung up a coat facing the wrong way. "Seriously? Don't you think Henry's kinda old to be hogging the game controllers?"

"Yes, but it's not my house, so I'm not making the rules. And you should be calling him Mr. LeBlanc."

"I tried, but he kept telling me to call him Henry, and I gave in so he'd stop talking. He's not the sharpest knife in the drawer, on top of being irritating. I mean, he thinks Elvis faked his death, and he keeps using the word 'irregardless.' Oh, and his favorite TV show is *Beavis and Butt-Head*." She lifted a corner of the sofa cushion, under which a collection of empty candy wrappers had been assembled. "These are all his, by the way."

She let the cushion fall, then plopped down on the sofa, jostling my leg and making me wince. "Sorry. I keep forgetting you've got a broken ankle." She gently patted the bandaged appendage. "And he talks way too much. He kept asking Felicity if she could talk to dead people—probably because he knows that Beau can—and if she ever communicated with her mom and dad. It was obvious he was upsetting her, but he kept at it until I asked Felicity what brand tampons she used for heavy-flow days and if she had menstrual cramps. That shut him up right away."

"Very smart. Just out of curiosity, though, what did Felicity say about seeing dead people?"

"She said she didn't. And I believe her. Because usually when there is more than one of us, we're like a lighthouse beacon to restless spirits—like when Beau is in the same room with me." She held up her hand and plucked at the rubber band. "Which is why I came prepared. This distracts me and breaks the connection. More subtle than when Mom starts singing ABBA songs, and works the same way."

She jumped up and lifted the cushion again to gather the wrappers.

"Ouch!"

"Sorry—I keep forgetting. I have to use the bathroom, and I thought I'd dispose of these before Mimi finds them. I think Henry and Camille are starting to wear on her nerves."

I grinned at her repetition of something Melanie said often about all three of her children and dogs. "Sure. I'll be here when you get back." I closed my eyes, trying to relax despite the throbbing in my foot, and I had just started to drift into a restless sleep when Sarah returned.

"Why do you think Mimi put this in the bathroom?"

I knew before I opened my eyes that she'd be holding Miss Pussycat. "I don't think she put it there. It just keeps . . . appearing."

"Ew." Sarah dropped the doll onto one of the side chairs. "Do you mean . . . ?"

"Yes. Someone from beyond is trying to send us a message, but we don't know who or why."

"Where did it come from?"

"An old house on Esplanade Avenue. Actually, it's the first project for Beau's murder-house-flip idea. I'm helping with the renovation, and Cooper wants to buy it."

She plopped down on the sofa again, dislodging my injured foot from the pillow it was resting on. "Sorry," she said again. "Do you want me to go find out who?"

I contemplated my little sister, who was the spitting image of our dad and like a younger version of myself but who'd inherited Melanie's psychic abilities and wasn't afraid to use them. I credited Melanie for instilling in Sarah a certain pride in this unique gift and teaching her a way to discern when and where to display it.

"I'm not sure. Beau's naturally distracted right now, so I would appreciate your help, but there's a very negative energy in the house and I don't want you messing with it. I'm pretty sure that it was the entity I saw in the backseat when the brakes stopped working and I crashed. I doubt Melanie would sanction your involvement."

"Well, we wouldn't have to tell her, would we?"

Before I could respond, Jolene and Camille entered the room with two trays full of steaming soup bowls, sandwiches, and freshly baked cookies—which Jolene had brought with her from her endless freezer supply—and set them on the coffee table.

"I hope you're hungry," Camille said.

"Nola's always hungry," Jolene said as she placed a tray in front of us and gave us each a napkin rolled expertly around cutlery. Then she carefully slid the coffee table closer to the couch and placed my pills on my sandwich plate. "So watch your fingers. I've got scars all over my hands from feeding her."

"Funny," I said, my mouth watering at the smell of the tomato soup. "And please tell me that's your pimento cheese on the sandwich."

"It is," Camille admitted. "And Mimi made the soup. I stay out of the kitchen as much as possible. I'm a terrible cook, as Henry keeps reminding me."

She settled herself in one of the chairs opposite the couch. "Aren't you going to eat anything?" I asked.

Camille shook her head. "Henry says I'm getting a little broad in the beam, so I'm skipping breakfast and lunch and just eating dinner. I did sneak a saltine in the kitchen, but don't tell him."

It didn't look as if she was joking, so I didn't say anything.

"Nice guy," Sarah said under her breath before turning her attention to the food.

"Have you heard from Mimi or Beau?" Camille asked. "They said it would be a brief meeting and that they'd be home within two hours."

I wondered about her impatience, but then I remembered that Adele had been her best friend, and that until Camille had read the newspaper article about Sunny's return she had been living with the assumption that Adele was alive and well. It must have been devastating for her to learn that her friend had been missing all this time and was now presumed dead. As if reading my mind, she said, "I just need to know if I should be grieving or searching for Adele. Or if there is any clue if Buddy . . ." She stopped.

"If Buddy what?" I asked, a bite of sandwich suddenly sticking to the roof of my mouth.

She shook her head. "I don't want to speculate. At least not before we know anything for sure."

I put my soup spoon down, my appetite gone. "Speculate about what?"

She closed her mouth and looked down at her feet, which were no longer swinging under the edge of the chair. "Nothing. I shouldn't have said anything."

"But you did, and I'm curious. What did you mean?"

Sarah pretended to be texting on her phone, while Jolene busied herself with tidying around the room.

Still looking down, Camille said, "It's just . . . well, if Adele is dead and has been found in New Orleans, then why hasn't Buddy been found? Or come forward?" Her eyes met mine. "Why is he hiding? I don't want to think it, because I loved Buddy like a brother, but what if . . ." Her narrow shoulders lifted inside her baggy sweater. "What if he hurt her? Whether or not he meant to. I mean, they could get into loud arguments, but I never saw him hit her. That's not to say it didn't happen, just that I never saw it happen. But wouldn't that explain everything?"

"No." I wanted to stand up and stomp around the room, the fact that I couldn't making me doubly aggravated. "It wouldn't. And I hope you haven't mentioned this to anyone besides me. Because . . ." I shook my head, not wanting to even try to imagine what it would do to Mimi and Beau. And Felicity. Learning that a beloved family member had been killed during historic flooding following a major storm was one thing. Learning that the family member had been murdered was quite another.

"No. Of course not." Camille's voice had shrunk to the volume she usually used in Henry's presence, and I felt bad that I had caused her stress. She continued. "I haven't even said anything out loud. Until now. You seem . . . safe."

"Good. And I promise that I won't be repeating this to anyone. There's absolutely no evidence, and nothing that I've learned about Buddy and Adele that would lead me to believe that Buddy had anything to do with Adele's death."

She held up her hands palms out, as if in surrender. "I know. That's exactly how I feel. It's just that, well . . ." Her voice disappeared.

"There are a million possible explanations as to what happened, none of them involving Buddy doing harm to Adele. I don't believe we should speculate until we have the facts. I think Mimi and Beau have accepted that they might never know what happened. And I'd like to leave it at that until we know more—for their sakes."

"Of course," Camille said, her head dipped low like a scolded child's. Her demeanor made me want to apologize, but I couldn't imagine what I needed to be sorry for. "Excuse me," she said. "I'm going to go tidy up the kitchen." She left the room before I could think of something to say.

Sarah's phone rang with the theme song from *Ghostbusters*. "It's Mom," she announced as she hit the red End Call button on her screen. She waited a moment before receiving the ding of an incoming text. After she read it, her fingers quickly tapped on the screen before she replaced the phone on her lap with a satisfied smile. "There. All good. Mom wanted to know if I'd given Jolene's mother the sweetgrass basket she sent as a hostess gift, and I told her I hadn't delivered it yet because Jolene had stuff to do, so we were still in New Orleans—which is all true, so she won't yell at me later for lying."

"Now, Sarah," Jolene said, "either you or Nola has to tell Melanie what's happened."

"I will," I said. "Promise. I'm just waiting for the right time."

The doorbell rang before Jolene could say anything else. "That should be Cooper," I said.

"I'll get it!" Sarah announced.

"No, you won't, missy," Jolene said. "You stay right here and quit jostling your sister, you hear? I'll be right back."

Looking properly chastened, Sarah took a sip of her tomato soup. "Cooper is *so* hot," she said. "And so is Beau. I don't know how you're going to choose."

"Choose? There's no choosing here. Cooper and I are just friends, and Beau is practically engaged. Besides, I've got enough going on in my life right now and don't have time for a romantic relationship."

"Right," she said, looking so much like Jack after I'd told him I was going to bed early while planning to exit through my bedroom window. She rolled her eyes. "And this house isn't haunted." She snapped the rubber band on her wrist twice while looking over my shoulder and into the foyer, where the portrait of Mimi's husband, Charles, hung on the wall. "It seems to me that they both need reminders, even if you think that you don't. But I'm prepared, and so far they're both nice. As for your situation, I suggest you cut off all your hair and stop bathing to avoid trouble. And don't brush your teeth for a week."

"On what planet have you been living to think that's a suitable solution for a woman who's not interested in anything but her recovery and restoring old houses?"

Sarah thought for a moment. "Nothing I can quote exactly, but Mom and I watch a lot of the *Housewives* shows." She peered out into the foyer again. "And who's the woman hanging around Cooper?"

A sharp wave of goose bumps rippled across my skin. "The woman?"

"Yeah. The angry woman. She wants to tell him something. Should I ask her what it is?"

I shook my head. "I don't know who it is, so I don't think that's a good idea. You shouldn't be opening yourself up to just anybody."

"I know. But, well, she's with Cooper, so I thought it might be okay."

"Beau saw her, too. He said she was angry, but I haven't had a chance to ask Cooper about any dead woman who might be mad at him."

Sarah frowned. "She's not dead."

I stared at my sister as goose bumps erupted over my scalp and down my legs. "What do you mean? If you and Beau are seeing her, doesn't that mean . . ."

She shrugged. "I'm telling you all I know."

The front door shut, and then Cooper, carrying a bouquet of red roses, entered the parlor with a blast of cold outside air. Dark circles sat beneath his eyes, and he looked exhausted even though he was clean-shaven and wore a suit and tie in preparation for the meetings that would immediately follow his flight. The new scratches the airbag had caused on his nose and forehead were scabbed over and, along with the old scar on his chin, made him look more like a prizefighter than like a businessman. He placed the bouquet on the coffee table before leaning over to kiss my cheek. As he straightened, I saw Sarah's *I told you so* expression.

"How are you feeling?" he asked.

"I'm okay. But you look exhausted. I hope you can sleep on the plane."

"I'll be fine. Seeing you smile will get me through the long flight."

I ignored Sarah's double thumbs-up behind Cooper. Sensing movement, he turned, but his attention was grabbed by something he could see from the window. From my perch on the sofa, I saw Mimi and her two grandchildren as well as the large, familiar figure of Uncle Bernie approaching the house from the front walk.

I studied their faces, vainly looking for any indication of the outcome of the meeting. "I hope this means that Adele can be at peace now."

Sarah cleared her throat. "I don't think so." I followed her gaze to a set of wet footprints in front of the window facing Prytania, as if someone else was watching the small group's approach.

"What do you think this means?" Cooper asked.

"Maybe Adele's waiting until after her funeral," I suggested, embarrassed by the way I ended the sentence with an inflection usually reserved for a question.

"No." Sarah shook her head, her gaze fixed on the spot by the window. "Her words are . . ." She stopped, frowned.

"Garbled," I finished, remembering the last time Adele had tried to communicate with Sarah. "Like she's underwater."

"No," she said again. "I can hear her clearly now. Like . . . she's now above water." She closed her eyes and inclined her head as if in prayer. "She's talking too fast and I can't . . ." Sarah tilted her chin, her eyes still closed. "I can make out the name 'Buddy.' And . . . something else."

Jolene, Cooper, and I held our collective breath, waiting for whatever came next.

Sarah's eyes popped open, her head pivoting to look at me. "Danger. She's saying we're all in danger."

CHAPTER 20

"I'll let them in," Jolene said, moving to the foyer, shattering the unholy silence that had settled over us.

More cold air entered the room as the group joined us, their faces somber and all eyes reddened. Cooper stood to help Mimi out of her coat before Jolene led her to a chair.

Mimi held up her hand. "I need to keep busy. Working in the kitchen is just what the doctor ordered, and I say it's time for lunch. If you all will excuse me . . ." Her gaze fell on the creepy doll. She drew back as if struck, her nostrils flaring.

"What is that thing doing here?"

"Sarah found it in the bathroom," I said. "We thought you might have put it there."

"Absolutely not." Her mismatched eyes blazed. Facing Beau, she said, "I thought I asked you to get rid of it."

"I did," he said through gritted teeth.

"I think it's trying to tell us something," Sarah suggested.

"Clearly." Felicity snatched it from the chair. "And none of us want to listen." She headed toward the front door. "I'm going to dump this in Beau's truck so he can return it to where he found it. Maybe that's all it wants."

Mimi's skin had turned the color of parchment. "Its message is contradictory. There's something evil attached to it. But there's . . . that's not what keeps moving it. There's another spirit. A benign one, I think. It's unclear to me why it keeps showing up unexpectedly."

I appreciated her judicious use of the word "unexpectedly." I would have used something more specific, like "horrifyingly" or "hellishly."

"Like they want us to pay attention," Sarah said quietly. The only other sound in the room was that of Beau snapping his rubber band against his wrist.

Felicity paused on the threshold, holding the doll upside down by its foot as if awaiting instruction. It seemed apparent to me that whatever paranormal vibes were winging their way around the parlor, she was immune to them.

"But it's not the evil part that wants us to notice it," Sarah continued. "It's . . . trying to hide, and the other entity, the gentle one, wants us to look."

"Is it connected to Adele?" Cooper asked.

Sarah shook her head, her gaze settling on Beau, her eyes distant, their usual bright blue faded now to a soft gray. As if they no longer belonged to her. "No. But she wants us to pay attention."

"Okay," Beau said. "Can you ask her to be more specific?"

"No. But she says you can." Her strange eyes shifted to Felicity. "And so can Sunny."

"All right. That's enough woo-woo for me," Felicity said, heading toward the front door, holding out the doll at arm's length so that it wouldn't touch her. "Sarah, I'm not sure what shows you're allowed to watch at home, but I think your imagination is just a little too wild." To the rest of us, she said, "I'll be right back." The lamps flickered as the door slammed behind her.

Without a word, Mimi turned in the direction of the kitchen.

Neither Sarah nor I pointed out that we had already eaten; we knew she wouldn't hear us.

Jolene motioned for Uncle Bernie to sit in one of the armchairs, then took his cane and carefully leaned it against one of the arms.

"Sorry about that, Sarah," Beau said. "Felicity is under a lot of stress, and I don't think she intended to be rude." He walked toward the bar cart. "I know it's early, but can I get anyone something to drink?"

"Bourbon on the rocks for me, please," Bernie said. Nodding at me, he said, "Begging your pardon."

"No need. It's been a stressful morning. I think I'd like an espresso. The stronger the better."

"I'll go make that espresso," Jolene said, grabbing the lunch tray to take it to the kitchen. "I think I'll have one, too."

"Make that three, please," Cooper said. "I didn't get a lot of sleep last night. I thought I was too old for nightmares."

"Why don't you help Jolene?" I said to Sarah.

"But . . ."

"Now," I said, sounding more like Melanie than I'd intended.

With a sigh, she carefully slid from the sofa so as not to disturb my ankle and left the room, each footfall heavier than the last.

"Almost makes me wish I'd had children," Bernie said.

"You can borrow her anytime," I said. "I'm sure my parents wouldn't mind. They might even thank you. Or make it a permanent arrangement."

"I heard that," Sarah shouted from the back hallway.

Beau handed Bernie an old-fashioned glass with a double pour before fixing a glass for himself, then turned to the spot beside me on the sofa, recently vacated by Sarah, but Cooper had already taken it. With a look of irritation, Beau settled into the armchair next to Bernie. "Let's fill Nola in."

Bernie took a long drink from his glass and swallowed, then paused until the warmth of the liquid had left his throat. My mouth watered at the memory of the comfort that could be found in a bottle of bourbon, and I had to look away. My good foot tapped with impatience as I waited for my espresso, hoping I could at least pretend it offered even a fraction of what I needed.

I felt heaviness in the air between Beau and me. I wished he were sitting closer so I could touch his hand, offer comfort. His craving for human touch was a palpable thing, my body absorbing it as if I were living through my own dark days all over again. When the police had arrived to tell me that my mother was dead, I'd wished for someone to show me I wasn't alone. But there'd been no one. My memories of that time in my life revolved around a feeling of loss I couldn't fully comprehend. An abyss over which I hovered without any sense that someone was holding on so I wouldn't fall.

As if reading my thoughts, Beau met my gaze and answered my unspoken question. "The coroner confirmed that my mom's dental records match the teeth of the skeletonized remains found at Charity."

"I'm so sorry." It was such an inadequately stupid thing to say, but it summed up all my thoughts and feelings about finally having at least a partial explanation of what had happened to Adele Ryan.

Bernie shook the ice in his glass, prompting Cooper to refill it. "Fortunately for the investigation, Adele's dentist was in Metairie Ridge, one of the highest points in the metro area, so none of their records were lost in the flooding. Which was extremely fortunate, since Adele had been seeing the same dentist since she moved to New Orleans, so all of her dental X-rays were kept in the same place."

I nodded slowly, trying to think like my dad when he was attempting to glean enough information to write convincingly about a historical mystery despite spotty evidence and no known eyewitnesses. "Was there anything else they could find out?"

Beau opened his mouth as if to speak, but no words came out.

Bernie cleared his throat. "So, the, uh, remains have been subjected to the elements for some time, and in addition, it looks like until this last bit of rain we had she was stuck beneath a lot of buried heavy X-ray equipment. Possibly from surging water or . . ."

"Or put there deliberately to hold her down," I said.

Bernie nodded. "Exactly. There aren't any corresponding wounds on the skeletal remains to indicate crushing, but that doesn't rule out entrapment or entanglement that might have prohibited movement."

"So you're saying the cause of death was drowning." I recalled what Sarah had said after speaking with Adele, how it sounded as if she were talking underwater. And how I'd thought the same thing when I spoke with her over a dead landline.

"Not necessarily," Beau said slowly. "They're not even sure if where she was found was where she died. Considering the hospital was evacuated and abandoned just days after the storm, it would be the perfect spot to bury a body. Nobody around and lots of sludge and heavy equipment to hide remains where they might never be found."

"Until Tulane decided to do a massive renovation project at the hospital complex," Cooper said, leaning his elbows on his thighs. "Which means that your mother's death might not have been an accident."

"It was murder," Bernie said. "Made to look like she was just another victim of the storm. And they might have gotten away with it except for the rain. And one other little thing. The hyoid bone."

"The hyoid bone," I repeated. "I know what that is." My father was a chronicler of true crime who, despite Melanie's protests, had never held back from sharing his more interesting discoveries. "It's that U-shaped bone in the front of the neck. Something like a quarter of all homicides by strangulation result in a fractured hyoid."

"Thirty-three percent, actually." Uncle Bernie drained the remainder of his drink. "But no drowning victim I've ever heard of had a fractured hyoid."

"So there's a chance that it was an accident, right? Maybe she fell on something, or something hit her that broke the hyoid." I wasn't usually such a Pollyanna. Maybe it was the pain in my ankle, or maybe I didn't want to witness any more grief. Learning that one's mother had died should be enough. The probability that she'd been murdered was too much.

"True," Bernie agreed. "Except for the wedding rings. They showed Mimi the rings, minus the diamond, and she verified that they were the same bands she gave Buddy for his bride. She let Beau have them for now, for safekeeping." His gaze moved to Beau, his expression apologetic. "When I studied the prongs that held the diamond on the engagement ring, they appeared to have been methodically bent away from the stone. If the diamond had been dislodged accidentally, the prongs would appear much less uniform."

"So you're thinking it's robbery?" I asked. "That's good, right? Doesn't that give you a better chance of finding those responsible?"

"It would," Beau said. "Except the diamond is well-known. If it were sold, it would most likely be sold in private and not at auction. Or it could have been divided, since no one would be looking for smaller diamonds. It's highly unlikely that we'll ever know if robbery was the motive or if the diamond was stolen after my mother was already dead."

Bernie cleared his throat. "There's one more thing. Strangulation is an unusual way to kill someone during a robbery. We normally see it in a personal attack where the victim and assailant know each other."

The room was silent as we mulled over the implications, until the front door opened and closed, announcing Felicity's return. She stood in the doorway, her eyes narrowing as she took in the silent group. Turning to Beau, she said, "Did you tell Nola everything?"

"Pretty much," he said, standing up so Felicity could take his chair.

Felicity gave him a dismissive wave and remained standing. "Does she know that my dad is being interrogated in prison to find out if he was involved with Adele's murder?" Felicity stood with her arms crossed tightly, so that she appeared to be hugging herself. And she'd referred to her mother by her first name.

Cooper and I exchanged a glance, both of us recalling the awful scene in the Ryans' dining room when her adoptive father had confessed to kidnapping Sunny when she was a baby, pretending she was his dead daughter, and then hiring a young actress to masquerade as the real Sunny. It had been as jaw-dropping as it was heartbreaking.

"Felicity . . ." Beau began.

"I'm just stating facts. In spite of his having admitted to kidnapping under extenuating circumstances, he is not a murderer." Her chin quivered as she attempted to control her emotions. I wanted to stand up and go to her, but I was almost relieved that my broken ankle meant that I couldn't. I didn't know Felicity well, but as I watched her now she reminded me of a wounded animal; her eyes were sharp and she was ready to bite if anyone came too near.

Bernie cleared his throat. "I've spoken with the detectives involved with the interrogation, and they've promised to call me when they're done. However, from what we know so far, it would appear that Robert Sabatier is innocent—of murder, at least. With the timeline of his whereabouts when Adele disappeared, as well as verified witness accounts and a paper trail that confirms the presence of both Robert and Angelina Sabatier in North Carolina and not here, it's doubtful that they will be able to connect him to what happened to your mother."

"Adele," she corrected. Felicity lifted her head and rubbed her eyes with the backs of her hands. "But she didn't accidentally bury herself on the grounds of Charity Hospital," she said, almost defiantly. It seemed as if she was trying very hard to be impartial. Maybe she thought that if she invested her emotions in the circumstances surrounding her biological mother's death, it would seem disloyal to the family who'd raised her and with whom she still felt enough of a familial connection to keep the name they'd given her and limit communication with the grandmother and brother who'd never stopped looking for her. She lifted her chin. "So we're looking at a murder."

"Most likely," Beau said before draining his glass. I licked my lips again, as if the memory would be enough.

"Do you want me to go see if Jolene needs any help?" Beau placed his glass on a side table outside of my field of vision.

As if summoned, Jolene and Camille returned from the kitchen with two trays containing small espresso cups and plates of biscotti, all beautiful antique Limoges china. I almost smiled at the image of Mimi, in the depths of her grief, still managing to be the consummate New Orleans hostess.

Jolene set a plate of biscotti on the coffee table in front of the sofa and handed me a delicate cup and saucer, two yellow pills tucked neatly against the cup. "There's plenty more where that came from, but you might want to take it easy on the caffeine, according to the instructions Dr. Longo sent with your pain meds. I made the executive decision that one little espresso couldn't hurt, and those of us who would have to live with an uncaffeinated Nola are all in unspoken agreement."

Cooper covered his laugh with a cough as he accepted an espresso cup from Jolene. "I wish I could stay to make sure she gets enough of both caffeine and pain meds, but I wasn't able to cancel my trip."

"Thanks, but I'll manage," I said. "Mimi has insisted that she and Camille will be on hand to make sure I have what I need, and Henry is living here now, so if I need assistance moving from the bed to the couch, he's here. Besides, I've got my crutches, so it's no big deal." The thought of Henry being in charge of anything did make me worry, but the knowledge that Beau would be nearby was more than a little reassuring.

"Where's Sarah?" I asked, sniffing the rich aroma of my espresso before taking a grateful sip.

"She's with Mimi," Jolene said. "They're talking about Beau's special gift—and why he has chosen not to speak with his mama. Sarah wanted to know if she could help."

I sat up straighter, wincing as my foot fell off the stack of pillows. "Help with lunch prep?" I asked hopefully. When I'd first asked Melanie if Sarah could join me for Thanksgiving, I'd received the oft-repeated speech that Sarah wasn't a party trick and that I needed to be mindful that she was only twelve. I'd been offended, because I'd known this without having to be told. As Sarah approached puberty her abilities would get stronger, as Melanie herself had experienced. We needed to tread carefully to prevent her being scarred for life, either by the spirits she'd encounter or by the clueless individuals who would think it cool that my sister could talk to the dead.

"I'm not sure," Jolene said with hesitation, picking up on the looks between Beau and me.

"I'm taking that to means she's *sensitive*," Camille said as she placed a plate of biscotti on the table between Bernie and Beau.

"She's what I like to call *intuitive*," I said. "She senses vibes from her surroundings. Like this house. All old houses, really."

I felt Beau looking at me but didn't say anything because he understood why I needed to protect my sister. She was young enough to be emotionally wounded by unwanted attention, even from someone as innocuous as Camille.

Camille stood behind Beau, blending into the scenery with her brown sweater and pants. Henry had been decked out in burgundy and plaid, his socks—no doubt washed and folded and put away by Camille—matching his shirt. She'd probably bought them for him and laid them out for him to wear.

She gave a little sniff and dabbed at her eyes with a wadded tissue, letting me know that Mimi must have told her everything. It was beyond my hope that Sarah hadn't been following the conversation. "So it was just a robbery? They killed Adele for her jewelry?"

"It's too soon to know," Beau said gently. He'd stood when Camille and Jolene had entered, and he remained standing.

"I need to let Henry know." Camille glanced around with the frantic look of a chipmunk avoiding an owl. Her monochromatic brown clothing meant that I would never be able to remove that analogy from my head. "Has anyone seen my phone?"

"Maybe you left it in the kitchen," I suggested. I wanted to add that it didn't matter; that Henry didn't seem the type to care one way or another that Adele had been confirmed dead and possibly been murdered.

She gave a quick nod of thanks, reminding me of a chipmunk again, and left the room with quick, silent steps.

My eyelids began to droop, either from the pain meds or from the weight of the recent revelations. Or, as my addled brain insisted, from Beau's emotions, which my body seemed to absorb. Which was ridiculous, considering that Beau and I weren't even what I'd call friends.

"Nola?" My eyes flickered open at the sound of Cooper's voice.

"Hmm?" I tried a smile, but only half of my mouth paid attention.

"I think I need to get you into bed."

"I hardly think I'm in any condition for that, but maybe later?" I listened in horror to my slurred words, wondering who had put them in my head and thought it okay to say them out loud.

Cooper made a strangled sound that could have been a laugh, and then another male voice—Beau's, I thought—said, "I'll help you."

"That's all right. I've got it." Cooper's voice sounded close to my ear, and then I felt gentle hands sliding beneath me. After the initial shock, I relaxed into him, feeling supported and comforted at the same time.

I nestled my face into his chest. "You smell good. Can I stay here all day?"

Cooper's chest rumbled against my cheek as he carried me out of the room, lights and faces passing in a blur through the slits of my drooping eyelids. I tried to raise my hand in farewell, but I managed only a slurred *"Byyeeeee."*

"Over here," Jolene said.

I smelled leather and old paper, and a distant memory of Mimi saying that she'd fixed up a bed in the library flashed through my head, along with an even older memory. I'd slept in a library before, when I was little—because I didn't know where my mom was and I didn't have a key to our apartment. I'd slept, huddled against a back shelf of thick volumes, until I'd been discovered and asked to leave. But this was different. I wasn't cold or scared, even when I'd felt Cooper lowering me onto a soft mattress and I had to leave the warmth of his arms.

"I'll go get extra blankets. She's really cold natured." Beau's voice again.

"I've got it," Cooper said, his voice close. "There's a pile here."

I felt the weight of a heavy blanket being placed on top of me. "There are more if you need them. I'll put one at the end of the bed to keep your feet warm. I know how you hate it when your toes get cold."

A tense undercurrent that had nothing to do with Adele or the evil spirit in the back of Cooper's car seemed to be circulating in the room. Whatever it was had its own energy, and I was too tired to acknowledge it, much less analyze it.

Gentle hands carefully lifted my leg beneath the covers and then slid pillows under my feet. "She needs to keep her foot elevated," came Jolene's voice. And then, closer to my face, she said, "I know you don't like sleeping on your back, but if I come back here and see you on your side and your foot off those pillows, there will be consequences." I tried to smile when I felt her kiss me softly on top of my head. "Sleep tight, and don't let the bedbugs bite."

Despite the soft mattress and warm blankets, there was definitely something missing. I let my hand fall to my side, touching only cool sheets. "Mardi," I managed.

"I'll get him," Cooper said.

"You don't have a car, and don't you have a plane to catch?" Beau's voice carried a note of smug satisfaction that I picked up on even in my extreme sleepiness. "I'll go get him and bring him back. I know where his food is kept, so I'll bring it, too."

"Don't forget his sweaters and bandannas," Jolene loudly whispered, as if I were asleep. "I've already packed his things in a little duffel bag for his trip to Mississippi. You might want to take out the Ole Miss football jersey, since he won't be needing it now. The bag has his monogram on it, so you can't miss it."

I stopped fighting to keep my eyes open and let them close completely, shutting off all light. The room might once have been the domain of a man whose benign spirit I'd encountered a few times, but at this point I doubted that anything would disturb my sleep even if all the restless spirits in New Orleans came to visit.

"Good-bye, Nola. I'll call as soon as I land." Cooper kissed me on the forehead, his lips lingering. I felt him straighten, sensed his absence before he'd stepped back.

Another familiar set of lips settled on the other side of my forehead. "Have a good rest," Beau said. "I'll be back shortly, with Mardi."

The room fell quiet before I heard the tapping of Jolene's heels, and then the flick of the light switch before the door softly snapped shut. And then, just before I fell into the oblivion of a drugged sleep, I imagined I could hear the soft humming of a woman's voice, the tune's words flitting past my drifting consciousness, the sound almost masking the soft footfalls of wet feet.

CHAPTER 21

When I awoke the house seemed to have fallen as silent as a mausoleum, the only light that of the streetlamps peering around the sides of the louvered blinds. My gaze skittered around the unfamiliar room, gradually becoming aware of a ticking sound from the small brass carriage clock on top of the mantel. Mardi's reassuring snores came from beside me, his warm weight pressed against me.

The memory of the sodden footsteps returned, along with a numbing fear. I wasn't afraid of Adele, I told myself. But I was terrified of the spirit that I'd seen in the rearview mirror before I'd crashed the car.

I tried to sit up, suddenly alert to an uncomfortable pressure in my bladder, but managed only to wedge my head and neck into an awkward position against the headboard. I recalled, in my semi-lucid state, Jolene placing a silver bell on a small table by the side of the bed, with instructions to ring it if I required assistance. I turned my head and spotted the glint of a reflection of the slender light from the window, highlighting the just-out-of-reach bell.

A noise like that of an animal rustling in the trash came from outside my door. The image of the creepy baby doll moving stealthily toward me on its stiff hands and knees left me paralyzed. I held my breath, wanting to hide my presence, but my heart hammered loudly enough to block out the soft ticking of the clock. Using my elbows, I inched my shoulders higher on the headboard, being careful not to dislodge my splinted leg from the stack of pillows it rested on. In desperation, and needing to draw a breath, I threw my hand out toward the bell. My fingers brushed the cold metal, knocking it from the table, causing it to crash to the floor with a sharp clang.

Mardi lifted his head as the door flew open and the blinding overhead light snapped on. "Get out!" I shouted, hoping the anger in my voice hid the terror.

"Nola, it's me. Beau."

The overhead light shut off right before the bedside light flipped on, revealing his familiar face, albeit with bed head and chin stubble. Although I'd need to have my feet held over a fire to admit it out loud, I'd never been so happy to see anyone in my entire life.

"Beau," I managed.

"Are you okay?" He touched my face with both hands before moving them down to my shoulders, his eyes doing a check of the rest of me, his concern turning my insides into warm putty.

"I heard something, and then I knocked over my bell trying to ring it."

He returned the bell to the table, a sheepish grin spreading across his face. "That was probably me. I set my pillow and blankets up on the floor outside your door so I could hear you if you needed anything."

"You were sleeping on the floor?"

"Yeah. I drew the short straw."

All the warm feelings I'd had moments before evaporated. "Just remember that at no point did I ask you to sleep on the floor, so don't try to bring that up later in an argument. Where's Jolene?"

"She took Sarah back to your apartment to sleep. Not to hurt your feelings or anything, but Sarah didn't appear to be disappointed."

"I'm sure." I tried to sit up a little further, but my bladder made it clear that no unnecessary movements should be made if I didn't want to embarrass myself. "What about Mimi and Camille?"

He glanced at the clock on the mantel. "It's three twenty in the morning, so I'm guessing they're both asleep upstairs."

"Where you probably should be." I looked at him closely. "You look terrible."

"Thanks for that, Nola. Today was one of the worst days of my life, so it's not entirely surprising."

"I'm sorry. I wasn't . . ." I shook my head, as if trying to rewind and start over. "What I meant to say is that I know losing a mother is tough. So if you ever need someone . . ." I gave him a one-shoulder shrug.

"Says the woman who still hasn't forgiven me for saving her from a fire."

"To the man who could have saved my guitar while I saved myself. I didn't ask to be saved, remember. By you or anyone."

"How could I forget? You remind me often enough. Maybe you can needlepoint it on a pillow and give it to me for Christmas just to make sure I remember." He dropped down onto the edge of my bed, my bladder shifting uncomfortably. "So. How are you? Really."

I might have still been feeling the effects of the painkillers, because my filters switched off and I began unloading my semi-dormant brain. "I'm conflicted. There's definitely something between Cooper and me, but I can't commit to anything because I really don't need the complications of a relationship in my life right now, not to mention that there's that angry woman who hangs around him. Who, according to Sarah, isn't dead, whatever that means. Then there's you, but we don't particularly like each other, and you're as good as engaged to Sam. I keep telling myself that I'm totally happy spending my energies on my day job and on the renovation of my house, but I'm not convinced. Maybe I feel like I'm cutting myself off from possibilities? Who knows? I would also like to find out what happened to your parents, and why your mom hasn't left yet, and solve the mystery of the lady at the Esplanade house who smells like Youth-Dew perfume and feels the need to protect the ghost boy—and anyone else, really—from the evil guy who tried to kill me. Except I can't do any of that without you, and I think it's best that we don't spend too much time together, *youknowwhatImean*? Of course, I don't know how that will work, since we're working together, doing the murder-house-flip thing, but we're both adults. I'm sure we can figure it out. And thanks for bringing Mardi."

It seemed as if he was trying not to laugh. He scratched himself behind an ear, just like Mardi. "I meant, how are you physically?"

The residual painkillers in my system did nothing to lessen my embarrassment. "Except for the ankle, I'm fine. A little shaken up, but otherwise okay."

"Understandable. What about Cooper?"

"Shaken up, too, but I think he's okay. It hasn't changed his mind about the Esplanade house, if that's what you're thinking. Although he's going to need your help cleaning out the negative energies."

"I'm going to ask Uncle Bernie for a little insight into that case. He can at least go through the police files for a fresh look."

"Good idea," I said, yawning, the movement reminding me that my bladder was at full capacity.

I turned at the creak and pop of old wood outside the door. "Is anyone there?" I whispered loudly.

"No," Beau answered, without bothering to look. "You know the drill. Old houses aren't authentic unless the floors creak. When the weather turns cold it's worse."

I wanted to mention the sound of squelching footsteps I'd heard earlier, but I couldn't be sure that it hadn't been the painkillers. "Do you think Felicity will stick around after the funeral? At least until you have answers?"

"Probably not," Felicity said as she pushed through the open door. Her feet were bare, but she'd thrown on jeans and a sweater. Static made pale hair strands undulate around her face like a Dr. Seuss character and made her appear much younger than she was. "We're really busy at work and I don't think I can take more time off, or I probably would." She closed the door behind her without latching it. "Sorry to interrupt, but it sounded like a couple of angry raccoons wrestling over a garbage can in here, so I decided to come down and investigate. I'm glad Mimi was able to sleep through it, but I thought Camille or Henry would beat me to it. I'm a little slow moving when I first wake up."

"Me, too." Beau's palms rasped against his unshaven cheeks.

"I'm glad to see you," I said. "I, uh . . ."

She held up her hand. "I get it. Beau, if you can help Nola out of bed, I can get her to the bathroom across the hall."

I sent her a grateful smile as Beau pulled me up with an exaggerated groan, which I ignored. Despite her petiteness, Felicity had no problem with me leaning on her as I hopped my way across the room after brushing away Beau's offer of help. "I got this," she said. "I work for an auction house where there's a lot of lifting and moving, so I've got major muscles. I've definitely lifted heavier crates."

"Thanks," I said. "You've got that Beau thing where compliments and insults are indistinguishable."

"Must be hereditary," Beau said with a grin. "But if you're good, I'm going to go make myself a snack. I'll ask Mardi if he wants to come with me, and I'll bring something back in case anyone else is hungry. Just give me a shout if you need me."

"Got it." Felicity didn't look up as she continued to propel me toward the bathroom.

With a nod toward where my jeans had been slit from the ankle to the knee, she said, "I guess you passed out before Jolene could change you into more comfortable clothes." She grimaced. "I hope those weren't your favorite jeans."

"They were. Which was probably why Jolene chose them for alterations. Not that it matters. It doesn't look like I'll be wearing normal clothes for a while."

"You'll manage. You seem the type of person who doesn't allow setbacks to become permanent."

I looked at her. "Me? I would say the same about you."

She shrugged. "Maybe. Michael says that you and I are a lot alike."

"Does he? And I was about to say that you and I should be friends. But only if you don't bring Michael up again."

"Sore spot, huh?" She opened the bathroom door to allow me in first.

"Seriously? Has he told you about our relationship?"

"I know enough."

"Great. Then you know why you should avoid mentioning his name in my presence."

"Deal—as long as you don't ask if I'm psychic. Everybody keeps asking me—and, for the record, I'm not. I'm totally fine with that, since seeing dead people would probably scare the crap out of me. I wasn't raised believing that sort of thing was normal."

"That's because it's not."

Felicity's movements were quick and efficient, and I was too relieved by not having to ask Beau for bathroom help to be embarrassed. As she was propping me up so I could wash and dry my hands, I asked, "Who do you mean by 'everybody'?"

"Mimi, Beau." Felicity held open the door as I hopped out of the bathroom. "Camille. I take it she and Adele were really close."

"They were best friends from childhood until Adele disappeared, and Camille blames herself for suggesting that Adele go look for Buddy—which is probably why she wants to talk to Adele. To ask for forgiveness, I guess."

Felicity snorted. "Forgiveness is overrated. All that really matters is learning how to live with yourself, and the rest will follow. I'm obviously still struggling with that, since I've been living in New York and pretending I don't have two families here in New Orleans. But I'm here right now, and that means I'm making progress, right?"

Despite her being Beau's sister, I decided that we could definitely be friends. But maybe that was the painkillers talking. I should have learned from the Sunny Ryan–imposter fiasco and practiced being less open and accepting.

"I'm sorry about your mom," I said, trying to bear as much of my weight as possible as I leaned against her while hopping across the hall.

"Me, too. I wish I could remember Adele and Buddy. From what Mimi has told me, they were both great people and great parents. I know Beau has a different take on them—which is fair, I guess. I wasn't the one left behind." Felicity pushed open the door to the library and allowed me to enter ahead of her.

"That's not really—" I let out a small shout. Highlighted in the glow of the overhead light as my gaze settled on the chair in front of the desk, the creepy baby doll, with her bonnet askew, sat perched on the worn leather, leaning drunkenly to the side while her blue eyes stared straight at me. I whipped around to face Felicity. "I thought you took that to Beau's truck!"

"I did. I don't know how—"

Beau burst into the room, followed by Mardi, with crumbs on his snout, an open bag of Zapp's Spicy Cajun Crawtator chips in Beau's hand. "Is everything okay?" His gaze followed Felicity's to the chair. He marched over to the desk and snatched up the doll. "I should burn it."

I was inclined to agree, but Felicity spoke up. "I'm kind of new to this, but don't you think there's a reason it keeps showing up? Like, maybe somebody's trying to tell you something?"

"Well, yeah . . ." Beau began. "But it's creeping me out now, too, and I'm not easily scared."

Felicity brought me over to the bed and gently helped me sit and prop my leg up. "Again, I'm not the expert here, but it seems to me that if a person is trying to tell you something from beyond the grave, you should listen."

I sent Beau a pointed glare. "Imagine that." Turning back to Felicity, I said, "So, if someone who *could* speak with the dead kept getting phone calls from the spirit realm, the person should listen, right?"

"Obviously. Unless the person has a really good reason not to. Although I can't think of any, because when it comes down to it, there will always be a choice about what to do with the information given. Just like in, well, normal conversations." She looked between me and Beau. "Unless I'm missing something here?"

"That's something you'll need to discuss with Beau."

The muffled vocals from ABBA's "The Name of the Game" rang out. Felicity reached into her back pocket to retrieve her phone. "Spam," she said, ending the call. "I figured either that or Michael. He's texted and called a few times today, and I haven't had a chance to get back to him. He was probably just checking to make sure I hadn't changed my mind about returning to New York."

"Have you?" Beau asked.

Felicity stilled, her eyes steely. "We agreed—remember? I'm here, and that's all I've got for now. I feel like I'm being pulled in half, and it's going to take time for me to figure out who I am, because I honestly don't know anymore."

Needing to cut the tension that seemed to bounce off the room's walls and swing from the ceiling, I indicated her phone. "So, you're an ABBA fan?"

"Isn't everyone?" she asked. "I mean, they're one of the most accomplished and talented musical groups ever. I get teased a lot, but whatever. It got me into a lot of trouble in boarding school, but it taught me how to throw a solid punch so that people would keep their stupid opinions to themselves."

Felicity wasn't much taller than five feet, and Jolene had described her as "a tiny slip of a girl." I couldn't imagine her getting into a fight, much less winning one. I decided to keep that to myself.

"ABBA's incredible," Beau said. "Even though she hates to admit it, Nola's also a fan."

"Cool," said Felicity. "You would know about good music, Nola. I actually loved that jingle Beau told me you wrote for Apple—even before I knew it was yours. And that song you wrote for pop legend Jimmy Gordon is on my playlist. I keep waiting for another one. Please tell me you're working on something?"

I looked down at the shredded denim of my once-favorite jeans. "I've started." I didn't mention that I couldn't get beyond the first line. It was hard enough admitting my failure to myself, much less out loud. "It's just . . ."

When I didn't finish, Felicity said, "Believe me, I get it. Life throws us curveballs sometimes. You'll get through it. You have too much talent not to. Beau was saying that a lot of the music venues on Frenchmen Street have open mic nights and that he thinks you should give it a try. We both agree that it's the perfect way to get back into your music, to sort of test out the waters and find your voice again."

I wanted to say thanks for her kind words, but I was too surprised that Beau had talked about me and had mentioned my curtailed music career. He studiously avoided my gaze, so our embarrassment was mutual. "I'll think about it" was all I could manage. I looked at the clock on the mantel. "It's after four in the morning. We should probably all go back to sleep."

Beau shoved his hands into his pockets, then looked surprised as he pulled out something in a plastic bag. "I forgot I had these."

I couldn't see what was inside, but I knew what they were without asking.

"Adele's rings?" Felicity asked.

Beau nodded. "I meant to put them in a safe-deposit box, but Mimi said she wants to hold them first. She just wasn't ready."

"Mimi told me about her gift," Felicity said. "When she was asking me if I had any sort of psychic abilities. She almost seemed relieved when I told her I didn't. I'm guessing her readings can be pretty traumatic."

"Trust me," Beau said. "Nobody sane asks to be psychic—and those delusional enough to ask probably don't know how it will affect their entire lives. I know I won't be able to stop Mimi from wanting to put her hands on these rings, but seeing what most likely were the final moments in the life of a woman she loved like a daughter . . ." Beau stopped. "I'm not even sure she should do it, but I don't think I could stop her. Maybe you and I should sit this one out." He looked at his sister. "Sometimes not knowing is better."

Felicity lifted her pointed pixie chin. "I get it, and I won't hold it against you if you don't want to be there. But I will be. I think Mimi will want one of us next to her." She stepped closer to Beau. "Can I see? I didn't get a good look at the coroner's office." She cupped one hand under the other and held them up to Beau. I listened to the platinum bands clinking against each other as they slid out of the bag. Using her thumb and index finger, Felicity held the wedding band close to her face to read the inscription. "'The past is never past; our love is eternal as time.'" She swiped at her eyes with a knuckle. "I'm not crying—I don't cry. But that's heartbreaking. I hope these weren't the reason she was killed. Because that would make her death even more pointless."

"I agree." Beau held out his hand for the rings. "We'll know for sure as soon as Mimi can get a reading on them. I think I'll keep them at Sam's until then. The bank's closed tomorrow, and with so many people coming in and out of the house to pay their respects, I'd feel better leaving them at Sam's. Her building has great security, and she's got a safe in her closet." He glanced at his watch. "And since it's almost time to wake up, I might as well take these over there now."

"What about Buddy?" Felicity asked, her voice barely audible.

"What do you mean?" Beau stared at his sister.

"Could he have done something . . ."

"No." They both looked at me. "I'm sorry. It's not my place to voice an opinion here. Camille suggested the same thing, but I can't believe it. I won't. Everything I've heard about your parents tells me that they loved each other and that your father would never have hurt your mother. I don't have any evidence either way. It's just . . ." I shrugged. "It's a gut feeling. My dad's always told me to trust my gut, and he's always been right about that. And Madame Zoe believes that Buddy is in danger. Which means that we need to find him. Soon. There's a reason why he hasn't returned, but we won't know until he's found."

Beau shook his head. "What if we find him and discover that he just didn't want to come back?"

Felicity put her hand on Beau's arm. "Then we'll know. And we can go on from there."

My ankle had begun to throb, distracting me from thinking about Beau and Sam and their missing father and their murdered mother. I was almost glad to feel a physical pain so that I could ignore all of it. "If it's not too much trouble, I could use another pain pill. I already skipped a dose, and I'm beginning to see stars."

"On it," Felicity said. "I'll go get you a fresh glass of water from the kitchen. Be right back."

I said good night to Beau while faking a huge yawn before leaning back against the pillows to wait. My eyelids drooped with exhaustion, but the pain in my ankle kept me from drifting off. When I was on the brink of passing out, my eyes snapped open and my gaze met that of the baby doll perched on the desk chair.

"Beau?" I called out, just in case he hadn't left yet. I mentally measured the distance to the desk and to the doorway of the library. With a soft groan, I pulled myself up using the wall and the side table, grabbed the creepy baby by her foot, and then hopped to the doorway. "Beau?" I called again, keeping my voice down so as not to wake everyone upstairs.

Except for the ticking of a multitude of clocks, and the faint noises from Felicity in the kitchen, the house remained quiet. I looked back at the side table where I'd left my phone, dismissing the thought of retrieving it as soon as it crossed my mind. My ankle felt as if it had been lit on fire, and I knew it would take the last of my strength to propel myself back to bed.

I turned in the doorway, mentally preparing for the hop back, then stopped. A floorboard creaked somewhere in the dark hallway behind me, the sound as sharp and loud as the crack of a rifle. I held my breath, listening for the sound of a footstep. Or the soft expulsion of a breath. But only the gentle ticking of the clocks filled the void, the absence of any other sound making it somehow more unnerving.

Feeling unseen eyes on me, I dropped the doll in the hallway, hearing a satisfying thunk when it landed on the wooden floor, and continued on my way back to the bed. It didn't matter where I put the doll. By morning it would have found its way to wherever it thought it needed to be.

CHAPTER 22

I awoke to the familiar smell of coffee and hot muffins and briefly thought that I was back in my apartment. But the absence of the hot, furry weight of Mardi, coupled with the throbbing pain in my leg, was an unpleasant reminder of why I wasn't.

"Good morning, sleepyhead," came Jolene's voice, along with the sound of rattling china, followed by the happy noise of coffee being poured into a cup.

My eyes shot open, focusing on the red of Jolene's hair and then moving down to the steaming cup she held in front of her. *"Mbmmmg."*

"She's never coherent before she has her coffee," Jolene said.

I shifted my gaze to see Mimi standing next to her and holding a plate with a muffin on it.

"Come help me sit her up," Jolene said to a large silhouette standing behind Mimi that I thought could be Beau or Henry. Not that I was happy to see either one of them first thing, but I'd have preferred Beau over Henry, hands down.

"I'll go find her brush," Sarah said, coming into view. "Her hair looks like a rat's nest."

I recognized Beau's scent before I saw his head looming over me as he and Jolene gently raised me to a sitting position and stacked pillows behind me, being careful to keep my leg elevated.

I heard the smile in Jolene's voice. "You're learning quickly, Sarah. A lot faster than your sister, although she does try, bless her heart."

"Mbbbbbbg," I mumbled, reaching for the coffee and smiling my thanks to Mimi as she placed the muffin on the table by my chair.

They all watched as I sipped my coffee, waiting for some of the caffeine to reach my bloodstream.

"Where's Mardi?" I said, my brain working hard to enunciate. I hadn't had my second cup of coffee yet.

"Henry is allergic to dogs, I'm afraid," Mimi said.

"Almost as allergic as he is to work," Beau added.

"You hush now, Beau," Mimi admonished. "Henry is my guest, and he's asked that Mardi not stay here. I'm sure we can find someone to keep him for now. We're keeping him in the kitchen, which he doesn't seem to mind, and that's a room Henry avoids."

"There are lots of hotels in New Orleans," Beau said. "I'm sure Henry would be comfortable in any one of them."

"Now, Beau," Mimi said, the softness of her tone doing nothing to mitigate the implied warning to behave.

"Mardi can come with me to Mississippi," Jolene said. "He had so much fun on our last visit. He sure gave Daddy's huntin' dogs a run for their money. Although they did seem to mock him for his wardrobe choices, which I found ill-mannered."

I wasn't sure if she was serious. "Thanks, Jolene. But I would prefer to have him with me. I guess you could say he's my emotional support animal."

"I understand," Mimi said. "Maybe if we keep Mardi in here and don't let him anywhere else, Henry won't mind." She tucked a strand of hair behind my ear. "Your color's a lot better than yesterday, and that's a good sign. Camille will be here any minute now with your pain meds and a fresh pitcher of lemon-infused water. She thought you might like it."

I didn't enjoy lemon in my water, but it was nice of Camille. "I appreciate that." I tried to move my foot and winced at the bolt of pain that shot up my leg. "And I'd like to hold off on the pain meds for now. I'm going to try to make it until the next dose."

"That's not recommended," Camille said as she entered the room. "Pain can contribute to stress and other negative emotional states, like anxiety. And unnecessary stress not only lowers your pain threshold but can also reduce pain tolerance and impact the immune system." She looked around apologetically. "Sorry. My mother was a nurse, so I picked up on a few things. Feel free to ignore me." She placed the pitcher and pill bottles on the table before stepping back.

"Don't be silly, Camille," Mimi said. She picked up one of the bottles, then looked through the bottom of her bifocals to read the dosage before dumping two small blue pills on her palm. "You've been more than helpful, and I know Nola appreciates it as much as I do."

Mimi handed me a glass of water with the two pills and watched as I took them. "Camille is making her mother's chicken soup, and it smells divine. I hope there's enough for me."

Camille's cheeks pinkened. "Of course, and if there isn't I'll just make more. But I made enough to feed a small army. Jolene said that Nola has a large appetite, so I made sure to double the recipe. Speaking of which, I need to go check on the stove."

As soon as she left, Sarah sat down next to me on the bed. On the other side of the room, Mimi and Jolene were having a conversation with Beau about food for the post-funeral reception, allowing Sarah and me to have a private moment.

She reached up and snagged something from my chin. "Muffin crumbs. Has anyone ever told you that you eat like a toddler?"

"Many times," I said. "And so do you." I plucked a crumb from her cheek. "It must run in the family."

She didn't laugh or even smile.

"What's up, Smatchen?" I asked, using the childhood nickname I'd bestowed on her and that I still used when she was acting like a small, irritable child.

"We're not alone," she whispered.

I knew better than to say that I knew Mimi, Beau, and Jolene were with us.

"Anyone I know?"

She gave a quick nod. "Beau's grandfather. He hangs out mostly around his portrait in the foyer. He likes to keep an eye on his family. He's a nice ghost."

"Okay. Anyone else?"

Sarah didn't respond right away. "There are a couple of spirits who are always around the doll. One is a nice lady who smiles a lot. She smells like Grandma Amelia, so I think she wears the same perfume." She pressed her lips together tightly, like a person who's afraid to say something out loud.

"And the other one?" I asked.

She wore a pinched expression, as if each word hurt as she spoke it. "He's not a nice man."

"Has he spoken to you?"

She gave a quick shake of her head, her face visibly paler. "No. He's very strong. And dark. I don't want to open myself to him. I think he wants to hurt people." Her fear had thinned her voice, making it high-pitched and reedy. "There's a little boy here sometimes, too. He wears old-fashioned clothes and a weird hat. He's the one who keeps moving the doll."

I looked at her sharply. "Did he tell you why?"

"He doesn't know. The man—the bad guy—wants to keep the doll hidden, which is why the boy keeps moving it even though the nice lady told him not to." She leaned closer, her voice so quiet that it almost disappeared. "The doll is part of a big secret, and the other two don't want anyone to know about it."

"Does he know what the secret is?"

"No. But the man really scares me. Please don't make me stay here. I don't want to go home yet, either. The little boy is stuck and needs my help."

I sighed. "Is there anyone else?"

"Adele's here," whispered Sarah. "She's really clear to me. Like, much better than before. I think because Beau and I are here together. And you know what Mom says when she and Jayne get together."

"'We're stronger together,'" I said, repeating the mantra I'd heard Melanie and Aunt Jayne and their mother, Ginny, say whenever they joined forces to combat less-than-friendly ghosts.

"Is she saying anything?"

Sarah shook her head. "She's waiting for Beau to notice her. He's pretending that she's not here, but he knows." She was silent for a moment, as if listening to something—or someone—that I couldn't hear. "Is Felicity upstairs?"

"I think so. She was up with me pretty late last night, so she's probably still sleeping. Why?"

"When she and Beau and I are all together, everything is very . . . 'crisp,' I think, is the word. Like, there's a veil between us and the other place, and it's sometimes pretty thick, but it wasn't yesterday when we were all here."

"I get that, except Felicity doesn't have any psychic abilities. At least that's what she says, and I believe her."

Sarah shrugged. "Maybe she doesn't know." She looked at me intently. "But that's why I don't want to stay here. The veil is very thin in this house. I think I make it too easy for the spirits to come through. Both kinds of spirits." Her eyes widened. "I can't help the little boy if I'm scared. And he really needs my help."

A quick knock on the doorframe was followed by Christopher's face peeking around the corner. "Are you okay with two more visitors?"

From the look on Jolene's face, she would have preferred to have more time to make me presentable, and I needed more time to become coherent. "Just give us a moment . . ." I began.

"The more the merrier," said Beau simultaneously. Trevor held a large, almost-flat rectangular item inexpertly wrapped with newspaper and tied up with a shoestring that had a bow at the top. Studying my bed head, Beau said, "Don't be scared. The accident wrecked more than just the car and her ankle."

Trevor let out a large snort of laughter but stopped when he caught Christopher's expression. I was glad that Jolene had removed the bandage from my forehead. She'd said that the wound there was just superficial and that the bandage would impede her ability to apply makeup to my face. At the very least, I wouldn't scare Trevor.

The young boy approached the bed, holding out the package. "This is for you. I fixed it up all by myself."

Christopher cleared his throat.

"Most of it," Trevor amended. "Go on. Open it. I can help if you need me."

"That would be great—thanks."

He didn't hesitate to rip into the newspaper, shredding it in three swipes and revealing a highly polished wooden backgammon board with intricate inlays around the edges, the triangles hand-painted and outlined with slivers of ivory. "It's stunning," I said. "You did a beautiful job refinishing it."

Trevor took it from my hand and flipped it over. "And this side is for chess or checkers, in case you get bored with backgammon."

"He did all of the sanding, staining, and polishing himself," Christopher said. "I just did some of the sanding in the trickier spots on the chess pieces. And Cooper gave us the idea."

"Yeah," Trevor said. "Cooper said you liked backgammon, so when I saw this at a garage sale me and Christopher was at—"

Christopher cleared his throat again, making Trevor roll his eyes. "Christopher and I. I bought it for a quarter, figurin' I could fix it up for free. It's suppose' to be for Christmas, but since you got hurt I thought you might could use it now. The pieces ain't gonna match, 'cause I'm having to search more junk shops and stuff, but I think that's cool."

I flipped through the torn pieces of paper on my lap. "The playing pieces?"

"I'm still workin' on 'em." He crossed his arms and frowned. "That dumb Henry say—"

Christopher placed a firm hand on Trevor's shoulder. "Remember what I said about calling people derogatory names, Trevor." To me he said, "Henry suggested that Trevor wait until he has all the pieces before giving them to you. That way he could make sure that the finish matched even if the pieces didn't. But I agree with Trevor that mismatched pieces add to the charm of the set."

" 'Cause he jealous I be better at math, and I tell him when he's wrong, like every time, in front of customers. That's why they like me better than him."

Sarah had begun brushing my hair, my eyes watering as she pulled the brush through the snarls, but I could still see Christopher's face as he mouthed, *It's true.*

"Thank you, Trevor. It's beautiful. I will enjoy looking at it until you finish the pieces. It will give me something to look forward to."

He grinned his winning smile, and it was clear why customers liked him.

"All right, young man," Christopher said. "We got to get you to school."

"Aw, man . . ." Trevor began, but Christopher was already guiding him out of the room by the shoulders.

"Since it's present time, I've got something for you, too." Jolene ducked out of the room before returning with a bright blue knee scooter. "Mary Alice at work broke her ankle last year and still had this, so she said we could borrow it for as long as we needed. Dr. Longo said you needed to wait until you get your boot on to use it, but I thought having it ready would remind you that you're getting better every day."

"I put the basket on," Trevor said from the doorway, " 'cause I know you like to tote stuff."

"And he only charged me twenty dollars," Jolene said, her smile not dipping. "I paid extra because it has flowers on it. And I added the pretty streamers on the handlebars. I got the sparkly kind so people can see you coming. I'm also making a monogrammed cushion, which should be finished before I head to Mississippi tomorrow."

"Oh, my gosh. What's today? Shouldn't you have already left?"

"It's Tuesday. And of course I couldn't leave. Not while you need tending to. Mama understands. She was fixin' to come here herself, but I said that between Mimi and me we got it covered."

"I feel terrible. I know how much you were looking forward to being home all week."

Jolene leaned over to fluff the pillows behind me, the fresh smell of her gardenia perfume pleasantly calming. "Please don't feel bad. I'll be home for turkey and sweet potato casserole and my grandmama's famous Jell-O salad. I'd bring some back for you, but there's never any left, so I'll have to make it for you when I get back. It probably doesn't travel well anyway."

"Wow. I can't say I've ever had Jell-O salad, but I'll look forward to it." I turned to Sarah, who seemed to be trying very hard to be inconspicuous by curling up on the floor in the desk's knee hole. "I need to come up with a story to tell Melanie and Jack about why Sarah needs to fly home early."

"I don't want to go home yet," came a small voice from beneath the desk. "Why can't I go with Jolene? I can chaperone her and Jaxson."

"You read too much Jane Austen, Sarah, and you can't go to Mississippi without me. Melanie is already going to throw a fit when she finds out about the accident, so let's not feed the fire by telling her that I sent you to have Thanksgiving with strangers."

"We're not strangers. We're not even that strange," Jolene said. "Well, except for Great-aunt Marvella, who threatens to take off her clothes and take her walker around the neighborhood if Alabama wins the Iron Bowl. And Cousin—"

"That's not what I meant," I said, interrupting her before she could really get going on her excessively leafy family tree. "I'm sure your family is . . ." I wasn't sure how to characterize a family whose members included a funeral director who only drove cars with trunks deep enough to carry seven bodies along with the shovels needed to bury them. However, the McKennas had somehow created Jolene, one of the most complex and wonderful people I'd ever met. "Lovely," I finished. "But Melanie will never allow Sarah to come visit again if I let her out of my sight. And we can't stay here and take advantage of Mimi's hospitality. That might set Melanie's hair on fire faster than if I let Sarah go to Mississippi."

Mimi took my empty cup and refilled it before returning it to me. "You are both welcome to stay here as long as you like. Although I do insist that you tell Melanie and Jack the truth, Nola. Don't make me call them myself."

With her gray hair tucked neatly into a bun at the back of her head, and with her matronly dress, pearls, and sensible shoes, Mimi looked like pretty much everybody's idea of a grandmother. Except, of course, for the mismatched eyes that hinted at her psychic abilities and didn't hide her will of steel. She had suffered through a great deal in her lifetime but hadn't let her losses define her. That was one of the things I admired about her. And why it was so easy for us to fall into the roles of granddaughter and grandmother.

"I will—I promise. As soon as they get back from the cooking competition with JJ next Sunday. I really don't want to ruin it for him. I'm in no danger, so there's no need for them to panic and fly here. They would, too. They'd immediately drop everything, which wouldn't be fair to JJ. So let's wait, okay? In the meantime, I need to figure out another living arrangement. I can't invade your home indefinitely, and over a holiday. Not to mention Adele's funeral. It's too much. I appreciate the offer, but I can't justify taking advantage of your hospitality."

"You're not taking advantage, Nola. I hope you realize that we consider you part of the family," Mimi said. "You and Sarah are more than welcome to stay as long as you need. Besides, I have Camille and Henry here to help me."

On top of Sarah's desperate plea to leave, the mention of Henry was enough to convince me that I couldn't stay. Trevor and I were in agreement on Camille's husband. It wasn't as if I knew Henry well enough to dislike him. It was more that what I did know convinced me that I didn't need to get to know him better.

"I know," I said, "but I couldn't sleep thinking about WWMD."

Mimi's thin gray eyebrows rose in question.

"'What would Melanie do?'" Sarah explained. "It's something my dad taught us to say before we did anything. It made life easier. And sometimes it even made sense."

"Especially as I've gotten older," I said, thinking about the spreadsheets I now used to organize my life. "It's an acquired thing, I think."

"I see," Mimi said slowly, although I wasn't sure she did. "But I can't think of where you could possibly go until you're mobile again. You don't even get your boot for at least two weeks."

"I've been thinking about it. Honestly, it makes sense that I should go back to my apartment and my own bed. You've made this room so comfortable, and I do appreciate it, but I think the familiarity of being home will speed up my recovery. I'm a runner, so my quads are pretty strong, which means that hopping up the steps on one leg won't be a problem, and I'll only have to do it once."

"She's got a point," Beau interjected, making me think that he also didn't consider relying on assistance from Henry a solid plan. "I could help haul you up the stairs, Nola, but leaving you alone in the apartment doesn't sound like a good idea."

I frowned at his use of the word "haul," but I decided to let it go so I could make my point. "I won't be alone—I'll have Mardi."

Sarah crawled out from under the desk. "And I can be there to help! And to take Mardi for walks. Then I can stay until Jolene gets back from Mississippi."

"I could make enough casseroles to stick in the freezer to last for a month," Jolene said. "Maybe more than that. You do have a healthy appetite, Nola."

I began to have a sense of what Caesar must have felt like when his friends betrayed him, but I could see Mimi's resolve wavering, so I let the insult slide. "Now that I have the scooter, I can make my way from room to room—very carefully until I get my boot. It's all wood floors in the apartment, and I'm sure Jolene won't mind rolling up the area rugs for the time being."

Mimi smoothed her hands on her lap, her fingers empty of rings. "I suppose that might work. But I must insist on being allowed to visit to make sure you're all right."

"Of course," Sarah and I said at the same time.

Beau's phone rang. "Excuse me a minute. It's Thibaut."

I could hear Thibaut's voice but couldn't understand what he was saying, but the frown on Beau's face made me worry that something bad was happening with my house again. I never envisioned that I'd have such a love-hate relationship with an inanimate structure. It had certainly chosen me, but sometimes I couldn't help but feel as if it had a questionable sense of humor, combined with a mean streak. To make me feel better after the recent roof fiasco, Jolene had started to use design software to plan the furnishing of the house. I hadn't even minded that she'd added labels like Jolene's Kitchen, Mardi's Wardrobe Closet, and Nola's Beauty Space. But now, listening to Beau and Thibaut on the phone, I began to wonder if any of it would ever become a reality.

When Beau ended the call, he wasn't smiling.

I felt bile rise in the back of my throat. "What is it now? Did the foundation split? Chimney collapse? Roof catch fire?"

"Not at your house, if that's any consolation."

"Is it the house on Esplanade?" Mimi asked.

Beau nodded. "Yeah."

I struggled to hide my relief. I had painstakingly reglazed each and every window in my Creole cottage, and my fingers almost bled from the memory. Not that I wanted anything to happen to the house on Esplanade, but we hadn't even begun the renovation yet, so there was a lot less to lose.

Beau continued. "Apparently that da—that doll showed up on the porch this morning, and when Thibaut entered the front door, the windows in the upstairs camelback addition blew out like a freak tornado. Jorge was so scared he left his toolbox and drove off in his truck."

My eyes met Sarah's, and I knew we were both thinking about the doll and its hidden secret.

He walked over to where Mimi sat and took her hand. "Could you and Felicity meet with the funeral director without me? I need to find out what's going on."

"You can't go alone, Beau." I had managed to forget that I had a broken ankle and had made like I was going to stand before Sarah tugged on my arm to hold me back.

"You're right," he said. "I'll take Sam."

"But . . ." I'd been about to say *But we're a team*, but I let the words dissolve on my tongue. Instead, I said, "Could you FaceTime with me when you get there? I need to assess how bad the damage is so I can tell Cooper."

"Sure." He looked uncomfortable, his eyes avoiding mine. "There's one more thing he told me."

I braced myself. "Yeah?"

"When they pulled up the rug in the upstairs room, it, um . . ." He scratched the back of his neck. "It revealed a large rusty stain. It could be paint. Or it could be . . . something else. They're going to get it analyzed. I called Uncle Bernie to see if he could put a rush on it. I know it's a cold case, but what happened in your car makes it urgent. Not that I can explain that to the police."

"Because it might affect your ability to sell the house to Cooper, or anyone else."

He met my eyes briefly. "Of course. This is our first murder-house flip. It needs to be a success if we want to make it into a viable project for a TV series—or for Mimi to invest in another house."

I wasn't sure what I'd hoped his motivation was, but his answer wasn't what I wanted to hear. "Right. So, the bloodstain on the floor was discovered upstairs, and not in the room where Sybil was found? According to Joan Wenzel, there was lots of blood in Sybil's room. She said they had to throw out the rug and bedclothes because there was so much. But nobody said anything about the upstairs room."

"Which could be why the bloodstain upstairs was missed," Beau said, his eyes serious. "The detectives at the time weren't looking for it."

Sarah's phone, in her purse, began to ring with an old-fashioned landline ringtone. She gave me a panicked look before pulling it out and holding it to her ear.

I couldn't hear a voice on the other end of the line, only a hollow *whoosh* sound like air moving through a pneumatic tube leading to nowhere. Sarah's eyes widened as she listened, sharp pops and crackles leaking from her phone along with what I had at first thought might be an errant wind. The sound unwound itself, materializing note by note, until I recognized the song. "Rolling in the Deep."

A thick leather-bound book flew off one of the shelves lining the wall, landing on its spine with its pages splayed like the wings of a felled bird. Sarah's phone dropped the call, the eerie song silenced as we looked at each other.

Jolene picked up the book from the floor, carefully keeping it open to the page where it had landed. "It's the Holy Bible. Not sure how it could have fallen like that, but the binding isn't broken, thank goodness—although the spine is creased, so it looks like someone really enjoys the book of Luke." She tried to smile.

Mimi took the Bible from Jolene and stared at the page as if waiting for it to speak to her. After a long moment, she replaced the Bible on the shelf and turned toward us. "I have a lot of details to take care of for the funeral and reception, so if you will excuse me . . ." On her way out of the room, she paused by the bed to kiss the top of my head. "Maybe it's a good thing that you're going back to your apartment now."

I regarded her closely, waiting for an explanation, but she turned to go. She'd barely made it out of the room when my phone began to vibrate and ring with "Rolling in the Deep." Mimi kept going even when her own phone began to play the same tune. I opened my mouth to call her back, only to become suddenly aware that the temperature in the room had plummeted, my breath swallowing the unspoken words in one single ghostly wisp.

CHAPTER 23

Later that afternoon, Beau helped me into his truck, along with two large containers of Camille's chicken soup and a small cosmetics bag for my meds. The bag had been borrowed from Jolene, which meant it was monogrammed with her initials and, on the reverse side, had a bedazzled depiction of Dorothy's red shoes.

Despite assurances that Beau didn't need help, Camille deemed it necessary to come with us so she could hold the soup and sit in the back to make sure I didn't slide off the seat. Considering how unassuming her personality was, I was surprised that she could muster a fierce forcefulness when she wanted to get her way. She'd probably mastered it from living with Henry for so long, as he didn't seem to be the kind of person who was good at compromising.

Mimi had stopped insisting that I stay, and she handed me a printed list of phone numbers—including hers, Beau's, Christopher's, the nearest hospital's, the police's—for me to give to Sarah, "just in case." I assured her that Jolene would be gone for only a few days and that she didn't need to worry, but her troubled expression didn't soften. I knew that she was thinking about the Adele ringtone playing on our phones, the same unanswered question in both of our minds. *Why is Adele still here?* I had no doubt that the answer lay with her wedding rings and what had happened to Buddy. All we could do was wait until Mimi was ready to hold the rings or for Beau to ask Adele directly—whichever came first. It felt like we were watching a tightly wound jack-in-the-box, knowing a big reveal was coming but still unprepared for the surprise.

Jaxson's car was parked at the curb in front of my apartment when we pulled up. After a quick introduction to Camille, he helped Beau pull me out of the seat and then up the stairs. We were all panting by the time we made it to the top, even after pausing on the landing.

The scent of something delicious cooking in the kitchen wafted toward us as Sarah appeared along with Jolene, who was holding Mardi. The small dog did a mad scramble to reach me as soon as the men set me down on the couch. He quickly asserted his place, pressing against my side like a furry comfort blanket. Jolene had already set up pillows for my foot and head, and draped blankets over the back of the couch, with the TV remote on a tray table within reach. A collection of magazines including *Southern Living*, *Garden & Gun*, *People*, and *Allure* was fanned out next to my laptop on the coffee table.

I scratched a happy Mardi behind his floppy ears, noticing that he was wearing a new fall-themed sweater. "Thanks, guys. And thank you, Jolene—this all looks wonderful and cozy. I know I'll be more than comfortable."

"I helped pick the magazines," Sarah said. "Well, *People*, anyway. I know you deny any interest in celebs, but that's always the magazine you pick up in doctors' offices. *Allure* was a compromise, since Jolene thought there might be something useful for you to learn inside and I figured I could learn something, too, but I vetoed *Vogue*. I can't see you or anyone we know wearing metallic conical breast plates to the grocery store or to walk the dog, you know?"

"Good call," I said. My gaze fell on an exuberant floral arrangement set on a tall pedestal table directly across from me, filled with fans of brightly colored blooms. "Where did that come from?"

"The table came from my bedroom. It's where I keep a framed photo of my grandmama and me standing in front of her funeral home, but I've moved that to my dressing table because we need to display these gorgeous flowers. Of course, I had to do a little bit of tweaking—my mama taught me how to properly arrange flowers, and I don't know what the florist was thinking—but aren't they just spectacular?"

"Yes, they are. But who are they from?"

She beamed at me and handed me a small white envelope. "Cooper."

Beau cleared his throat, then reached for the soup that Camille was still holding. "Here, let me take that to the kitchen." He quickly disappeared into the other room.

Jolene tucked the corner of a blanket around my injured ankle. "What do y'all say we give Nola a bit of privacy for a minute? Sarah and Camille, I could use some help setting the table. And, Jaxson, could you please help me get my nice dishes from the top shelf? Sometimes being petite is a real disadvantage."

"I think you're perfect just the way you are," Jaxson said.

Jolene's cheeks reddened before she turned away.

The note was brief, but it still managed to send a tingle down to the toes I could still feel.

I wish I could be with you. I promise to make it up to you when I get back. And I'm not talking about a rousing game of backgammon.

Love, Cooper

I stared at the signature line, reading it over and over. *Love, Cooper.* And then back to the word "rousing." If I weren't only in my twenties,

I could have sworn I was having a hot flash. I'd have to ask Melanie about it, although she was still denying that she was anywhere near menopause.

I considered calling Cooper for a discussion, or at least an explanation, but I had no idea what the time difference was between New Orleans and Malaysia. Besides, he had already told me that finding availability in his schedule to talk would be problematic and that he would call me as soon as he was stateside again, on Friday.

"Supper's on the table," Jolene announced.

I placed the card and envelope on the tray table and pulled myself up to a sitting position.

"Oh, no, you don't." Jolene rushed over to my side, followed quickly by Sarah. "This is the sort of thing I told you that you need to watch out for," she said, looking at my sister. "Nola puts mules to shame with her hardheadedness, and if she didn't sing so beautifully I'd say she was deaf, too, because she apparently didn't hear a word Dr. Longo said about taking it easy. And she is *not* to put any weight on that foot." Jolene scowled at me, making me surprisingly grateful that she was leaving the next day.

She crossed the room to retrieve my scooter, sparkly streamers flying from the handlebars. "This is a special treat, so as soon as your last bite of dessert is gone, you're going right back to the couch and elevating your foot, you understand? I know you're thinking that once I'm headed to Mississippi you can do what you like, but I've already had a long sit-down with Sarah so that she understands her responsibilities. I've also bought two rolls of duct tape just in case."

"I really don't think—"

"And she taught me how to use them," Sarah said, her face serious.

Jolene turned down offers of help from Beau and Jaxson. "We gotta see that Sarah can do this on her own, or back to Mimi's we go."

Sarah sent me a desperate glance, and I gave her a brief nod. "We got this." That was something my mother used to say, and it surprised me that it was the first thing that came to me. "My other leg is very strong, so you don't have to support all my weight, okay? Just hold the scooter steady and maybe take my elbow to help me stand."

With minimal effort, Sarah and I managed to pull me off the sofa and onto the scooter. It helped that Sarah had a lot of upper-body strength owing to being on the Ashley Hall archery team. She was also tall for her age. We wore matching smiles of satisfaction as we faced Jolene.

Beau actually clapped. "Well done. Everybody make room so Nola can practice navigating to the dining table. Watch out, because she might run you down. We all know how much she appreciates Jolene's cooking."

I aimed the scooter directly at him, but he stepped out of the way in time, so I unfortunately missed him. Two chairs had been set up for me at the table so I could elevate my leg on one. After I'd sat down, I patiently waited for Jolene to place a napkin in my lap even though it was clear that I was more than capable of doing it myself. I didn't want to give her any reason to suggest going back to Mimi's again.

"You didn't have to do this, Jolene. Sarah and I would have been perfectly happy with a pizza or frozen dinners."

"Speak for yourself," Sarah said, reaching for Jolene's homemade dinner rolls.

"You know how much I love to cook, and it's a pleasure to see so many faces at my table." Smiling graciously at Camille, she added, "Especially a new face. I suggest that you serve yourself before the food comes to Nola, or you're likely to miss out. She's so skinny that she has to run around the shower to get wet, but she has the appetite of a linebacker, bless her heart." Jolene handed the bread basket to Camille just as Beau's phone rang.

He excused himself and stood. "It's Sam. Go ahead and start. I'll be right back," he said before stepping into the kitchen.

I could hear the low rumblings of his voice but couldn't make out the words he said. Not that I was trying to eavesdrop, of course, but it wasn't like he was whispering. When he returned, he wore a grim expression.

"Everything all right?" Camille asked with concern.

Beau sat down again and pulled up his chair. "Sort of. There was a fire today at the complex where Sam lives. Fortunately, it was in the middle of the day, when most of the residents were at work, but it seems it was set deliberately in another part of the complex to distract first responders from a burglary call that had gone out from Sam's building fifteen minutes earlier."

"Oh, no. Is Sam all right?" Camille pressed her hand against her heart.

"She is. The door to her apartment isn't, though. Hers was one of two apartments where forced entry was attempted. Unfortunately, they succeeded with hers." His eyes met mine. "Don't worry. The rings are still there. The burglar made it to the closet where the safe is but didn't manage to open it—if he, or she, even tried. Police are dusting it for fingerprints. Only Sam's AirPods and a small Bluetooth speaker were taken—probably because they were the only things of value that were portable."

"Well, that's a little too close for comfort," I said. "Maybe you should put the rings in a safe-deposit box?"

"That was my original plan, but the funeral is tomorrow, so I can't make it to the bank before it closes for the holiday. I'd rather put them someplace where I can easily access them night or day and on weekends so that when Mimi says she's ready I can retrieve them."

"You can keep them here," I said, "since now we have alarms on the doors. And a Barbie head. Besides, we have nothing of any value here except for Jolene's *Wizard of Oz* collectibles."

"And my fine china, don't forget," Jolene said.

"I don't think anybody's going to break in to steal china," Jaxson said. At Jolene's hurt expression, he amended, "I mean, if it were a robber with any sense of taste and style, that's the first thing they'd go for. But for most criminals it's too fragile and heavy to grab and go. My guess is that fine china is very low on the list of items stolen during robberies in this city."

"Well, that's a relief," Jolene said, passing a bowl of her mashed potatoes with candied bacon bits to Camille. "And I think it's a good idea to keep them here for the time being. The room at the back of the apartment that Nola uses as her office and music-writing room looks like a hurricane tore through it, and even she can't find anything in it. I think she uses the mess as an excuse not to write any songs, since her guitar is completely buried, but that's a conversation for another time."

I narrowed my eyes at her and didn't bother to hide dropping a piece of ham on the floor for Mardi.

"Anyway," she said, sending me a scolding look, "anybody who's read the news article about the rings will never suspect they're here. And then, when Mimi has a sudden hankering to hold them and see what they can tell her, the rings are only a hop, skip, and jump away."

"That makes sense," Beau said, reaching down to scratch behind Mardi's ears. He apparently knew better than to feed the dog from the table. "Let me check with Mimi, and if she agrees, I'll bring them early in the morning. I'll stay at Sam's tonight to make sure everything's safe, then drop the rings here first thing in the morning, before the funeral."

"Are you sure they'll be safe here?" Camille asked quietly. "They're our only chance to find out what happened to Adele, and I don't want them to disappear. Don't you think they'd be safer back at the house?"

Beau reached for her hand and squeezed. "I know. And I understand—believe me. But Mimi was adamant about removing them from the house. She wants to find out what happened as much as we do, but reading objects takes a huge mental toll on her. She doesn't want to jeopardize orchestrating the perfect funeral and goodbye for my mother."

"Of course," Camille said, looking down at her hands. "Mimi

always knows best. We just have to be patient. The truth will out eventually."

"'Truth is like the sun. You can shut it out for a time, but it ain't goin' away.'" Jolene smiled. "The King said that. I have to say he was wrong about a lot of his fashion choices, but he sure was spot-on about that."

"King Charles?" Beau asked.

"No. Elvis." Jolene stood and began collecting dishes, motioning everyone to remain seated while she brought them to the kitchen and got dessert. Sarah joined Jolene, obviously on her best behavior so I wouldn't have second thoughts about letting her stay here. As Jolene picked up my plate, she said, "Carly has asked me to go wedding-dress shopping with her as soon as I get back. Isn't that exciting?"

I could think of a lot of words to describe wedding-dress shopping with Carly, but "exciting" wasn't one of them. "Too bad I can't go, too." For the first time, I considered my broken ankle in a positive light.

"Maybe we can FaceTime," Jolene suggested as she walked into the kitchen.

"Maybe," I said, then turned to Jaxson. "Doesn't Carly have other friends or bridesmaids who can go dress shopping with her?"

"She does, but half of them live out of town and the other half can't make the appointments Carly has already scheduled. And she doesn't want her mother there at all—because, Carly says, she's too opinionated. We're both really grateful that Jolene can do it."

"I bet." I turned awkwardly in my chair so I could point my finger at his chest. I was unfortunately too far away to jab it where I could leave a mark. Lowering my voice, I said, "Look, Jaxson, I trust you. And I trust Jolene. I even think that the two of you believe you can spend the holidays with her family without any funny business." I waggled my eyebrows so he'd understand what I meant by "funny business," because I wasn't going to use the word "sex" in front of Sarah—not because she didn't know what it was, but because she would definitely tell Melanie, and then my sister would never be allowed to visit me again.

I leaned as close to Jaxson as I could. "But if Jolene sheds one tear on your behalf, or you lay a finger on a single strand of her red hair, I promise you will live to regret it."

CHAPTER 24

Later that night I lay in bed, on my phone, flipping through the comments on the company's latest YouTube video, which showed Thibaut and Jorge replacing the insulation in my attic. I couldn't hop on my bike and go see my house, but this was the next best thing. I felt like a mother watching a nanny cam to check on her baby. The random comments about Mardi's supposed owner had stopped being posted, or Jolene was very vigilant about deleting them before I saw them. Either way, they weren't on public view. I'd have to ask if she would be checking the comments over Thanksgiving or if she'd want to delegate the task to me. I would be doing little besides sitting on the couch with my leg raised until my doctor's appointment the following week.

I glanced at the time on my phone and confirmed that it was well past midnight. I'd been put to bed hours before by Jolene and Camille, the latter making sure I had my pain meds set out on my nightstand, along with a full glass of water. My ankle throbbed, but despite what Camille had said about pain management, I was, for reasons I chose not to share with her, reluctant to take a pill.

In case I needed anything, my bedroom door had been left open a crack, despite Sarah sleeping on an air mattress next to my bed while Mardi, the traitor, curled up against her side. I could hear Jolene moving around in her room, her humming accompanying the sounds of drawers opening and closing as she planned her wardrobe for the coming days and found miraculous ways to condense twenty outfits, plus accessories and makeup, into two suitcases. I made a mental note to ask her to make a video of her packing hacks for the YouTube channel. If we made sure Mardi was visible in the background, we'd get thousands of likes. Social media was a strange beast, but as long as it garnered more customers, Mardi and I were game.

"Nola? You're not snoring, so you're awake, right?" Sarah asked quietly from the floor.

"I don't snore."

"Yeah, you do. I've recorded it, if you want to hear it."

"That's not necessary. And if I do, it's only because I'm on my back because I have to keep my leg propped up. Otherwise I don't snore. Maybe it's Mardi. I think he might need a C-PUP machine." I laughed at my own joke.

"Uh-huh."

"Is there anything you need?"

There was a brief pause, and then I felt Sarah gingerly sit on my bed. A soft woof soon followed, along with the warmth of dog fur next to me on my pillow. "Yeah. I wanted to talk to you. About . . . dead people."

I lifted my head. "Any in the apartment I need to know about?" I asked with alarm.

"Dead people are everywhere. The ones here are just passing through, I think. They're only here because they sense my presence, but if I ignore them, they mind their own business and go on their way. It's like they were just hanging out and saw my light and had to come see what it was all about—sort of like how a shark can detect a drop of blood from a mile away."

"That's encouraging." I pressed my head back into the pillow. "I don't want you bothered by lost spirits. It was hard for Melanie when she was your age and didn't have anyone to explain it to her. She doesn't want you to go through what she did."

"I brought the peacock pin just in case."

"Good." The pin had belonged to Melanie's grandmother Sarah, and my sister used it for the same purpose that Beau used his rubber band.

"And I've been memorizing lots of ABBA lyrics and songs."

"Even better," I said, unable to keep myself from smiling. "Hopefully you won't have to resort to using either the brooch or ABBA. We're just going to have a chill weekend filled with lots of pizza, popcorn, and chick flicks. Doesn't that sound like fun?"

When she didn't say anything, I lifted my head again. "Sarah? Are you regretting not calling Melanie? Because I can call her right now and have you on the first flight home if—"

"No. It's not that."

I did my best to scooch back in the bed to rest against the headboard without my foot coming dislodged from the stack of pillows it rested on, and I waited for her to say something.

"I want to help. With Beau's mom. And with whatever is haunting that creepy doll."

I didn't add Cooper's ghostly female companion. Even I couldn't grapple with all the lost and lonely spirits that were inhabiting my world at the moment, and I was presumably an adult. "You shouldn't have to worry about any of it, Sarah. You're a kid, and one day soon you'll be all grown up, and then you'll have to worry about stuff. Enjoy it while you can."

"When you were my age you were on a Greyhound bus all by yourself, moving across the country."

"Yes, but—"

"Sometimes we know what's best for us even if other people think we're too young. You have bravery on steroids, and I can talk to dead people. It's, like, our superpowers, you know? And I think we have them so that we can help others. I would feel selfish if someone needed my help and I said I couldn't help because I wasn't old enough."

We lay in the dark without speaking, with only the sound of Mardi's snoring interrupting the silence. Eventually I said, "What is it you want to do that you think I'll say no to?"

"How did you know?"

"I was once a dumb preteen, too. I know how you think. So, what is it?"

"Since you asked, I need you to tell Beau to let me help him talk to his mom. He needs to. There's something . . . not right in Mimi's house, and I think it's about Adele. And how she died. She wouldn't let me see anything, but I felt it. Felt *her.* She really needs to talk to Beau. He needs to find his dad before they do."

Chill bumps bounced along my spine. "Who are 'they'?"

She lowered her voice to a whisper. "The same people who hurt Adele."

I lay against the pillow. "Madame Zoe said the same thing. And why are you whispering?"

"Because I don't want anyone else to hear," she whispered back.

By "anyone else" I knew she wasn't referring to Jolene.

Mardi left my pillow and stepped across me to settle into Sarah's lap, as if he sensed that she needed comfort and support. In the same low voice, she said, "Something's building—something real bad. It's like a pimple right under the skin getting ready to pop."

It was refreshing to be reminded sometimes that Sarah was just a preteen with a grown-up gift.

She leaned closer to me. "Beau's in real danger."

My apprehension turned into full-blown panic, and I had to force myself to keep my voice calm. "All right. And if I convince him to talk to Adele, you believe that you can help him with what's next?"

"Yeah. Pretty much."

"If I do that, you have to promise me that if you are in any kind of danger, you will stop immediately and let me send you home. Melanie would kill me just for having this conversation."

"I know. But since she didn't make you disappear when you were a teenager, or me when I was a colicky baby, I think we're safe."

"That's very dark, Sarah. Very dark."

"It comes with the territory."

I sighed. "What makes you think Beau will listen to me?"

"Seriously?" I imagined Sarah rolling her eyes in the dark. "Do you really need me to answer that?"

Instead of responding with something even I wouldn't believe, I asked, "Why can't you just be another adolescent girl who's obsessed with selfies and Instagram likes?"

"Because social media sucks. And if you don't want to sound even older than you are, call it IG."

I let the dig about my age slide. I hated social media, too, mostly because I found it to be a time suck filled with curated pictures and inane prattle about things I didn't care about. Except for accounts about dogs and old houses. Those I followed religiously. "Are girls picking on you again?" Melanie had shared that Sarah had become very low-key about her abilities since letting it slip that a classmate's deceased grandmother was standing in the classroom.

"Duh. Why do you think I closed my social media accounts? They practically exist only for bullies, and I've got better things to do with my time. Not that it stops them from inviting me to slumber parties so I can be the free entertainment."

"I'm sorry. That stinks."

She stretched out her legs. "It's all right. It's fun to freak them out. Like once, at lunch, when I made a scared face looking behind one girl and wouldn't tell her what I saw. She had to go home for the rest of the day."

"Sarah, that's not nice."

"I know, and I felt bad. But she's the one who started the nickname Scary Sarah."

"Well, in that case, she deserved it. But still. Did you apologize?"

"Yeah. And I told her that one day she was going to be really famous."

"Wait—you can see the future?"

"No. But she doesn't know that. And we won't be in school together anymore when she finds out, and now she's being nicer to me. So it's a win-win."

I didn't want to encourage her, but I couldn't help but laugh. "Have you shared this with Melanie?"

"Of course, but not until I figured out how to present it to her so I wouldn't get in trouble." She was silent for a moment, and then we both said together, "WWMD?" before bursting out laughing.

We'd lain in silence for long enough that I was beginning to drift to sleep when Sarah spoke again. "There's one more thing."

"I'm almost afraid to ask. What?"

"I want to go see the house on Esplanade. After I saw that doll, the lady came to see me after I went to sleep."

I jerked my head off the pillow. "Here? In this apartment?"

"Yes. I already told you. Dead people are everywhere."

I pulled my sheets closer under my chin. "What did she say?"

"She needs my help to protect Lynda."

I was fully awake now. "Lynda? Did she tell you how that's spelled?"

I felt Sarah sit up. "Uh, no. We weren't doing a spelling bee. She just said 'Lynda,' so however you spell it works, I guess. Why? Do you know who she is?"

"Yeah, I'm pretty sure. I have no idea what it means, but I know two people who might know. We'll have to find someone to drive us to see the house. I can ask Cooper if he can take us after he gets back on Friday. But only if you're sure. There's another spirit in the house who isn't nice at all. I think he's the one who wrecked Cooper's car."

I felt her steady gaze on me in the darkness. "I know. The lady told me. The man doesn't like her talking to me."

That unexpected comment chilled me to the bone. "She saved me, I think. In the crash, I felt someone cushioning me. Did she give you her name?"

"No. I got the feeling that she might not want me to know. But she did say she saved your life. She doesn't know how much longer she can keep protecting everyone. She's not getting any stronger, but the bad man is. That's why I need to help her. There's no one else."

"I don't think it's a good idea, Sarah. I don't understand how this works, but I've been around Melanie and Beau enough to see how nasty things can get. Maybe we should ask Beau."

"You don't think finding out who killed his mom and what happened to his dad is enough for him right now? Maybe I was wrong and you actually don't like him."

"I do like him. . . ."

"Ha. I knew it!"

I would have smiled, but I was too busy trying to stop my teeth from chattering. The thought of dead people in my apartment talking to my sister was more unnerving than I would have imagined. And the notion of the entity in Cooper's backseat getting stronger was nearly enough to send me over the edge.

"Very funny," I managed. "But you're right. Beau does have a lot on his plate." Briefly, I considered suggesting that we bring in Melanie. But being allowed to move to New Orleans by myself had been premised on the assurance that I was completely ready to live on my own, without any financial or emotional support from my family. It wasn't that I felt I would let them down if I asked for help; I didn't want to disappoint myself.

"So, you'll ask Cooper to take us?"

I didn't respond right away; I wasn't sure what the correct answer was. After thinking it through from all angles, I said, "Yes. I can ask. And we should see if we can meet with the previous owners, too. If Cooper wants to buy the house, he should be part of figuring out what happened to the people who used to live there."

Sarah and Mardi resettled themselves on the floor, and I resumed drifting to sleep. A needling memory of something Sarah had said brought me fully awake again. "Do you really think I'm brave?"

"Don't let it go to your head or anything, okay? But yeah. You're a freaking icon of bravery."

I paused, letting her words sink in. "I'm not sure if I agree, but thanks. So are you, you know."

"Or maybe I'm just too dumb not to be afraid."

"Maybe it runs in the family." I stared out into the darkness, wondering if anyone besides my sister was there, and decided I didn't want to know. "Good night, Sarah. I love you. And please disregard every mean thing I said to you when you were little and annoying. I'm glad you're my sister."

"Same," she said.

I listened until her breathing slowed and Mardi began snoring again before I closed my eyes, knowing that, at least for a moment, all was right in my world.

CHAPTER 25

I tried not to feel insulted that Jolene seemed more disappointed to be leaving Mardi behind than to be leaving either Sarah or me. She also spent a lot more time explaining the care and feeding of Mardi to Sarah than she spent explaining mine. Granted, I could speak and explain my needs, but still.

Despite the cooler weather, Jaxson was sweating when he climbed the stairs after loading all of Jolene's luggage into Bubba, including at least three covered casseroles in insulated containers and an entire cooler filled with her homemade breads and cookies. Since an equal amount of food and goodies had been left in the kitchen, I wondered yet again when—and if—Jolene ever slept.

"Is your mom's oven broken?" I asked.

Jolene gave me a confused look. "Not that I know of," she said as she carried out the door yet another dish covered in foil.

Since I couldn't go down the stairs, we said our good-byes on my perch on the couch. Jolene hugged me twice while delicately wiping tears from her eyes. "I hate to leave you, Nola. Maybe I should call Mama—"

"Don't even think about it. Sarah and I will be fine, and Cooper will be back on Friday. In case I need anything before then, Mimi and Beau will be on call, with Camille and Christopher on backup."

"What about Henry?" Sarah asked. "I noticed his name wasn't on the list of phone numbers."

I shared a look with Jaxson while Jolene said, "Because that man is as handy as a screen door on a submarine. Now, come hug my neck so we can be on our way. Mama's called me three times already this morning, seeing if we've left yet. Daddy's going to deep-fry the turkey this year, and Mama's a nervous wreck. He just about burned down the house last year, but he swears he knows where he went wrong. Which reminds me—we need to stop at the Walmart and get a couple of fire extinguishers, just in case."

We said our final good-byes, Sarah waving Mardi's paw, while I narrowed my eyes at Jaxson to remind him of last night's conversation. "Don't forget to call Carly!" I called after him.

They'd been gone less than five minutes when the doorbell rang. I checked the Ring app on my phone and saw Beau standing on the doorstep. "It's Beau. Could you—"

"On it!" Sarah was already racing down the steps to let him in.

He was dressed for the funeral, wearing a dark suit and tie, looking a lot better than any man on the way to his mother's funeral should. "You clean up good," I said. "Your mom would be proud."

"She is," Sarah said, matter-of-factly.

We both looked at her, and I was reminded of what I'd promised Sarah the night before.

"Do you have a minute to talk? I promise it won't take long."

He looked at his watch, and then at Sarah and me. "I still have to pick up Sam, but I can spare a minute. Unless it can wait?"

Sarah shook her head. "I don't think so." She stepped closer to him and looked up into his face. "You know what I want to talk about, don't you?" Closing her eyes, she tilted her head and breathed in deeply through her nose. "That smell—I remember it from the cemetery tour. It's like dirt and rotting leaves. And—"

"Death," Beau finished for her. "I know. I smell it, too. It's been getting heavier and heavier and sometimes I feel like I can't breathe. Like I'm being buried alive."

"Me, too," Sarah said. She took his hand. I thought I'd imagined the ripple of static electricity that smudged the air around them, but then I saw them jerk their hands apart as if they'd both been shocked.

Beau stared at her. "What was that?"

"We're stronger together," Sarah said, echoing what I'd heard Melanie, Jayne, and their mother, Ginny, say whenever it was time for battle.

"Oh, no," he said, holding his hands up between himself and Sarah. "I'm not getting you involved in my family drama. You're just a kid."

Sarah looked back at me for encouragement. "She is, Beau," I said, "but she wants to help." I paused. "Adele asked her to."

Beau began to shake his head. "No. No, Sarah. That's not okay. She doesn't have the right—"

"You need Sarah's help," I said. "You're in real danger. And so is your dad. From the same people who killed Adele. You don't have much time, and if we can keep Sarah safe, I think we should let her help you."

"Keep her safe? I don't even know if I can keep you safe. You almost died in that attic—remember? Because you wouldn't listen to me to stay away. And let's not forget the car accident." He scratched the back of his head. "This is nuts. I can't believe I'm even having this conversation."

"She's your mom," I said. "And hasn't she already saved your life once? Maybe she thinks she has to do it again so that you will believe that she and your dad love you and that they didn't abandon you. You should be jumping at the chance to find out what really happened to them so that you can finally stop blaming your parents for your abandonment issues."

I didn't realize how cruel the words sounded until I'd already spoken them and it was too late to call them back. But they were true. And sometimes the truth hurt.

His eyes darkened as he glared at me, his expression exactly what I imagined he'd wear if I'd physically struck him. "You would know, wouldn't you?"

I sucked in my breath and held it until my lungs burned. "Touché," I said.

He pulled out a clear baggie from the breast pocket of his jacket, the two rings visible inside, and handed it to Sarah. "I don't have time to argue right now. Please hide these until Mimi asks for them. I've got a funeral to get to."

Beau walked quickly to the door and I felt the thud of each angry footstep.

"You're wrong," Sarah said quietly.

Beau came to an abrupt stop before turning to face my sister.

"She said good-bye when she left. You were sleeping but you heard her, even though you always tell people that she didn't say good-bye."

He looked back at Sarah, his anger dissipating when he realized he was looking at a child. Without a word, he headed down the stairs and out the front door, slamming it behind him on his way out.

Sarah and I spent the day parked on the sofa, bingeing HGTV's *House Hunters* and the Investigation Discovery channel, which was having a *Southern Fried Homicide* marathon. We also watched *The Sound of Music* from start to finish, something I didn't think I'd ever done. We spent at least twenty minutes arguing over whether the song "My Favorite Things" is about Christmas and, if not, how it shouldn't place the movie in the same category as *How the Grinch Stole Christmas* and

Christmas Vacation. It was as if we were both looking for a distraction from the lingering unease following Beau's abrupt departure and Sarah's unsettling last words to him.

I'd expected him to text or call, and I'd found myself constantly checking my phone until I caught Sarah watching me and forced myself to ditch the phone face down on the floor. When Sarah retreated to the kitchen to make yet another batch of microwave popcorn I checked my phone again but found only more pictures from JJ's bake-off, along with the news that he'd made it into the next round. These messages had been sent by Melanie to the family group text chain that Sarah had named "Addams Family." Melanie had yet to figure out how to change it, so it remained. I tapped out a string of thumbs-up emojis, then found myself hesitating before hitting Send. I could easily tell Melanie now that I had been in a fender bender and had hurt my ankle, if only to appease Mimi and everyone else who kept insisting that I needed to tell my parents about the accident.

I hit Send without adding anything, then put my phone down on the floor again and shoved it under the sofa so I wouldn't be tempted to pick it up. I'd call Melanie and Jack on Sunday, when Sarah was on the plane flying back home and Cooper and Jolene were back in town, so they wouldn't think that I'd been abandoned to my own devices. The last thing I wanted was for Melanie and Jack to fly to New Orleans and try to fix everything. As many times as they'd told me that they had faith in me, my recovery, and my dogged determination to see my transition through, they were still my parents. I had a strong feeling that, no matter how many years had passed and how much older I'd become, they still saw me as that lost little thirteen-year-old wearing a halter top and a bad attitude and standing on Melanie's porch.

The rings lay on the coffee table, where Sarah had put them while she considered the perfect spot to hide them, which she'd promised she'd do before bedtime. She'd held them in her hands for a long time, hoping to feel a spark.

"Nothing," she'd said. "I think it's a matter of dialing the right channel, like on Grandpa's old radio when he tries to find his favorite AM talk station. Ginny can always fine-tune it, which makes sense, and I'm sure she could read these rings, too. But they're on a frequency I can't find."

"Good, because that's not something I want you to be doing. If Melanie didn't disown me outright, she'd find another way to punish me—like making me wear Kate Spade and Lilly Pulitzer for a year."

"Where do I sign up?" Sarah asked.

I rolled my eyes. "Bottom line is that Beau and Mimi will take care of Adele. You did your part and told Beau what you needed to. The rest is up to him."

"But we still get to go to the Esplanade house, right?"

"Yes. With Cooper. But if we see that guy from my backseat, we're noping right out of there, okay?"

"I guess. But I might need to stay here longer to make sure everyone who's been searching for the light finds it."

"Good try, but no. You've got school on Monday. Besides, Melanie has probably already bought matching Christmas outfits for you, JJ, and the dogs, and I know you don't want to disappoint her."

She didn't smile. "I just want to accomplish one special thing this year, you know? And we're almost in December."

I stared at my funny, smart, and beautiful sister and it was like my words were coming out of her mouth. Every painful memory of what it was like to be caught between childhood and adulthood hit me like a blow to the solar plexus. "Put those down, and then I want you to sit and listen carefully. I'll be blunt because my ankle's hurting and I'm feeling crabby." She'd been juggling the wedding rings—as if that in itself weren't a skill to be proud of—but immediately stopped and returned them to the plastic bag on the coffee table.

"Sarah, you have many talents. One of your most stellar ones happens to be communicating with the dead. Sure, you won't get a school trophy or certificate for it, and you might actually hate it sometimes, but I know without a doubt that one day you will be grateful for it. At some point you might even get a little proud and smug that you can do what so few people can. You have the ability to change lives. Not many people can say that. And if any of your classmates make fun of you or try to make you feel like less than the wonderful person you are, it's because they're jealous. Hitting a home run in softball is nothing compared to what you can do."

"So then why can't I—"

"Because you're not yet even thirteen. And also because I'm not your mother. Can we leave it at that, please?"

"Whatever." Her phone beeped, and she groaned when she read the screen. "It's JJ. He thinks he's going to win in his age bracket." She threw herself back on the sofa in a dramatic sprawl. "At least I don't have to respond. I texted Melanie saying that Mississippi has bad cell reception and not to expect to hear from me until Saturday."

"The whole state?"

"Nobody's questioned it, and that means we're good, right? Mom, Dad, and JJ won't think it weird if we're not replying to their messages."

"Good plan."

She studied me with a contemplative expression. "You know how Dad says it's always better to rip off the Band-Aid and get it over with?"

"Yes," I drew out slowly. "But waiting a few more days won't change a thing except that I will have had a few more days of rest and recovery. So let's enjoy this time together now and let me figure out the rest later."

"You sound just like Mom." She didn't make it sound like a compliment.

"I think Mardi needs to go out. It's starting to rain, so please put on his raincoat, which is hanging with his leash on the peg by the downstairs door. Jolene's *Wizard of Oz* umbrella is in the stand beneath it in case you need it."

She pried the sleeping dog off the sofa and began carrying him toward the door. "I don't think Beau's the only one who needs an intervention."

"I have no idea what you're talking about."

She put Mardi on the floor and I listened as they walked down the steps, Sarah loudly singing the lyrics to "Lips Are Movin." It was my favorite Meghan Trainor song, even if it was about lying.

I settled back into the sofa and checked my phone for the time. My ankle was throbbing, and I'd already missed two doses of my pain pills. I'd been waiting to take one dose before bedtime so that I could sleep, despite Camille's warning. I extended my hand for the bottle on the tray table but only managed to knock it over. The cap fell off and several pills rolled out, but all of them settled just outside of my reach.

After several failed attempts to grab one, I leaned back against the pillows to wait until Sarah returned.

CHAPTER 26

Sarah and I were debating whether to stick one of Jolene's casseroles in the oven or order pizza when the doorbell rang. I opened my Ring app with more anticipation than I should have felt, but instead of Beau I spotted Felicity on the doorstep.

"I'll get it," Sarah said, already heading down the steps. Mardi surprised me by staying at my side, his ears and posture indicating his full alertness.

"It's okay, Fluffer-butt," I soothed, stroking one of his silky ears. "It's just Aunt Felicity. You're friends, remember? She gives you treats."

We listened as footsteps climbed the stairs, both of us looking through the open door toward the landing. Mardi's tail thumped against me when he spotted Felicity but slowed when he spotted the man behind her.

"Henry," I said, not bothering to hide my surprise. "I wasn't expecting you."

"Or me, either, I'm guessing," said Felicity. Sarah followed them in, giving me a discreet shrug before closing the door. "I basically grew up in New York City, so I don't know how to drive. I was going to take an Uber, but Henry insisted on bringing me."

Henry stopped in front of me, reeking of cigarette smoke. "Yeah, it was getting pretty crowded at Mimi's with all the people from the funeral," he said as he helped himself to the bowl of popcorn Sarah and I had been sharing.

"I guess I should have called," Felicity said, "but it was sort of last-minute. Beau didn't want to leave Mimi, but he wanted someone to physically check in on you to see if you were all right and if you needed anything."

"Beau said that?"

"He did. He also wanted me to let you know that he's been thinking about what you and Sarah said."

I exchanged a glance with Sarah. "Wow. Thanks for letting us know." I could tell by her face that she wanted me to say more, but I was reluctant to share anything in front of Henry, including how many times a day I brushed my teeth. He seemed to be the type of person who would take any glimmer of information, twist it, then use it against you. I had no proof except for Trevor's opinion, and that was enough for me.

Henry edged his way behind the sofa, nudging my side table with his leg and jostling the loose pills as he peered out the window. "I offered to drive because I wanted to see where you and Jolene live. I'm not gonna lie—I kinda expected something a lot nicer. It's kind of a dump, isn't it?"

"Thanks for noticing," I said. "Jolene's done a great job of decorating and has made it homey, which is all I need, and it's also all I can afford right now. I'm spending most of my money and energy on renovating my Creole cottage, which will hopefully be done around New Year's." It was unclear why I was trying to justify myself to this man. There was just something about him that made me bristle. Apparently he had the same effect on Mardi, since my sweet dog growled when Henry tried to scratch behind the dog's ears.

"How's your house hunt going?" I asked. "I know Mimi loves having you stay with her, but I'm sure you and Camille are looking forward to getting your own place."

Henry grabbed another handful of popcorn and shoved it into his mouth, stray kernels falling to the floor. Mardi stayed close to my side instead of licking them up like he usually would. "I've been busy working, so Camille's supposed to be taking care of that," he said with a full mouth. "Not sure why nothing's happened yet, but we're pretty comfortable at Mimi's. I think she appreciates having me around for security, too."

"I thought she had an alarm system," I said, unable to stop goading him. It was too easy. Besides, he deserved it. I wanted to ask about Camille's working, too, but Felicity cut me off.

"Your water glass is empty—can I refill it for you?"

"Yes, please." She picked up the glass before disappearing into the kitchen.

"Looks like y'all have been having a party in here," Henry said, indicating the dirty plates and loose pills.

"If you're offering to help clean up . . ."

"Nah. That's women's work. Wouldn't mind having a tour of the place, though. Beau's been talking about me joining JR Properties, to help with construction, so I'm studying up on old places like this, to figure out what doesn't work for modern living."

I'd heard Beau say that exact thing, and it didn't surprise me that Henry would simply repeat what he'd heard instead of coming up with an original thought.

Henry brushed off his hands over the popcorn bowl, and I caught Sarah's look of horror behind his shoulder. He continued. "I had a year of engineering at Louisiana Tech before I realized I knew a lot more than those so-called professors and dropped out to forge my own path."

"And how's that working out for you?"

Felicity appeared with my water and placed it next to my pills on the side table. "I'd love to see the place, too," she said. "I mean, the company is named after me. I should probably know more about what it does, right?"

Sarah began leading Felicity and Henry to the back hallway that separated my bedroom from Jolene's. "There's just one bathroom," Sarah said. "So if you're talking about modern living, I'd highly suggest having more than one, just in case there are boys living in the same house. I have to share a bathroom with my brother, JJ, and I can't describe the trauma."

I closed my eyes, listening to Sarah's voice as she moved through the small apartment. I focused on deep breathing to distract myself from the pain in my ankle, telling myself that I could wait two more hours for my bedtime dose.

I must have dozed off, because when I opened my eyes again Felicity was gently nudging my shoulder. "You okay?"

"Fine. Just tired from lying here all day. What did you think?"

"It's a dump," Henry said.

Ignoring him, Felicity said, "I love what Jolene's done with the décor! It's hard when you're renting, because you don't want to invest in anything permanent, but the *Wizard of Oz* décor in her room is adorable."

"She takes her devotion to the Emerald City very seriously. Wait until you see her plans for my cottage. She's done an amazing job of exchanging shout-outs and other promo on our social media channels for goods and services. Jolene is truly a gem. As is Trevor. He made a breakfront for my kitchen out of an old antique. He's a genius."

Henry coughed. "More like a troublemaker, if you ask me."

"No one did," I said, not caring whether I sounded belligerent. There was only so much I could take, and his saying something mean about Trevor pretty much took me over the edge. To Felicity, I said, "I'm hoping to get Cooper to drive Sarah and me to the property on Esplanade on Friday. If you'd like to come with us . . ."

"I'd love to," Felicity said.

"If it's as much of a dump as this is, I think I'll take a pass," Henry said. "Now, if you ladies will excuse me, I need to use the little boys' room."

Sarah raised an eyebrow and pretended she was trying not to throw up.

"Are you sure you're okay to ride in a car?" Felicity asked.

The alarm on my watch sounded. "Time for me to move." I sat up and Felicity and Sarah, one on either side of me, pulled me onto my scooter. "I've already figured out that it takes fifteen minutes to go to the kitchen and back. If I do that four times a day, that's the one hour I'm allowed off the couch. I'm already going stir-crazy, so I'd say a field trip would be just what the doctor ordered. Traveling by car won't be much more strenuous than sitting on the couch."

Ignoring their dubious expressions, I began my trip to the kitchen, followed closely by Felicity and Sarah. "It takes me fifteen minutes because I always pause to see what else Jolene left for me in the fridge. I mastered opening the fridge without falling over in the first hour." I happily demonstrated by opening it and pulling out a mystery tin with a lid on it.

I closed the door with my head, then scooted over to the nearest counter to drop the tin and pry it open. Smells of sugar and chocolate wafted toward me. "Jolene's famous peanut butter balls! I should do fifteen extra laps to burn off the calories, but it will be worth it."

"Should I put some on a plate?" Sarah asked.

"Nah. Just bring the whole tin and put it on the coffee table."

"So," Felicity said, "Mimi said that Thanksgiving dinner tomorrow will be small, which makes sense under the circumstances, but I'll be happy to come back and bring you food."

"Please don't," I said, scooting over to the freezer and flinging open the door. Foil-covered dishes in all different shapes and sizes had been stacked inside like blocks in a game of Tetris. "We haven't even gone through everything she left in the fridge yet. I think she was planning on the world ending. So we don't need any food, but thank you. Actually, would you like to take some with you?"

Felicity laughed. "Nah, I think we're good. Friends and neighbors have been bringing over casseroles ever since Adele was identified."

I didn't question why she didn't refer to Adele as her mother. I'd been calling Melanie Mother for a long time, and when I thought of the mother who'd given birth to me, I thought of her only as Bonnie. It wasn't an either-or thing but more of a before-and-after. I'd long since realized that the human heart was big enough to contain all the love from the succession of important people in our lives, but the human mind was much more limited. We made up hierarchies to help our hearts cope with loss.

"I'm sure," I said. "How was the funeral? How are Mimi and Beau holding up?"

"They're doing well, considering. There were so many people there to support the family. And a lot of press, too, as you can imagine. They're calling her 'the last Katrina victim.' Although whether that's true or not remains to be seen."

"Speaking of which—did Mimi mention the rings? We have them, and you're welcome to take them back with you."

Felicity shook her head. "She didn't ask, so if you don't mind keeping them here for a little bit longer . . ."

"It's fine. For me, anyway. But I'm sure you'd like some answers before you head back to New York."

"Yeah, well, my return is sort of open-ended right now. My boss is pretty understanding, and he told me to take as much time as I need. My mom and Michael have been living in New York to be with me, but I know they both want to come back to New Orleans. The house on Audubon Place has been rented for a year, and they have until the end of the lease to decide what to do. With my dad's trial pushing them into the spotlight, it just got ridiculous. But this is their home. Michael's been running the Sabatier Group from New York, but he'd be much more effective if he were here."

"So you think you might move back?"

She shrugged. "I doubt it. This isn't home to me. And I have a life in New York. New Orleans will always be the place where my mom died, and where my dad disappeared."

"I get that. Charleston will always be my home, but New Orleans is home now, too. I don't think there's a rule written anywhere that says you can have only one. Unless you're Jolene, who is more Mississippi than the river."

Felicity gave me a lopsided grin. "Yes, well, I'll remember that. And thanks. I'm glad to know I have at least one friend here in New Orleans. You have to promise me that you'll show me your cottage before I leave. I'm not going to step on Jolene's toes, but I know a thing or two about interiors. It comes from working estate sales for the auction house for so long. I know everything from Mafia gaudy to Jackie Kennedy Parisian chic."

"I'll keep that in mind." Her smile vanished, and she looked so sad that I wished I had two good ankles so I could stand up and hug her.

"Are you going to hog those peanut butter balls all for yourself, or can I have one?" Sarah reached for the tin and I let her have it, ignoring Melanie's voice in my head reminding me to make sure that Sarah didn't gorge herself on junk food. Sarah's love for sweets was a surprise to no one.

After Felicity and Sarah resettled me on the sofa, I noticed that Henry was missing and must still be in the bathroom. Sarah caught my gaze and made another gagging pantomime with her finger in her mouth.

Felicity sighed. "I have no idea what Camille sees in him. There's only so much a pretty face can compensate for before the jerk inside shines through." Turning toward the closed bathroom door, she shouted, "Henry—it's time to go!"

Henry emerged from Jolene's bedroom. "Sorry—I didn't have time to really look at all of Jolene's collectibles. Some of them might be worth something. Please let her know that if she is up to selling anything, I'd love to talk."

"Sure," I said, "but I doubt she'll want to part with any of them." I shivered, suddenly aware that the temperature in the room had dropped. Felicity noticed and grabbed a blanket that Jolene had placed on the back of the couch and settled it around me.

"Feels like there's a window open," she said. "It's been pretty windy—maybe one of the casement windows in the back room got blown open."

"I opened the bathroom window to air it out," Henry said without embarrassment. "But the door's closed, so it's probably not that."

"I'll go check," Sarah said with rounded eyes, then disappeared into the back hallway, the air in the room warming as soon as she left.

I watched Felicity's expression change, as if she'd noticed, too.

"We'll let ourselves out," she said. "Don't hesitate to call if you need anything at all, and definitely let me know when you're planning to head to the Esplanade house."

"Will do. Speaking of which, has Beau said anything about the bloodstain they found in the upstairs room?"

"He hasn't said anything, although he and Uncle Bernie spent a lot of time talking after the funeral, so maybe there's news."

Henry was already headed toward the stairs. "Let's go. There might still be food left."

Felicity shook her head. "Remember—anything at all, I'm here. And tell Sarah I said good-bye," she said as she rushed to catch up to Henry.

As soon as the door shut downstairs, Sarah reappeared. "No open windows. I still need to check the bathroom, but I'm going to give it a little more ti—" She stopped, her eyes focused on something behind me.

I turned to the small tray table where I kept my water glass and pain pills. The first thing I noticed was the pill bottle, now righted and with its top screwed on, all loose pills presumably returned inside. But it was the glass that Felicity had recently refilled and that sat next to the pill bottle that made me lean back as if to get away from it. It now appeared to contain solid ice, its sides frosted over.

Sarah reached up to stroke the peacock brooch on her sweater.

"Do you know what this is about?" I asked.

She didn't answer right away, which scared me more than any answer would have. "I don't know. But I saw the same thing happening in the kitchen when we were in there with Felicity. The coffee in the glass pot froze, too. We had the freezer and refrigerator doors open, and I thought maybe that was why. . . ." Her voice drifted away as she realized how much that didn't make sense.

"Are you're saying that Felicity has powers she's unaware of?"

"Maybe." She bit her lower lip. "It's like how when Beau and I are in the same room together there's this sort of static electricity that *bing*s in my head."

I didn't ask her what she meant by "bing"; Melanie had used that exact word when describing how it felt when she and her sister, Jayne, were together. She likened it to the spark given off when striking a match.

"She—Adele—came in with Felicity, but Felicity didn't seem to be aware of her mom's presence. Or maybe she was but she's so used to ignoring it that she doesn't notice it anymore." Sarah frowned. "I don't think Adele likes Henry very much. She kept poking him in the back to annoy him. Anyway, there goes our theory that once Adele was put in the family mausoleum her spirit could rest. Her funeral was hours ago."

"True." My gaze strayed to the side table. "I think she tidied up my pills, too—unless you did that?"

Sarah shook her head. "Wasn't me."

My gaze immediately shot to the coffee table, where Adele's rings had been inside a plastic bag. Except they weren't there anymore.

"Don't panic," Sarah said. "I found the baggie in my sweater pocket when I went to check on the windows. So I hid it for safekeeping. And I'm not going to even try to guess how it got into my pocket."

"Good thinking." I took a deep breath in an attempt to calm my racing heart. If the rings had disappeared, they could have been taken only by Felicity or Henry, and both scenarios were equally disturbing.

Sarah plopped down in the armchair across from me. She looked exhausted, her skin appearing pasty, with a thin sheen of sweat on it. I wished that I could call Melanie and ask if this was normal. Instead, I decided to wait for thirty minutes to see if Sarah improved. If she didn't, I'd figure it out. Forcing a smile, I said, "So, pizza or one of Jolene's casseroles for dinner tonight?"

Before she could answer, the unplugged landline phone—the same one that wouldn't stay hidden in my closet—rang, making us both jump. "I guess you want me to get that?" she asked.

"No. I don't think you should. And I don't want to break my other ankle trying to get to it before it stops ringing. Stay where you are—it'll stop eventually."

We stared at each other, listening to the incessant ringing. Finally Sarah stood. "I can't take it anymore." With heavy steps, she approached the desk and picked up the receiver. I could hear only the faint sound of static and the echoing of a high-pitched voice that seemed to be coming from deep space. Sarah didn't speak, but she closed her eyes to concentrate on listening. After she hung up, she approached me wearing an expression of confusion. She fell back into the chair, her face even paler than before.

"It was Bonnie," she said quietly.

"Bonnie," I repeated. The name unsettled me, the sound of it foreign to my ears. I hadn't heard my mother's name spoken out loud in a very long time, and I had to think for a moment to recall where it fit.

Sarah nodded. "Yeah. She said Sunny told you that she was watching out for you."

I recalled the note Sunny had made for me and stuck in my purse before she'd skipped town after we'd discovered her true identity. In it she'd said that Adele and Bonnie were watching over me to help fight the demons that hadn't stopped chasing me. I'd used the purse a couple of times since then, the wrinkled note still at the bottom.

"Why? Am I in danger?" I was only half-serious; danger seemed to be a running theme of the conversations on that phone.

"She kept saying the same thing over and over, but it didn't make any sense."

I hesitated, not knowing if I really wanted to know. "What was it?"

"'Find the stones.'"

"What does that mean?"

Sarah shrugged. "I have no idea. I'm just the messenger." She leaned her head against the back of her chair and closed her eyes.

I'd made the executive decision to order pizza for dinner and was pulling out my phone when I heard a loud *thump* coming from the direction of Jolene's bedroom. I glanced over at Sarah, but her deep and heavy breathing told me she'd fallen asleep.

Not willing to wake her up, or wait until she woke up on her own, I slid down to the floor and crawled to the back hallway. When I was halfway there it occurred to me to be wary of an intruder, but I reassured myself that I had my phone and could dial 911 if I needed to.

I peered around the corner of the doorframe and immediately spotted the source of the sound. Jolene's Bible, usually perched on her bedside table, lay on the floor five feet away from where it should have been. I crawled closer and slid the book toward me. It was open to the middle of the book of Luke.

Even if I believed in coincidences, I would feel sure that two Bibles falling open to the same place in separate locations within days of each other wouldn't qualify as one. I was tempted to call my dad but I discarded that idea almost as soon as it came to me, for the same reason why I couldn't call Melanie.

Instead, I called Cooper. I had no idea what time it was in Malaysia, but I had an urgent need to talk to someone who understood as much as I did that puzzles were meant to be solved. He was also someone who'd known me for a long time and liked me anyway. The call went directly to voice mail, and I hung up without leaving a message. Wherever our relationship was, it seemed desperate to leave one, so I told myself that he'd see that I'd called and would get back to me when he could.

Then I crawled back to the sofa and ordered pizza while I waited for Sarah to wake up.

CHAPTER 27

By Thanksgiving, my dream of endless days of blissfully doing nothing productive had changed, and Sarah and I had become stir-crazy and eager to escape the small space of the apartment. Even Mardi seemed despondent, his plumed tail, usually held proudly aloft along his back, now hanging low and limp. The weather had been chilly and damp, which meant we couldn't entice him to spend more time outside than was necessary for him to do his business before he pulled at his leash to return inside.

After a nap following our feast of Jolene's turkey casserole and homemade buttermilk biscuits and almost an entire pecan pie (pronounced *puh-CAHN* by Jolene, who was the authority on such things), we opened our eyes to sunshine in an almost perfectly blue midday sky, temperatures hovering in the low sixties.

Mardi began pawing at the door, and I watched with envy as Sarah stood and shrugged on her sweater.

"I'm coming, too." I pushed myself up to a sitting position. "If you'll bring my scooter down the stairs, I can go down on my rear end, step by step."

At her look of doubt, I said, "It's just my ankle, Sarah. The doctor didn't say anything about not getting fresh air. I just need to keep my weight off of it."

"That's not—"

"I know. I'm supposed to be keeping it elevated. It will be—sort of—on the scooter. And we won't be gone long—promise. I'll put my leg up as soon as we get back. We can just go around Tulane's campus, since there are smooth paths everywhere and you won't have to lift me out of any potholes."

"That's not what I was worried about." Her eyes traveled to my head. "Your hair . . ."

I rolled my eyes. "I'll wear a hat. And I think you've been hanging around Jolene too much."

After Sarah had helped me bundle up in a thick sweater, jacket, hat, and gloves, I positioned myself at the top of the stairs and began the process of descending, Mardi considerately matching my slow progress. I'd made it to the landing when my phone rang. I was so grateful for the reprieve that I didn't check to see who was calling before I answered it.

"Is this Nola?" came Uncle Bernie's familiar voice. "Did I interrupt you in the middle of a run?"

"No," I panted. "I mean, yes, this is Nola. But no, I'm at my apartment."

"Good. I was hoping I could stop by. I've got some interesting information about the house on Esplanade that I wanted to share. I could probably tell you over the phone, but I'm going through a bout of cabin fever and would welcome an outing. I didn't want to bother Beau so soon after the funeral, but I didn't want to wait, so I thought I'd try you."

I remembered that Jaxson's parents were on a Caribbean cruise for the holiday, and that must have left Bernie and his wife to their own devices. Since they didn't have children of their own, Thanksgiving must have been lonely.

"Believe me, I get it. My sister and I have been cooped up here, and we were just getting ready to go for a walk through campus while the sun is shining. If you give me about an hour, I can meet you here at my apartment. Your wife is welcome to join us."

"Well, that's very kind of you. But how about meeting on that bench behind Gibson Hall where we met last time with Jaxson? Since campus is deserted, I can have my friend Frank park in the circle in front, and then I can walk around the building. The wife says I need to get more exercise anyway."

We made plans to meet in thirty minutes, and Bernie was already waiting when Sarah and I made it across campus to the bench in the small memorial garden. A giant live oak shaded the area, but Bernie sat on the end of the bench bathed in a swatch of warm sunlight.

"Hello, Bernie," I called out. "We've got to stop meeting like this."

He grabbed his cane to stand. I hopped off my scooter and situated myself next to him on the bench so he wouldn't feel obliged to get to his feet. I gave him a peck on the cheek because he looked lonely, sitting by himself, with only trees for company. I looked around. "Where's your wife?"

"She wanted to stay home and tidy up. I can be a bit of a slob, I guess."

"I can see why you and Nola are friends," Sarah said as she placed the scooter on the smooth paver in front of me and propped my ankle on top of it.

"Ignore her," I said.

"Good to see you, Sarah," Bernie said with a smile. "And here we are again, working together to solve a mystery. Just like in a Nancy Drew book."

"Or Hardy Boys," Sarah amended. "Since you're a guy."

He chuckled. "Maybe we should write our own series."

Sarah nodded, but I noticed that her gaze kept drifting over his shoulder. Even Mardi's attention seemed focused on something behind Bernie. I turned to look but saw nothing except empty air.

"What happened to your leg?" he asked.

"Oh, just a minor accident. I'll be fine in no time. The doctor just wants me to stay off of the ankle for a bit, until it's better."

I could feel Sarah's eyes boring into the side of my face but I ignored her. "So, what do you have?" I indicated the manila folder in Bernie's lap.

He handed it to me. "I don't know if you'll be able to decipher any of this, but I thought you might like to have it anyway. If your dad ever decides to write a book about the murders at the house on Esplanade, he'll be wanting this. It's the DNA tests they did on the stains your construction guys found under the rug in the upstairs room."

"Thank you." I flipped through the pages of what looked like hieroglyphics and technical jargon before closing the folder. I'd give it to Beau to see if any of it would make sense to him. "I didn't realize you were a fan of my dad's books."

"Jaxson got me started—he's a true fan. I'm pretty new to the club, but I have to say that a lot of the old cases you've been working on would be perfect subjects for his future books. I think having an old and crusty retired police detective as a character could add a lot of flavor, too."

I grinned. "I'll let him know. Would you mind summarizing what you learned about the bloodstains? I'm afraid my line of work doesn't include crime-scene analysis, and I doubt watching a lot of true crime counts."

He grinned. "Bottom line, the stains are human blood. Unfortunately, the sample is too old and degraded to extract any viable DNA. A cleaning agent such as bleach might have been used at some point, which would make DNA collection nearly impossible."

I leaned against the back of the bench. I had hoped, for Sarah's sake—and my own—that we'd get the answers needed to set free the spirits of the little boy and the woman who'd been protecting him. I especially wanted to send the dark spirit back to where it came from.

Of course, the bloodstains might not be related to any of the spirits, but, as my dad had drilled into me over and over, there was no such thing as coincidence.

"That's disappointing. I'd really hoped this would lead us somewhere."

"Now, hang on. I'm not done yet. I said the bloodstains weren't able to give us any information. However, it's usual in cases of violent death—as this appears to be, with such a large blood spill—for there to be other sources of DNA."

"Like saliva," Sarah said. "And hair."

"Bingo. Good job, young lady."

Sarah smiled proudly. "Thank you. Nola and I have been bingeing *Cold Case Files* on Netflix."

"Your hard work is showing." He winked at her. "They were able to retrieve hair samples from the cracks in the wooden floor beneath the stain. The strands were contaminated with blood, so it appears that the hair could have come from the victim. We can also use the process of elimination to identify the source by getting hair samples from people who were known to be in the house. So, Sarah, what part of the hair might contain DNA?"

"The roots," we said in unison.

"He wasn't asking you," Sarah said.

"Yeah, sorry. I got carried away."

"You are both right," Bernie said magnanimously. "But the hair samples we retrieved didn't have roots attached. In the absence of DNA, what else might hair found at a crime scene tell us about the victim?"

Sarah thought for a moment. "Well, the color and length could be used for victim identification. And if it's curly or straight."

Uncle Bernie nodded. "Correct. Go on."

"It could tell us the person's race. Or if the person colored their hair," I said.

"All correct." He looked at us expectantly. "What else?"

Sarah's eyes narrowed. "They could tell if it wasn't human, right? Like, if it came from a doll. Or a dog."

"Or . . ."

There was a long silence. "A wig!" Sarah and I shouted at the same time.

"Another bingo for both of you. It appears the hair is synthetic, like that found on dolls and in some wigs. One with short, brown hairs, to be more specific."

"So the victim or someone else associated with the crime scene wore a wig," I said.

"Possibly," Bernie replied. "The good news is that this new clue might lead to reopening the case."

"But how long will that take?" I asked.

He shrugged his large shoulders, the buttons of his corduroy jacket straining from the pressure. "You know how it is. Current cases keep the NOPD pretty busy, so it won't be a priority."

"But that doesn't mean I can't get a head start on the investigation, right?" I asked. "I could talk to the previous owners and ask them if they know anyone who wore a wig."

"Nobody's stopping you." He looked at his watch. "I have to go now—I told Frank I'd meet him in ten minutes, and it's going to take me that long to walk around to the front of the building." Using his cane, he pulled himself up with a little assistance from Sarah. "Ladies, it has been a pleasure, as always. I'll let you know if I find out anything else, and I'll ask you to do the same."

"Of course," I said. "Would you like me to share what you just told us with Beau, or do you want to tell him yourself?"

He leaned heavily on his cane. "I should probably tell him in person. I need to speak with him about another matter anyway, and I really hate giving information over the phone. There's always a chance it will be misinterpreted. I can make an appointment to see him—unless you're going to be seeing him soon?"

"He'll probably stop by tonight or tomorrow, and if you'd like me to pass anything along, I'm happy to do it."

"Yes, well, please tell him that I found some information on that fellow he asked me about. I think you know him—Cooper Ravenel."

I took a moment to respond, surprised at the mention of Cooper's name. "I'm sorry—what?"

He looked confused. "I, uh, thought you, uh—that there was . . ."

I felt a burning sensation in the pit of my stomach. "Did Beau ask you to check up on Cooper?"

Bernie's neck reddened, and he looked so uncomfortable that, if I hadn't been so angry at Beau, I might have felt sorry for the old man. "Oh, dear," he said. "I shouldn't have said anything. I was under the assumption that Beau was asking for you. I shouldn't have assumed, and now I've gotten you upset. I'm so sorry."

Picking up on the agitation in my voice, Mardi had begun to pace around the bench. Forcing a calm I was far from feeling, I said, "It's not your fault, Bernie. It's Beau's. And I'll talk to him later, when I don't feel like killing him with my bare hands. For the time being, I'll tell Beau about the wig if I see him first, but please don't let him know that you told me about Cooper. I'll need to deal with him myself."

"That's fair. And I really and truly am sorry." He studied me without moving away.

I hated myself for asking, but the words were out of my mouth before I could call them back: "Is there something I should know?"

Bernie raised his bushy gray eyebrows. "Depends on how close your relationship is. If it's as close as Beau thinks, then probably. Maybe you should just wait until you see Mr. Ravenel again and ask him yourself."

"About what? You can't just drop that on me and walk away. Cooper and I have known each other for a long time and his sister is one of my best friends. If there's something I need to know, please tell me. I can handle it." I said that only because I assumed that if it was anything bad, Alston would have already told me. Even though I'd just had a lesson on why people should never assume.

He glanced at Sarah and Mardi, who were hanging on every word.

"It's all right," I assured him. "Say what you need to, because my sister knows that if she repeats any of it to our parents, I will never allow her to visit Mardi and Jolene ever again."

Bernie remained reluctant to speak, and he kept looking ahead on the path as if he wished he were already halfway down it.

With forced calm, I said, "I know you're just the messenger, so I won't hold it against you. So please tell me, and I promise I won't tell Beau that you told me anything. I personally don't want to speak with him ever again, so I doubt that will be a problem."

He pressed his lips together and nodded. "Well, then, I'll just say it. Cooper Ravenel is engaged to be married to a woman who is currently in a coma and has been for a couple of years. He was driving the car that led to the accident that caused her current condition. He has power of attorney and will not allow her to be taken off life support, even though her doctors and the experts he's called in have all confirmed that she is in a permanent vegetative state, with no hope of ever waking up. He pays for her twenty-four-hour care in an upscale nursing home outside of Los Angeles and visits her once a month. He's been doing that for two years now."

I heard wind rushing in my ears even though the leaves on the oak tree remained still. My heart pounded heavily in my chest, my breath suspended as my world slowly dismantled itself around me. I recalled how Cooper had avoided talking about the scar on his chin, recalled his shutting down whenever I joked about my driving. I was heartbroken over Cooper's pain. But I was equally angry about his silence.

"Nola? Are you all right?" Bernie asked. "I can ask Frank to drive you and Sarah back to your apartment."

I gave a quick shake of my head. "No. I'm fine." My voice even managed to sound normal. "Do you remember the woman's name?"

He nodded. "Lilly Hoffman."

"Lilly Hoffman," I repeated, the name weighted and strange on my tongue.

Bernie turned his head at the sound of a car horn honking.

"Thank you," I said. "For everything. Now go find Frank. I'll be in touch if I find out anything about the wig. And you do the same."

He gave me a thumbs-up and then continued down the path around the stone building.

Sarah sat down in his vacated spot next to me on the bench, neither of us speaking as we watched him disappear around the corner of the building.

"I told you she wasn't dead," Sarah said softly.

I looked at my sister, not needing to clarify who she meant. "But how did you see her if she isn't dead?"

"Because she's not alive, either. Maybe that's why she's angry. Maybe she's ready to die and Cooper is keeping her here."

The sky had already begun to darken, heralding an early sunset. It would be fully dark before we'd made our way across campus. "Let's go," I said.

She steadied the scooter while I placed my knee on the cushion, and then we headed down the path toward Percival Stern Hall, its midcentury windows and stark architecture appearing even more brutal to me than usual. I barely noticed the streetlight as we crossed Freret Street at the crosswalk.

"There's one more thing you should probably know," Sarah said, sounding out of breath as she jogged to keep up with me and my scooter. "But I don't know if you can handle one more thing."

I stopped to catch my own breath and faced her. "On a scale of one to ten, how bad is it? Because I can only take a one or a two right now."

She thought for a moment. "It's a one or two."

I continued propelling the scooter as she jogged to catch up. "Then go ahead. I'm ready."

"Have you ever met Uncle Bernie's wife?"

I thought for a moment, trying to remember. "No. I don't think I have. Although he talks about her a lot whenever we meet, so I feel as if I know her."

Sarah's eyes became serious. "That's because she's dead. I saw her last time I was here, too. In Jackson Square. She's sad because he's so lonely."

In the grand scheme of things, this tragic revelation was a one or two on my scale of personal disasters. But it was also the tipping point of my emotional state, which over the past several months had accumulated such baggage as my move to New Orleans, managing my addiction, buying my new house, starting a new job, getting into a car crash, and being swarmed by numerous spirit energies despite my reluctance to engage them.

The only thing I was sure of at that moment was that I wouldn't cry. I'd dealt with much worse events in my life and hadn't shed a tear. Tears were for those who had the time to wallow in their misery. After each major disaster in my life I hadn't had the luxury of falling apart. I'd needed to remain standing just for my survival, and it would take a lot more than simultaneous betrayal by the two men in my life to make me break down.

But that didn't mean I wasn't stewing in anger and hurt. Clenching my teeth together so hard that my jaw hurt, I kept my scooter moving forward, heedless of the stares of passersby and Sarah's running footsteps and the jingling of Mardi's tags behind me as my sister continued the apologetic litany that followed me all the way back to the apartment.

CHAPTER 28

The following morning I awoke to multiple texts from Jolene. I could tell they were hers from the sheer abundance of emojis. Only Sarah used them with the same frequency, but she was twelve.

"Awoke" was too strong a word following the fitful restlessness and tossing and turning—as much as I could toss and turn while keeping my foot elevated—that had occupied the majority of the time I'd spent in my bed. More than once, I'd begun to dial Melanie's number before changing my mind. I needed advice, but I couldn't call her. Instead, I'd texted Jolene and fallen asleep while waiting for a response.

I imagined her having fun with her extended family members, all of them sounding just like her, and I felt a stab of homesickness for my own family. Or maybe Jolene was having too much fun with Jaxson, something I preferred not to think about. I'd finally turned off my phone around midnight, since waiting for it to beep was part of what was keeping me awake.

By morning my eyes were crusty and swollen from crying and lack of sleep, and I had to wash my face in cold water to clear my vision and my head so that I could attempt to read Jolene's texts. Flipping through them, I saw that she'd sent me multiple pictures of what appeared to be a red car. Despite the smiley-face and heart emojis that accompanied the photos, my stomach did a sick somersault when I realized they were pictures of the Ford Mustang that Jaxson would be driving back to New Orleans for me.

I considered staying in bed and turning off my phone again. I didn't want to talk to Beau or Cooper, because despite going over various scenarios in my head instead of sleeping, I hadn't come up with a single one that could adequately express my anger and disappointment. And my hurt.

Maybe it was a good thing that Sarah was with me, because otherwise I would have rolled over and shoved my face into my pillow so the world would go away at least for a while. But Sarah was probably awake and waiting for me. *You have bravery on steroids, and I can talk to dead people. It's, like, our superpowers.* I had serious doubts about my bravery, but for her I had to at least pretend.

Using my crutches, I went in search of Sarah. She was still in her pajamas and wearing a pair of fluffy dog slippers that looked a lot like Mardi, who was curled under her chair at the dining table.

Sarah jumped up, pulled out two chairs for me, and helped me sit. "Hang on. I'll get your coffee. Jolene warned me what might happen if you weren't caffeinated first thing." She ran into the kitchen and returned with a coffee mug with Dorothy's ruby red slippers dotting its pink ceramic surface. It was Jolene's favorite mug, but I wasn't coherent enough to mention that. I'd just need to make sure that it was washed, dried, and returned to its spot before Jolene got back, or there would be repercussions. Like being forced to wear false eyelashes. Or pantyhose (something I'd never seen before I'd roomed with Jolene).

Sarah put the mug in front of me and I took a grateful sip.

"Are you feeling better?"

"Well, the good news is that my head hurts and my eyes sting, which means I'm not noticing the pain in my ankle as much. Which, now that I think about it, is actually hurting more than before."

"That means it's healing, right? Can I get you a pain pill? It will probably fix the headache, too."

I shook my head and immediately wished I hadn't, as it felt like my brain was slamming against the sides of my skull. "I'm good," I said.

She looked at me with serious eyes. "Dad doesn't like taking anything, either. He says he'd rather suffer through it."

I wasn't sure how much our parents had shared with her about the addiction tendencies I shared with Jack, so I was careful how I responded. "I just don't like depending on anything to make me feel better. The pain's not that bad. Really." I took another sip of coffee so she wouldn't see me grimace.

Sarah pushed a plate of Jolene's reheated muffins toward me. "Are we still planning on going to the Esplanade house today with Cooper?"

I felt physically ill. "I'd rather not. I'm still trying to process everything, and I don't think I'm ready to see him. I haven't heard from him, either, which makes it easier not to think about him."

She placed a muffin on her own plate and began picking at it, pinching off bites and putting them in her mouth. "You sound like Mom. She's, like, the queen of procrastination. Not that I would ever say that to her face."

I grunted, not yet ready to engage before I'd had at least a full cup of coffee. I opened my phone to my messages, then slid it over. "Could you please read these texts from Jolene and paraphrase for me? My puffy eyes are messing with my vision."

Sarah scrolled down the page, pausing occasionally to smile or frown, before finally looking up. "Bottom line: She's had a great time and so has Jaxson, but she's coming home today because she feels guilty about leaving you and me here to fend for ourselves." Sarah shrugged, examining the muffin crumbs on the table and the remnants of our meals and snacks in the living room. "Not sure what she means, since I don't think we've been in starvation mode or anything. Anyway, she just left, so it's too late to tell her to stay."

I struggled to assemble my brain cells. "She's on her way? Now?" I looked around at the mess and at the forbidden mug in front of me.

Sarah had already jumped up and begun collecting dirty plates and glasses. "Don't worry. I have a lot of practice with making a room look ready for inspection. Dad and I do it all the time when Mom tells us she's coming home early." She paused, her eyes wide with excitement. "And now we'll have a car, so we can go to the house on Esplanade. As soon as we tell Jolene why we want to go, she'll be happy to drive us. Maybe we can stop by to talk with Joan and Honey first, to ask them about the wig. Do you want to call before we leave?"

"I don't . . ."

She picked up my phone again and typed in the password—it wasn't surprising that she knew what it was—and began scrolling through the contacts. "Their last names are Meggison and Wentzel, right? I don't see them on here."

"That's because I don't have them on my phone. I guess we'll have to wait."

Sarah regarded me with a look of hurt and disappointment. "I know you don't want to do this now, but I'm leaving on Sunday. And you did promise."

I sighed heavily. "Fine. You're right. Honey wrote her number on a piece of notepaper that should still be in my backpack."

She jumped up and retrieved the backpack from the hat stand in the front room, then handed it to me. "Keep tidying up while I look. The living room isn't going to clean itself." Ignoring her exaggerated groaning, I stuck my hand into my backpack, searching for the small, folded piece of paper. I rarely cleaned out my backpack except in moments like this, when I was trying to find something in the mess, or when it became too heavy. I began pulling out the contents and placing them on the table—my wallet; my travel coffee mug, which probably needed washing; an empty pack of gum; a full pack of gum; a lipstick. I examined the lipstick, not having to wonder who had put it in there or why. I found the crumpled paper at the very bottom, wedged into the creases of a cloth bag held closed with a tied string.

"I found the phone number," I called out as I placed the paper on the table. Then I opened the bag and watched as two stones—one black and one pink—fell onto the table. They'd been given to me by Madame Zoe, and just as quickly forgotten. I looked inside the dark crevices at the bottom of the backpack and pulled out the second pouch. I remembered Beau handing it to me, outright dismissing the stones and everything Madame Zoe had told us. I'd tossed his pouch into my backpack and forgotten it along with mine.

I untied the string and watched as a green stone and a purple crystal slid out of the bag. I picked up the purple one—amethyst, Madame Zoe had said. Used for enhancing psychic powers. No wonder Beau had wanted nothing to do with the stones.

"What's that?" Sarah asked, pausing next to me while carrying two folded tray tables to the stand on which they were kept in the corner of the dining area.

"Some kind of psychic-healing stones. Madame Zoe gave them to Beau and me."

Her eyes widened as she looked at them, making me uneasy.

"What is it, Sarah? What's wrong?"

"That phone call. From Bonnie. She said to 'find the stones.'" Her worried eyes met mine.

I picked up the obsidian and rose quartz the psychic had given me, and I rubbed them together in my hand. "But why would Bonnie want us to find them? It's not like they were lost or anything. I've been carrying them around in my backpack ever since Madame Zoe gave them to us. I would have discovered them sooner or later."

I closed my fist, as if I could squeeze out the answer like juice from a lemon. But when I opened my fingers, the stones remained cold and mute on my palm.

Sarah returned the trays to the stand, her expression thoughtful. "Can you think of any other stones? Just because you happened to pull these from your backpack doesn't mean they're the ones Bonnie was talking about. I mean, maybe she's referring to stones you're using on one of your renovation projects?"

I rubbed the stones together again as I thought, wishing that I could call Cooper to discuss possibilities. My dad thought that Cooper was excellent at unraveling perplexing mysteries. He'd even earned an acknowledgment in one of Jack's books for decoding the cryptic markings in an old mausoleum.

As if I had conjured him, my phone buzzed with a text from Cooper. At the sight of his picture, my head was barraged by too many emotions to name, leaving me mostly numb.

"Want me to read that?" Sarah asked, peering over my shoulder at my phone.

"No need," I said, pressing the face of my phone against my chest. "You're too young to be exposed to this kind of emotional trauma."

"Too late. He says his plans have changed, and he won't be back until Monday at the earliest. He says he has business in LA, but it's only a three-hour time difference, so he'll call once he's stateside. And then he says that he misses you, but there aren't any emojis, so I can't translate exactly."

"He's a grown man. He doesn't use emojis." It sounded as if I were repeating something I'd read or said before. I couldn't think of anything original to say as my thoughts were circling around the meaning behind Cooper's text, and around his business plans, which most likely included a visit to the fiancée he hadn't thought to mention to me. And neither had his sister. Either Alston had been sworn to silence or he hadn't mentioned his fiancée or the car accident to his family.

"He's probably going to LA to—" Sarah began.

"Don't say it," I said. "It's bad enough that I'm thinking it, so just keep it to yourself, all right? And the living room isn't going to clean itself."

Sarah sighed and rolled her eyes, but she returned to tidying, leaving me to stare at the stones and wonder what my mother had meant by *Find the stones.*

At the sound of a car door shutting, Sarah and Mardi went downstairs to greet Jolene. I listened to the squeals and barks of greeting from my position on the couch with my leg propped up on cushions, leaving me feeling left out and sorry for myself for the first time since the accident.

Jolene and Sarah, along with Mardi, emerged from the stairway with arms overladen with bags, suitcases, and Tupperware. Jolene dropped her load in the middle of the floor so she could embrace me, the scent of hair spray enveloping me along with her warm hug.

I squirmed under her close inspection and quickly diverted her attention. "How are you? Did you have a good time?" Her green eyes were bright and clear, her perfect complexion even rosier than usual, and my untrained eyes could tell that the enhanced color had nothing to do with cosmetics.

"That's like asking a fish in the ocean if he has enough water! I've just spent time with my whole family, and I think my neck has just about been rubbed raw from all the hugging. We had plenty to eat, and the weather was fine, which was really a blessing, because the whole McKenna clan likes to play some football on the lawn after we eat, to make room for dessert. Even Mama and Grandmama get into the game, although we know we're not supposed to tackle them, but that doesn't stop either one of them from tackling us, which is always a sight to see. . . ."

"What about Jaxson?"

"Oh, Jaxson had a wonderful time, too. Mama and Daddy loved meeting him and were all too happy to have him there. Mama put him right next to her at the dining table, and Daddy even showed him his gun collection. He doesn't even trust his brother, Harold, enough to let him come within spitting distance. Isn't that a hoot?"

"Yes, but I meant, where is Jaxson?"

"Oh, right. Like, *Where's Jaxson?*" The color in her cheeks intensified.

"Exactly." I must have been watching too many true-crime shows, because the first thoughts that flitted through my mind were of her grandmother's funeral home and Jolene's access to formaldehyde and other dangerous chemicals. And shovels. "Wasn't he supposed to come back with you?"

"Yes, but then I came back early to check on you, and he needed to stay another day to finish up with the business part of his trip. He'll be back on Sunday." She smiled and it almost seemed like a normal smile. Almost.

"What about you, Nola? Are you feeling all right? You look thin." Redirecting her gaze to Sarah, she asked, "Has Nola been eating? Don't you think she looks thin?"

"I think she looks the same, Jolene. Maybe, since you haven't seen her in a couple of days, she looks different to you."

When Jolene turned back to me, Sarah hastily picked up two foil cups—left over from the previous night's cupcakes—off the rug and discreetly hid them in her jeans pocket. Studying me closely, Jolene said, "It looks like you've been crying. What's wrong?"

Lying to Jolene was pointless, so I didn't even try. "I found out that Cooper has a fiancée. She's been in a coma ever since a car accident two years ago. Beau . . ." I stopped, again feeling a surge of anger and sadness gripping my throat and rendering me speechless.

Sarah finished for me. "Beau asked Uncle Bernie to dig into Cooper's past and that's how we found out. From Uncle Bernie, I mean."

Small creases of concern appeared between Jolene's red brows. "Well, that's not good."

I waited for her to hug me or say the right thing. Maybe even offer to call up one of her Mississippi cousins to knock some sense into Beau or Cooper or both of them.

Instead, she folded her arms and gave me a level gaze. "So, what are you going to do? Besides crying and avoiding speaking with Beau and Cooper, hoping that the problem will go away."

I opened my mouth, but she cut me off. "Sarah, would you please take all this food back to the kitchen and put it away while I have a little come-to-Jesus meeting with your sister?"

Sarah sighed. "Whatever." Stepping heavily, she grabbed the handles of two tote bags and began dragging them across the floor toward the kitchen, Mardi following at her heels.

"Nola, honey. What are you going to do?"

I blinked back stupid tears. "I was hoping you were going to tell me. You always know the right answer."

She smiled. "I don't, and knowing the answer isn't always what you need. Sometimes you just need to try hard enough to figure something out, and then the answer will come to you. Just know that it's usually not what you expected."

"I'm just so angry."

"Well, then." Jolene straightened. "As my grandmama would say, that's as good a start as any. What should we do first?"

"'We'?" I said hopefully.

"Of course. I never said you'd have to do anything alone. I've got your back. As soon as you pull up your big-girl pants, I'm here to help."

"Yay!" Sarah said, coming out of the kitchen. "We need you to drive us to Honey's house. I just called her, and she and her sister will be home if we can be there in the next hour."

Jolene looked at me. "Well, what are you going to do?"

I looked from Jolene to Sarah. "Do I have a choice?"

"You always have a choice," Jolene said. "Just first make sure it's one you can live with."

I sighed. "I guess I'd better go put on some color."

CHAPTER 29

Jolene helped me down the stairs—muttering something about how angry Dr. Longo would be if she knew I wasn't on the couch with my foot elevated—while Sarah carried my crutches. We were leaving later than planned because I'd needed to change out of my pajamas and it had taken longer than anticipated to get a brush through my hair. I'd feigned surprise when the brush got stuck for the third time, and Jolene had commented that it didn't look like my hair had been brushed in days.

Jolene opened the rear passenger-side door for me. I looked into the open door and spotted a large cardboard box with untaped flaps resting on the seat next to the opposite window. "What's that?" I asked.

She followed my gaze. "Oh, right. I forgot that was there. I can bring it upstairs if you like, but I think the backseat's big enough for both of you."

"Don't worry about it. There's plenty of room, and it gives me something to lean against." I crawled headfirst into the backseat and made myself comfortable, with my leg propped up along the seat.

The seat belts in the back had long since disappeared into the crevice at the rear of the seat, and I didn't have a door handle to hold on to. I just kept reminding myself that I was in a steel tank, and that because of the holiday there were fewer people on the road for Jolene to hit.

During the drive, Jolene shared stories from her visit to Mississippi, and she even sprinkled Jaxson's name in several times. She seemed her usual bright and cheerful self instead of the heartbroken mess I'd half expected to see. She didn't mention Carly and Jaxson's engagement party, either, and I certainly wasn't going to bring it up and spoil her mood.

When she took a sharp turn, I heard the sound of multiple objects shifting in the box behind my back. "Hey, Jolene—what's in the box? And if it's from your grandmother's funeral home, I don't want to know."

"It's actually from Trevor. He gave it to me before we left for Thanksgiving. He asked me to keep it in my car for safekeeping and said that he'd get it back from me when I returned."

"Like, specifically in your car? Did he tell you what was in it?"

"Yes—he didn't want me to go to the trouble of bringing it up to the apartment, and he said it would be fine in the backseat. And he didn't say what was in it, just that it's odds and ends from the storeroom at the Past Is Never Past. He's tired of straightening the shelves and then seeing the next day that Henry has gone in and made a mess and poor Trevor can't find anything and Christopher blames it on Trevor—at least that's what Trevor thinks. So he decided to mess with Henry by taking some of the personal items that Henry has left in the storeroom and in the desk and putting them in a place where Henry will never find them."

I grinned. "Trevor is a genius. Bubba is the perfect hiding place, since Trevor knew you'd be driving to Mississippi for Thanksgiving. So, what's next? The stuff magically reappears and sends Henry over the edge?"

"That's the plan." Jolene glanced over her shoulder at me. "We shouldn't be laughing, but it is funny. Henry does seem to enjoy antagonizing poor Trevor. I don't blame the boy for wanting a little mild-mannered revenge on his tormentor."

"Just as long as Henry doesn't find out who's behind it. I think he has a mean streak, and I wouldn't want to see Trevor hurt in any way."

Jolene bumped over the curb in front of Honey and Joan's house. "We're here." After exiting the car, she retrieved my crutches from the cavernous trunk before opening my door.

"Hey, look." Sarah pointed out a gray Honda sedan pulling away from the opposite curb two houses down. "They've got South Carolina plates. Do you think Mom and Dad are keeping tabs on us?"

The car passed us, traveling slowly enough that I recognized the two occupants I'd spotted when Cooper and I had been looking at the house. "Not unless you let slip that you weren't in Mississippi," I said as Jolene handed me my crutches.

As I watched the car continue down the street, I felt sure that it was the same gray Honda I'd seen before.

"You look like someone just walked over your grave," Jolene said.

"I have no idea what that means." I indicated the moving car. "Have you seen that car before?"

She peered after it, squinting her eyes to see it better before shaking her head. "I could have, but it's not that memorable, you know? Not like a red 1967 Ford Mustang. Now, that's a car people remember."

"Speaking of which, can we talk about that? I've had a lot of time to think since my accident, and I don't think I'm ready for a car of any kind, much less a classic like—"

"Oh, look." Jolene waved in the direction of the house. "Honey's at the door. Let's not keep her waiting. It's getting chilly." She gave an exaggerated shiver, then led the way to the front walk.

I'd reached the front steps before I realized that Sarah wasn't with us. I turned to find her tapping her fingers against the peacock brooch on her sweater while staring at a window on the left side of the house. "Are you okay?"

She was humming a familiar tune, ABBA's "Fernando," her lower lip clenched between her teeth. Slowly, her eyes drifted down to meet mine. "Sure. But let's not stay too long, okay?"

"You got it. This should be quick, but just in case, give me a signal if you need to leave. I'll say my ankle's hurting or something and we need to go, all right?"

Honey met us at the door, yellow and green paint drops in her hair and on her oversized shirt. A finger smear of orange paint blazed across one cheek, and Zeus perched on her shoulder, his dark eyes watching us calmly. "Come in, come in. I'm sorry that you just missed Joan. She has a standing appointment at the beauty parlor every other Friday so she couldn't stay."

"No worries. We won't stay long." I turned and pointed to the house where we'd spotted the car pulling away from the curb. "Do you by chance know anyone on the street who owns a gray Honda sedan? Maybe new neighbors from South Carolina?"

"A gray Honda?" She shook her head. "Not that I know of. Besides, isn't Honda the most popular car brand in America? You probably see them everywhere."

"Probably. Just thought I'd ask. I've seen what I think is the same car enough times to notice."

"It's just coincidence," Honey said, her smile cracking the dried paint on her cheek.

Sarah and I looked at each other, raising our eyebrows like our dad did whenever someone brought up a coincidence.

Honey opened the door wider and stepped back into the foyer so my crutches and I would fit. I introduced Honey to Sarah and Jolene before indicating the bird on Honey's shoulder. "And this is Zeus. I don't think you've met him before, either."

Sarah eyed Zeus warily, as if he were a copperhead instead of a harmless avian.

"Right," I said, staring at the bird with apprehension. I remembered him going into attack mode when Beau had taken Annabelle from my backpack during our visit.

Honey smiled. "It's a pleasure to meet you, Sarah. And, Nola, I'm so glad you reached out. I initially thought it was to tell us about the doll."

"Excuse me?"

"Lynda's baby doll. We've been hoping to hear if Mimi had had a chance to examine it yet." Honey closed the door behind us.

I exchanged a glance with Jolene. "She's, um, not done examining it yet. Her daughter-in-law's funeral was the day before yesterday."

"Of course. I did read about that in the paper. I hope they find out who was responsible so the family can get some closure. Joan and I know exactly how that feels, of course. An unsolved murder and missing loved ones are difficult burdens, aren't they? And here you are, in the middle of both. I suppose there's some sort of reason for that, don't you?"

"Probably," Sarah said at the same time I said, "I doubt it."

"Your house is lovely." Jolene began walking toward the living room with the large picture window, its wide sill covered with framed family photographs.

"Is your Beau not with you today?" Honey asked, following Jolene.

"He's not *my* Beau," I clarified. "And no, it's just us today."

"Well, that's a relief, because I'm not dressed for male company. Joan doesn't approve of my artistic endeavors, so I choose times when she's not here to work in peace. May I offer you anything to eat or drink?"

"No, but thanks. I promise we won't keep you. As Sarah mentioned on the phone, we're on our way to the house on Esplanade, so we won't stay long. This could have been a quick phone conversation, but if you don't mind, I also want to look at your framed photos again."

"Of course," she said. She fluffed a cushion on the couch and gestured for me to sit. "Sarah told me about your ankle, and I'm so sorry. And I'm sure your doctor has told you that you should be keeping it raised as much as possible."

"It's more trouble to get up than to sit down, so if it's all right with you, I'll remain standing so I can make my way around the room."

Jolene shook her head and wore her *bless your heart* expression. "Just in case you couldn't tell, Nola has terrible listening skills, but we love her anyway."

Honey laughed. "I believe my sister shares the same affliction."

My phone beeped with a text from Beau. We need to talk.

I closed my screen without responding and placed my phone in my back pocket. Hobbling over to the windowsill, I said, "I don't know if you've been told yet, but the coroner's office has had a chance to investigate the bloodstain found under the rug in the upstairs room."

Honey clutched a strand of chunky turquoise stones at her neck. "Yes. They let us know that it was too old to be useful to the investigation."

I slipped out the frame Beau had borrowed and replaced it on the sill before picking up a photograph I remembered from my previous visit; it showed Joan and Honey with their stepmother, Sybil, and their sister-in-law, Jessica, along with Lynda as a baby. "The blood sample was. But hair samples were also discovered, in between the floorboards, and might be useful. I have an in with the NOPD, which is why I found out first, but I'm sure you'll be updated shortly. That's why we're here. They won't be able to pull DNA from the hair, because it's synthetic, not human."

Honey blinked up at me as I replaced the frame and picked up a photo of Jessica and her husband's mother, Sybil—the woman who was murdered in the back room of the Esplanade house. Sybil had short silver hair worn in an attractive bob, and Jessica had long blond hair. Neither appeared to be wearing a wig, let alone a short brown wig.

"Do you remember anyone being in the house around the time of the murder who might have been wearing a short, dark wig?"

Honey thought for a moment before shaking her head. "No. Not that I remember. But maybe Joan will."

"Hopefully." I put down the frame, then picked up one with a photograph of Lynda as a towheaded toddler, Annabelle dangling from her hand. I brought the frame closer to my face to study the doll. But the doll in the photograph seemed devoid of all the creepiness I now associated with it.

My ankle throbbed from my being upright for so long. I placed the frame back on the ledge, then looked at the collection of photos, arranged three-deep, not a single one looking like its subject could be wearing a wig. "Thanks so much for your time and for letting me look at the photos again. Please let me know if Joan remembers anything about a wig."

"I will. And please let us know as soon as Mimi has something to tell us about that doll."

"Of course." My phone buzzed again, at the same time that I registered the sound of bird wings flapping around my head.

I turned to see the bird circling the ceiling before coming to rest on Sarah's outstretched arm. "Be careful," I said. "Zeus tried to attack Beau when we were here."

"He won't hurt me," Sarah said matter-of-factly.

The hooked yellow beak opened wide and a rusty, disused voice said, "Hide the key. Hide the key. Hide the key." Then Zeus fell silent, staring at me with the round black eye on the right side of his head.

Honey's mouth opened with astonishment. "That's the first time I've ever heard him speak! Oh, my goodness. Joan won't believe it."

"Do you know what he means?" I asked.

"I have no idea," Honey said. "I'll ask Joan, but I can't for the life of me think of what key he's talking about. Or why we'd want to hide it." She held out her arm and Zeus flew to her, settling again on her shoulder, his head turning while his obsidian eyes surveyed the room.

Sarah watched the bird closely. "He's repeating something he heard, right? Isn't that how parrots work?"

"Yes, that's right." Honey stroked the bird's small head. "But since he's been completely silent ever since we got him, I don't know when he might have learned it."

"Maybe he means the key to the armoire," Jolene said.

"Maybe," I agreed. "Although we've opened the armoire and haven't found anything of value, except possibly the doll. And it's not like the armoire is impenetrable without a key—it has just a single lock that's easily picked by a locksmith, or anyone else with the right tools. Or a hammer if someone doesn't care about antiques and just wants to find out what's inside."

"Where did you find the key?" Honey asked.

I was spared from answering by my phone's buzzing.

Please call. I talked to Adele. You're in danger.

I shoved my phone back in my pocket. I might have become desensitized by all the warnings I'd been exposed to from beyond the grave in recent months. Especially any coming from Beau. I doubted that I'd ever believe anything he told me again.

"Thank you, Honey. It was great to see you. Please let us know what Joan has to say about the wig. And if she knows what Zeus meant by 'the key.'"

"I will. And I'll ask her about the Honda, too." She clasped her paint-spattered hands in front of her. "I feel so invigorated! For the first time in so long, I feel hopeful about getting answers. And about sweet Zeus. It's like he's finally coming alive again."

"I'm glad. We'll talk soon." Using my crutches, I hobbled to the front door, where Sarah was already waiting, eager to leave. "Are you okay?" I asked quietly.

"Just hurry," she said as she opened the door and stepped out onto the porch.

We said our good-byes and headed toward the car. The front passenger-side door lock no longer worked, so Sarah just yanked the door open. She gave a small yelp, then stepped back.

Jolene ran to see what was wrong, and I struggled to keep up. She'd already reached inside the car and pulled the familiar doll off the front seat by the time I caught up to them.

"Can you put it in the trunk, please?" Sarah asked. "It's giving off conflicting vibes and I'm starting to get a headache."

Jolene unlocked the trunk and dropped it inside. "I think we should put it back where we found it," she said. "Maybe it just wants to go home."

I looked at Sarah, waiting for her to agree. But her gaze was focused on the box in the backseat, her eyes narrowed in concentration.

"What is it?" I asked.

It took her a moment to raise her eyes to meet mine. And then, in a woman's voice I didn't recognize, she said, "Find the stones."

CHAPTER 30

It was several minutes before the glassiness in Sarah's eyes dissipated. She remained standing by the car, frozen in place by visions and voices no one else could see or hear. And then she blinked and she was Sarah again, looking around as if wondering where she was and why she was there.

"I'm fine, I'm fine," she insisted as she climbed into the car. "I'll explain later. Right now we need to leave."

Jolene helped me into the backseat before sliding into the driver's seat. "Maybe we should go home. . . ."

"No," Sarah said. "I'm fine. I have a lot of voices in my head right now and I'm trying to figure out stuff. And I only have until I leave on Sunday, so I don't want to waste any time."

"What did you mean by 'Find the stones'?" I asked.

Sarah turned to look at me. "What?"

"That's what you said—when you got to the car. You were looking at the box in the backseat, and that's what you said. But it wasn't your voice."

She returned to facing forward, her gaze on the windshield in front of her. "I don't remember," she said quietly. "But I thought we already found the stones. In your backpack." Sarah leaned her head back. "Apparently those aren't the stones we need to figure out whatever it is we're supposed to figure out." She paused. "I think we should call Beau for backup."

"Between you, me, and Jolene I'm sure we can figure this out without him. Besides, I'd rather set my hair on fire than ask for his help."

No one spoke on the drive to Esplanade, the only sound that of Jolene's cassette tape of Dolly Parton's greatest hits playing through the car's speakers. Beau called twice, but I silenced my phone and let his calls go to voice mail. I still hadn't heard from Cooper, but instead of being disappointed I was grateful for the reprieve. I considered calling Alston to get any background on Lilly Hoffman, but decided against it just in case Cooper hadn't told his family. As angry as I was, it wasn't my secret to share.

Jolene parked at the curb in front of the house on Esplanade Avenue. I hadn't seen it since the windows in the upstairs room had shattered for no known reason, and the boards temporarily nailed across them gave the house a shade of ominous neglect.

I wasn't one to feel negative vibes from a house, and I hadn't felt anything but hopefulness about this one since I'd first seen it. Maybe it was the dumpster at the side of the house that tinged my feelings now; it was filled with old plumbing fixtures and outdated lights and other detritus of past lives. More than likely it was the evil entity whose presence at the side of the house had been captured in a photograph. And the creepy baby doll that we'd found in the house—and that seemed determined to go where it wanted to—most definitely altered my perception. It was clear that the doll was trying to tell us something. I only hoped we could figure it out before someone had a heart attack looking in their rearview mirror.

Sarah was the first to get out of the car. While she helped me out of the backseat, Jolene retrieved the doll from the trunk. As we made our way to the front door, she held the doll at arm's length as if it were covered in wet paint, then dropped it on the porch so she could open the door with the key I'd given her.

"Do you smell that?" Sarah whispered.

I nodded. "Youth-Dew perfume. A bottle of it was found in the armoire. Joan told us that it's the same perfume her stepmother, Sybil, wore."

Sarah nodded. "The one who was murdered here."

"Yes." I swallowed. "Is she alone?"

Sarah gave an abrupt head shake. "They're all here."

The door swung open and the three of us peered inside. Drop cloths covered the wooden floors, and abandoned ladders and construction tools sat scattered around the front room. Formica countertops from the kitchen were stacked against a wall, ready to join their out-of-date friends in the dumpster. Sarah picked up the doll and led the way into the house, with Jolene and me following close behind.

Sarah's gaze was focused on the doorway leading to the kitchen, from which a staircase rose to the upstairs room. "He doesn't want us here," she whispered. "Sybil is keeping us safe, but we don't have much time."

The sound of small feet scampered across the floor above us. I froze, listening as a footfall above followed and an icy chill blew through the room. "We have to hurry." Sarah began walking quickly through the kitchen to the back bedrooms as the small running footsteps came down the stairs. "Stay here."

"Not while I've got breath in my body," Jolene said as she followed Sarah and I hobbled after both of them. I looked over my shoulder toward the stairs as I passed, telling myself that the dark cloud forming at the top was only in my imagination.

We found Sarah sitting cross-legged on the floor in front of the armoire, the doll cradled against her chest. I watched the reflection of her face in the full-length mirror appear to shift as if I were seeing through raindrops on a window. Her eyes darkened as she leaned forward, her lips moving silently. Jolene looked at me, and I held my finger to my lips and shook my head. I'd seen Sarah converse with empty rooms and vacated corners ever since she was a baby.

I watched small puffs of white escape from her mouth as she spoke through pale blue lips. Jolene's teeth chattered as she pulled off her coat and draped it around my sister. Sarah didn't move.

"What key?" Sarah asked, her voice barely audible. Another footfall came from above, followed by a creak. I found myself wishing it were a living, breathing intruder's footfall rather than the alternative.

"What key?" she asked again, her voice more urgent. She looked over her shoulder toward the doorway. She closed her eyes, listening to something no one else could hear. Her eyes snapped open and she jumped up. "We have to leave. Now."

The air in the room had chilled so much that frost had formed on the mirrors and the window glass. Without waiting to be told twice, Jolene took one of my crutches and made me lean on her as she propelled us quickly toward the back of the house.

"Don't you need to leave the doll here?" I called to Sarah.

She didn't turn around or slow down but headed toward the back room and the door to the outside. She flung it open and ran out into the small backyard, Jolene and me following like a pair of ungainly ducklings looking for their mother.

Sarah continued moving, through the small side yard and toward the front of the house, not stopping until she'd reached the car.

"If you can make it on your own, I'll meet y'all at the car," Jolene said. "I need to lock up the house, although it's unclear to me if I need to keep people out or in."

I nodded, then hobbled the short distance to the curb. When I reached Sarah we were both out of breath and my ankle was throbbing, meaning that there was a reason why I was supposed to be resting and keeping it elevated. Like I had a choice.

"What just happened?" I asked. I immediately regretted my harsh tone when I saw that Sarah was close to tears.

"I'm sorry, but the woman told me we needed to go because we were in danger."

My breath stilled. "From whom?"

"From him." She indicated the house with her chin. "He won't come farther than the front porch now, because he doesn't want to leave the woman and the child. They're giving him his strength, which is why he's keeping them here. And because they know his secret." She paused. "He will do anything to make sure we don't discover what it is."

I looked down at the doll. "Why didn't you leave that in the house?"

"Because he wanted me to."

Nothing else she could have said would have chilled me as much as that.

Jolene's phone rang as she reached the car. She answered it as she slid behind the wheel and slammed the car door behind her. Her greeting was followed by a long silence. "All right. We're on our way now."

She tossed her phone into her handbag before facing me. "That was Beau. He's been trying to reach you. He went to the apartment to talk to you and found that the alarm was sounding and the back door had been forced open. The police are on their way, but he already checked to make sure no one was inside. He thinks the alarm scared whoever broke in, because it doesn't look like anything's been disturbed."

Jolene turned the key and Bubba rumbled to a start. "That's a relief," I said. "I hate to think of some stranger pawing through all our things. But what on earth were they thinking they might find of any value? It's not like we're in a high-rent building. I mean, when I showed my family a picture of the outside, Mama thought we were living in the projects."

I sat up. "Oh, no. The rings. Adele's wedding rings. Beau gave them to me for safekeeping."

Sarah turned to face me. "Don't worry, Nola. They're safe. I put them where nobody would ever think to look."

I tried to think of a secret hiding place in the apartment and could come up with only the obvious. "The freezer?"

"Of course not. That's, like, Burglary 101. Everybody thinks that's the safest place to hide valuables, but every robber knows that now, thanks to all the true-crime shows, so that's the first place they look. I'm a lot more creative than that." She turned back around, a smug grin on her face.

"You hid them in the Barbie head, didn't you?" Jolene asked.

Sarah jerked her head toward Jolene. "How did you know?"

"Who do you think drilled that hole in the bottom? It's where I used to hide my favorite lipstick from my little sister because she kept borrowing it and wouldn't return it."

Relieved, I sat back against the box and looked out the window to prepare what I was going to say to Beau. We were passing Café Degas, where I'd gone with Beau and Cooper, when I spotted a gray sedan parked facing away from us on the adjacent perpendicular street. I might not have even noticed it except for the recognizable South Carolina license plate.

"Turn the car around!" I shouted. "I just saw the Honda!"

Sarah's screams and mine intermingled with honking horns and screeching brakes as Jolene took an immediate illegal U-turn over the neutral ground before bumping over the curb to travel down Esplanade in the direction we'd just come from.

"Slow down," I said as she approached the intersection. "It was parked right there." I pointed to the now-empty curb and the equally empty street. "Turn here," I instructed, belatedly remembering that Jolene's focus behind the wheel didn't include other vehicles.

We barely avoided being sideswiped by a delivery truck as she turned, and although we made a thorough three-block search for the car, it had disappeared.

Beau's truck was already parked in our driveway when we pulled into the parking pad behind the apartment building. Beau and Jaxson were both working on the back door, which they had removed from its hinges and placed on cinder blocks. A new doorknob, still in its packaging, sat on top of a bag from Freret Hardware.

"I'll go make sure the rings are still where I put them," Sarah announced before she and Jolene climbed out and closed their doors, apparently forgetting that I was still in the backseat and that the creepy doll was with me. Not wanting to wait until they remembered me, I unlatched my door, then used my good leg to kick it open. I was struggling to get out of the car without my crutches, which were in the trunk, when Beau appeared.

"You look like a roach on its back," he said as he reached for me. "Let me help you."

"I can manage." I kept my hands out of his reach as I maneuvered myself toward the edge of the seat.

"Come on, Nola. Let me help. You're not even supposed to be off the couch, and I know falling out of a car isn't part of your recovery plan, either."

"I'd rather break my other ankle than accept anything from you." I succeeded in putting my good foot on the ground and grabbed the doorframe to hoist myself up.

He stepped back. "Why are you so mad?"

My anger kept scrambling the words in my head, so no sentences would form. In frustration, I lifted my right hand to grab him by the collar of his shirt, just to get his attention, but I missed, sending me lurching sideways out of the car. He grabbed me before I had the chance to steady myself using my damaged ankle.

Gently, he stood me up and leaned me against the car. "Are you okay?"

I was breathing heavily from the exertion and my emotions, and all I could think was that it was a good thing for Beau that I had a broken ankle. "Am I okay?" I shouted. Jaxson, Jolene, and Sarah had all turned and were watching us. "Let's just say that I'm a lot better physically than I am mentally. Because you"—I jabbed my finger in the direction of his chest but couldn't poke him because he'd stepped back—"are a jerk who thinks I need protecting, and asked for a background check on someone I care about without even telling me."

He looked surprised. "You weren't supposed to know."

On the list of all the stupid things he could have said, that was at the very top. "Yeah, well, I do. And I don't appreciate your interference."

"Come on, Nola. The guy's hiding something pretty major from you. Aren't you glad you now know he's got a fiancée?"

It felt as if my head might spin off my shoulders. "It isn't any of your business. Cooper would have told me. In his own time." I wasn't sure that was the truth, but I wanted to believe it. It also helped justify my anger with Beau. "But you had to go and interfere and mess everything up. Why can't you just leave me alone? I don't need your help. Ever."

I wanted to storm into the apartment and slam the door behind me, but I couldn't walk and the door was no longer attached to the frame. Seeing my distress, Jolene approached. "I think Nola needs to rest. It's been a busy day."

Beau looked like he might argue but, seeing Jolene's expression, he remained silent.

Jaxson retrieved my crutches from the trunk. "I can help you up the stairs if you'd like me to."

"Thank you for asking," I said, throwing a glare at Beau. "I happily accept your offer to help."

We headed toward the open doorway, and Jolene called back to Beau, "I still have a few things in the car from my trip that I need brought inside, if you would be so kind as to bring them up. But leave that doll in the car. I figure it's going to show up wherever it wants, so no point in moving it."

Jaxson and Jolene settled me on the couch. My ankle was in full-on throbbing mode, but I didn't say anything because I knew

Jolene would make me take a pain pill. I kept talking, hoping to distract myself from the pain. "We weren't expecting to see you today, Jaxson."

"I guess I couldn't stay away. Too many things to take care of here."

I happened to look up as a glance was shared between him and Jolene. It wasn't anything I'd call searing, but there was some unspoken meaning being communicated that they weren't interested in sharing with anyone else. I tried to catch Jolene's gaze while she tucked a blanket around me, but all I could see was her cheeks' soft pink glow, which didn't come from a bottle.

Sarah emerged from the back hallway. "The rings are still there. Nobody will ever guess where I hid them, so don't tell anyone."

Jaxson said, "The good news is that I finished up my business early enough to make it back in time to take your car to be detailed. It had a little bit of road dust on it from the long drive."

I felt an uncomfortable pull in my chest at the reminder of the Ford Mustang I was supposed to take possession of. "Thank you, but you shouldn't have bothered. It's just going to be sitting in the driveway until my ankle is better."

"Luckily, the previous owner had a car cover, and his widow has generously included it."

Sarah's expression grew apprehensive. "So Nola's going to be driving a dead guy's car? I don't think that's a great idea."

I waited for Jolene to say something, but she seemed preoccupied with rearranging the magazines on my tray table.

"I drove it all the way from Mississippi, and it runs like brand-new, and I didn't see any hitchhiker in the backseat." Jaxson chuckled, but his smile faded when he noticed that nobody else found his comment amusing. "Sorry. Too soon, I guess."

"It will always be too soon," I said.

"Duly noted. Anyway, as I was saying, the car was meticulously maintained, and if I were that guy and I was looking down at my most prized possession, I'd be thrilled that someone beautiful and responsible like your sister was the new driver."

"Thank you," I said. "But I'm still not crazy about being behind the wheel of any car again. My boss is letting me work from home, so there's no fieldwork. And that's all good, because I'm so behind on paperwork right now that I'll never catch up."

Jaxson helped Jolene out of her coat. "Isn't that what you were supposed to be doing while I was gone?"

Turning to Jaxson, she said, "Thank you," then gave him a look like the organizer of a surprise party might have right before opening the door for the victim.

Beau appeared from the direction of the back stairs carrying the box from the backseat, with two paisley quilted Vera Bradley totes stacked on top. "Where should I put these?"

I opened my mouth to tell him exactly where I wanted him to put them, but Jolene cut me off. "Thank you so much, Beau. Please put the totes in my room, and you can just drop the box right next to that armchair. And I apologize—I don't know where my head is lately—but I should have told you to leave the box in the car. It's fine just where it is, though. We can keep it here until Trevor asks for it back, and in the meantime I can find a doily to cover it so we can use it as an end table."

"Trevor?"

After Jolene explained the whole Henry story, Beau laughed. "Good for Trevor. Henry's getting on Mimi's last nerve, but she doesn't want to say anything because Camille is so nice and such a great friend. We're all hoping they find their own place soon, but Camille's been a real comfort to Mimi."

"That is an unexpected blessing," Jolene said. "It's like Adele orchestrated it all, isn't it? Her best friend appears right at the moment Mimi, you, and Felicity need her most."

Beau nodded. "I'm going to agree, since otherwise it would be a coincidence, and we all know there's no such thing." He sent me a meaningful glance. "She's also a pretty amazing salesperson. Our numbers at the store have skyrocketed since Camille started. . . ."

The pain in my ankle radiated all the way up to my head, but it was still hours before I'd want to take one of my pills.

Beau had stopped talking and was reaching for the bottle on the tray next to me. "You haven't taken one in a while, have you? It looks like you need one now."

I glared at him. "Don't you have someplace else to be? Someone else's life you can interfere in?" The hurt look on his face barely registered as I snatched the pill bottle from him and opened it. I tipped it over, and only five pills spilled out onto my palm. I upended it to make sure nothing was stuck on the side, and when nothing else came out I held it up to my eye and confirmed that the bottle was empty.

"That's not right," I said, putting four of the pills back into the bottle. "I think I've had maybe three since I've been here, and hardly more than that while I was at Mimi's." I looked at Mardi, whose eyes were as alert as ever. "Sarah—did you pick up all the pills after I knocked over the bottle? I don't want Mardi to eat any."

"I didn't see any," Sarah insisted. "I even got down on my hands and knees to be at Mardi's level to make sure there weren't any on the floor. And I vacuumed before Jolene got here, so if I missed any, they'd be in the vacuum bag."

I sat back, relieved. "Thank goodness." Sensing my need for reassurance, Mardi came to stand next to the couch, within petting distance, and I accommodated him with a scratch behind one floppy ear.

Jolene handed me a water bottle she'd pulled from her bag. "Here. Take your pill and wash it down with this. You'll feel better soon."

I did as instructed, then rested my head against the pillow, willing the medicine to work quickly.

"You should be taking them as prescribed," Beau said. "It's important that you get ahead of the pain so—"

My phone rang, preempting the response that was burning on my tongue. I didn't recognize the number, though it had the local 504 area code. I had a fifty-fifty chance of it being a call from someone I actually wanted to talk to rather than a sales call. But if I answered, I wouldn't have to talk to Beau.

"Hello?" I deepened my voice so that if it was a sales call I could pretend they had the wrong number. Being able to avoid sales calls was the main advantage of having a lifelong nickname.

"This is Joan Wenzel. Am I speaking with Nola Trenholm?"

"Hello, Mrs. Wenzel. This is Nola."

"I'm sorry. It didn't sound like you when you answered."

"I think I might be getting a cold," I said, to avoid explaining. "Did you have a chance to speak with Honey?" I put the phone on speaker.

"I did. I'm thrilled that Zeus came out of his shell, but he hasn't said anything since I've been home, so who knows if he's cured?"

"Do you have any idea what he meant by 'the key'?"

"I have no idea. The only key in the house that I was aware was missing was the one from the armoire, but you found that."

"And he hasn't said anything else?"

I heard her heavy sigh. "No. I just told you. He hasn't said anything in our hearing since he spoke while you were here. I'll be happy to let you know if he does."

"Thank you. What about the wig?"

"I'm afraid I don't have anything to add, sadly. Sybil was quite proud of her silver hair, and she most definitely would never have worn a wig. And Jessica and Lynda certainly didn't—Lynda because she was just a little girl, and Jessica just wasn't the fussy type with her looks. All-natural and never wore makeup or heels. My guess is that the wig hair could be very old—perhaps dating back to my grandparents and my numerous aunts and uncles. I don't know of any deaths in the house prior to Sybil's murder, except for poor Uncle Patrick falling down the stairs."

"Wait—I thought he died from influenza."

"No. Although I suppose technically you could say that. He was sick when he fell down the stairs and died. I'm sure it played a part."

"That's horrible," I said.

"It is. A child dying from anything is horrible. And that leads us to the bloodstains under the rug. They could be from an accident—you know how children are—and not anything nefarious at all. The police haven't come up with anything?"

"No. Not yet. It's a cold case, so it's not a priority, but at least it's brought their attention back to your stepbrother and his family's disappearance. I hope you and your family can get some closure."

There was a short pause. "I do agree, but I've also begun to think that maybe we should just let it go. Honey and I aren't getting any younger, and this entire incident keeps us in the past. I want us to only be looking forward as we enter our golden years. I believe Sybil would understand."

I frowned at my phone, wondering at her change of heart. Maybe it was all about growing older and moving on. Maybe. "Of course. Although, as representatives of the new owner of the house, we need to do our due diligence and make a full disclosure when we sell it. Which means I need to see if I can find anything else."

"That's perfectly reasonable," Joan said. "Please let us know if you discover anything new."

"Of course. And likewise." I was about to hang up when I remembered something else Honey was supposed to ask her about. "One more thing. Do you know anyone who owns a gray Honda sedan with South Carolina plates? I think it's a recent model."

"I don't. It's most likely someone looking to buy the house on Esplanade. It's off the market, but if they have an out-of-date listing, they wouldn't know that, would they?"

"No," I said slowly. "But that wouldn't explain why the car was in front of your house."

There was an extended pause. "Well, you know, with the Internet these days you can find all sorts of personal information, such as who owns a particular house." There was a brief silence, and I pictured her shrugging her thin shoulders. "Perhaps they were hoping to make a private offer but changed their minds. Or, you know, Nola, it could just be a coincidence."

I looked up as she said that last word, my gaze immediately meeting Beau's.

"Yes, well, I promise to keep looking. I am so very sorry I couldn't be of more help. I'll be in touch if Honey or I—or, for that matter, Zeus—comes up with anything to add."

"Thank you. I'll be in touch." I ended the call, my eyes still locked on Beau.

"There's no such thing—" he began.

I held up my hand. "I know. There's something I'm not seeing here. And if I had to guess, I would say that Joan Wenzel would be more than happy to keep me in the dark."

CHAPTER 31

It was still dark outside when I finally gave up on sleep and slid out of bed, careful to avoid stepping on Sarah and disturbing Mardi. I checked my phone again to see if Cooper had texted or if I had missed a call, but there was nothing. I'd texted twice, asking him to call me, so his silence meant that he was avoiding me. I might have tried to tell myself that he'd lost his phone, but the entire incident with Michael had at least taught me never to be that naïve again.

I sat on the edge of my bed for a long time, watching the gray light creeping around my window shades shift to blue and then yellow as the sun began its climb. I'd been going over all the unanswered questions about what had happened to Adele and Buddy Ryan, as well as about the odd disappearances of Mark, Jessica, and Lynda following the murder of Mark's mother, Sybil. After the harrowing events at the Esplanade house, I was glad Sarah would be leaving and getting far away from whoever was lurking upstairs in the room where a rug had hidden a bloodstain for decades. They said that the dead kept their secrets, but a select few of us knew that wasn't true.

For the first time since moving in with Jolene, I was up before her.

Despite the noise I made trying to figure out the coffee maker, she remained in her room. Because I hadn't ever actually seen her sleeping, and I thought that maybe she was a freak of nature and didn't need any sleep, I cracked her door and verified that she was sound asleep in her bed.

I closed the door quietly, hoping she wasn't coming down with something. Jolene lived for the Christmas season, and she'd be disappointed to miss even half a day of the preparations and hoopla that surrounded the holidays. Before we'd gone to bed the previous night, she'd suggested going tree shopping with Sarah today, with a promise to FaceTime me so I could be part of the excitement (her word) of choosing our first tree for the apartment.

Since today was Sarah's last full day in New Orleans, I didn't want to keep her cooped up inside with me, so I'd feigned enthusiasm and told Jolene it was a great idea. Fortunately, Jolene had then begun discussing our matching outfits (including Mardi's) for our joint Christmas card and didn't notice the lukewarmness of my response or Sarah's hesitance.

Sarah entered the kitchen rubbing her eyes, with Mardi trotting in her wake, and took over the coffee maker without any resistance from me. As she scooped coffee grounds, she said, "I'm leaving tomorrow, and nothing's been resolved. I didn't help figure anything out. So much for my psychic abilities. That creepy baby doll has given you as much new information as I have."

I squeezed her shoulders. "Sarah, as I know Melanie would tell you, you have very little control over your abilities. And, as I'm sure she will also tell you, sometimes you won't know what you've learned right away. It's like you're only allowed a tiny scrap of the whole picture at a time. Whether or not the people in the spirit realm are sadistic jerks is not for me to say, but I can only hope that there's a purpose behind their stingy doling out of information."

Sarah's blue eyes were serious as she carefully poured coffee into my mug. "Has Beau told you what Adele told him?"

"I'm in danger, apparently. That seems to be the running theme from the netherworld these days. Too bad the spirits can't be more specific."

"You know that's not how it works." Sarah looked at me hopefully. "Maybe I should stay longer. I can call Mom and Dad and tell them that you need me here."

"Thanks, but no. That's sweet of you, and I know it has nothing to do with skipping school, but I think between Jolene, Jaxson, and me—"

"And Beau."

"We don't need him."

"You sure about that?" Sarah asked quietly.

"Very." I put my mug down on the table, next to the two bags of stones I'd pulled from my backpack the previous day. I untied the string of the one Zoe had given me and spilled the stones out onto my palm.

Sarah placed a plate of frozen waffles in front of me, along with a tub of margarine with a knife protruding from the middle, and I was glad Jolene wasn't awake to see the sacrilege. Sarah sat down in the chair next to me and used her index finger to mix up the stones.

"I feel like I'm letting you down leaving you without any answers."

"Oh, my gosh—really? We don't have all of the answers, but I think we're getting closer because of you. I'm sorry you got stuck babysitting me over your Thanksgiving break."

She grinned, and she looked so much like our dad that it made me homesick. "I had fun. I'm glad you let me stick around."

"Me, too."

"Still no idea what 'Find the stones' means?"

Before I could answer, Jolene emerged from her bedroom. She was in her nightgown and robe, her hair a red cloud around her head, and her face devoid of makeup. She was holding the Bible that I had found on her floor.

"Jolene, are you all right?" I asked.

"Yes, thank you. I'm sorry—I think I overslept. Too many late nights catching up and chatting with my family." She held out the Bible. "Did y'all put this on my bed?"

Sarah and I shook our heads.

"But while you were gone it did fall off your nightstand and onto the floor," I offered. "It landed open at the book of Luke."

Her face paled. "Do you remember which chapter?"

"Yes, actually. I figured someone was trying to tell us something, so I paid attention. The first chapter number that appeared on the page on the left was in a large, bold font, so I think I remember it. I'm pretty sure it was twenty-two."

Her face paled even more. "Twenty-two? Are you sure?"

"Pretty sure. Why?"

"Verse forty-seven is where Judas betrays Jesus. When Mimi's Bible flew off the shelf in front of everyone, it fell open at the exact same chapter. I didn't think it meant anything at the time, but now . . . but now . . ." She gave us an anguished look before she clutched the Bible to her chest and ran back to her room. Despite the drama of her exit, her good manners wouldn't allow her to slam the door.

Sarah looked at me with raised eyebrows. "Should I go see if she wants to talk?"

"Don't worry. I will. But not yet. She'll want to get dressed and put on her makeup first. But you could put Mardi in her room. He's really good at offering comfort—better than any man I've ever met."

"Ew." Sarah picked Mardi up, then walked over to Jolene's closed door and tapped. "Jolene? Can Mardi come in?"

The door opened and Jolene reached for the dog. "Thank you, Sarah. I'll be ready to go tree shopping in an hour. Wear the pretty plaid hair band I got you. I've got one, too, and we can match." After offering a wobbly grin, she closed the door.

Sarah returned to her seat and rested her elbows on the table, her head perched on her hands. "That was weird."

"It was." I took a sip of coffee, wishing the caffeine would reach my tired brain faster. I needed to think. There were so many loose pieces of information floating around like alphabet soup in my head, and none of them would come together to make sense. And behind them all was the awareness that Cooper hadn't returned my calls or texts, and that he was in California, where his fiancée lay in an irreversible coma. The fiancée he'd neglected to tell me about. And I knew about her—Lilly—only because Beau had decided to do a background check on Cooper.

Maybe it was a good thing that I was so distracted with the unanswered questions surrounding Adele's murder and the disappearance of Jessica and Lynda, because it meant that I wouldn't have to dwell on the facts that I was too trusting and that I hadn't learned a thing from my mistakes. The overwhelming need for a drink hit me like a punch, and I quickly took another sip of coffee to make it go away.

"So," Sarah said, interrupting my thoughts. "You know that Adele song that keeps playing on our phones and stuff?"

"'Rolling in the Deep'?" I felt encouraged that I remembered the name.

"Yeah, that one." She looked over her shoulder at Jolene's door to make sure it was still shut. "I'm not good at lyrics like you are, so I Googled the song to find out what it's about." She paused. "It's about betrayal. Just like that Bible verse that keeps popping up."

"Betrayal?" I looked at Jolene's closed door, my mind tossing the implications about. Lowering my voice, I said, "Do you think it's about Jolene?"

She shook her head. "No. Because it's a message from Adele. The dead Adele, not the singer," she clarified. "That's why she's using Adele's songs, and that one in particular. The dead Adele is trying to tell us something, and I feel so stupid because I can't figure out what it is about her death that's somehow related to a betrayal. I think it's urgent, because she keeps trying to get the message across to us, but we're not getting it."

"A betrayal," I said, feeling a tinge of the PTSD from my recent encounter with Michael. "Speaking from personal experience, I'd say that a betrayal is a great reason to stick around and seek justice."

"Or revenge," Sarah said.

We stared at each other, sorting through the implications. Eventually, Sarah stood. "I need to get dressed. Hopefully you or I or both of us will have figured something out by the time Jolene and I get back with the tree."

I held out my empty cup. "I can't think if I'm undercaffeinated. Could you please fix me another cup before you go?"

She sighed heavily and took the cup before going back to the kitchen. Pausing in the doorway, she turned and said, "One more thing. I don't think it takes a psychic person to notice, but there's something weird going on between Jaxson and Jolene."

"Thanks, Sherlock. I have noticed. Maybe you can get her to talk while you're looking at trees. Speaking of which, I know she wants a big one, but I'm thinking tabletop. Remember that it has to come up those stairs and I can't help. So it's your job to talk her out of anything over three feet tall."

She rolled her eyes and began heading to the kitchen just as the landline phone on the desk began to ring. Our gazes locked. "Should I answer it?" Sarah asked.

I wanted to tell her no, but I couldn't force the word out of my mouth.

She slowly approached the desk, but before she reached it, the ringing stopped. Sarah stared at the silent phone for a moment, then turned away from it. "I'll get that coffee for you now."

I looked at the innocuous phone and wondered who could have been calling and what the message would have been. And if the ringing alone was just another warning of danger.

CHAPTER 32

As soon as Jolene and Sarah left, I made my way to the table and clumsily arranged my crutches and myself in front of my laptop. I'd had such grand plans to get ahead with my paperwork, and now I found myself even further behind. Judging by the boxes of decorations Jolene had brought back with her from Mississippi, I suspected that she would want to turn the apartment into a Christmas wonderland, so I was determined to focus and get as much work done as I could before she and Sarah returned.

The table still held the two bags of stones from Madame Zoe—in addition to remnants from breakfast, including crumbs and the margarine tub. The mere fact that Jolene had left the apartment without it being pristine was a chilling sign that things were not all right. I decided that I couldn't work with the mess around me, so I collected the stones into their respective bags and stuck them into one of the desk drawers. Still not satisfied, I used a cupped hand to corral the crumbs into a pile and sweep them into my waiting hand.

I'd made it to the edge of the table when I noticed a long strand of blond hair, wavy at the end, and clearly not belonging to Jolene,

Sarah, or me. My dad had once shown me how a human hair burns slowly and gives off a distinctive odor, whereas synthetic hair would melt and curl up into a frizzy ball. I considered hopping to the kitchen to retrieve Jolene's candle lighter for easy determination of whether the hair was natural or synthetic.

It took me ten whole minutes of thinking—clearly I was procrastinating—to realize that the hair was probably from the Barbie head that had sat on the table more than once. It could have fallen out on its own when the head was there. Or maybe Sarah had been messing with it in Jolene's room and a strand had clung to her sweater and traveled to the table.

Hobbling back and forth between the kitchen and the table, I continued to clean up while telling myself it wasn't procrastination if I was simultaneously working on resolving the puzzles despite all the missing pieces. Sarah had left her sweater on the back of a chair, and when I picked it up I saw strands of her own long dark hair next to blond Barbie hair. I was on my way to the coatrack to hang up her sweater, and stopped when I breathed in the strong scent of Youth-Dew perfume, as if someone wearing it had just passed by.

I held the sweater up to my nose, but it carried only the scents of Sarah and wool. Maybe the perfume had been my imagination. Or maybe I wasn't paying enough attention. Pulling the sweater away from my face, I examined the strands more closely, wondering what I might have missed. I needed to talk this out with someone like my dad. Or Cooper or Beau. But I rejected that thought as soon as it crossed my mind. My dad was busy with JJ. And I would rather shave my head than ask Beau or Cooper for help.

I took another step, then stopped again, my whole body tingling with the image of my shaved head and what I'd look like bald. And then the room seemed to shrink, becoming just big enough for me and the sweater with the strands of hair.

I stumbled back to where I'd left my phone on the table and quickly scrolled through my contacts to where Sarah had dutifully entered the numbers for Joan and Honey. Recalling the unsettled feeling I'd had after speaking with Joan, I called Honey's number first. She picked up on the third ring.

"Hello, Honey. This is Nola. I'm sorry to bother you, but I have a random question for you that I hope you might be able to answer."

"Please don't apologize, Nola. I'm happy to speak with you. Joan has been gone a lot the last few weeks, so it's nice to have someone to talk to. And, oh, I so love randomness. I use it as a theme in my paintings."

"Great," I said. "Do you recall if your brother ever wore a toupee?"

"Oh, my. Yes, yes, I do recall. I'd forgotten about it until just this moment. He started losing his hair in high school and was very self-conscious about it. He wore hairpieces ever after, which is probably why I forgot that he lost a lot of his hair in his twenties. It's almost like he was born wearing a wig, and we got used to it. He was also very tall, and it wasn't all that noticeable to those of us much shorter than he."

"So he wore wigs even after he married Jessica?"

"As far as I know, yes. Remember that we were estranged, but every time we did see him he wore one, and Jessica once joked that he wore it as a disguise, since nobody knew the real man beneath the wig. I recall how awful those wigs were, because Mark would never splurge on any hair-restoration products or procedures. He was stingy that way—isn't that funny? He'd spend all his money on cars and houses and boats, but not on something like personal care. That didn't bother Jessica, since that sort of thing wasn't important to her. That might have been what attracted them to each other, because I honestly couldn't see anything else they had in common."

I thought back to the family photos arranged neatly on the sill of the picture window in Honey's house, and I recalled that only one of them was a picture of Mark. "Was Mark's wig dark brown?"

"Yes, it was. It matched his natural color, which was just like our father's." There was a lengthy pause. "Oh, dear. Are you thinking the wig hair found in the bloodstain might have belonged to Mark?"

"I don't know. Not yet. I'm still figuring it out. I'll call you once I know something."

I ended the call without saying good-bye, my hand shaking so much that I dropped my phone. It was the comment she'd made about Mark losing his hair and wearing a toupee at a young age. Synthetic hair.

If Mark was dead, possibly murdered, that put a whole new spin on what had happened in the house on Esplanade. What if only Jessica and Lynda were missing? What if they'd gone into hiding to cover up another murder?

I shouted out Sarah's name, belatedly recalling that she'd left, along with Jolene, my only form of transportation. I thought about calling Jolene and asking her to come back, but I hesitated, not wanting to interrupt her fun, especially if she was having an emotionally hard time at the moment. If anyone deserved a little fun, it was her.

I considered calling Cooper, then immediately dismissed the idea. I wasn't ready to talk to him. As much as I'd appreciate his problem-solving skills, I was happy to postpone the inevitable conversation about his fiancée. He'd texted me earlier in the day, saying that he'd missed me and he would call as soon as he could. I'd deleted the text without responding.

That left the last person on earth I wanted to ask for help. Beau's psychic abilities might be useful, but that didn't override my reluctance to call him. Because we officially worked together, I'd stopped short of deleting him from my contacts—because, like most people my age, I didn't have anyone's phone number memorized. I figured texting him might let me remain in neutral territory, whereas a phone call would be an olive branch. Which was why I needed to make sure that he was the one to initiate the call.

Smiling to myself, I began to type. *I think Mark was murdered. Call me. And I need a ride.* I sat back, pleased with the casualness of my text, and waited for the three dots to appear to let me know Beau was replying.

I was still waiting ten minutes later when I started thinking about a plan B. I considered calling an Uber, but I wasn't up to going on this trip alone, especially since I was handicapped by my broken ankle and needed assistance to get into and out of a car, as well as up and down steps.

I was staring at my phone when another possibility popped into my head. I opened my contacts and clicked on Felicity's number. She couldn't drive, but she could ride in the Uber with me and help get me in and out. I did the thing that no one under thirty did anymore—waited until voice mail answered.

"Hi, Felicity. This is Nola. If you get this in the next half hour, could you please call me? I need to check something out at the house on Esplanade and would welcome your company. Please—"

The call was picked up by a man saying hello.

"Oh, I'm sorry. I'm trying to reach Felicity. I must have dialed the wrong number. . . ."

"No, no, this is her phone. It's sitting here on the table, and the ringing was distracting me from my game."

I groaned inwardly as I recognized Henry's voice. "Sorry," I said, knowing the sarcasm would be lost on him. "Is Felicity around?"

Electronic shooting noises came through the phone, and I pictured him with his feet up on Mimi's coffee table while he played a video game. "Probably not, because she didn't answer her phone."

"Thank you, Captain Obvious." I didn't care if I was being rude. So was he, and besides, he wasn't paying any attention. I wanted to ask him why he wasn't at work, but that would involve prolonging our conversation. "Would you mind going to look and giving her the phone? She can't be far if her phone is there."

His heavy sigh reminded me of Sarah, but she was only twelve, so it was allowed. "Whatever. Hang on." I heard a rustling sound as he hoisted himself off of the couch and presumably stood before shouting, "Felicity! Come get your phone! Nola wants to talk with you."

We both waited for a moment before he spoke again, this time to me. "Nope. She's not here. And by the way, I want you to tell your friend Trevor that I better have my things that he stole from me returned no later than tomorrow night or I'm going to have him arrested."

I jerked back from my phone, surprised at his vehemence. "It's not stolen and it's not your stuff." I winced, realizing I'd just admitted Trevor's being the responsible party. "Look, I'll make sure everything's put back the way you left it by tomorrow, all right?"

"You make sure it is or I'll call the cops."

I rolled my eyes. "Got it. When you find Felicity, could you please tell her to call me? It's important."

He sighed again, as if I'd just asked him to roll a boulder up a mountain. "Yeah, sure."

"Thank you, Henry. And please—" I stopped, realizing he'd already ended the call.

I went ahead and got dressed so I'd be ready when Felicity called, and when she hadn't called an hour later, I sat down at the kitchen table again and tried to lose myself in my backlog of paperwork. But my thoughts kept going back to the wig and the doll, and I spent more time checking my phone to make sure I hadn't somehow not heard it ring and readjusting the volume to ensure that it was loud enough.

My stomach had begun grumbling, alerting me to the lunch hour, but I was reluctant to go into the kitchen and heat something up or make a sandwich in case Felicity called and was ready to go right away.

I was in the process of standing up, with the goal of snagging from the kitchen a plate of cookies to tide me over, when the front doorbell rang. I opened my Ring app and was surprised to find Camille on my doorstep. I hobbled to the top of the steps and shouted down toward the door, "I'll be right there!"

I'd become a pro at maneuvering myself down to the bottom of the stairway using my arms, rear end, and left foot, so it took me just under two minutes to reach the door, pull myself up, and unlatch it.

"Camille, it's so nice to see you." I looked behind her. "Is Felicity with you?"

"Hello, Nola," Camille said sweetly, her arms wrapped around a large Thermos. "Felicity said she needed to stay with Mimi, so she asked if I'd stop by. I made some of my chicken soup for you."

My stomach grumbled in response. "Wow—that was really nice of you. Thank you. I'm absolutely starving. I only had a bite of frozen waffle for breakfast. It's a good thing Jolene's back, so I don't starve to death." I hopped backward to open the door wider and allow her inside.

"Oh, is Jolene back already? I didn't think she was due in until tomorrow."

"Yes, she came back early. I'm sorry you missed her and my sister, Sarah. They're out looking for our Christmas tree and getting a head start on their shopping. I don't expect them back until suppertime."

"Well, then," she said, "I'm glad I stopped by. I can feed you and keep you company at the same time."

I spotted her car in the driveway before I shut the door and locked it. "I really appreciate it. You go on up—it will take me a minute to join you."

"I can help. . . ."

"No—but thanks. I've got it. If you don't mind, could you please put some of that soup into a couple of bowls while you're waiting so we can have lunch together? I think there's a few of Jolene's dinner rolls still left, too. They should be in a baggie on the counter. You can stick them in the toaster oven to heat. I promise it won't take long."

She appeared worried. "Only if you're sure . . ."

I gave her a thumbs-up and began my one-legged hop up the stairs while holding on to the banister with both hands. When I made it back into the apartment, my laptop had been pushed aside and two bowls of steaming soup were waiting on the table. The toaster oven beeped as I hopped toward the table. Camille helped me sit and then propped my leg up on a chair before placing the bread on a plate next to me. She pulled out a chair, but before she sat down she noticed the corrugated box sitting in the front room.

"Is that from the shop?" she asked.

I turned and, for the first time, noticed the store's name and logo stamped on the side. "Sort of," I said slowly. I didn't want to get Trevor into trouble, and I didn't know Camille well enough to know if she'd get the joke.

"'Sort of'?" she said.

"Yeah, um, it was accidentally put into Jolene's car and then carried upstairs. It's not inventory or anything—just miscellaneous stuff from the desk. Don't worry—Beau knows about it, and I'm positive he'll make sure everything's put back where it belongs."

She frowned. "Henry did say some things were missing from the store. Nothing valuable, so I didn't report it and just assumed we'd find it moved someplace. Henry was upset mostly because some of the items were of a personal nature, but they wouldn't mean anything to anyone but him. Do you know if anyone's gone through the box?"

"I couldn't say. I don't know how long Jolene's had it or who's had access to it. I do know it traveled to Mississippi and back in her car over Thanksgiving."

"That's just bizarre, isn't it? So, what on earth is it doing here?"

I shrugged and took a large spoonful of soup, along with a bite of butter-slathered bread. After swallowing, I said, "I have no idea. But you should ask Beau. He'll know." I smiled to myself, having dodged a bullet so that it landed firmly in Beau's backside.

"Well, if it's all right with you, I'll just take the box down to my car when I leave, and I can take it back to the store on Monday. That'll save Beau the trouble of bringing it back."

"Sounds like a win-win," I said as I scooped up another spoonful of soup. "And you're being so kind that I hate to ask you for a favor."

Camille patted my forearm. "It's what I'm here for, Nola. Just tell me what you need and I'll be happy to take care of it."

I took a spoonful of soup and thoughtfully chewed the chicken and vegetables while savoring the broth before I responded. "Would you mind driving me to the house on Esplanade? I promise I won't keep you very long, but I need to check something out."

"I'd love to. I've heard Beau and Mimi talking so much about this 'murder-flip' project that I'm intrigued. I just hope I don't find it too scary. I've never been one of those people who like ghost stories or haunted houses."

"Same," I said, recalling the heavy footsteps, the terrible smell, and the feeling of dread from the last time I was in the house on Esplanade. "I think it's an acquired taste. Fortunately, it's broad daylight outside, so it's the best time of day to visit an old house."

"Why? Because ghosts don't like the sun?"

"No, because you can see and appreciate all the architectural details."

"Ah," she said, nodding. "Not that I believe in ghosts, of course. Or haunted houses."

Noticing that my bowl was now empty, she said, "Would you like some more?"

"I'm stuffed—thank you. I think I ate too much, but it was really delicious." I looked at my phone. "We should get going. It won't take us long, but sunset comes pretty early this time of year."

Camille began to clear the table. "Let me clean up, and you go elevate your leg. I'll be quick."

I listened to the clang of dishes from the kitchen as I hopped to the living room. As I sat down on the sofa, my gaze fell on the box, its unsealed flaps folded into one another. Being my father's daughter, I couldn't not open it now, especially after the conversation with Camille. I slipped down to my knees, crawled over to the box, and pulled open the flaps.

The box was only partially filled, making it easy to move things around and see what was contained inside. I laughed when I noticed a game controller, knowing how much its absence must have frustrated

Henry. That was the only item from the house, as far as I could tell; the rest of the objects were office items—including a stapler, a box of paper clips, a rubber-band-wrapped stack of hangtags, several catalogs for upcoming estate sales, and an inventory book—the pilfering of all of which was intended to annoy rather than harm. I admired Trevor's cleverness as much as I appreciated his victim selection, and I couldn't help smiling as I rummaged through the box, almost laughing out loud when I found opened bags of Doritos and Oreos and a six-pack of Coca-Cola cans. Henry would not have been happy being deprived of his stash of junk food.

I'd reached the bottom of the box when I spotted a familiar cloth bag, closed with a string at the top. It was identical to the two bags that had been given to Beau and me and that I'd rediscovered in my purse and put away in the desk drawer. I pulled the bag out of the box, feeling hard, round stones through the thin cloth, and I opened the top. Three crystals—one pink, one green, and one blue—lay nestled inside.

I stared at the bag, confused. Had Henry gone to see Madame Zoe? He didn't strike me as the type of person who would seek out a fortune teller, but I'd misread people before. I just had to think about Michael Hebert to confirm that. I'd dropped the bag back into the box and was folding the flaps up when Camille spoke.

"You ready to go?"

I looked up to see her in the kitchen doorway, drying her hands on one of Jolene's *Wizard of Oz* dish towels.

"Yep—ready." I crawled back to the sofa to pull myself up. "I was curious about what was in the box. Nothing valuable—just bits and pieces—but I can understand why Henry would be annoyed."

Camille frowned. "I just don't understand why Trevor would want to do that. Perhaps Christopher should have a talk with Trevor's grandmother."

I looked at her to see if she might be joking, but I quickly dismissed the thought. Camille didn't seem the type to joke. Or, apparently, to find fault with her husband.

"Nola, before I forget, I know you and Beau aren't getting along right now, so if you'd rather give me the rings to hold until Mimi's ready, I'd be more than happy to help. That will save you the awkwardness of dealing with Beau. I promise they'll be safe with me."

"Actually, I would—but I don't know where they are." I wasn't sure why I lied. Probably because she was married to Henry, and I didn't trust him. I gave her a reassuring smile. "After the attempted break-in I asked Sarah to hide them, and I guess I've been too distracted to find out exactly where she put them." I pulled out my phone. "Hang on—I can ask."

I called Melanie's landline in Charleston, knowing that nobody would be there to answer it, and I let it ring several times before hanging up. "She must have the ringer off."

"Can you call Jolene and ask her to pass her phone to Sarah?"

"I could, but I really don't want to bother them. It can wait. And no need to worry—Beau and Jaxson fixed the door and added more locks, and I'll set the alarm on our way out. I'll ask Sarah later."

Camille slid on her jacket and picked up the box. "Don't want to forget this. I'll go first and open the car doors. I'll be right back to help you down the stairs."

"Thank you," I said, stifling a yawn. "Sorry," I said. "I haven't been sleeping well."

"Understandable. I'll be right back."

It was nearly three o'clock when we pulled out of the driveway and onto Broadway—plenty of time before sunset, around five o'clock. I sat with my leg propped up in the backseat, the box with its curious contents stored in the trunk.

Not surprisingly, Camille was a cautious driver, staying below the speed limit and taking corners more slowly than necessary. It took us fifteen minutes longer to get to Esplanade than it took with Jolene or

Beau at the wheel, and I must have fallen asleep at some point, because I wasn't aware we were there until Camille shook my shoulder. I never slept in cars, probably because of my childhood, during the lean times of which a car was our only shelter and someone needed to be on the alert. Even on the long bus ride from Los Angeles to Charleston I didn't remember actually falling asleep.

Now I found it difficult to hold my eyes open, every limb revolting at the notion of being forced to move. I wondered if this was a natural reaction to physical trauma, and if my brain was just now trying to catch up.

Camille had parallel parked at the curb, making it easy for me to exit the car. We stood there for a minute looking at the faded facade, the house backlit by the late-afternoon sun, its front in shadow. The brown grass and the dying leaves still clutching tree branches gave an appearance of a house in mourning and waiting for a miracle.

"I'm sure it was beautiful at one time," Camille said. "I can see why you're so attached to it." After handing me my crutches, she said, "Give me your key and I'll go open the door."

I did as instructed, then slid my backpack over my shoulder before making my way through the door and into the front room. "I'll be quick," I said. "I just need to get something from one of the bedrooms."

"Take your time—it's still daylight, and I want to see the house. Although it's such a shame."

I wanted to ask her what she meant, but she was already climbing the steps to the second floor. I paused at the threshold of the kitchen, remembering the feeling from before, the sense that something evil was coming down the stairs toward us. Which was foolish right now, since Camille had already made it up the stairs and was now walking slowly around the room upstairs without any sign of fear.

I made my way to the closed armoire, turned the key, and opened it. The doll had disappeared from Jolene's car and it hadn't shown up anywhere else, so I fully expected to find it where I'd first discovered it—especially since hearing what Sarah had said about the evil entity wanting the doll here. The doll—or whoever was manipulating it—seemed to be of a different opinion.

I lifted my hand to open the small compartment at the top, where I'd first found the doll. I froze, my fingers suspended in midair.

Words had been written with a fingertip in the dust on the mirror. My dry tongue stuck to the roof of my mouth as I read the three words: *FIND THE STONES.*

I jerked back, knocking over my crutches and causing them to crash to the floor, the sound deafening in the almost-empty room. The words hadn't been there before. I would have seen them.

Looking past them, I opened the small door. There was the doll, its glassy blue eyes staring at me, the expression almost challenging. I grabbed hold of her, and I could have sworn she blinked at me, maybe because she was aware of what I was about to do.

Despite the chill in the unheated house, dots of perspiration beaded on my forehead as a wave of nausea passed over me, making me wonder if I was coming down with something. I sucked in a breath. "Sorry, Miss Pussycat. Zeus told someone to hide the key. I don't know what key or where it goes, but considering your annoying habit of showing up everywhere, I'm going to guess you've been hiding it all along."

Leaning against the armoire, I took the doll's head in both hands and used what was left of my strength to twist it until it popped off. The head hit the wooden floor and rolled out of reach. A wave of dizziness overtook me and I thought I might fall. I waited for it to pass and then looked down at the headless torso in my hands.

Embedded in the soft stuffing of the body lay a silver key attached to a small chain with a plastic fob. GUIDRY MOVING AND STORAGE was printed in red, with a 504 phone number beneath it. I clasped the key tightly and let the doll's torso drop to the floor. In the part of my brain that was still functioning, I thought that a storage room would be a great place to hide a body.

I blinked, unspoken words swimming in front of me. I needed Beau. Even in my current mental state, I felt embarrassed by the admission. I needed him, and not just because of his psychic abilities. But not right now. Because all I could do at that moment was stay upright and not pass out.

Scampering footsteps ran down the stairs, followed by the heavier tread that I remembered from the last time I was there. A stench of rot sent an avalanche of fear through me, making me retch. "Mark? Are you here?"

I wasn't sure when the pieces of the puzzle had finally clicked into place. Maybe when I'd learned that Mark wore a toupee. And that synthetic hair had been embedded in the bloodstained wooden floorboards. The blood wasn't Sybil's, and there had been a lot of it, with strands of the hair stuck in the congealing and drying blood. Which could mean only that the blood came from the person who'd worn the wig. Mark. And there was only one reason why he would have been murdered by someone who was supposed to love him.

Ice-cold air swept through the room, and my limbs vibrated with fear. The spirit emanated pure evil. The evil of someone wicked enough to kill his own mother. I blinked hard, trying to clear my vision, which had suddenly become blurry. *Think. Think.*

I remembered the family photographs lining the windowsill in the elderly sisters' house, how only one was of Mark. He was their brother, yet they had chosen not to memorialize him in photographs. I squeezed my eyes shut so I could focus on a single train of thought. I recalled what the sisters had said about his relationship with Jessica and about how she'd moved out with Lynda to live with his mother, Sybil. How Sybil had been brutally murdered and the rest of the family had disappeared on the same night. But had they really disappeared? Maybe some of them had simply escaped after retribution for Sybil's death had been exacted. Opening my hand, I looked down at the key chain in my sweaty palm and wondered what secret it might hold. And why the dark presence in the house didn't want it revealed.

"Mark?" I said his name out loud without knowing why. Something was muddling my brain, but not enough not to know that I had just made a grave error.

A familiar scent of perfume wove its way through the gagging stench. I shoved the key chain into my jeans pocket while my fingers still functioned. I felt drunk but couldn't remember drinking anything. *What is wrong with me?* An idea floated above my head, out of my grasp, unwilling to be dissected.

Heavy footsteps sounded from the adjacent bedroom as fear constricted my throat. I knew better than to say Mark's name again. Irrationally, I thought he might forget about me and move on. Smaller footsteps scampered around the room like a child was playing hide-and-seek. I didn't turn to look, my gaze fixed on the words on the mirror. They floated in and out of focus, as if I were looking at them underwater. An overwhelming exhaustion consumed me, and all I wanted to do was lie down on the floor and go to sleep. But I couldn't. There was something . . . a memory. Or a thought. A piece of information that whirled around my exhausted brain, telling me to pay attention.

I tried to focus on the mirror as it caught an image of something behind me. But I couldn't turn. I could barely stand on my one good leg. I braced my arms against the armoire so I wouldn't fall.

Pay attention. The words came from a voice inside my head. A woman's voice that I hadn't heard in a long time. It made me want to cry. "Mom?" I said, the single syllable slurring.

Pay attention. Forcing my eyes to stay open, I focused hard on the memory or thought that wouldn't stop poking me. I looked back at the mirror and saw a face behind me. I blinked, and the face disappeared. And that's when I remembered.

Beau. And me. And Madame Zoe. She was giving us the bags of stones and telling us that she'd given some to Adele. Right before she disappeared. I squeezed my eyes shut, trying to think. My good leg buckled, and I slid down the armoire onto my knees.

I had found the stones. Adele's stones. She'd had them with her when she died, and her killer had taken them along with the diamond in her engagement ring. The diamond was long gone, no longer evidence of a murder. But the stones remained with her killer, a telling clue. As the wedding bands would be if Mimi got ahold of them. And I had just told Camille that only Sarah knew where they were.

I wiggled out of my backpack and struggled to stay awake as I dug into the outside pocket for my phone. I needed to call Sarah and warn her.

"You look sleepy." Camille's sweet voice came from somewhere above me as I felt her tug on my backpack to slide it off my arm.

I blinked up at her, each blink slower than the last.

"That's right, Nola. Go to sleep. I put enough of your pain meds into the soup to make you sleep like a baby."

My cloudy brain struggled to understand what she was talking about. What was it about the soup? I could still taste it in my mouth, feel the grit on my teeth.

"Nobody will question why there's so much of the meds in your system when they find your body, since you have a history of substance abuse. Not your usual poison, but not uncommon."

The word "body" echoed in my head, but I couldn't latch onto its meaning. I just wanted to go to sleep. I closed my eyes, but a cold, icy hand on my cheek startled me awake. The scent of Youth-Dew was stronger now, hovering close to me. "Sybil," I tried to say, but only air emerged.

"I like you," Camille said in a friendly voice. "I really do. Which is why I don't want it to hurt. I hoped if you were sound asleep you wouldn't feel a thing."

She raised something that reflected the weak light from the window, and I recognized my phone. I tried to reach for it, but my hand wouldn't obey.

Camille's features came into focus. "I'm not a fan of technology, but facial recognition sure can come in handy." She held my phone over my face. I tried to distort my features so it wouldn't recognize me, but from her look of satisfaction, I knew she'd gained access. "I'm texting your sister so she can tell me where the rings are and I can clean up that loose end."

I felt her tugging on my feet, and then the sensation of being dragged across the floor. Searing pain from my ankle shot up to my brain, bringing a cold blast of clarity. My head bumped against the strip of wood at the threshold, jolting me fully awake. I struggled to keep my eyes open, only barely aware of Camille stepping over me.

With one last futile effort, I tried to grab hold of the doorframe, but I felt myself sliding farther into the kitchen, next to a pile of salvaged millwork. "Just give in, Nola. Go on and go to sleep, and you won't feel a thing."

Somewhere on the floor above us, small feet ran in circles. With a punch of dread, I heard the heavy thud of bigger feet following them. I opened my mouth to scream, expelling only a small whine of air.

Camille straightened, and my phone slipped from her hand and hit the floor next to my head. "Is there anyone up there?" she shouted, a hint of fear in her voice. I listened as her footsteps cautiously ascended the bottom steps. I smelled the perfume and felt small hands on my cheek. They were sticky, as if they belonged to a small child. Two female voices whispered loudly, the location of the source changing with each word, like in a magic trick.

"Mom?" I murmured, nearly delirious with the struggle to stay awake.

"Nola." The word sounded inside my ear, radiating warmth on my cheek. I smelled the briny aroma of sea creatures and river mud, something I'd come to recognize as Adele's signature scent. A tear rolled down my cheek. I wasn't alone.

A patter of small footsteps descended the stairs, brushing by us and leaving a cold breeze in its wake.

"Is anyone up there?" Camille called again.

I would have laughed if I'd been able. The dark presence was all around us, pressing on my chest and making it hard to breathe. Assuming my puzzle-solving skills remained intact, Camille had nothing to fear from him. In her quest to hide her own sins, she was about to inadvertently destroy all the evidence of the crime Mark had committed. I was the dangerous one, the single person who could expose the shameful secret he'd been hiding for over a decade. If anything, he'd want to help Camille.

"Mom?" I said again, wondering if, in my delirium, I had imagined my mother's voice.

"Your mama's dead, Nola. But you'll be joining her soon enough and can catch up."

I waited for Bonnie's voice again, even if it had been only in my head. The silence felt like a physical blow.

My phone began to vibrate on the floor. With my last thread of energy, I turned my head, then lifted the phone to face me. An unflattering picture of Beau—which I'd taken while we were installing the bathroom fixtures in the upstairs of my un-air-conditioned cottage—stared back at me. If I'd had the energy, I would have cried with relief. With all the strength I had left, I swiped my finger across the screen to unlock it, then selected the one character that was guaranteed to let him know that something was horribly, terribly wrong.

CHAPTER 33

A jarring blow to my head, along with excruciating pain from my ankle, woke me up. I opened my eyes to see a blurry Camille dragging me toward the stairs. The cloying stench of putrefying flesh gagged me as the heavy air crushed my chest. My head hit the first stair tread as she tugged on my legs, beginning to drag me up the stairs one by one. I felt absurdly grateful for the overdose of pain meds Camille had dumped in my soup.

Her face hovered over mine. “I’m so sorry to wake you.” She smiled warmly. “Go back to sleep. I’ve got a nice bourbon waiting for you.”

That one word sent a familiar craving through me, the shame of it stinging my eyes. She grinned down at me as if I’d given her the right answer.

Camille dragged me up another step before dropping me again. *Thud.* She let go with one hand long enough to swipe her forehead. “Don’t worry. I’ll make sure you’re good and numb before you accidentally fall down the stairs. Your family and friends will be disappointed to know that you lost your battle with the bottle, but at least you won’t feel any pain.”

I ran my tongue over my parched lips and tried to turn my head to hide my humiliation. Camille spoke with her soft Southern voice so that anyone not paying attention might have thought she was discussing the proper place settings for an afternoon tea. "It's your one weakness, you know. I had to do a lot of thinking before I figured out how to take care of you. Just like with Adele. Except her weakness was her children."

Sticky fingers brushed my cheek again as the scent of Youth-Dew permeated the rot, not softening the stench but at least reminding me that I wasn't alone. Sybil was here, protecting little Patrick and keeping Mark at bay. For now. And Bonnie was here, too. Somewhere.

There were so many bits and pieces of questions spinning in my head, but one circled on repeat. I reached out and grabbed it. "Why?"

She dragged me up another step, then dropped me, my head and legs thumping in sync. "Because your mama never taught you to mind your own business. Even before you found Adele's stones, I knew you were trouble. You wouldn't give us Adele's rings."

Adele. She'd been warning Beau of danger for years—for as long as he'd been ignoring her. We'd thought she'd returned to help Beau find his lost sister. Until we'd discovered that Adele's death hadn't been accidental. If I somehow managed to survive this, I would make sure he knew it was all his fault.

Thump. My head hit another step, offering me momentary alertness. My ankle was now numb from the pain, something for which I might have been grateful in different circumstances. I needed more time. I needed Beau to understand my text. With a sinking feeling, I realized that even if he did, he would have no idea how to find me.

"You're a lot heavier than you look," she gasped.

I was too weak to feel insulted.

"I have no idea how I'm going to get you up so I can give you a proper shove. But, as dear Adele used to say, where there's a will, there's a way."

Those had been Adele's words. It was like she was there, speaking directly to me. *Where there's a will, there's a way.* It was trite and overused, but right then I needed desperately to believe it. A reel of memories flashed behind my closed eyelids. Memories of Beau and me, of all the times we'd finished each other's sentences and how we'd known each other's thoughts before we said them out loud. There had always been an unseen—and largely unwelcome—connection between us. I forced my eyes open and stared at the room, at the bed and nightstand, imprinting it in my brain while I thought about Beau. I might have dismissed such woo-woo practices only yesterday, but right now it was all I had. I only needed more time.

"Where there's a will, there's a way."

Camille whipped her head around to see where the voice had come from. "Adele?"

It seemed to have come from everywhere—the ceiling, the floor, the walls—blanketing me with love and warmth. I tilted my head, listening. There were two voices now. Both female. They seemed to be chanting, the words familiar to me, yet undistinguishable. The rhythm reminded me of Melanie and Aunt Jayne when they joined psychic forces, their chorus as powerful as it was memorable. *We are stronger together.* I felt hands on my head, protecting it from the hardwood floor, while another set held me down, slowing Camille's progress.

"Mom?" I wasn't even sure if I'd spoken, but I felt a reassuring touch on my cheek to let me know she'd heard.

Camille managed to wrestle my limp body over the last step before collapsing onto the floor next to me.

A wave of sleepiness washed through me. I forced my head up, let it bump back down on the floor. "Why . . . Adele?" My words slurred and sloshed against each other.

Camille sat up. "Sweet Adele. I did love her like a sister, you know. We were so close. When Henry lost yet another job, it was Adele who invited us to move to New Orleans and start over. She even got us our jobs at the Past Is Never Past. That's what kind of a friend she was. In return, I tried to be the same kind of friend to her."

I attempted to snort but could only hiss air from my nose.

"I was an excellent salesperson and bookkeeper. Just ask Mimi or Christopher. When I started giving Henry and myself well-deserved bonuses, they didn't even miss the money. And they wouldn't have had all the excess income without me, so it was really a win-win. It could have gone on forever without anyone knowing—I also did the taxes for the business, of course, and knew all the tricks—but Adele got it into her head that it would be a good idea for me to have a backup person. She said she didn't want me to have to think about work while I was on vacation. That was Adele. Always thinking about others."

She got to her feet and walked out of my field of vision. I heard the once-familiar sound of a bottle top being twisted open. Her footsteps neared and I smelled the beloved scent of bourbon.

She stood over me, a bottle filled with amber liquid in her hand. "I was able to hold her off until one day when I visited my parents in Alabama and Adele took the opportunity to start going through the books. She found the discrepancies right away—I almost think she was looking for something. She told me that she was going to tell not only Mimi about it but also the police. She was always about doing the right thing. Adele gave me the chance to tell Mimi myself, because that's the kind of person she was.

"Henry thought we should confess to Mimi. He's not the sharpest knife in the drawer, bless him. But I love him. I have ever since I first laid eyes on him. We had such a good thing going, and we even had money in the bank for the first time. I couldn't let Adele ruin all that."

She groaned as she propped my torso against the newel at the top of the stairs. Being upright made it easier to stay awake, but now I could see the red stain on the floor where the rug had been, and I could see the black shadow creeping along the wall near the ceiling. The temperature plummeted as fear billowed inside me. It was Mark, guarding his secret. With a sinking feeling, I knew that dealing with Camille might be the least of my worries.

To stay awake, I began chanting an internal litany to the tune of "Dancing Queen"—the first tune that came to mind. *Hurry, Beau, please just hurry, Beau. . . .*

"Open your mouth, Nola," Camille said sweetly. "You'll like this part. This will be over quickly. You won't feel a thing, just a little snap of the neck when you accidentally fall down the stairs."

I felt her hands on my face, forcing open my mouth, and then there was the warm liquid taste of bourbon on my tongue. It burned as it slid down my throat, and my stomach betrayed me with the familiar hug of warmth that I'd missed. She held my head while I gagged until I swallowed.

Liquid dripped down my chin and neck and onto my sweater. She used my sleeve to wipe it, then dropped my arm with a look of satisfaction. "Sorry to be so messy, but it adds a realistic touch to this story, doesn't it?"

She set the bottle next to me on the floor, the smell of it now entwined with the putrid stench and the perfume. I retched, feeling a mixture of soup and bourbon come up, then dribble down my chin. My shame and embarrassment were quickly drowned by terror as I looked down the steep, narrow stairs. *Hurry, Beau. Please just hurry, Beau. . . .*

Camille struggled to lift me to a standing position as two sets of invisible hands held me down, thwarting her efforts. She stepped back, breathing heavily as she looked at me, seemingly unaware of the oily shadow oozing along the wall and of the drop in temperature. I struggled to breathe through the stench of death mixed with Estée Lauder perfume as small white clouds blew out of Camille's mouth while she talked. "Little Sunny's kidnapping was the best thing that could have happened to us, because Adele could barely eat or sleep, much less think about any bookkeeping improprieties. I couldn't have planned a better distraction."

Leaden weights seemed to have attached themselves to my eyelids, and each blink grew longer and longer. But I needed to hear the rest of the story, if only so I could repeat it later and see Camille punished.

She swiped her hands against her pants. "My work here is almost done. I just need to catch my breath so I can lift you. I suppose you wouldn't be interested in helping me, hmm?" She gave me the warm, sympathetic expression I'd grown used to. "I am sorry, Nola. I really like you. You remind me of Adele, you know. Too smart for your own good. And much stronger than you look. I hope Beau can get over losing you. I'm glad he has Sam, although I can't figure why he's wasting his time with her when he's got you. Poor Buddy, though."

"Buddy?" I managed. Not just because I needed to keep her talking, but because I really needed to know.

"That's a long story, and I'm afraid we've both run out of time. Good night, Nola. Sleep well."

She leaned down to hoist me high enough for leverage. A loud crash came from behind us, and she dropped me. I fell forward so that I lay across the top of the stairs, my legs against the newel. Shards of milk glass from a broken lamp were sprinkled across the wooden floor like snow. Camille wiped a drop of blood from her cheek where a fragment had hit her.

"Who's there?" Camille shouted.

I heard the chanting of the two women again, louder now, and seeming to come from the corner of the room where the humanlike shadow had grown and now covered the wall like a black stain. It was spreading, as if the dark energy was drawing strength from Camille as Sybil's strength faded along with the scent of her perfume.

My hope dwindled as I cast about for something to hang on to. *Where there's a will, there's a way.* I turned my head, focusing on the women's chanting. It had grown softer, yet the tone had changed to one that taunted the growing entity. This observation brought a small glimmer of optimism.

Camille stood and hooked her hands under my arms, attempting to pull me up to a seated position at the top of the stairs. I strained to lift an arm to stop her but my limbs were useless. I closed my eyes, surrendering to sleep, willing it to be quick.

Wake up, Nola. Wake up. He's coming.

My eyes snapped open. *Mom?* I wasn't sure if I'd spoken the word out loud. I felt Camille's hands trying to pull me up at the same time the two other sets of hands pushed me back, their efforts growing weaker. I was helpless, the bourbon and pain meds having done their job.

Camille began to rock me back and forth. "One, two, th—"

Downstairs, the front door crashed open against the wall. Camille loosened her hold on me, my head falling backward. My landing was cushioned by what felt like a soft lap.

"Nola?" *Beau.* I would have felt crippled with relief if I'd had any feeling left.

Camille clamped her hand over my mouth when she heard the sound of footsteps approaching the stairway.

"Nola?" Felicity's voice rang out. "I got your voice mail. Are you still here?"

After a moment, I heard Beau say, "Camille's car is here. Maybe they're in the backyard."

I lay limp listening to them walk through the house, each step diminishing my remaining hope.

Where there's a will, there's a way.

I struggled to open my eyes, wanting to believe Adele was right.

Fight, Nola, baby. We got this.

My eyes sprung open. *We got this.* It was what my mother used to say every time she had a setback. It was what gave us the good months. I'd hated it then, that reminder of her failure. But maybe that wasn't what it had been to her. Maybe it had been a rallying cry of hope. If we were together, we could face anything.

A glass vase filled with Mardi Gras beads flew off the dresser, over our heads, and down the stairs, landing with an explosive crash. Camille jumped, but she didn't release her grip on me.

"Did you hear that?" Beau's face appeared at the bottom of the steps; he looked up and spotted us. "There you are. Everything okay up there?"

"She's drunk," Camille said. "And I think she tried to overdose on her pain meds." Camille grabbed my arm and spun me around so I faced the stairs.

Felicity appeared behind Beau, her eyes wide as she took in the broken glass and me. "Who else is up there?" She was looking past us, into the room where the icy chill pressed against my back.

A low growl sounded behind us, the resonance vibrating deep in my marrow. Tumbling down the stairs almost seemed like a welcome alternative to being near whatever that was. Camille moved to stand behind me, pressing her knee into the middle of my back and holding me upright.

"Camille, is everything okay?" Beau put his foot on the bottom step, his gaze never leaving my face. I tried to mouth the word "No," but my facial muscles acted as if they belonged to someone else.

"Nothing I can't handle. I told her to stay off the stairs, that they were too steep, and far more dangerous because of her inebriated condition, but you know how headstrong she can be. And she's got a broken ankle. It's almost as if she has a death wish."

I tried to speak, to defend myself, but only gurgled.

Beau's gaze shifted from my face to whatever was standing behind us, and judging by the look on his face I was more glad than usual that I couldn't see ghosts.

The women's chanting continued, the words slipping over the cliff of my memory, eluding my grasp.

"We're stronger together," Beau said, still looking behind me.

"Adele?" Felicity whispered.

Beau faced his sister. "You can see her?"

Felicity nodded, her eyes wide. "Do you see the other woman, too?"

"Yeah. And they're not alone."

The growl rumbled in the air again, my chest vibrating with it.

Beau put one foot on the next step. "Adele's here, Camille. She's been talking to me for years, and I finally decided to listen to her. I know what you did."

"I don't know what you're talking about. Adele's dead." Camille's knee dug harder into my back.

Beau's face hardened. "You killed our mother, and we can prove it." He took another step up the steep stairway. "Adele told me to talk to Henry. He's your weakest link, Camille, as I'm sure you know. It took him all of five minutes to cave. He told me how you lured my mother to the flooded Charity Hospital with the promise of finding Sunny. And how he strangled her and then pried the diamond from her ring because the two of you are the worst kind of predators. She loved you, Camille, and you murdered her."

Camille went still, oblivious to the creeping black shadow that now covered the stairway walls. "Henry killed her—not me. She was my friend. I loved her like a sister."

Beau took another step. "Right. Which is why you asked him to kill her and then rob her. You didn't have the guts to do it yourself. And then you told him where to hide her body. You are as guilty as he is."

Camille reached down and grabbed a handful of my hair. "Stop where you are. Or I will shove your drunk girlfriend down the stairs and she will take you with her."

The dark entity emitted another growl as the shadow oozed down the wall and touched the steps. Fear was the only thing keeping my eyes open. And anger over what Camille had done to Adele. And to her children.

"Please don't make this any worse," Beau said. "I've already called the police, and they're on their way."

"You can't prove anything," Camille said, her voice taunting like a playground bully's. "A ghost's testimony won't stand up in court. Neither will anything Mimi has to say about the rings."

Camille shifted me closer to the edge of the top step, my head lolling forward, my eyes cast toward the bottom of the stairway, where Felicity had now joined Beau on the same step. I watched as she linked arms with her brother. *We are stronger together.* The words being chanted were now clear to me, and if I could have, I would have joined in.

"Actually, we *can* prove it," Beau said. "A strand of hair was found stuck in a prong of the engagement ring. It's been sent to the lab for forensic analysis, but we all know whose DNA we'll find, don't we?" Beau took another step toward us. "Let me help you get Nola downstairs, and then we can talk."

I felt Camille shift her stance, getting into position. *We got this.* This time the words hadn't been inside my head. Bonnie was here, and I wasn't alone.

With energy reserves I didn't know I possessed, I flung out my arms, attempting to grab onto anything I could. One hand grasped at the railing, my fingertips barely gripping the wood. Camille's knee struck me in the middle of my back, expelling all the air from my lungs while knocking me forward and dislodging my frail grasp on the railing.

I had no wind left to scream. In eerie silence I was propelled down the steep stairs in what seemed like slow motion. Beau lifted his arms, reaching for me. Our eyes met right before I shut mine, unwilling to see what happened next as I prepared for the inevitable collision.

Except there wasn't one. Something pulled me back, suspended me in the air for what felt like minutes, just long enough for me to grab onto the railing to keep myself from falling.

Camille, on the top step, teetered from the momentum of her kick. Her arms circled like small propellers as she lost her balance and fell headfirst down the stairs. Beau turned his back to the railing, somehow managing to slow her fall. She landed on her shoulder, striking the kitchen floor with a loud crack. She screamed, then rolled over on her back, her good hand clutching her shoulder, which sat higher than it should have.

I looked down the stairs at her, trying but failing to feel sympathy through the nausea and dizziness that were currently spinning inside me. I slid down onto the top step and gulped in air, refilling my lungs and attempting to clear my head. Small, invisible feet ran past me and down the steps, leaving behind a feeling of panic. The scent of Youth-Dew had evaporated completely, letting me know that Sybil had exhausted her strength. And that this nightmare was far from over.

Felicity rushed to Camille's side. "I'll call nine-one-one and say we need an ambulance."

Beau took the steps two at a time to reach me. He knelt next to me, then pushed back my hair and looked into my face. "Are you all right?"

I managed a nod. "I didn't . . ." I slurred, then stopped, knowing he could smell the bourbon.

"I know. You don't need to explain anything to me."

"My mom . . . was . . . here. Bonnie."

"Yeah. I figured that's who it was. I saw Adele, too."

"And Sybil. Mark . . . killed her."

The last light of the day filtered through the windows, a frost now covering the lower corners of each pane, on the inside. I shivered.

"He's here," Beau whispered.

I nodded as my eyes drifted closed. "I need to . . . sleep."

He shook me gently. "Not a good idea," he said, keeping his gaze trained on something behind me. "Let me get you outside."

An icy finger touched the back of my neck as Beau leaned toward me. Then a tug on the hem of my jeans bolted me out of my inertia. My mouth opened in a silent scream as I was yanked across the room into the dark corner where the bed stood. I grabbed at whatever I could, splinters and broken glass stabbing my palms, blood mixing with nervous sweat.

I slammed against an old console TV and snagged a brass ring pull with my index finger, jerking me to a temporary stop.

"Nola!" Beau shouted, crawling toward me and grabbing my wrists just as my finger slipped out of the ring pull. He hooked his foot on the leg of a heavy oak bookcase as something small landed on my head and then on my arms and Beau's fingers. The dying light from the window was reflected by the dark, glossy wings of hundreds of flying cockroaches falling from the ceiling.

I screamed. And screamed.

"It's okay, Nola! I've got you!" Beau shouted over the fluttering of papery wings and the din of hard-shelled bodies hitting the wooden floor.

Felicity appeared at the top of the steps. She dropped to her knees and crawled to us, her movement slowed by unseen currents of viscous air as she swatted at the large insects without flinching. She grabbed hold of the back of my shirt with one hand, then put her free hand on Beau while hooking her feet around the other front leg of the bookcase to protect her from the suction pulling us all toward the bed.

"We're stronger together," she said. With her eyes on Beau, she said, "Mom said that. When we were on the steps." A roach fell on her head, and she shook it off as another ran over my arm. I shuddered but dared not pull away. "That's how I knew. That . . . I'm like you."

"We're stronger together," Beau repeated as a percussive wave of air swept through the room. Four bright orbs of light, one smaller than the others, hovered around us. *We've got this.* The echo of the silent words reverberated around the room and through the invisible currents.

"They're still here," Beau said, close to my ear. "Their energy is depleted, but they're here."

One of my sneakers flew off my foot as unseen hands pulled on both legs, and I began to slip away from Beau and Felicity. I looked behind me, through the falling rain of cockroaches, and saw, beneath the bed, the dark abyss that was sucking me closer like a hungry mouth.

"Nola—close your eyes!" Beau shouted.

I shook my head. I couldn't see spirits, but it didn't matter. Working together, we were all stronger. I drew from my anger at the pointless deaths of Patrick, Bonnie, and Adele. And Sybil. Anger at the sheer waste of their lives. I turned my face to the unseen force gripping me. "Mark! We know what you did. You will be stuck here forever unless you ask for forgiveness and let Sybil and Patrick go."

The pulling on my legs intensified. One hand slipped out of Beau's grasp, but Beau held on with this other hand, his fingers digging into my skin, letting me know that he wasn't letting go. I didn't know what waited for me in the dark maw behind me, but I was beyond sure I didn't want to go there.

Felicity kept her grip on Beau, and small electric fibers danced around where their limbs touched. The muscles in Beau's neck bulged as he struggled to hold on. "Mark! Let us help you find your way to the light. You don't have to stay here. You have no more secrets to hide."

The pull intensified more, tugging me backward. Beau's grip loosened, my wrist slipping.

I pushed down the rising bubbles of panic. "Sybil is here, Mark. She and Patrick want to go to the light. You can go with them. You only need to ask for forgiveness."

The fluttering of insect wings filled the room as the air shifted almost imperceptibly, my body now being shoved from side to side like a mind weighing a decision.

"There's a better place," Beau said, his voice wavering with strain. "A place where there is light and forgiveness. You don't need to stay here. All you need to do is ask your mother to forgive you for what you did. She can lead you to the light."

My fingers slipped through Beau's and held on to his hand. One by one, they began to slip. "I . . . can't . . . hold . . . on . . ." I gasped.

"Yes, you can." The words were forced from between his gritted teeth. "Mark, listen to me. All you have to do is ask," Beau shouted. "Your mother loves you. No matter what, your mother will never stop loving you."

The heavy waves of air slowed, like water in a departing boat's wake. The hold on my legs loosened by a degree.

"Sybil's here, Mark," Beau continued. "She's waiting for you."

A shimmer of gray light broke through a corner of the room, near the ceiling, a sparkling ray of sunshine cutting a swath out of the growing darkness. I looked toward the almost blinding light and I recognized Sybil from Honey and Joan's framed photographs. She looked younger than in the pictures and had her arm around a little boy dressed in clothing from the turn of the previous century.

"Do you see her, Mark? She's looking for you. She wants to set you free."

A loud roar blew past us, my skin vibrating with the sound, my ears ringing. It was rage and regret and sadness and remorse all at once. Intense enough that my eyes stung with tears and my heart hurt from the kaleidoscope of emotions.

The roaches had stopped falling from the ceiling, their corpulent bodies vanishing from the floor, and the pulling on my legs came to an abrupt end, leaving only a throbbing pain in my ankle. I kept my eyes on the woman and boy in the corner as the light grew, bathing the entire room in a buttery glow.

A black shadow appeared on top of the bloodstain on the floor, and I scrambled in my half-awake state to get closer to Beau. The shadow expanded, its head, torso, and limbs morphing into the figure of a man. He stared at us with hollow eyes before turning to face the woman and child in the corner.

The light grew as the man shed his dark shadow, becoming more human as he walked toward the corner. He stood in front of the woman until she extended her hand. After a brief moment, the man took it. Mark, Sybil, and Patrick turned as one, and without a glance back, they moved away from us just as the stream of light withdrew to wherever it had come, leaving us in dark silence.

I lay on the floor, breathing heavily and feeling on my hip the pressure of the storage-room key and fob in my pocket. Something cold that felt like a kiss brushed my cheek. I turned my head to see a small orb, its light dimming, its energy diminished. "Mom?"

We got this, Nola, baby. You're gonna be okay. I'll always be a part of you. Every time you make music, you'll find me there.

I reached out toward the orb, wanting to capture it and hold it and keep it safe. But it was already gone.

Felicity switched on her phone's flashlight and moved the beam around the room. "No more roaches. I thought I was back in New York City for a while there, although these cockroaches are bigger." Her feeble laugh bumped with nerves.

Too tired to laugh, I turned my head and watched Beau crawl toward me. He sat down and pulled my upper body into his lap. The distant sound of sirens, not an unfamiliar noise in New Orleans, punctuated the night.

"I'll go check on Camille and wait for the ambulance and police," Felicity said. I listened as her footsteps pounded down the stairs.

Beau looked down at me. "Are you okay?"

I nodded, almost expending the last of my energy. "How did . . . you know . . . to come?"

He grinned, and it managed to shoot a bolt of electricity through me even in my current state. "You left the voice mail on Felicity's phone, so we knew where you'd gone. But it was the kissing emoji you sent in your last text. That's how I knew there had to be something terribly wrong."

I smiled and closed my eyes, the sound of sirens growing louder as I finally succumbed to sleep.

CHAPTER 34

The following day I was awakened by Sarah jumping on my bed and Mardi barking. I'd been forced by Beau and Felicity to listen to Dr. Longo and stay overnight in the hospital for observation and so my ankle could be resplinted but had returned to the apartment before dawn so I could go back to sleep in my own bed with Mardi curled at my side. The doctor had scolded me almost as much as Melanie did after Jolene, acting on my wishes, had called my parents and let them know all that had happened since Sarah's arrival.

I was still foggy headed when I'd spoken to Melanie, but I vaguely recalled her saying she wouldn't fly to New Orleans immediately if I would promise to continue the conversation when I was home at Christmas. I agreed only because it gave me time to make other plans. Especially since I didn't know if Cooper remembered offering to drive me to Charleston for the holidays. I'd heard nothing from him since I'd ignored his last text. That one act must have told him that I'd learned his secret. Not that it mattered. There was too much to think about, so in true Melanie fashion I decided to think about it later.

The toxicology report confirmed my suspicion that Henry had

swiped some of my pain pills when he dropped by with Felicity to check on me and that Camille had added them to her soup. Fortunately, her goal had been only to incapacitate me and not to kill me outright, so it would appear as if I'd overdosed on pain pills and alcohol and fallen down the stairs. After all my efforts to remain sober, that was the part that hurt the most.

"Time to get up, sleepyhead," Sarah said, mirroring Melanie's morning greeting. "I'm all packed and ready for the drive to the airport. Jolene has a muffin and coffee waiting for you."

The image of both did perk me up. Sarah threw off my blanket and quilt. "She says you have exactly forty-five minutes to make yourself presentable and to put a fire under your rear end—her words, not mine. You'll get your coffee and muffin as soon as you're done."

I groaned but allowed her to help me out of bed, and I didn't even complain when she made me use my crutches instead of hopping.

As I exited the bathroom, dressed in my jeans and a sweater, the doorbell rang. Like Pavlov's dog, I immediately ducked into my bedroom to apply lipstick before I even knew what I was doing.

"It's Cooper," Sarah said, looking at the security app on my phone. I really needed to change my password.

Jolene emerged from the kitchen with a steaming mug of coffee and a muffin on a plate. She pulled out a chair at the table and motioned for me to sit. "I'll go tell him that he's not welcome here. I wish I had my daddy's shotgun to show him I mean business."

"That won't be necessary, Jolene. I need to talk to him."

"I'll let him in," Sarah said, already heading toward the door.

Jolene and Sarah discreetly retreated into the kitchen as Cooper joined me at the table, his good manners dictating that he remain standing until I told him to take a seat. Which I didn't.

"I'm sorry," he said. "I should have texted or called when you didn't respond."

I looked up at him, the scar on his chin appearing more vivid. "Yes, you should have. Not that it would have made a difference."

Maybe I was more foggy headed than I thought, because I had the uncharacteristic urge to lay everything out then and there. "I know about Lilly."

I gave him points for not trying to pretend he didn't know what I was talking about. His fingers absently brushed the scar. He didn't ask how I knew, and I didn't volunteer the information. I was still too hurt to add Beau's part in how I'd learned.

"I've been wanting to tell you for so long. It's like I'm stuck between the past with Lilly and the possibility of a future with you, but my feet are glued to the ground and I can't move. I've been trying, but . . ."

I wanted to lash out at him, tell him to leave and never let me see him again. But his face reminded me too much of my mom, of how sincere her apologies were during her rare sober moments. "But guilt and remorse are terrible things. Some of us turn to alcohol to smother those feelings."

He dipped his head. "And some of us drown ourselves in denial and work." Raising his eyes to meet mine, he said, "So. Are we over?"

"Did we really ever begin?"

He attempted a smile. "I'd like to think so. I think we both felt . . . something. Something more than just getting over someone. Could we start over—as friends? I need someone to talk to. I haven't even told my family about Lilly. They knew I was dating someone, but they don't know the rest. It's all so . . . awful. I don't think I could handle their disappointment in me."

He sounded so desperate. And so much like me that it hurt my heart. I reached over and took his hands in mine. "I think we could. I think we could be good friends. For now."

"Good." He sighed with relief. "I have a rental car. Can I drive Sarah to the airport? I figure that would give you and me a chance to talk on the way back. There's so much I need to tell you."

"Same," I said, needing to tell him about what had happened at the house on Esplanade, and about the doll and the key and Camille and the rest of it. I also needed to tell him what Sarah had said about Lilly. About why she was angry. And why she needed him to let her go. I checked my watch. "If we hurry, we'll have time to make a stop. I just need to make a quick phone call first."

Honey was waiting on the steps when Cooper pulled his rental car up in front of the house. The gray Honda sedan—from this vantage point I could tell it was an Accord—sat parked facing the empty carport, its owner no longer attempting to keep it hidden. Joan's Cadillac was absent; Honey had told me Joan would be gone, at Bible study.

Cooper helped me out of the car and handed me my crutches. "Are you sure you don't want me to come with you?"

"I'm sure." I began making my way toward Honey, and she met me halfway.

After greeting me, she said, "It's best that you don't come inside. And it's important that you leave before Joan gets back. I won't call it a conspiracy if you won't, but the fewer the people who know, the better."

"Agreed." I dug into the hip pocket of my jeans and withdrew the storage-room key and fob that had been hidden inside the doll. "I'm guessing you already know what's in the storage unit."

She took the key but didn't answer. I glanced at the elusive gray Honda. "How long have you known that Jessica and Lynda are alive?"

Honey regarded me with her large, round eyes, cobalt blue mascara dusting her eyelashes. "Are you sure you want to know?"

"Yeah. I do. I think the trauma of what I went through at the house yesterday grants me the privilege."

"I suppose it does. I'm not supposed to believe in . . . all that. But I've experienced enough things I can't explain to know that there's so much we don't understand. What you told me about Sybil, about how she protected you and our uncle Patrick . . . that's exactly who she was. And Mark . . ." She shook her head. "I loved him because he was my brother, but there was something loose inside of him. Our father was a wonderful, kind, and gentle man, unless he was drinking. Then he became a cruel brute. Joan and I were spared the worst of his brutality, but poor Mark, who had the misfortune of being his only son, wasn't as lucky."

She looked over her shoulder at the house, then took a step closer to me. "Mark learned things he shouldn't have. Jessica told me stories . . ." Honey pressed her lips together. "He was violent toward women his entire life, including to his wife and daughter, so it's no surprise that death didn't change him."

She took a deep breath. "To answer your question, I've always known Jessica and Lynda were alive. And that Mark was dead. I've known since the night of the murder. Jessica called me, hysterical. Mark had hit little Lynda, and when Sybil tried to stop him he killed her. His own mother! And then he turned back to Lynda. So Jessica did what any mother would do." Honey's face softened. "I couldn't place any blame on her, and I knew I had to help her. If she called the police, she could go to jail, and then Lynda would go into foster care. Joan and I could apply to be her guardians, but that would take too long. And Lynda was too traumatized to be separated from her mother. I did what I thought was right."

A small tear escaped from the corner of her eye. "I gave Jessica the name and address of an old friend in Summerville, outside of Charleston, where she and Lynda could go and be safe. And then we had to hide Mark's body. I immediately thought of the storage facility. I got the lease on it after my husband died and I moved in with Joan and needed a place to store my things. My husband was a big hunter, so we had a giant meat freezer."

I did my best not to focus on the last two words.

"I told Jessica to hide the key somewhere just in case they were stopped, because we couldn't have the key being found anywhere near her. I didn't know she'd hidden it in the doll until yesterday, when Jessica came to see me. She was worried that the key would be found now that the house was sold. That's why you kept seeing their car. Jessica was trying to find a way to gain access without breaking in. Getting arrested wasn't something she could afford."

I nodded slowly, absorbing everything she'd just told me. "You did a good job of pretending you didn't know anything—probably for your sister's benefit. I'm guessing Joan doesn't know any of this?"

Honey took a deep breath, her penciled-in brows knitting together. "My sister most likely suspects the truth but doesn't look too closely because she doesn't really want to know. She would feel compelled to alert the authorities if she knew the full story. Not because she doesn't love Jessica, but because she has an exaggerated sense of right and wrong. She doesn't understand the gray area between black and white." With surprising strength, she gripped my upper arms. "Do you?"

I'd never seen the world in just black and white. I was a musician. A lover of old houses. Both things meant that I saw the world in terms of the possibilities that existed in the gray areas. I considered for a moment the men who'd used and abused my mother and had never been held accountable. She'd been an absent mother, her focus always on nursing her career disappointments with illegal and legal substances. But she'd been there yesterday, helping to protect me. Maybe this was the one chance I had to take a stand in her memory.

I took a deep breath and looked Honey in the eyes. "The truth is that I haven't seen Lynda or Jessica. And I've never been to Guidry Moving and Storage. That's all I know. And I would suggest destroying what is left of the doll before Mimi changes her mind and wants to hold it."

She stood on her tiptoes and kissed me on the cheek with a loud smack. "I knew you were good people the minute I met you." She stepped back. "You should be going. I need to say good-bye to my guests before Joan comes home."

Our gazes locked in mutual understanding. "Good-bye, Honey." Then I made my way back to the car where Cooper and Sarah waited.

"Did you learn anything new?" Cooper asked as he and Sarah helped me into the backseat.

"Not a thing."

He looked at me for a long moment, waiting for me to say more, while I spent more time and concentration than necessary adjusting my seat belt and getting situated in the backseat. He'd known me long enough to know that I was a terrible liar.

Without a word, he closed my door and returned to the driver's seat before putting the car in drive, then pulling out onto the street. I didn't look back.

CHAPTER 35

During a spate of balmy weather two weeks later, Jolene and I sat in the rocking chairs on the front porch of my Creole cottage sipping hot chocolate with red and white peppermint sticks protruding from the tops of our mugs. On the floor between us lay Mardi, wearing yet another monogrammed sweater; this one had Santa hats with white pom-poms. Across the street, the Christmas trees in our neighbor's coffin planters were festooned with fleur-de-lis ornaments and coated with sparkling tinsel that danced like a Las Vegas showgirl in the breeze.

We were waiting for a delivery of bedroom furniture for the two rooms upstairs. It was coming from the Past Is Never Past as a housewarming gift. Seeing as how bedroom furniture was the last thing I needed to move in, I gratefully accepted despite the fact that the items were antiques and Melanie and Sarah might have something to say about it.

I stretched out my leg, miraculously not too much worse for wear from my escapades in the house on Esplanade. My new boot was wrapped in a festive green-and-red-striped cover monogrammed with a silver letter N on top—an early Christmas gift from Jolene. I was getting so used to not having full use of my right leg that I realized I might miss the boot when it was gone. Especially because then it would be time for me to learn how to use a stick shift and begin driving the Mustang convertible. The thought made my stomach churn. I couldn't think about it now. Christmas was approaching, and I was finally going to spend my first night in my own house.

"I can't believe I'm going to say this," I said, "but I already miss Sarah. I'm actually looking forward to going home for the holidays. Cooper's still planning to drive me, which could be interesting."

"Hmm," Jolene said noncommittally. She took a sip from her mug. "Sarah and I think a lot alike. If we were the same age, I'd say we were separated at birth. And then you and I would be sisters! Wouldn't that be amazing?"

"That's one word for it," I said. "But I think one sister is enough for me. Besides, I like you as my roommate. And judging by the state of our love lives, we'll stay roommates until they move us to a nursing home."

She didn't say anything, which surprised me. Usually she was ready with a strongly (for her) worded lecture about not thinking negatively. Instead, she gave me a smile that seemed perilously close to her *bless your heart* smile.

"Is something wrong?" I asked.

"Actually, I think there is." She looked inside her mug. "This tastes funny to me. Does yours taste funny?"

"No. I think it's delicious. I can tell it's homemade and you didn't use a mix."

Jolene wrinkled her nose. "I wonder if the milk was bad."

"It's fine," I said. "Maybe you're coming down with a cold. Colds always affect my sense of taste."

She didn't say anything but remained focused on the contents of her mug.

"Speaking of our love lives—or lack thereof—you're not still planning on throwing Jaxson and Carly an engagement party, right? Or going dress shopping? Just say no and she'll take the hint."

Jolene turned to me, and for the first time since I'd met her, her mouth opened but, despite several attempts, she seemed to be unable to speak.

I looked up when I heard the sound of a vehicle approaching. Beau pulled up to the curb, and he and Felicity exited the cab.

"Hey, y'all," Jolene said with a wave, appearing to be overly eager for a chance to speak with someone besides me. "Come on up and join us. It's supposed to get cold again tomorrow, so this might be the last chance we have to sit outside for a spell without getting chilblains."

Beau leaned against the porch railing while Felicity sat on the recently delivered joggling board—a housewarming gift from Melanie and Jack, and as much a nod to my hometown as the front door painted Charleston green and sporting a palmetto-tree knocker.

Felicity bounced up and down on the wooden board. "It's nice to see you in one piece, Nola. I'm not going to lie. There were several moments there when I doubted that we'd make it out with all our limbs attached."

"Same," I said. "Thanks for being there. I don't know what I would have done without you and Beau. That was the perfect time to discover your dormant psychic abilities, and I for one am very grateful."

She didn't smile, and when I looked at Beau I saw him slicing his finger across his neck.

"I'm sorry . . ." I stammered.

"It's all right," Felicity said. "I'm still coming to terms with it. I find it very weird and I'm not at all excited about it. I'm just going to ignore it for now."

"That sounds like a page right out of Nola's playbook," Beau said.

I shot him a look. "You'll figure it out. And if you need some guidance from someone other than Beau, I know that my stepmother,

Melanie, would be happy to help. She used to be closeted about her abilities, but now she's very open. That change happened when she realized how many people she could help."

"Thank you. I'll keep that in mind."

I drained my mug and noticed that Jolene's was still nearly full and that she was eating the peppermint candy cane. Turning to Felicity, I asked, "When are you going back to New York?"

Felicity exchanged a glance with Beau. "I haven't decided. I'm working remotely for now and staying with Mimi while I figure things out. My mom—I mean, my other mom, Angelina—has offered me a job with Sabatier Properties. She and Michael have taken over as CEO and CFO and are restructuring everything. She thinks it's time to add more women to leadership roles in the company, and I agree. Nothing is final yet, but I'm excited. I would be working with Michael."

"That's terrific," I said. "The part about staying in New Orleans." I bit my tongue so I wouldn't say anything I'd regret.

Jolene stood. "Excuse me for a minute, please. I'm going to go inside and make a new batch of hot chocolate and bring out two new mugs. And I just made a mess of reindeer poop, so I'll bring a big bowl of that, too."

Despite its name, my mouth salivated at the thought of Jolene's concoction of Corn Pops covered with melted chocolate, peanut butter, and other yummy stuff.

"I'll help," Felicity said, sliding off the joggling board and following Jolene inside—with Mardi in their wake, hoping for a treat.

An awkward silence fell after the door shut. I hadn't spoken to Beau since the incident at the Esplanade house, or for a while before that, because of his digging up dirt on Cooper. But he'd saved my life. Again.

He spoke first. "I heard you, you know. Asking me to hurry. I knew it was you because it sounded like an ABBA song." He sent me a sidelong glance. "I don't know what this thing is between us, Nola.

If it's a good thing or not. But if there's one thing I've learned, it's not to question the out-of-the-ordinary. Which is why I listened and came running when I heard you."

"I'm glad. It might not have ended well if you had ignored me."

"I was just afraid that you'd yell at me. I know how much you hate it when someone steps in on your behalf. At least this time I didn't let a guitar burn."

I rolled my eyes as I tried not to laugh at how absurd that sounded. But also how true. I glanced at him, and he seemed to be waiting for me to say something. "What?"

He tilted his head in the same way Mardi did when I fake-threw a ball. Like I owed him something.

"Oh. Right. Thank you. I owe you one."

"No, you don't. I'm not keeping a tally. I'm just glad I was there to help a friend."

I met his gaze. "Is that what you call this thing between us?"

He continued to regard me for a moment before looking away. "Yeah. It's why I did the background check on Cooper. There was something . . . not right with the woman's spirit I saw hanging around him at the restaurant. I didn't want you hurt."

"The jury's still out on whether I should hit you or thank you, so let's just call it even, okay?"

"I did it because I care about you, Nola. You're important to me." He reached into his shirt pocket and pulled out a ring box. I stared at it, confused and surprised at the same time.

He snapped open the lid to reveal the familiar platinum band of his mother's engagement ring, but it now displayed a large round diamond held in place with new prongs. "The stone is from Mimi's maternal grandmother's ring, so it's still a special heirloom, even without the original diamond. What do you think?"

"Oh . . . it's beautiful. It's just . . . I don't . . ."

I felt his eyes on me and I found myself hoping that he couldn't see the inside of my mind and the tightly coiled ball of conflicting emotions. Or maybe I wished he would, so that he could explain them to me.

Beau snapped the lid shut. “I hope Sam likes it. She loves old things that have a past.” He slipped the box back into his pocket. “I know you do, too, which is why I wanted to show you. I’m going to ask Jolene to help me plan a surprise proposal party.”

“Well, then,” I said, feeling motion sickness from riding the roller-coaster of relief and disappointment. “I’m sure she’ll love it.”

I sat back in my rocker, glad to return to somewhat familiar ground. “I’ve been meaning to ask you—was there really DNA evidence on the rings? The police wouldn’t tell me anything about that when they interviewed me. I have a call in to Bernie, since he’s got his ear to the ground and seems to know what’s going on before the police do.”

Beau grinned. “No, there wasn’t. Hair DNA has kind of lost favor in the court of law anyway, but I wagered on Camille not knowing that. Which was a solid bet, because she ended up with a broken shoulder and collarbone, along with a shattered knee and more charges against her than just murder.”

His expression sobered. “I did have a chance to talk with her while we waited for the ambulance, and she told me what happened to my mom. Maybe she wanted to clear her conscience, or maybe she thought confessing to me would make it easier on her later. Regardless, she told me that for days following the storm Charity was only accessible by boat, and the bottom floors were flooded. That’s why she told my mom she could find Sunny there. Adele didn’t question that, since it was Camille, and she didn’t hesitate. Henry was waiting for her. Unfortunately, so was Buddy. He’d returned to the shop right after Adele left, and Camille told him where to go. Henry had a gun, so Camille assumed he’d take care of the problem.”

“But that’s not what happened.”

Beau shook his head. “No. Buddy arrived too late, but not too late to see Henry strangling my mother. Dad tried to save her, but Henry hit him on the head with the gun. Henry thought he was dead, but when he returned to bury Adele, Dad was gone. When Dad didn't show up again, they assumed he was wandering around with a head injury and didn't know who he was. That's why Madame Zoe warned us that we needed to find Buddy before anyone else did. Out of his mind or not, he'd witnessed Henry killing my mother, and that was a loose end they couldn't afford."

He spoke without emotion, separating himself from the story.

"By then Charity Hospital had been more or less abandoned, so it was the perfect place to hide her body. They didn't plan on it ever being found." He rocked back and forth, the sound of creaking floorboards mixing with that of the rustling leaves in the yard.

Beau continued. "I'm not sure if I should be grateful to Camille for telling me or angry and sad that all of that happened to my mother."

I put my hand on his arm. "I think you should be feeling both. That's pretty much life in a nutshell, isn't it? The universe is pretty good at settling opposing emotions on us and then treating us like players in a spectator sport when we try to figure out what we're supposed to do."

"You think?"

"Do we have a choice? It's not like we're given a comment box for complaints. We have to go with whatever we're given and make the most of it."

He surprised me by grinning. "You know what, Nola? I wouldn't call you an optimist by any stretch of the imagination, but I do love to hear your observations."

"Thanks. I think." I sat back, withdrawing my hand. "Has Adele gone, then?"

"I haven't seen her."

I didn't point out that he hadn't answered my question.

"At least we know what happened to her, and she's home now."

He nodded slowly, his gaze focused on the street in front of us. "I'm just glad it's over."

"But it's not, is it? Not until you find your dad and bring him home. Assuming he's still alive."

"He is. That was the last thing Adele told me. Right before she told me to find him." He stood suddenly, his chair rocking in his wake.

I followed his gaze to the street, and I immediately recognized the woman with the gold hoop earrings and the long salt-and-pepper hair.

"Madame Zoe," I said, trying to exit my chair using just one leg and failing miserably. I watched through the porch railing's balusters as she approached, each step bringing with it the sound of tiny ringing bells. She stopped at the foot of the steps. I wasn't entirely surprised to see her at my house. She'd found me here once before.

Without preamble she said, "Do you still have the stones I gave you?"

"Actually—" Beau began before I interrupted.

"Yes. I have both pouches. And Adele's stones, too."

"Good. You'll be needing them." She pointed a finger with a long black-lacquered nail at my front door. "Bring your sister to come see me. We have much to discuss. You will need her help to find Buddy."

Beau frowned. "Felicity? But I don't—"

"She's stronger than most. And much stronger than you." She walked back to the street, then turned around. Directing her attention toward me, she said, "You have a new car."

"Yes," I said slowly. "Although technically it's not new, nor is it mine, but—"

"Be careful." Without another word, she turned and left.

Beau and I stared at each other. "I'll go and see if there's anything Jolene needs." He disappeared inside, leaving me alone on the porch. My gaze traveled to the red Ford Mustang parked at the curb, where Jaxson had thoughtfully delivered it the day before.

Even I, who knew nothing about automobiles, found it almost sexy in a red, shiny, retro kind of way. I stood and hopped up to the porch railing to get a better look. It didn't have airbags or antilock brakes, which might have been what Zoe was warning me about.

The car's radio suddenly turned on and began playing the Rolling Stones' "Honky Tonk Women" at full blast, the song audible through the white vinyl convertible top. A dog being walked across the street suddenly bolted, pulling the leash from its owner's hand, and took off down the sidewalk.

I retrieved my crutches, then hobbled to the front door. I would think about it later. *Later* was always so much better than *right now.* I managed to open the front door and get myself and my two crutches inside before the door slammed shut behind me.